Duchess

Duchess

A NOVEL OF
SARAH CHURCHILL

SUSAN HOLLOWAY SCOTT

NEW AMERICAN LIBRARY

New American Library
Published by New American Library, a division of
Penguin Group (USA) Inc., 375 Hudson Street, New York, New York 10014, USA
Penguin Group (Canada), 90 Eglinton Avenue East, Suite 700, Toronto,
Ontario M4V 3B2, Canada (a division of Pearson Penguin Canada Inc.)
Penguin Books Ltd., 80 Strand, London WC2R 0RL, England
Penguin Ireland, 25 St. Stephen's Green, Dublin 2, Ireland (a division of Penguin Books Ltd.)
Penguin Group (Australia), 250 Camberwell Road, Camberwell, Victoria 3124,
Australia (a division of Pearson Australia Group Pty. Ltd.)
Penguin Books India Pvt. Ltd., 11 Community Centre, Panchsheel Park, New Delhi - 110 017, India
Penguin Group (NZ), cnr Airborne and Rosedale Roads, Albany,
Auckland 1310, New Zealand (a division of Pearson New Zealand Ltd.)
Penguin Books (South Africa) (Pty.) Ltd., 24 Sturdee Avenue,
Rosebank, Johannesburg 2196, South Africa

Penguin Books Ltd., Registered Offices:
80 Strand, London WC2R 0RL, England

First published by New American Library,
a division of Penguin Group (USA) Inc.

ISBN 978-0-7394-7396-2

Set in Minion
Designed by Daniel Lagin

Printed in the United States of America

Prologue

ST. JAMES'S PALACE, LONDON
NOVEMBER, 1688

It is no easy trick to overthrow the King of England.

One must be blessed with courage and conviction, a dash of reckless-ness, and passion beyond measure. And in my prime, on the night I helped my friend the Princess Anne escape, I do believe I had all that, and more.

I needed every bit of it, too. I was staying at St. James's Palace in the lodgings of my brother-in-law, the Earl of Tyrconnel, and because he and my sister were gone to Ireland, I was alone in the apartments save for the servants. I had just finished dressing for the day, my pearls still cool against my throat, when one of the maids burst into my bedchamber, tears in her eyes and her apron knotted in her hands.

"Oh, my lady, my lady, there's soldiers at the door!" she cried, her voice shrill with panic. "They called General Lord Churchill a traitor, and they say they must see you at once!"

I hooked the last pearl through my ear before I answered, determined to be calm. I'd known the king's soldiers would come. There'd never been any doubt. My four children were safe with friends in the country in preparation, our estates as secured as they could be. Yet though my heart raced within my breast, I would not turn flighty and fearful, but instead do as John and I had planned.

"The soldiers may say what they please about His Lordship," I said as I rose from my dressing table and shook out my skirts. "We know the truth. I shall see the officers in the parlor."

I waited upstairs until the men had been shown into the parlor, and then I waited a little longer, to give them time to consider their actions against my husband and me. By most lights, neither John nor I would seem the sort to be arrested as traitors to the crown. John had served in His Majesty's household and in his army since he'd been a boy, rising from a mere page to a lieutenant general, his accomplishments acknowledged with the title of Baron Churchill of Sandridge. Although I was still a young woman, not yet thirty, I had lived in the eye of the court for nearly fifteen years. I'd begun as a maid of honor to the Duchess of York, before she'd become queen, and now I served as Mistress of the Bedchamber to Anne, the Princess of Denmark and His Majesty's younger daughter. John and I had been well rewarded for our loyalty, and we were wise enough to appreciate our good fortune.

But to the sorrow of the country, James Stuart had again and again proved himself unworthy of the throne he had inherited from his brother Charles II. He had silenced the voice of the people by dismissing Parliament. He had chosen to serve his own Roman faith and be guided by the pope, to the fear and detriment of his own Anglican country, and he had vowed to make Catholicism again the state religion. He had imprisoned the Archbishop of Canterbury and other leaders of the Anglican church in the Tower and charged them with seditious libel. Worst of all, he had replaced Protestant leaders in the government, the army, and the navy with papist Frenchmen, letting poor England be pushed towards the greedy, grasping hands of our great enemy King Louis of France.

James's actions left no recourse for any Englishman who cared both for his country and his faith, and so my husband and I and many others had turned to the Protestant Mary Stuart, James's older daughter and the Princess of Orange, and her husband William for deliverance, and meant to put them on the English throne in James's place.

Yet as I walked slowly down the stairs, I could not help but think how irrevocable each step might be. My husband and I had together agreed that this was the right course to take for our consciences, but the risk was fearsome indeed. If the rebellion failed, retribution would be swift for those who had supported it.

We would forfeit all our property and estates and have our titles and privileges stripped from us. We would be imprisoned in the Tower until tried, and when—not if—we were convicted, we would be beheaded for all the world to watch. The only legacy we would leave for our little son and three daughters would be poverty and disgrace, and as for the poor innocent babe I now carried within my womb—why, I could not even guarantee birth and life, or the eternal salvation of a Christian baptism.

The lieutenant waiting for me in the parlor was very young and respectful, so young he flushed like a girl when I greeted him. That was the power not only of my rank, but of my beauty as well, displayed to best effect in a rich green velvet gown with deep cuffs of Venetian lace. He wore the yellow coat of the old Duke of York's regiment, the first with which my John had served, too.

"So what has brought you here with your men, Lieutenant?" I asked, smiling. I wished to put him at his ease, the better to coax from him whatever news he might know. "I don't believe you've come simply to ask after my health."

"No, my lady." He took a deep breath and looked down at the floor, shying away from my gaze, the way most people do when bearing ill tidings. "My orders are to confine you here to Lord Tyrconnel's lodgings, my lady, and to admit no one other than your servants."

"Am I to know the reason, Lieutenant?" I asked lightly, for John had warned me to pretend as little knowledge as possible. "An officer and six of his men seem quite excessive for the care of one lone baroness."

"No, my lady." At last he did raise his gaze to meet mine. "I regret that I must inform you that your husband General Lord Churchill has betrayed His Majesty in the most grievous manner possible. Yesterday His Lordship and His Majesty George, the Prince of Denmark, fled to the camp of William, Prince of Orange, at Axminster."

Speechless with surprise, I felt my knees weaken beneath me, and I dropped into the nearest chair. Of course I'd known that John had planned to go to William once the prince had landed on English soil, but not so soon as this. He was supposed to have sent me word, a sign, so that the Princess Anne and I could have left London first, to be safely with our husbands and beyond the king's reach. But no word had come, and now

I was left with soldiers to watch me close as a hungry cat at a mouse's hole in the wainscoting.

The lieutenant hurried to my side, bending on one knee beside my chair.

"I am most sorry, my lady, very sorry," he said, his voice full of the hand-wringing helplessness that young men seem to feel when confronted with unhappy women. "Shall I send for your maid, my lady?"

I shook my head, gathering my wits as well as my courage. At least I knew now that John was safe. I could take comfort in that, and I would be strong. I *must* be strong, for John's sake as well as our children's. "You say Lord Churchill has been denounced as a traitor. Does that mean you have come to arrest me for the sin of being his wife?"

The lieutenant hesitated. "No, my lady. Those are not my orders."

But the words *not yet* hung between us, unspoken yet understood. I would have to act as swiftly as I could.

"Might you tell me this, Lieutenant?" I asked. "How many other officers and lords have gone with Lord Churchill to Axminster?"

The young man hesitated, his fingers working nervously over the pommel of his sword being all the answer I needed to my question. The rebellion *was* succeeding, and fast. John had guessed that support would be strong in the army and in the navy, and that the great lords, too, would reject James and choose William in his place. Thank God he'd been right.

"They say the king means to hold fast here in London, my lady," the lieutenant said instead, freely giving me what I would have begged next. "They say he is on the road now, with two thousand of his most loyal troops. But as long as you remain here, my lady, following His Majesty's orders, you will be safe."

Oh, yes, I was safe, I thought with grim certainty, as safe as any prisoner locked away in a cell. But this young man's opinion was of little consequence. My duty next was to rescue the princess.

I drew my handkerchief from my cuff, dabbing it weakly at my temples.

"You are most kind to watch over me, Lieutenant," I whispered, making my voice faint. "These are troubled times, and I will feel much safer with you and your men here."

He puffed out his chest beneath his green sash, the little cockerel. "No harm will come to you while we watch over you, my lady."

"Thank you," I said tremulously. "I will be sure to give orders to the cook that you and your men are to have whatever you wish to fortify yourselves for your duty."

"That's not necessary, my lady," he said, though I guessed he'd be the first at the kitchen table when the joint was pulled from the spit.

"Oh, but it is," I said, my gratitude as cloyingly sweet as May honey. "It *is*. Yet I fear I must ask a small favor of you in turn. You say I am not to leave here."

He frowned. "Those are my orders, my lady."

"But you see, Lieutenant, I have an appointment that must take me from this part of the palace." I hesitated, as if from modesty. "I am with child, and I was to call upon my midwife to consult about—"

"You may go, my lady," he said hastily, his expression every bit as squeamish and discomfited as I'd expected. "You have my leave for that small freedom, but you must give your word that you'll return."

A half hour later, I was hurrying across St. James's Park towards Princess Anne's quarters in the Cockpit at Whitehall, the oldest part of the royal palace. I took care not to draw attention to myself, wearing a plain dark woolen cloak with the fur-lined hood drawn up and my head bowed, and a black scarf wrapped over my face as if against the chill November air.

I entered Whitehall not by the front hall, where there were sure to be more of the king's soldiers, but through the apartments I kept in the Cockpit below the princess's, for the times when I attended her. In the summer, when the first hints of a rebellion had risen, John had urged the princess to have a tiny back staircase constructed between our bed-chambers, secret to all but us, and now I made good use of it.

"Oh, you've come, you've come!" cried the princess as soon as she saw me at the staircase's door. I tried to curtsey, as was fit, but she was too distraught for ceremony and instead grabbed my hands and pulled me upright.

"My dear, have you heard?" she cried, throwing herself into my arms and blurring the difference in our ranks, as she often did with me. "The prince and Lord Churchill have gone to William, and left us behind! Oh, God help us, whatever are we to do?"

"That's why I've come, Your Highness," I said, disentangling myself so I might look at her squarely. She was trembling, her doughy face even more pale than usual with fear, and I spoke slowly to calm her, the way one would with a terrified child. "We will solve this together. Where are your other ladies?"

"They are in the parlor with the queen," she said, belatedly lowering her voice so she wouldn't be heard. "I came here to use my closet. But what can we do? How can we get away now, with my father returning to London? I would rather throw myself from the window than have him find me here!"

Her voice broke into a sob, and I slipped my arm around her shoulder. She knew what was at stake as well as I. While her father had fallen into Romish ways, she'd been raised as good an Anglican as any woman in the country, a decision that was a long-standing torment to the king. But it wasn't only her father's wrath that she feared; if William succeeded in seizing the English crown, then Anne would become second in the succession after her sister Mary. She would be a great prize for each side to possess; the sooner she could be taken to safety in William's camp, the better.

That had always been planned for me by John and the others, my special assignment, to spirit Anne away from the palace. Ah, how fast it would break the king's heart and spirit, to see both his daughters turned against him!

"What shall we do?" Anne asked again in a helpless wail. "What will become of us?"

"Pray listen to me, Your Highness," I said, my voice soft and urgent. We had known each other for so many years, since we'd been girls, that I understood the times when she needed me more as a friend than as an attendant. "You must retire to your bed early tonight, and lock your bedchamber door so no others can enter. I have already sent word to Bishop Compton, and he has promised to—"

"The bishop will help us?" Her eyes lit with hope. Lord Henry Compton was not only the Bishop of London, but also Anne's preceptor and advisor, and the cleric who had presided at her wedding to Prince George. The bishop had been forced into hiding for his criticism of the king, but I had known where to find him, and known, too, that he would risk his own life for the princess and our cause.

"He and I and Lord Dorset, too, will return later this night for you, Your Highness," I said, reciting our careful plan. "We'll have a hired coach waiting on the other side of the park, near Charing Cross. I'll come for you again myself, up the back stairs, and lead you away. Then we'll journey to Lord Dorset's house in Epping Forest for the night."

"What if we meet my father's soldiers on the road? What if we are stopped? What if—"

"His Majesty is coming from the west," I said. "If we leave with haste tonight, we should outpace them."

She gasped with wonder. "Oh, my dear, you have it to every detail!"

"Because we cannot afford any detail to go astray, Your Highness," I said firmly. "You must say nothing to anyone else, not to any of your ladies or servants, and you must bring nothing with you. Our escape must look sudden, unplanned, as if you'd been carried off against your will."

She nodded slowly, her expression still taut with trepidation. "My father sent orders for you to be arrested for treason and taken to the Tower. I begged the queen to stay them until tomorrow."

Even though I'd already suspected such an order would come for me, I felt the chill of it run through me like a river of ice. When the king's nephew the Duke of Monmouth had tried to lead an earlier rebellion and failed, James had ordered all of us at court to watch the execution. It had taken six clumsy strikes of the axe to sever poor Monmouth's handsome head from his body.

"You could well have saved my life, Your Highness," I said slowly. "However can I thank you for so great a favor?"

"It was no favor to you, Lady Churchill, but to me." Her eyes filled with tears. "How could I ever risk losing you, my dearest friend?"

I took her familiar hand in mine, her fingers heavy with her rings and her palm moist with fear.

"I risk everything for you, Your Highness," I said softly. "We both know the dangers if we fail."

Her mouth twisted, and I quickly offered her my own handkerchief.

"So much danger!" she cried forlornly as she pressed the handkerchief to her eyes, then buried her face against my shoulder. "Oh, so much peril for me to bear!"

I patted her plump shoulder, praying for both our sakes that tonight she'd find the strength to make good our escape. A royal princess can be the most selfish creature alive, cosseted and protected from the cradle to her grave: what would Anne know of perils or danger? If we were captured by her father, the very worst James would do to her would be to confine her to her rooms here at the palace or hold back her allowance. For me, there'd be no mercy, and that certainty made my voice sterner than perhaps it should have been.

"Have courage, Your Highness," I said. "We can't be weak now. We must be brave if we are to succeed."

She lifted her face, her cheeks flushed and wet with tears of misery and fear. "I will try," she said contritely. "I must trust you as I always have when I've needed you. Now I must trust you again, for I have no other course."

I smiled and smoothed the lace scarf around her throat.

"You must trust me because you are my dearest friend, too, Your Highness," I said, offering the gentle assurance she needed most to hear. "We will be brave together, you and I, and because we have right on our side, we will succeed."

Chapter One

When I had been a tiny girl and living in the country near St. Albans, I had listened with rapt fascination to the stories my older sister Frances had told of her life at the court of King Charles II. Perhaps it was because we were poor for gentry that her stories seemed so dazzling, or perhaps it was that the pall of England's recent sorrows still shadowed our lives in the debts my father could never escape. All too well my parents recalled the grim rule of the Puritans, when Oliver Cromwell and the rest of his sour zealots had led England into twenty years of civil war and misery. They'd cut off the head of poor King Charles I and banned every merriment and pleasure as sinful, and ruined the lives and fortunes of those who still remained loyal to the exiled royal family.

But I was born in 1660, the week after Charles Stuart returned to England to reclaim his martyred father's throne, and for me there was no other London than the one my sister described. Frances was thirteen years older than I, and in the manner of little sisters, I breathlessly believed everything she told me.

King Charles was the most handsome and glorious ruler ever to grace the throne. The ladies in his court were all great beauties, celebrated for their grace and charm; the gentlemen to a man were handsome, brave, and bold, and even the palace of Whitehall itself rivaled every other such great house for grandeur and nobility. Oh, how eager I was to journey there, too, and find my own place among so many splendors!

But my path was not so easy, nor so grand. My father died the winter

I was eight, and what little property he'd preserved passed to my older brother John. My sister Frances had long since wed Sir George Hamilton and retired from court to the country with a growing family of her own. My mother and I were left with nothing but my father's debts. To keep us from the chill grip of Newgate, she had thrown herself upon the mercy of the king and secured lodgings for us within the protection of St. James's Palace, where no creditors could follow.

I know that makes for a pretty tale, the resourceful widow and her daughter saved from disgrace to live in a palace, but I assure you, it was not half as grand as that. My mother had borne me so late in her fecundity that she'd always regarded me as an inconvenience and a hindrance, and age hadn't sweetened her temper. She was quick with blows if I crossed her or disobeyed, which only served to strengthen my natural spirit and resolve to make my own way apart from hers.

Nor did the quality of our lodging lessen the ill feelings between us. We had our sanctuary from the bailiff, true, but it was far from the grand quarters of the court. Instead we were like scores of others from around the kingdom, rewarded for our loyalty with the meanest of spaces in the distant corners of the palaces of St. James's and of Whitehall. My mother and I lived together in a single room near the stable yard, where despite the lack of a window, we still were assaulted by the racket of comings and goings day and night, and the stench of manure and other offal.

In this place, my mother took in worn smocks and other linens from the gentlewomen to mend towards our support. She had always been able to stitch a fine seam and fancywork, and tried to teach me the same. But I recognized this sorry education for what it was, training to be as sub-servient as she, and instead I labored to improve myself for greater things.

Now I have heard that in the time of clever Queen Bess, a hundred years before, ladies were encouraged to read and parse away at Latin like greybeard scholars, but such an overwrought education was no longer the fashion. I learned to read tolerably well, yes, and write a pretty hand for letters, but ciphering and foreign tongues remained beyond my sphere.

Yet who can fault me, when there were so many other accomplishments to acquire that would bring me more favor? From the palace's galleries and in the park, I observed the court's grand ladies. I practiced their graceful walks and curtseys, and how best to hold my head and arrange an open fan in my hands. I learned to tell this duke from that earl, and which held more favor with the king. I washed my hair in honey-water to preserve its golden color, and I took care to keep my visage from the ravages of the sun. I saw how even the most beautiful and indulged mistress must give way to the plainest wedded lady, and resolved that I would barter my maidenhead for marriage and nothing less.

And finally, directly before my thirteenth birthday, I was rewarded. I never knew why my mother's incessant applications on my behalf were finally answered, if I was honored because of my sister's old place with the former Duchess of York, or because of my father's long-standing loyalty to His Majesty. Perhaps I'd simply been noticed while I walked in the park. I was a pretty child and I knew it, with bright blue eyes, fair skin, and an upturned nose, and though not tall, I had a pleasingly confident carriage that made gentlemen turn and look after me with interest. That was the sum of my dowry, and I knew that, too. Unlike other young girls with aspirations, I'd no grand family name or fortune to ease my way, nor a patron to sponsor me at court.

All I knew to be certain was this: I had been called to the newly wed Mary Beatrice, Duchess of York, to be considered for a place as a maid of honor in her household. James, the Duke of York, was the king's only brother and heir, and the court he and the duchess kept at St. James's was nearly the equal of His Majesty's, across the park at Whitehall. To belong to the Yorks' household would be splendid for me indeed.

For the first time since I'd come to London, I proudly entered the palace beneath the tall brick towers built long before by the eighth King Henry. I wore my best gown, dark blue wool piped with yellow, with rows of tucks at the cuffs and hem of my petticoat to make up for the absence of more fashionable lace which I could not yet afford. I held my head high and reminded myself that I'd been born into the gentry, and that my father had once owned property in three counties.

"My name is Miss Jennings," I said, showing the treasured letter to the porter who stopped me at the door. "I've come at the invitation of Her Grace the Duchess of York."

The man scarce deigned to notice me or my invitation, beckoning to a page to be my guide.

"Show Miss Jennings to Her Grace, Wilkins," he said, already turning to the gentleman behind me. "Be quick about it, too."

"So you are to be the new maid of honor, Miss Jennings," the page said as he led me down the hall. He was not much older than I, his skin so ablaze with pimples that it matched the scarlet coat of his livery. "You look fresh and sweet as new cream."

"I'm nearly thirteen," I said as grandly as I could. Like every girl my age, I was eager to put aside my childhood for what I was certain would be better. "That's quite old enough to be a maid of honor."

"Old enough for mischief, that's for certain." He looked me up and down with approval. "His Grace'll make short work of a little morsel like you."

"That's impudent talk!" I said, shocked he'd dare say such a thing. "Where's your respect for your master?"

"It's there before His Grace's face whenever I need it," the boy said, unperturbed. "He doesn't pay much heed to us lads, anyway. It's the women he likes. If you're wise, you'll keep yourself to company and away from his path. Unless that's why you're here. There's plenty that are. Mark you, here comes the Countess of Fitzwilliam. You know how to make your curtsey, don't you?"

"Of course I do," I whispered sharply as I stepped to one side and lowered my eyes. I put my heels together, bent my knees, and dipped deeply as the countess and her two attendants passed us by.

"You must learn every lady and lord at court, by sight and by rank," the boy said, "and who deserves which salute. You'll lose your place if you don't. Mind the dog, there."

"Must I curtsey for her, too, if she's a peer's dog?" I pulled my petticoat to one side of the large yellow bitch sprawled across the floor before me, languidly flopping her tail with a steady *thump*.

"Oh, it's worse at Whitehall," the boy continued as we turned to climb a staircase. "Both His Grace and His Majesty are mad for beasts, but His

Majesty fair worships his dogs. They say there's more dogs than whores in that palace, and all of them lolling about wherever they please."

I didn't answer, unsure exactly how to reply to this flippant link between dogs and royal mistresses. Besides, there *were* dogs everywhere here, and it seemed that I'd only traded the stench of the stable for that of the kennel. There was another familiar smell, too, one of too many chamber pots and too many people living too closely together regardless of their rank, though here at least it was mingled with the sweeter, wafting stink of perfume.

"Have we much farther to go?" I asked as we turned down another long, dark hall. Perhaps things would improve when we drew closer to the royal quarters.

"Around this corner," he said, and my hopes sank. I'd dreamed so long of visiting the more noble part of the palace that the reality was sadly disappointing. The halls were more spacious here, true. The benches beneath the leaded windows were covered in dark red plush, and the ceiling overhead was a fairy-tracery of cast plaster. Yet these same ceilings were smudged with soot from candles and fires, and even the dark paneling along the walls, carved to mimic folded drapery, was filmed with the fine grey dust that drifted from the breweries near Charing Cross.

But then my eyes widened as I saw something far, far different, hanging there on the wall before us, and I forgot the dust: an enormous painting, with figures sized near to life, and beyond a wisp of drapery, every last one was without clothing.

"Ahh, that won't be the last of those you see," the boy said, laughing at my embarrassment. "His and Her Grace do like their paintings, and sculptures made from marble, too. Her Grace brought crates and crates of them with her from Italy, along with her own cooks and confessors. That one's supposed to be an allegory of pagan love."

I frowned with disapproval at the lascivious, unclothed people. I'd no notion what an allegory might be, but I wanted no part of one, nor of pagan love, either. "I thought Her Grace was supposed to be a pious lady."

"She's a papist," he said, as if that explained everything. "They say she wished to bury herself away in a nunnery, too, but that the pope himself made her marry His Grace and come to London. They say he's ordered her to save our English souls from hell, and betray us all to King Louis and the French."

"I should like to see her try!" I remembered the bonfires and burning straw effigies in protest of the duke's marriage to the Italian Mary Beatrice of Modena, and the ugly prints that were posted about the city, portraying the new duchess hand in hand with a crook-backed pope and a leering French King Louis leading England to unholy ruin. "My soul does perfectly well in the keeping of the Church of England, thank you."

But the boy shook his head. "Take care, Miss Jennings. Most folk in England may be like us, but His Grace already leans towards his wife's Romish faith, and they say he'd even have his daughters the princesses raised in it if His Majesty would let him. Best to keep your own beliefs close if you wish to prosper in this household. Here we are."

We'd stopped before tall double doors, flanked by a pair of guardsmen in the uniform of the duke's own company. They took no notice of Wilkins or me, or perhaps because they recognized him, they judged us not worth bothering over. The boy rapped on the door, and my heart thumped in my chest. I smoothed my skirts one last time and bit my lips to make them redder.

"Remember me, duck," Wilkins whispered behind me, and just before the door swung open, he reached down and pinched my bottom through my skirts.

"Your Grace, Miss Jennings," the footman announced, and I only just managed to close my gaping, gasping mouth and curtsey.

"Come, come, Miss Jennings, let me look at you." The young woman in the tall-backed chair smiled at me, her needlework in her hands and a half-dozen richly dressed attendants sitting about her on low cushioned stools, called *tabourets* at court. I'd known the duchess was young, only sixteen, but somehow I'd expected the weight of her title and responsibilities to have given her gravity beyond her years. Instead I found Mary Beatrice to be warm, her smile eager, and despite the dark coloring to her hair and skin that were the legacy of her d'Este ancestors, she had a natural elegance and grace. I guessed she'd also be an easy, obliging mistress to serve, and my desire to be chosen rose even higher.

I stepped forward and swept my woolen skirts gracefully as I curt-seyed, presenting myself for her approval.

"You were recommended as a true English beauty, Miss Jennings." She chose her words with great care, bending her tongue around a language that must still be so foreign to her. "That judgment is most correct."

"Thank you, Your Grace," I murmured, taking care to venture no more. The main role of a maid of honor was to be an agreeable ornament to the court, and I was determined to prove I could be precisely that.

She leaned a little closer, studying me. "How many years do you have, Miss Jennings?"

"I am thirteen, Your Grace."

"So young!" she exclaimed, and a shadow of sadness crossed her face. Was she thinking of her own tender age? Or was she regretting how, like every princess, she'd been married off for political gain, and her own sweet youth squandered on a husband twenty-five years her senior? "You shall make a fair companion to Lady Mary and Lady Anne, too."

I nodded again, barely able to hide my excitement. These two princesses were her stepdaughters, His Grace's children by the first duchess. To be companion to them would be as great an honor as with Her Grace herself.

The duchess looked down for a moment, wrapping a strand of silk floss around and around her fingertip. "You have no lover, Miss Jennings, do you?"

"Oh, no, Your Grace!" I flushed, my cheeks hot at such a question, and the other ladies laughed slyly behind their hands or fans at my discomfi-ture. "Not at all!"

The duchess raised her hand, and at once the laughter stopped. "I am glad," she said. "I do not like bold intrigues in my household, Miss Jennings."

Someone sniggered, barely turning the sound into a cough. Later, when I knew more, I understood the jest, for there was never a household more given to intrigues of every sort than this one, with the master him-self leading the whole sordid parade.

But at the time all I did was nod. "No, Your Grace. That is, I shall not be bold."

"I wouldn't think you would." She smiled again, her teeth as fine and regular as the pearls around her throat. "We find you most acceptable, Miss Jennings. When will you join us?"

"Oh, at once, Your Grace, at once!" I cried, swept away by my enthusiasm. "A thousand gratitudes, Your Grace, and I promise I'll never give you cause for regret!"

"Never, Miss Jennings?" she said archly, laughing, and the others followed her and laughed as well. "How pleasing that would be if true!"

Behind me I heard a door open and the rustling of skirts, and Mary Beatrice's attention shifted away from me to the newcomer. Of course I could not turn to look; to show my back to Her Grace or any other of a higher rank was strictly forbidden at court.

"You are done with your music master, Lady Anne?" the duchess asked with that same eagerness to please, holding out her hand to the girl who'd entered with her governess. "Was he content with your new piece?"

Coming before me, Lady Anne only shrugged and brushed her pursed lips across the duchess's presented cheek with as little affection as possible. She was just eight, tall and plump for her age, with dun-colored hair and a plain face above a gold-colored silk gown that echoed those of the other ladies in miniature. Her eyes were famously weak—everyone in London had heard of the foreign surgeons and failed cures—and her constant weeping squint gave her a look of cross displeasure.

"Did you play well, Anne?" the duchess persisted, and again the only answer she received from the girl was another silent lift of her shoulders. Of course this did not make Mary Beatrice happy, her arched black brows drawing together as she watched the girl walk away from her.

I watched them thoughtfully. It was clear there was no excess of love between them, something I would do well to remember.

"We have a new maid of honor, Anne," the duchess said with a cheer that seemed forced. "This is Miss Sarah Jennings."

She pointed to me, and as the princess turned, I curtseyed yet again. Lady Anne considered me with wary interest, the way she might a new puppy that could perhaps bite.

"I get sweetmeats with my tea when I play my harpsichord piece without mistakes," she said. "They're bringing me a dish of them now. Do you like sweetmeats, Miss Jennings?"

"Yes, Lady Anne," I said carefully, suspecting this royal puppy might bite, too. "I do."

"Then you shall eat them with me." Without waiting for my reply, she headed for the small mahogany tea table that had been set for her near the window. I glanced back to the duchess, who motioned for me to follow, and as I joined Lady Anne, a footman magically appeared with a second chair for me.

"Sit, Miss Jennings," Lady Anne ordered, swinging her legs gently as she surveyed the silver dish of little cakes placed before her. "You have my leave. I like these ones with the jam centers the best."

"Thank you, my lady." I sat gingerly on the edge of the chair. Choosing sweetmeats with a princess was far beyond my experience, and I feared desperately that somehow I'd err and lose my new position before I fair had it.

"Eat." Lady Anne popped one of the sweetmeats into her mouth, licking her fingers. "I wouldn't have asked you otherwise."

I plucked the nearest sweet from the plate and took the daintiest of bites, not wishing to be caught with my mouth overfull.

Lady Anne took another, squinting at me closely. "You haven't told me how fortunate I am."

"Fortunate, my lady?" I asked, mystified. Though the other women had begun to speak among themselves again, I suspected they were listening, too.

"To have Mary Beatrice as my new mother," she said. "Because she is young and beautiful and clever. Everyone tells me I am fortunate that she married my father, but you did not."

Careful, Sarah, careful! "It's said that a mother is impossible to replace, my lady."

She turned her hand to lick a stray dribble of red jam that had fallen onto the emerald ring she wore on her little finger. "My mother is dead, and my aunt, and my grandmother, and all four of my little brothers."

"We live in perilous times, my lady." This was sadly true. In the last half century, poor England had suffered through a civil war, a great fire that had destroyed much of London, and a hideous plague that had claimed thousands of lives across the country. "My father died five years ago."

Strangely, that caught her interest. "How, Miss Jennings? How did he die?"

"He had long suffered a weakness of the heart, my lady," I said. "The final attack seized him with great pain, but his last suffering was quick."

"May God have mercy on his soul." She nodded, satisfied. "My mother died of a wasting cancer that ate away her breasts and bowels from within. Her agony was so great that my father brought her priests to comfort her, and gave her last rites in the Romish church. My mother would never have tolerated that if she hadn't been so ill. My father thought no one would find out, but we did."

She smoothed the cuff of her embroidered linen cap between her fingers, heedless of the jam she smeared upon it. Lady Anne was testing me, and I knew it as well as she did herself. Did I side with her, who had been raised like me in the Church of England, or with her stepmother, my new mistress, who followed Rome and the pope? I thought of what the boy Wilkins had told me of keeping myself free of the question of faith in this household, yet here that same question had already dug its claws into me.

"If Her Grace your mother was out of her wits from pain, my lady, then what she said or did would not count, would it?" I reasoned, not really sure myself.

Lady Anne nodded solemnly. "Dr. Compton says it doesn't, and he's the Bishop of London."

"Then it must be so, my lady," I said, trying not to think of how odd this conversation was. "Her Grace's soul must be safe."

"I believe it is, too." Lady Anne sighed and bit into another sweet, the red jam oozing from the corner of her mouth. "I believe she's safe with the angels in *our* heaven."

She leaned over the table towards me, lowering her voice.

"You told me the truth, Miss Jennings," she said. "No one else does that. You didn't tell me what you thought I should hear, or what I wanted to, like everyone else does."

Was this a compliment or not? "Yes, my lady," I said at last. "I *was* truthful, my lady."

She smiled, her teeth speckled with sticky raspberry seeds. "I like that, Miss Jennings. I like you. You must be here each day, for me."

"Yes, Lady Anne," I said, keeping my amazement to myself. Because I didn't yet possess a courtier's sense of what to say to best please those I served, because I was still so guileless and had spoken only the truth, I'd managed to please the princess and win her favor.

I smiled back and slipped the rest of my sweetmeat into my mouth. If making my way at court was to be this easy, I thought with the foolishness of my youth, why, then, how could I do otherwise than prosper?

"You must watch yourself in that place, Sarah," my mother said, watching my preparations with her hands clasped at her waist. She hadn't offered to help me pack my belongings, nor did I wish her to. "There'll be plenty of villains waiting to prey upon you."

"I'm only a maid of honor, Mother." I began laying my clothes into my trunk: a small, neat stack of plain petticoats and smocks, rolled knots of stockings, silken garters coiled like brightly colored serpents. It wasn't much for a lady going to court, where new fashions were slavishly followed, but the duchess would help dress me in a fitting way once I was in her household. A porter to carry my chest and a footman to escort me were waiting outside to take me to my new quarters in the palace, and in a way I felt as if I were already there. "I'll scarce be noticed at all."

Mother sniffed, her expression sour beneath her starched widow's hood. I'd thought she'd rejoice for my good fortune, but ever since I'd returned this last time to gather my things, she'd been shrill and full of dire complaint, and I was wary of the temper that too often rose from her displeasure.

"With your fair hair, they'll notice you quick enough," she warned. "You'll be no more than another pretty tidbit to that pack of wolves."

"I'm not so foolish as that, Mother," I protested. "I know my worth, and I mean to make the most of it."

"Now that I'd like to see, Sarah," she said, "you playing at being as grand as that Romish foreign duchess!"

"You won't be able to see me at all, Mother, not once I'm a part of the Duke of York's household," I said warmly, without thinking of the consequences. "You won't be allowed past the guards without an express invitation."

"That's bold talk to your own mother, isn't it?" she said, her voice now brittle with anger and her face turning livid. Others whispered that my mother had a witch's powers, and when her temper took her like this, I could almost believe it myself. "You'll see. You'll be no better than all the other hussies when the first gallant whispers his pretty words into your ear."

"I will be different." I began tossing the last of my things into the trunk willy-nilly, desperate to be gone. "And I'm not another hussy."

"You are if I say so, daughter." She grabbed me by the wrist, pulling me around to face her. "You think you know so much more than I! What do you know of the court? What do you know of the world?"

I thought of how well I'd done earlier with the duchess and with Lady Anne, and with brave if unwise defiance I raised my chin. "I already know more than you do! The Duchess of York herself has invited me to join her household, while you—"

Her hand caught me hard across the cheek, striking the very words from my mouth, and though I'd felt such blows many times before, the sting was always doubly sharp because it came from my mother. I pulled free and stumbled away, putting the bed between us.

"Ungrateful little baggage!" she shouted, her eyes full of the familiar old fury. "Go to your fine new friends, and see how long they want you! Just don't come back here whimpering to me when some noble rascal's filled your belly with his bastard and cast you off without a penny!"

I slammed the lid of my trunk shut and fled into the hall. I told the porter to fetch the trunk, ignoring how he stared at the red mark of my mother's hand that I knew must be blazed on my cheek.

"You're a proud, ungrateful wench, Sarah!" my mother shouted after me from the door. "You always have been, and you'll never be anything else!"

With my head high as if nothing were amiss, I nodded to the page and the porter with my trunk on his back, and together we started towards the far side of the palace and the royal apartments.

And I never once looked back.

* * *

I stretched as tall as I could to look over the wall, the hem of my satin petticoat snagging on the rough bricks. The privy garden behind the palace was empty except for the moonlight, a pale wash over the marble bench and bare branches of the espaliered pear trees pegged flat to the walls.

"Where is this great show you promised, Lady Anne?" I whispered, my words coming in little puffs of warmth in the cold night air. I rubbed my hands together, wishing I'd brought gloves. "I see nothing extraordinary."

"She *will* come, I vow," Anne insisted, though the anxiety in her whisper showed no such confidence. "You'll see with your own eyes, Miss Jennings. Like the great whore of Babylon herself, she is."

I could hear the princess's excitement in the tremble of her voice, whispering the forbidden word aloud there in the dark. Of course King Charles's court at that time was so wicked that even a swaddling babe would soon know of whores and bawds and jades of every rank. But because of who we two girls were, in the company of others we were expected to feign the blindest innocence, as was proper for ladies of our tenderling age and station.

"There she is, Miss Jennings," Anne said, her whisper squeaking upwards. "There—there! Exactly as I promised!"

"Hush now, or she'll mark us!" I jerked Anne down lower beside me, so only our eyes peeked over the mossy-topped wall.

The lady—for a lady-whore she must be, to have found her way into this garden—moved with swift purpose to the bench, the gathered tail of her skirts catching on the rough crushed shells of the path. The silver-shot silk of her gown glistened in the moonlight, and her deep Flemish cuffs swung back and forth as she fluttered her fan before her face, more from nervousness than from need on this chilly night.

Even through the screen of leaves and branches I recognized her, and I wondered that Anne didn't, too, or why she would pretend otherwise. The lady's name was Arabella Churchill, and she was, like me, a part of our own household here at court, another maid of honor to the duchess.

But that wasn't the reason I'd no wish to linger here to spy. I took

Anne's arm, meaning to lead her away. "We've tarried here long enough. Come, my lady, we'll be missed if we don't return to the others."

"No, we won't." Anne pulled her arm free, willful and stubborn. "Not yet. Look, there is the whore's lover now!"

Against all my better judgment, I obeyed, looking to where she pointed. The man was more difficult to see through the branches, his wig long and full and flopping over his shoulders, hiding his face from us in shadows. His coat and waistcoat glittered with gold, the flaring star of his rank embroidered over his heart.

I'd been wise to worry. "Come, my lady, this is not proper, nor right."

But again Anne shook me away, instead intent on the couple before us.

"She cares not who watches, nor does he," she said, paying me no heed. "I know. I've been here before. She was one of my mother's maids, the *whore.*"

Even through the veil of the trees, we saw it all. There was no courtship, no wooing. The gentleman hooked his thumbs into the wide neckline of the lady's gown, sliding the stiffened collar over her shoulders and down her arms until her breasts popped free. He filled his hands with the yielding flesh, bending to bite at her throat, and though her black-gloved hands clung to his back, she turned her head away, towards us. By the moonlight I could see the resignation in the lady's face, the same that I'd seen once on a stag at the end of its run, waiting with the huntsman's knife at its panting throat.

Anne's fat little fingers moved restlessly around mine, her palms turning moist. I told myself I should not look to see more, yet still I was Anne's sorry match in guilty fascination, pulling her closer to me against the brick wall. She was trembling, my poor lady, and I would comfort her however I could.

With rough force the gentleman turned the lady and shoved her face-first over the arm of the bench. He threw the drapery of her petticoats over her hips and unfastened the fall on his breeches, and with a low wordless grunt plunged his member deep within her, jerking against her like an alley mongrel with his bitch.

I turned away, unable to watch any longer, and pressed myself against the wall to steady my shaking knees.

"I would never let a man use me like—like that," I said, fair spitting the words. My heart raced and my face felt hot with shame for Anne and for me, and for Arabella Churchill, too. "I'll never grant a man that power over me. Never, my lady. *Never.*"

Anne twisted closer to me, her rounded body feverishly warm where our skin touched in the cold night air.

"You would if they forced you to," she said. "Women must do as men say."

For Anne that was sadly true. A princess is no more than a pawn in worldly games, a pawn who must take whatever convenient prince is pushed into her bed. But not I—I was only Miss Jennings, poor and fatherless and common-born, with no dowry beyond my face and my cleverness and my desire to play my part grandly on the stage of life.

"I'll not bend to any man's whim, my lady," I vowed fiercely. "Never."

"You will swear to it?" Her pleading eyes were too bright, too desperate, in her childish face. "Everyone says that that—that *whore* in the garden barters her body to better her situation at court. But you would not do that, Sarah Jennings, would you?"

I know now that I had come to King Charles's court too young, and lapped up the heady poison of corruption and deceit with my innocent tongue. Now I know that I learned too soon to judge and value others first by what they could do for me, and I learned as well to find no wrong in the practice. When I looked at Anne's round face, I saw not only my youthful companion and the princess I was bound to serve, but also a protector for my future, a link in the golden chain that ran directly to the throne itself.

"I will not leave you, Lady Anne," I promised, my words soft as velvet. It was easy to make such reckless promises at thirteen, and easy to keep them, too. "I swear to you I never will."

She twisted her fingers deeper into mine and pressed her lips, sticky from spun-sugar sweets, to the back of my hand.

"I trust you, Sarah," she whispered, her voice ripe with fervency. "You are my friend, and I'll trust you like no other."

I kissed her dimpled hand in return and felt the warmth of her loyalty, and her love. I didn't dream that, like every good courtier, she might have played me as I sought to play her.

On the other side of the wall we heard voices and laughter, and with guilty haste we brushed the twigs and flecks of dirt from our petticoats.

"Come, Miss Jennings, hurry," Anne whispered as we cut our path beneath the hanging boughs, back to the gallery. "As soon as the whore is done pleasuring Father, he will leave her and return to the company."

Oh, yes, I had come to court too young.

Chapter Two

"James was away from his lady for nearly a month," Lady Ainsworth said as she shuffled the playing cards, "and Mary Beatrice was most eager to see him when he returned here last night. *Most* eager. I'd wager a guinea that she'll keep him abed for the rest of this day, and likely tonight as well."

Across the table from her, Lady Simonton smiled and idly twisted one of her long chestnut curls around her fingers. I was sitting with the two older ladies-in-waiting in the duchess's gallery, the afternoon sunlight streaming in through the long row of arched windows while they played ombre. After six weeks in Her Grace's service, I'd learned what was expected of me. We ladies were ready if Mary Beatrice had need of us, but until she did, our time was our own to squander or make use of as we chose. Most played cards with a relentless passion—loo, all fours, ombre, piquet, ruff, and honors—but I kept away from the table, unable to play for the enormous stakes that the other ladies wagered, as much as a thousand guineas in a single night. Instead I sat to one side on one of the tabourets with a book of sonnets open in my lap, pretending to read while I listened shamelessly to the conversation around me.

Lady Simonton took her cards and fanned them in her hand, her pearl bracelets slipping down her wrist. As idle as we were, she was still dressed in the most costly French fashion, the folds of her silk lutestring skirts falling gracefully around the nipped toes of her damask-covered mules.

"His Grace had no right being apart from his wife for so long," she said, "no matter what business may have kept him abroad. Not unless, of course, he'd left her with a babe on the way."

"Oh, I'll venture James has done his duty by her." Lady Ainsworth arched a single brow. Her husband had been a supporter and boon companion of the king from the time of his exile in France, and Lady Ainsworth had benefited from his loyalty, too. "He is a Stuart, after all, and he's sired enough brats to know how it's done. But did he go to Arabella's house first, I wonder, or Mary Beatrice's?"

My cheeks flamed, remembering the shameful scene that Lady Anne and I had witnessed between Miss Churchill and the duke.

But Lady Simonton misread my shame. "Hush," she said, and glanced pointedly at me. I knew her caution wasn't so much for my youth and innocence, but because they still didn't know whether I was to be trusted. "Mind your words, sweet."

But the other lady ignored the warning. "Who can fault him for turning to his mistress? Neither of his wives has graced him with a son who's lived longer than a few breaths. I say it's God's own curse, the same as with the poor king and queen. Not even the Stuart seed can find purchase in a barren Catholic womb."

Lady Simonton sighed and laid her first card on the table. "The duchess isn't like the queen. She's not barren. She's already been with child once."

"And lost it."

"But she's taking all the right precautions for the proper outcome next time," reasoned Lady Simonton. "You see her each morning, too, holding her nose as she chokes down those vile concoctions the midwives have made for her. She wants a child as much as the rest of us."

"What we want is not only a boy, but an Anglican heir to the throne." Lady Ainsworth nodded, her dimpled chin bobbing up and down. "That's what England needs, and what she was brought here to do. You know the king would embrace his brother's son as if he were his own."

This was hardly news to anyone at court, or in London, for that matter. While Anne and Mary, the two princesses, had been safely raised as Anglicans, a male heir to the throne was most sorely needed.

But how could any Englishman or woman with a clear eye for our country's future wish differently? As young as I was, I still feared what would become of tiny Protestant England if pitted against the great Catholic powers of France, Spain, Portugal, and Rome. I feared their intolerance and their hateful persecution of others unlike themselves. And most of all, I feared what would happen to the rest of us Anglicans if a Catholic king were ever again to sit on the throne of England.

But at least now I knew that these two ladies were Protestants as well. While it was easy to tell that the duchess's Italian attendants—among her ladies-in-waiting was her childhood friend the Countess Lucrezia Pretonari Vezzani, while her confessor was Father Antonio Guidici—were sympathetic to her faith, guessing among the English ones could be more hazardous.

"Grant the duchess a bit of time," Lady Simonton was saying. "She'll bear James his son when she's ready. You forget how young she is, and that her body still needs time to ripen for childbearing."

But Lady Ainsworth only sniffed to show her disregard for the duchess's lack of a son. "Sixteen's not so very young," she said. "There's plenty of wives younger than that with a ring of children around their knees. How old are you, Miss Jennings?"

Startled, I just remembered to look up as if I'd been pulled from my book. "Yes, my lady?"

She smiled indulgently, running her fingers back and forth across her bracelets. "How old are you, poppet?"

"Thirteen, my lady," I said. "Fourteen in June."

"Truly?" she asked, the surprise now hers. "I thought you were older than that. Certainly the gentlemen will, you know."

Most people did believe me older, especially since Her Grace had replaced my plain wool clothes with the more elegant finery that was more suitable to my new place in her household. She particularly liked me in the gown I wore today, broad red and green stripes cleverly mitered and pleated to show off the narrowness of my waist, with the fine border of Venetian lace on my linen smock peeking above the gown's low neckline. I'd learned to lace my stays more tightly, too, like the other ladies, and was proud of how round and womanly the whalebone made my budding breasts appear.

"Thirteen, you say." Lady Simonton studied me over her cards, her blue eyes full of doubt. Neither of these ladies could be more than five or six years my senior, though I'd grant that they were vastly older in worldly experience. "Has the duke met you yet?"

I shook my head, and the smile they exchanged between them said much that excluded me.

"Miss Jennings, Miss Jennings," Lady Ainsworth said, her voice like a tigress's purr. "His Grace's welcome to you will be very warm. *Very* warm."

"Oh, stop!" Lady Simonton laughed, holding her cards up to her face. "Don't frighten the poor lass!"

"I don't mean to frighten. Only . . . *inform.*"

Lady Simonton made a face, then turned towards me. "Tell us, Miss Jennings. Did your mother speak to you of how women conceive babes? Do you know how such things occur?"

"Yes, my lady," I answered promptly. Mother had been so afraid that I'd be led astray by some low apprentice or stableboy that she'd begun lecturing me on this same subject long before I needed it. "I know what men do with their wives."

"With their wives," Lady Ainsworth said, teasing, "*and* with their mistresses, *and* their scullery maids, *and* any other female with half a breath left in her body."

Again they laughed together, their heads tossed back and their jeweled ear-bobs dancing against their cheeks, making me flush with shame for my ignorance. Was I that great an innocent fool, for them to find such amusement at my expense?

Lady Simonton reached out and patted my shoulder. "What she's saying, my dear, is that at court the gentlemen often have many more opportunities to—to *indulge* themselves than other men might."

Lady Ainsworth chuckled, her eyes heavy-lidded and sly. "So do the ladies, if they wish it."

"*If* they wish it," said Lady Simonton sternly. "You will be much pursued, Miss Jennings, not only because you are so fair, but because you are so young. You'll find a great many gentlemen who believe that plucking a virgin's maidenhead is the best sport in the world."

The heat in my cheeks grew warmer still, and I marveled that they could speak with this freedom and ease about such things. "I don't wish to be any gentleman's sport, my lady."

"Nor should you," she said firmly. "No matter how much a gentleman presses, Miss Jennings, you don't have to grant him so much as a kiss unless you're willing, too. You're not some milkmaid ripe for tumbling behind a hedgerow. You're a lady, a maid of honor to Her Grace. Even if it's the duke himself—hah, even His Majesty!—you can refuse him."

"*Especially* if it's the duke, the randy old goat." Lady Ainsworth wrinkled her nose with disdain "But 'tis not all so bad, little Miss Jennings. If you find a gentleman who does please you, no one here or at Whitehall will look askance if you decide to take him as your lover."

"Thank you, my lady," I said, "but I—I don't believe I will."

That made her smile, though I'd never intended it should. "You're only thirteen. Wait until you've danced in the Great Hall at the palace and had all the handsome young bucks come panting and pawing after you."

"But you must take care, Miss Jennings," warned Lady Simonton. "Maids of honor must appear to be maids, even if few enough of them are. If you get caught with some gentleman's child swelling up beneath your smock, why, then Her Grace will have no choice but to send you home."

"Or into keeping," Lady Ainsworth said blithely, "if that's the game you choose. It depends upon your circumstances. You are quite poor, aren't you? No portion to speak of?"

"My father lost nearly everything because he supported His Majesty's cause, my lady. I have no gold, nor land, nor title to bring to a husband." I knew they pitied me because I *was* poor by their standards, if not those of the rest of the world. I didn't care. I was still proud of who I was, and I raised my chin as high as I dared. "My fortune lies in my person, and my wit."

"So it does, Miss Jennings," Lady Ainsworth said, appraising me. "So it does, and a splendid fortune for a woman it is."

She turned up one of the cards before her, a red queen, and with a half smile held it up between two fingers for me to see. "You're clever enough to make some besotted wretch pay quite dearly for your favors. This court—even this household—has seen its share of women who've bettered themselves that way, and not all of them have been actresses, either. Lady Castlemaine is a Villiers by birth, yet with every bastard she bears the king, she increases her power and her wealth."

"But that's not what *I* want, my lady," I protested unhappily. "Not at all!"

"Of course you don't, pet, not yet," Lady Simonton said easily, "and who can fault you for it?"

I shook my head in silence, unable to explain. Yes, I wanted wealth and power and the other worldly benefits that could come to those at court. But I didn't want them at the price of my soul, nor was my heart so avaricious that I would put aside all thoughts of love and common happiness, and spread my legs for a powerful man for the sake of gold or a title the way that Arabella Churchill had. What I longed for more was a partner, a friend, a gentleman to share my life and my love, as well as my ambitions, and if such a paragon did not exist, why, then I'd be like the great Virgin Queen herself, and never wed.

But these noble ladies didn't begin to understand my silence, nor, truly, did they wish to. I offered much more amusement otherwise.

"You know, Miss Jennings, there *are* ways to stay the whole wretched process," Lady Ainsworth said with that same knowing half wink that I was beginning to dread. "Not that your mama would have told you. No, no. But *I* know where one can purchase small linen casings made to cover your lover's staff and keep his essence from mingling with yours to make an inconvenient babe. Or you might prefer to follow the French manner, and receive the gentleman into your mouth instead of—"

"Please, please, spare the poor innocent!" Lady Simonton exclaimed, her gaze rolling up towards the heavens in feigned distress worthy of the stage. "Next you'll fetch the Aretino from beneath your pillow, by way of illustration!"

They laughed uproariously at that, while I prayed the queasiness I felt did not show upon my face. Though a virgin still, I'd thought I'd known all there was about the act between wedded women and men, but now it seemed I was as ill schooled in this as I was in Latin and Greek.

I frowned, determined not to be ignorant any longer. "Please, my lady, might I ask what is this Aretino, and what does it illustrate?"

They laughed again, with Lady Simonton forced to clap her hands over her mouth to stop.

"It's a wicked, wicked book," Lady Ainsworth explained, "brought to me from Venice by a certain wicked gentleman. It explains all the postures and positions most advantageous to lovemaking, and the illustrations show them."

From the way her eyes sparked and her tongue rolled around the word *wicked*, I realized with shock that the wicked gentleman was most likely her lover, not her lordly husband. Her *lover*: I knew that nearly all the great gentlemen here at court kept mistresses in addition to their wives, but I'd yet to meet a lady who'd done the same to her husband.

"Oh," I said faintly, now hoping very much that she didn't produce the book for me to see. "Thank you, my lady."

But Lady Simonton was laughing still, pressing her fingers to her lips as if she could feel her own mirth bubbling out.

"More correctly it's a book about swiving, Miss Jennings," she said, pausing just long enough to nip the tip of her finger between her small white teeth. "There's precious little to do with love anywhere in *those* pages!"

I looked down at the book of sonnets by an Italian poet that the duchess had given to me, sonnets that were full of love and honor and noble deeds. There was nothing in them about linen casings or curious postures, and nothing, either, in my own dreams of a gentleman who'd make me his wife. Hearing these highborn ladies speak so wantonly reminded me of the dog-leavings scattered throughout the palace halls, sordid reminders that there was an ugly side to the lives of even the most noble folk.

"*Cazzo dritto non vuolt consiglio.*" The foreign words spilled salaciously from Lady Simonton's lips, words she then translated for my reluctant benefit. " 'One cannot quarrel with a standing cock.' Surely you must have heard *that* little proverb by now, my dear."

"I could send for Maestro Aretino's book for you, Miss Jennings," Lady Ainsworth said, as if she was daring me, and perhaps she was. "It would take but a minute to fetch. Then you could judge the quality of the dialogues and the pictures for yourself."

"What book?" Lady Anne asked, joining us unannounced, with her governess and a page trailing after her. "I should like to see a book with pictures, Lady Ainsworth, for I cannot abide reading. The words make my eyes hurt."

Hurriedly we three rose to our feet, our heads bowed as we curtseyed in near unison to the princess.

"Good day, Lady Anne," Lady Ainsworth said, her manner now sweet enough to lure a honeybee. "Permit me to venture that the book in question would be of scant interest to you. It's a dry book for scholars, my lady, full of foreign words and expressions."

Anne scowled, suspicious. "If the book is so boring and tedious, then why were you offering to show it to Miss Jennings? Why won't you show it to me?"

"Lady Ainsworth perceived a lack in my education, my lady, that needed correction," I said quickly, praying that Lady Ainsworth would follow my lead, despite the difference in our ranks. Not only would it be unthinkable for her to show her wicked book to the princess, but the pious young duchess would be furious if she learned one of her ladies kept such a volume for her amusement. And as for me—if at my age I were to be linked with this Aretino, then I was quite certain my first month at court would become my last.

I smiled at the princess. "Lady Ainsworth only wished to improve my knowledge by showing me a book brought from Venice. She meant nothing more."

"Oh, so it's *Italian*." Anne wrinkled her nose with disdain for her stepmother's country, her interest in the book instantly gone. "I'd rather play cards, anyway."

She came to the table, her high red lacquered heels—a subtle sign of her nobility—clattering over the bare floor. Without a thought, she took Lady Simonton's chair and began to push the cards left from their game into a stack.

I looked over her head to Lady Ainsworth, expecting that she would give me some silent sign to show her gratitude for what I'd just done. But instead her expression was cold and haughty, and in place of the ally I thought I'd made, it seemed I'd somehow gained a fresh enemy instead.

"Miss Jennings, sit," ordered Lady Anne. "I will play with only you, for I feel sure you won't try to cheat me, like everyone else does."

"Yes, Lady Anne." I moved to the chair on the other side of the table and waited for the princess to finish shuffling the cards.

"Mary Beatrice's maid dressed my hair differently this morning," Anne said suddenly, pausing with the cards in her chubby, childish hands. "Do you like it?"

"It's most becoming to you, Lady Anne," Lady Simonton said eagerly, nodding for extra emphasis. "And quite the latest fashion, too."

Anne ducked her chin low, her mouth set into a tight stubborn line. "Regard me, Miss Jennings, and tell me the truth. Does the dress of my hair become me?"

I looked at the princess's fine, light brown hair, now scraped back from her wide forehead and twisted into tortuous curls stiffened into place with sugar-water.

The princess already knew the truth, and so did I.

"No, my lady, it does not," I said softly, wishing to gentle my verdict. "But then, not every fashion suits every face."

Her response came so slowly that I feared I'd misstepped, but when her smile finally broke across her plain little face, it was as bright and full of wonder as the sun rising over a mountaintop.

"You are right, Miss Jennings," she said, her words coming in a shy rush that was almost a whisper. "My hair *is* ugly. Oh, Miss Jennings, why is it that you are the only one I can trust to tell me the truth, the only one who will treat me as a friend would?"

I nodded and smiled in return, the only answer that would do. Perhaps I should have rejoiced at having won the princess's trust again, and again simply by telling her the truth as I'd seen it. But already I'd learned that at court truth meant nothing, and trust even less, and though I was glad that the princess believed she could trust me, I wondered how much—or how little—I in turn could ever trust her, or anyone else.

Two days later, I finally met my new master, the Duke of York.

I had gone walking with Mary Beatrice and several of her other ladies in the park. Snow had fallen in the night, just enough to cover the pointed blades of grass and dust over the statues and benches. The Italian-born duchess was fascinated by our English snow and insisted on going out-side soon after dawn. With most snowstorms, the palace gardener's boys would be sent out with brooms and shovels to clear the paths for the ladies, but on this day the duchess had ordered that the paths remain un-touched. She bundled herself in furs and veils against the cold, and urged her sleepy ladies to hurry from their beds to join her.

With her small pack of flop-eared spaniels leaping around her skirts, Mary Beatrice set out into the snow. She took one deliberate step, then another, lifting her skirts so she could see the footprints her high-heeled shoes left in the unblemished snow. I was the only one of her ladies who'd followed closely, the rest slow and grumpy at being roused so early on such an errand, and Mary Beatrice turned to look over her shoulder at me, her cheeks pink from the cold.

"The snow is most delightful, Miss Jennings, is it not?" she asked mer-rily, her accented words turning to little clouds in the chilly air. "Come, follow me!"

She laughed and plunged ahead into the snow, heedless of how her silk-covered shoes were being ruined. But I laughed, too, and ran with her like the young creatures we were, and for those few moments I almost forgot that she was my mistress and the Duchess of York and a foreign-born papist.

The little dogs raced in mindless circles about us, just as glad to be free of the stuffy palace, and yipped and yapped at each other as they tossed bits of snow into the air.

"Here, Jip, here!" the duchess called to one of her favorites. But when she bent to brush the snow from its muzzle, the little dog leaped up and caught her glove in its teeth, pulling it free of her fingers. With a small fierce growl, the dog worried the glove, then bolted off across the snowy grass with its prize.

At once I drew off my own glove and offered it to her. "Take mine, Your Grace," I said with a quick curtsey. "You must keep your fingers warm."

But she waved away my offer, her bare hand cocked over her eyes against the sun as she looked for the rascally dog.

"Tell that to Jip, Miss Jennings," she said, laughing again. "Spoiled little beast! I won't chill your hand, too, because he's being so ill behaved. Run back to my dressing room, Miss Jennings, and ask Pellegrina to give you another pair."

"Yes, Your Grace," I said, backing away from her through the snow. I ran up the stairs to the duchess's apartments, eager to be done with this errand so I could return outside. With the fresh gloves in my hand, I hurried back through the withdrawing room.

And there, so directly in my path that we nearly collided, stood my master, James, the Duke of York.

"Your Grace!" I gasped, dipping low. "Forgive me, I did not see you!"

"No harm done, sweetheart," he said, and smiled. "None at all."

James was nearly as tall as his brother the king, though there was scarce other resemblance between them, or between him and his daughter, Lady Anne, either. At past forty, the duke was still a handsome man, his jaw firm and his blue eyes clear, and he'd yet to put on the extra flesh that most men his age acquired. He must have come from his bedchamber, for he wore a voluminous Indian gown of gold and plum silk damask, his shirt beneath it open at the throat and his feet in black silk mules. He had not yet put on his wig of shoulder-length auburn curls for the day, and his shaven head was covered by a kind of nightcap or turban made of fur. While he was not at all perturbed to be seen in such obvious undress, the intimacy of it shamed and confused me, and I swiftly looked down and away from that pale triangle of his bare chest between his open shirt and gown.

"You are Miss Jennings, aren't you?" he asked. "My wife's newest maid?"

The warnings I'd had from Lady Ainsworth and others regarding the duke rang an alarm in my head, and my one thought was to escape back to the other women.

"Yes, Your Grace," I said, as stiff as a block of alder wood. "I am Miss Jennings, your servant, Your Grace."

"More likely the duchess's servant, eh?" He grinned as if this were the greatest witticism imaginable and took an idle step closer to me, blocking my way to the door. "She sent you to fetch her gloves?"

I looked down at the green kidskin gloves, trimmed with white fur, that were clutched tightly in my hand. "Her Grace wished to keep her hands warm."

"And what of yours, Miss Jennings? Weren't your little hands cold, too?"

"I had my muff, Your Grace." I held the muff up for him to see, pushed up over my wrist, as if somehow he would not have noticed it himself. I was inordinately proud of that muff, my first gift from Mary Beatrice: a narrow barrel of black clipped beaver fur, luxuriously puffed inside with swansdown and lined with pink silk. "My fingers were warm enough."

"Were they." He reached out and lightly stroked the muff's soft fur. "What of the rest of you? Your arms, your thighs, your breasts? Is all of you as warm as it should be?"

I blushed, unable to mistake either his meaning or the suggestiveness of his caress, and I shifted the muff away from his touch. "Yes, Your Grace."

"You know I wouldn't want you cold on account of my wife's whims. Perhaps you need a cloak lined in this same fur. You'd like that, wouldn't you?"

I swallowed hard, my heart thumping, and thought of how he wanted me to betray Mary Beatrice, laughing with her spaniels in the snow.

"Thank you, Your Grace," I said, "but I am content with what I have."

"I cannot believe that. Ladies always wish for new baubles and fripperies, don't they?" He chucked me beneath my chin, forcing me to look up and meet his eye. "What a pretty little piece you are, Miss Jennings. What a joy it will be to have you in this household!"

"Thank you, Your Grace," I said, pulling my chin away from his hand. The greedy hunger I'd seen in his eyes frightened me, and I knew I must find a way to leave him as soon as I could. "Forgive me, but Her Grace will want her gloves, and I should—"

"Not yet, my dear." His voice ruffled with irritation as he inched closer still, so close that now I could smell the scent of his tobacco and the chocolate he'd had for his breakfast, lingering on his breath. "My wife can spare you. Tell me of yourself instead. Has that sweet mouth of yours been tasted yet, I wonder? I can't recall when I've seen a blush as innocent as yours."

The other ladies had told me I'd always the right to refuse a gentleman's attentions, but they'd never explained how it was to be done. I made an unhappy little whimper of fear and tried to scuttle sideways, but he deftly turned his body to trap me.

"Tell me, Miss Jennings," the duke said, his own face now flushed with lust as he leaned over me. "What of your own little muff, eh? Have you sprouted a pelt of your own, the softest of fur?"

Before I could answer he'd reached down and pressed his hand low below my belly, cupping my woman's place through my petticoats. I gasped at his boldness, and forgetting his rank, I put my palms on his chest and shoved him away as hard as I could.

"No, Your Grace!" I cried, my fear now mixed with anger that he'd dare try such freedoms with me. "No, I say!"

"What in blazes are you doing, girl?" he demanded, breathing hard. "Quiet yourself!"

"Forgive me, Your Grace," I cried, "but I will not listen to such shameful questions from you, nor permit such—such liberties with my person!"

He kept back and frowned, clearly so perplexed by my reaction that I wondered if no other woman had ever rejected his advances.

"There's no reason we cannot be friends, Miss Jennings, is there?" he asked at last. "The two of us, eh?"

"Forgive me, Your Grace, but I—I should return to the duchess," I said, making a stiff-backed curtsey, though by rights I could not leave the room without his permission. "She—she will wish her gloves."

I bowed my head, suddenly overwhelmed by the enormity of what I'd just done. I had not only spoken first to a personage of royal blood, but sharply, too, to a man who might someday be king. I had scolded him, and I'd put my hands upon him to push him away. Had the other ladies advised me wrongly, for the amusement of seeing me disgraced and sent away? Should I have let the duke do whatever he pleased instead, and accepted his hateful fur-lined cloak as payment?

For now I would most certainly lose my place, perhaps even be put in prison for such grievous disrespect. I slipped my wayward hands back inside the muff to hide their trembling, my eyes swimming with tears as the melting snow dripped from my skirts to the floor in a ring around me.

I heard the scratching of a pen as he wrote something at the nearby desk, the rustle of the sheet as he folded the paper. Then he was there beside me again, and I had to force myself not to jump away.

"Here, Miss Jennings," he said, his voice far more kindly than I'd expected. "This is the name of a mantua-maker skilled with furs. She will make you whatever kind of cloak you fancy, and a gown or two to match, if you wish. Tell her you are my guest, and you may have anything in the shop that pleases you."

I looked up quickly, in time to see him slip the folded paper into my muff, his fingers sliding in so deeply that they brushed against my own. As he did, the door behind him opened and three of Mary Beatrice's ladies returned, with Lady Ainsworth first. I could see from her face how swiftly she'd noted every guilty detail of the scene before her, from James's undress and flushed face to my own obvious misery, and I knew no good would come of it.

"Good day, ladies," the duke said pleasantly, as if he weren't pulling his fingers from deep inside my muff. "Was the morning air too chill for you?"

"Too chill, Your Grace, for any pitiful mortal with blood in his veins." Lady Ainsworth blew on her hands to warm them as she looked slyly at me, then slid her gaze back to the duke. "But then it would seem, Your Grace, that you've found entertainment enough indoors."

The duke only laughed and looked down at me with such unabashed lust that I could not keep still.

"I believe you mislaid this, Your Grace," I said, pulling the obviously unopened and unread note from my muff and handing it back to him. "It is yours, is it not?"

He frowned down at the scrap of paper. "Are you sure, Miss Jennings?"

"Yes, Your Grace," I said. "It's yours, not mine."

He grumbled crossly. "I suppose it must be mine," he said, stuffing the note into the deep sleeves of his Indian gown. "However could I have lost it?"

Then he turned on his heel and left, his displeasure hovering like a fading storm cloud in the chamber.

"Her Grace is still waiting for those gloves, Miss Jennings," Lady Ainsworth said. "That is, if her fingers have not been bitten clean away by the frost."

"Yes, my lady," I said quickly, and with relief I began towards the door. But to my surprise, Lady Ainsworth caught my arm and held me back, waiting to speak until the other ladies had moved from hearing.

"You could not have done that any better, little Miss Jennings," she said. "Poor James must be half mad from wanting you."

"I don't care if he is, my lady," I said. "I do not want *him*, not at all."

"Oh, but that is of no consequence," she said with an airy wave of her hand. "What matters is that you rejected the duke's billet-doux before us, and returned it to him purposefully unread. Which casts you, Miss Jennings, as the truest of innocents."

"But I *am* innocent, my lady," I protested in an indignant whisper. "He tried to be—be familiar, but I would not let him."

"You could have granted him every last favor he sought," she said, "yet from the way you comported yourself just now, no one would ever believe it. You have outwitted him, and set yourself beyond reproach. This tale will be reported everywhere in St. James's and Whitehall by nightfall, and you—you will shine like the purest diamond."

Suddenly she smiled at me, with more warmth than I'd ever dreamed possible, and something close to admiration, too.

"You are learning, Miss Jennings," she said thoughtfully. "I misjudged your aptitude. Already you've discovered how to coax others to follow your whims and make them believe it was their wish, not yours. Perhaps in time we'll make a proper courtier of you yet, yes?"

"Yes, my lady," I said softly, even as I turned my smile into a perfect mirror of hers. "I believe you will."

Chapter Three

By the time my fifteenth birthday neared a year later, I was able to claim that I knew my way about the court better than any other lady my age. I'd learned whom to trust and whom to avoid, when to curtsey and when to stand instead of sitting, whose gifts were safe to accept and whose would bring unpleasant obligations. I was much praised for my cleverness as well as my beauty, but better than that, I had earned the trust and protection of Mary Beatrice, the Duchess of York, and the devotion of her stepdaughter, Lady Anne.

I'd also remained that rarest curiosity at court, a virgin maid of honor, with my innocence a banner of challenge to every gentleman from my master the Duke of York down to the lowest page. But I knew my worth. Familiarity with the court hadn't changed that. The only fortune I had to barter with was my face, my wit, and my maidenhead. All around me were the sorry lessons of ladies who'd let themselves be ruled by flattery or passion, and I'd no intention of being one more left with a big belly and a handful of jewels and forgotten promises. I wanted more, and I meant to get it.

And then, at last, I met the one man destined to be my match.

In honor of Anne's older sister Lady Mary's birthday, the younger members of the court were to perform the masque *Calisto* before His Majesty and the rest, a last frivolous extravagance of Shrove Tuesday before the solemnity of Lent dulled London for forty nights and days. As a cast we had been chosen less on account of our talents for theatre, and

more because of our rank or our beauty, with each of us still in the freshest flower of youth and attraction.

But now, too late, each one of us here in the Great Hall of the palace
had realized that our rehearsals these last weeks might have been better
spent in learning our roles, instead of amusing ourselves with flirtation
and foolishness. Those with speaking parts like mine—I played Mercury,
that quicksilver messenger—forgot both our words and our cues, while
the dancers misstepped and collided and cursed each other's clumsiness.
It seemed we would indeed give a most memorable performance, but
scarce the one that Mr. Crowne, the poor playwright, had envisioned for
his work.

I stood to one side while I waited for my scene, and silently recited the
words of my lines over and over, moving my lips without giving them
voice.

"You seem anxious, Miss Jennings." His Grace the Duke of Monmouth came to stand beside me, so close that I alone might hear his low,
teasing voice. At twenty-six, his manner was still lighthearted and free of
care, with a handsome face to match. "I should never have expected such
a weakness of you."

He smiled down at me, his dark eyes full of the same knowing Stuart
charm as his father's. There was a great deal of His Majesty in him, in
both his person and his manner, so much that many whispered what a
pity Monmouth was only a bastard son raised to his title, and not a true
heir to the throne or Charles and his barren queen.

"You honor me, Your Grace," I said with the curtsey that even a pinchbeck duke merited, "but the sad truth is that this day I can recall but half
of my lines. What if tonight, with the lights bright upon me, I forget every
word? Look, see how I already tremble!"

I held my quivering hand out for proof, and he took it for a moment,
frowning with mock gravity as if he were a surgeon and I his patient.

"Now this is very curious, Miss Jennings," he said. "I'd always thought
you the bravest of ladies—a veritable lioness. I'd never thought to see you
quake with fear."

"You should, because it is true." I pulled my hand back from his, suddenly more conscious not of how my hand shook, but of how purpose-

fully he was pressing my palm, running his thumbnail lewdly between the juncture of my first two fingers. "If you falter in your dance, Your Grace, then those watching will laugh, and excuse you for having had more useful concerns to distract you from your practice. But I—I shall receive no such indulgence."

He smoothed the deep lace on his cuff and winked, sly as any fox. "From me you would, Miss Jennings."

"Better I might have studied my lines with more care, Your Grace, than to rely upon others' indulgences." I knew from experience to let his gallantry pass unacknowledged, for, again much like his father, Monmouth believed that every lady was susceptible to his persuasive charms—which, in truth, most were.

"But you are only a maid of honor, my dear," he said, "not a scholar. No one expects you to study."

He took a small single step of great elegance, as if practicing his own dance, while at the same time placing himself closer behind me, so near that he pressed into the skirts of my petticoats. I did but smile in polite deference, no more encouraging than in other times past when he had sought me out, and deftly swirled a step away from him.

"But if my Mercury stammers or falls mute tonight before the court, Your Grace," I said, "then I shall be cursed as a failure, for not being the proper pretty ornament you say I should be."

He laughed, though I had meant every word. "Anyone who believes so little of you, Miss Jennings, would be sorely surprised by the truth. I know, because I've felt your lioness's claws."

I didn't blush, though I knew he expected me to. One night not long before, he'd caught me alone near the Banqueting House after he'd taken too much wine, and whispered slurry poetry as he'd tried to thrust his hand inside my bodice.

"Is not a lioness permitted to defend her virtue, Your Grace?" I asked, remembering how he'd yelped when I'd struck his hand aside. "Is not that part of her nature?"

"Her nature, and her power." He leaned forward and kissed me lightly on the cheek, a feathery salute and no more. "For luck, Miss Jennings, so you may shine tonight."

"Thank you, Your Grace," I said as he left me to find another more welcoming lady.

"What was my cousin saying to you, Miss Jennings?" Lady Anne came beside me, sipping some sweet-smelling concoction from a pewter tumbler. She was wearing a tall golden helmet with nodding plumes, part of her costume for tonight, but much at odds with her dark wool day gown, and with her childish face. She had grown taller lately, and even without the benefit of the plume, we were near equal in height now. "He seemed most attentive to you. What did he want?"

"His Grace was asking after my preparations for tonight, my lady, that is all," I said. There'd be nothing gained in telling her more. "What is that you're drinking?"

"Honey and orange-water to encourage my singing," she answered proudly. Her uncle the king had declared her to have a fine voice, and so she'd been given a song of her own. "Mrs. Davis said it would soothe the throat and make my notes ring."

"Mrs. Davis would know of such matters." Mrs. Davis would know of a great many other matters, too, being not only one of the professional actors brought in to bolster our meager performances, but also one of the king's favorites, with a house in Suffolk Street to prove it. Her presence on the stage tonight would both improve the quality of our little company, and vex poor Queen Catherine. Not that Charles would give a fig. He seldom did.

But Anne was watching Monmouth as he coaxed another lady into dancing with him, making her laugh as he spun her on her toes so her skirts flared high around her ankles.

"So it seems my cousin James enjoys your company, Miss Jennings," she said. "Everyone says so."

"What, His Grace?" I shrugged elaborately. "He enjoys every woman's company, and because he's so pleasing, most don't notice he's not very clever. I've heard that his greatest accomplishment is being able to walk upon his hands."

"He can do that?" Anne's face lit with interest. She was only ten, after all, and likely hand-walking was still a great recommendation in a gentleman. "I must make him show me."

"He's also married," I said, a more important drawback to me, "and I like Her Grace too much to let him coax me into mischief."

Belatedly I realized this was as entertaining news to Anne as the hand-walking. Besides, she knew me well, my little friend Anne, and she was quick to see past any dissembling.

"He has asked you, then?" she asked with eager curiosity. "My cousin?"

I sighed, wishing I'd never begun this conversation. If I'd been interested in being kept, then I suppose Monmouth would have been as fortunate a choice as any peer I'd met, not that I'd confess that to Anne. "Every gentleman at this court seems to ask every lady one time or another, my lady. You know that, just as you know I have always declined."

She dipped one chubby finger into the sweetened drink and licked the syrup from it, her unfortunate squint-eyed gaze still following her dark-haired cousin across the Great Hall. "They say my cousin is most generous to those he loves."

"Only because he's spending his wife's fortune, my lady." Pointedly I returned to studying my lines instead of Monmouth's flirtation. The duke's wife had been made Duchess of Buccleuch in her own right, in honor of the vast Buccleuch fortune that she'd brought to the marriage from Scotland, and yet she was still as helpless as any other wife to stop her husband's pilfering from her portion for the sake of his mistresses. "It's no wonder he's so generous."

"Maybe that's why he's coming back here," Anne said. "Maybe he's going to try being generous enough to tempt you."

"He's coming back?" I looked up quickly, too late to escape. Monmouth was in fact returning to where the princess and I stood, his arm slung over the shoulders of another gentleman in the brash, familiar way that men do.

"Is it true you can walk upon your hands like an ape, James?" Anne demanded. "Miss Jennings says you can."

I was most sorry she'd repeated that, but Monmouth didn't care.

"It is most certainly true, Anne," he said, winking at me instead of at his plain little cousin. "I'm a man of many accomplishments, and I thank Miss Jennings for her acknowledgement. Alas, if she'd only do the same for my friend Churchill!"

The other man disentangled himself from the duke's arm and bowed grandly to me and the princess, the elaborate silk knot on his right shoulder—the sign of his rank in the Duke of York's Guards—falling forward across his crimson sleeve. Of course I already knew John Churchill. In our little court at St. James, John served the Duke of York just as I served the duchess. He had come from a middling family in Devon, then to Whitehall as a boy, hoping to make his way in the world much as I had myself.

But his path had taken him into the duke's regiments, where he'd earned much honor on Dutch and French battlefields, and into the bed of the king's favorite mistress, the Duchess of Cleveland. Although he was only twenty-four while the duchess was at least ten years older, it was whispered he'd been rewarded with certain financial gifts for his ardor, as well as a baseborn daughter who in turn was good-naturedly accepted by the king. That his older sister Arabella had continued as the Duke of York's favorite mistress—though no longer a member of the household— bearing several of James's bastards, only muddied the scandalous waters around John even further.

But those were all things I reminded myself of later. Now, when John Churchill smiled at me, I forgot all but how he had grown handsome as any angel, tall and well made in his crimson coat laced with gold, and graced with a rare spark to his eyes that would make any woman sure they shared a secret jest between them.

"Good day, Captain Churchill," I did manage to say, and with a well-practiced composure that hid my interest. "We have not seen you here at Whitehall for some time."

Monmouth groaned. "Come now, Miss Jennings. Grant the gentleman the honor he's due. He's saved my life more than once, you know, and there's no other man I'd want beside me with a sword in a fight."

"How fortunate," I murmured, having heard this before about John Churchill. He was said to be monstrously brave and daring, never shying from any danger in battle. He must be canny, too, to always be so adept at saving the life of the king's son.

"It's pure courage, Miss Jennings, not fortune," the duke declared, warming to his subject with such enthusiasm that others across the room turned to listen. "And he's more than my savior, my friend, or any mere captain, but a newly minted lieutenant colonel, fresh from the fields of honor and King Louis's court."

"I did not know, Your Grace." I finally let myself smile back at the colonel, in recognition of his honors. And I *was* impressed, too. He was young indeed to have earned such a rank, and with every prospect and merit for continuing on such a comet's course. "You have my congratulations, Lieutenant Colonel."

"Thank you, Miss Jennings." The corners of the colonel's mouth twitched with amusement, showing he'd much rather be thanking me for something more tangible, granted in private. "You are most kind."

Anne made a snuffly sort of noise beside me, and to be true, I'd near forgotten she was there. "Miss Jennings isn't always kind. Sometimes she's not kind at all."

"Oh, lamb, who of us is?" the duke said to the princess, though his knowing eyes kept watching the colonel and me. "Shall I show you how I walk on my hands?"

"Yes, James, at once!" The princess pointed imperiously. "Do it here."

Monmouth laughed, teasing, and tapped his fingers on her round cheek. "Not here, little queen. This rehearsal's been upset enough. Come with me into the hall, and I'll show you there."

Anne gulped the rest of her orange-water, set the empty tumbler on the window's sill, and looped her hand through the crook of the duke's arm.

"If you cannot do it, cousin," she said as they left us, the plume on her helmet nodding, "then I shall tell everyone you are a liar."

The colonel grinned. "I see the Lady Anne is no longer a child."

"I'm not sure she ever was." To keep from meeting his eye, I looked after the duke and the princess as they made their way towards the hall.

"You've changed, too, Miss Jennings," he said, and placed his hand extravagantly over his heart. "When I first saw you again on the stage today, I had to ask Monmouth the name of the astonishing beauty playing Mercury."

"I'm not so great a fool as to believe that of you, Colonel Churchill," I scoffed, unable to keep myself from speaking plain. Suddenly it had become much easier to remember his scandalous dalliance with Lady

Castlemaine. "Nor am I so changed since you last left London, and you know it, too. Or has some grievous battle-wound stolen away your memory?"

"Oh, I always recalled the girl that you were, Miss Jennings." He smiled still, not the least discouraged. "But I was dazzled into forgetfulness by the beauty you've become."

I tipped my head, skeptical. "But what is it that you've become, Colonel? You're so brown, you scarce look an English gentleman at all. Did King Louis make you toil in the sun in his vineyards?"

He held out his hand to me, shoving back the cuffs of his shirt and jacket so I could see his bare, brawny arm. "That's not been browned by a French sun, but by a Mediterranean one in Tangier."

"Tangier?" I hadn't expected so exotic an answer, and it intrigued me, as did he. "So you have dallied among the heathens, Colonel, and lolled in their harems?"

"I fought for His Majesty's cause there, beneath an English flag and an African sun," he said, pushing down his sleeve again. "I've been posted to the garrison in Tangier, fighting Moors and Algerian corsairs. Should you like to see the scars that prove it?"

I recognized a dare when I heard one. "But are they the scars won by the soldier in Tangier, I wonder, or the courtier at St. James's?"

"Ah, Miss Jennings, if you must judge my scars, then you judge me as a man." He grinned so wickedly I could not help but smile back. "Come walk with me, and decide."

"Forgive me, Colonel, but no." I held up the crumpled sheet with my lines as proof, as much to remind myself as him. If I shamed myself tonight on the stage, it was because I'd squandered my rehearsal time like this. "I must practice my lines for tonight."

I turned away, but he caught my arm.

"Wait, Miss Jennings, if you please," he said, his voice suddenly firm, and his gallant's palaver shrugged aside like an old coat. "Stay, and tell me of other things that have changed here since I've been away."

I sighed, feigning impatience. "His Majesty has continued his improvements of the City since the Great Fire. The work on St. Paul's is—"

"Not that," he interrupted. "Tell me of your life. If Lady Anne demands too much from you, or what dish you liked best at the table last night, or whether it's true that the duchess lets her Italian priests come and go boldly through her chambers."

"Hush, hush, Colonel, mark what you say!" Now I was the one taking his arm, pulling him from the hall and the rehearsal to the alcove of one of the tall windows, a place where we were less likely to be overheard. "These are not things fit to discuss among so many others."

He studied me intently. "You're young to realize the difference. But then, Monmouth did tell me you were a wise and clever lady."

From a man as notoriously shallow as the duke, that was no compliment, and I narrowed my eyes. "Likely he told you a great many things about me."

"He did, but I prefer to judge for myself."

"So we are back to the docket again, Colonel?"

"It seems we are." He leaned against the window's sill, folding his arms over his chest. The pale winter light filtered through the leaded diamond panes and crisscrossed his handsome face with shadows. "So tell me, Miss Jennings. Are you in sympathy with the duchess and her priests?"

Careful, I thought, careful, careful. "I'm loyal to my mistress, Colonel, just as I believe you should be loyal towards your master, the Duke of York."

He smiled, pleased, I think, by what I'd said. "You're scolding me, Miss Jennings."

"If you need scolding, then I shall do it," I said warmly. "The duchess has been very generous in her kindnesses to me."

"Nothing in Whitehall is given for free," he said. "You must have worked hard to earn that kindness."

"I have," I said, "for isn't that one of the purposes of coming to court? To make oneself agreeable to those in high places, so that they will be agreeable and obliging in return?"

He laughed. "You're an ambitious lass."

I didn't join his amusement. "I *am* ambitious," I said. "As are you, Colonel Churchill."

"True enough." His laugh had changed to a thoughtful smile: another judgment, and I passed. "Most maids of honor would say they've come to find a husband, or a protector."

"I'm not like most maids." Why was it suddenly so important that I make him understand exactly how different I was? "Her Grace trusts me, and favors me because I'm one of the precious few of her ladies who has managed to keep clear of the duke's bed."

This time he didn't laugh, and I wondered if he was recalling how his own sister had made the hasty tumble from maid to the duchess, to mistress to the duke. "That's no idle accomplishment."

"It's not an easy one, either." I cast my gaze towards the ceiling to show my disgust at the duke's endless pursuits. "But I still do not think it wise to discuss Her Grace's devotions where others might overhear and misunderstand."

I meant that, too. Mary Beatrice was a gentle lady who had favored me with much kindness and many favors in return for my services. Thanks to her, I'd enough money both to put aside and to send to my mother. Why should I care how she worshipped her Maker while alone in her own rooms?

But to see her husband James, King Charles's heir to the crown, kneel at her side in the small Romish chapel she had made beside her bedchamber— that was a different matter altogether.

"There is not much to misunderstand, Miss Jennings, not if one cares for the peace of this country," the colonel said, as if reading my thoughts. "Those of us who are friends of a Protestant throne long for reassurances."

I paused, troubled, as I searched his face. "How did we get here, Colonel?" I asked softly. "From Tangier to this?"

His expression didn't change nor lose its intensity. "If I have made you uneasy, Miss Jennings, then I'll—"

"No," I said quickly. I'd never had such a conversation with another gentleman, but I didn't wish him to stop, either. "Go on, please."

"Very well," he said. "If you're half as clever as Monmouth claimed, then I don't have to tell you more."

"I understand this 'more' of yours, Colonel Churchill," I said, my whispered words rushing with urgency, "just as I understand the consequences. 'More' being the Duke of York, who makes no mystery of his sympathy to Catholicism. 'More' being him as a future king who would take his orders from the pope himself, and rule over an England in such a turmoil of hatred and violence as to make the last civil wars seem as nothing."

"So you agree with Lord Clarendon?" he asked, naming the king's chief minister.

"I agree with those who would put England's safety first," I said. "There is a difference between tolerance and carelessness."

He nodded, thoughtful. "I wonder how many of your fellow maids and ladies even know who Lord Clarendon is?"

"They should," I scoffed, though I knew he was likely right to doubt. I'd formed my opinions by what I'd overheard from the conversations of gentlemen, and from reading on my own. Alas, while most of my fellows could cite the three best shops in London for point lace and ribbons, I knew most could not name the Earl of Clarendon, at least not in his role of determining policy.

"So where does that put your loyalty, Miss Jennings?" The colonel's face was solemn, as was right for such a question. "If forced to choose, would it be your mistress, or your country?"

"I do not know." I looked down at the wrinkled sheet of paper in my hand, the ink smudged and the words blurred. How foolish and vain tonight's masque now seemed! "I pray it will never come to that."

"As do I," he said quietly. "But for once I must grant that Monmouth was right. You *are* both wise and clever, Miss Jennings, and not merely beautiful."

For the first time in his company, I blushed. I was so often called beautiful that I no longer believed it, thinking—most rightly—that it was the first easy compliment to come from a man's coaxing tongue, and often the least sincere. But to be admired for my intelligence, my perception, and by one of the most handsome young officers at court—I ask you, what lady could resist such heady praise?

He reached for my hand and I let him take it, just as I let him draw me closer.

"Miss Jennings," he began, and I waited breathlessly for whatever he'd say. "Miss Jennings, I—"

"*Here* you are, Miss Jennings." Lady Anne's small cherry of a mouth was stern and disapproving, her squint more of a scowl. "Everyone is waiting for you."

"Forgive me, my lady." I pulled my hand free of the colonel's. I'd never been caught with a gentleman like this, especially not by Lady Anne. My curtsey was clumsy and the guilty flush spread from my cheeks clear down to my bodice. Now, too late, I pictured Colonel Churchill with the worldly Lady Castlemaine, and how beside her I must seem the most empty-headed little fool imaginable, ripe for the plucking. "I'm coming directly."

Anne didn't move. "Come *now*. I cannot do my piece without you."

"Yes, my lady," I said, beginning to leave, but the colonel stopped me. "When will I see you next?" he asked with such fervency that my blush flared hot again. "Tell me, Miss Jennings. When?"

"If you come to the performance tonight, Colonel Churchill," I said, striving to sound haughty, even a little bored by his attentions, "then you shall see me on the stage with the rest of the company."

And then I did leave, hurrying along beside Anne where I should have been all along.

"Am I truly so late, my lady?" I asked, looking ahead to where the others were still rehearsing. "Did many miss me?"

"*I* did," Anne said. "You know that he is still Lady Castlemaine's lover?"

I wanted no more reminders of Lady Castlemaine. "It was a conversation, my lady, nothing more."

Anne sniffed and pulled off her helmet, holding it cradled in her arms like an infant. "Lady Castlemaine is *old,* Miss Jennings, at least thirty-five years. Did you know she gave him four thousand pounds because he pleased her, and another thousand guineas beyond that to buy his commission?"

I thought of how I'd smiled so winningly at the news of that promotion. "He wouldn't have been promoted as high as he has been without merit or courage. Monmouth says he owes Colonel Churchill his very life."

"Oh, Monmouth." Anne wrinkled her nose at her reflection in the polished metal of her helmet. Her pale brown hair was mussed from the helmet, sticking out every which way around her face like a scarecrow's straw. "He can only walk four steps on his hands before toppling over, which is scarce walking at all. And you shouldn't care if he's courageous."

"No one has ever said that Monmouth's courageous, and if he—"

"Don't pretend to be thick-witted, Miss Jennings, because I know you're not," she said crossly. "I meant Colonel Churchill, and you knew it, too. He won't do for you, for he hasn't a farthing to his name. At least, not that Lady Castlemaine hasn't put under his pillow."

I stopped abruptly, short of the others. "My lady, if you please, I'd—"

"He won't appreciate you, Miss Jennings," she said, her round face full of mournful sorrow. "Not like I do."

"Oh, my little dear," I said with remorse, realizing too late what I'd done. "Forgive me, please, please! How can you ever conceive of Colonel Churchill replacing you?"

She stared glumly down at the helmet. "I'm going to forget my words in my piece tonight, and everyone will laugh, and Mary will hate me for ruining her masque."

"If they laugh at you, my lady, then they'll laugh at us all," I said. "You've been to our practices. We haven't improved one whit, and I'm scared nigh to death of what a shambles I'll make of quick-footed Mercury."

"Not you, Miss Jennings!" she cried. "You're never frightened of anything."

"Of course I am." I was, too—frightened not only of the performance ahead of us that night, but of the gravity of what I'd discussed with Colonel Churchill. It was so much easier to worry only about the color of my gown, or whether I should part my hair on this side or the other, and not consider the greater problems that threatened us. And yet, with him, it had seemed the most natural thing in the world. No other man I'd met had ever treated me with such regard, and I let myself dream of what my life could be with such a man to share it. But I was also frightened by how easily I'd been taken in by his charming ways, and worse, much worse, of how dearly I longed to see him again.

I held out my hand to her, showing her what was left of the sheet with my lines. "There's your proof of my fear, and a sorry sight it is, too."

Anne's chin rose, heartened by my weakness as I knew she'd be. "Then we must now practice together, Miss Jennings. I'll make you learn your part, and you'll make me learn mine, so that neither of us will have anything to fear."

I reached out and smoothed her hair, then set her helmet back on her head.

"Yes, Lady Anne," I said, wishing everything could be settled with such ease. "Yes, my lady, we shall."

Chapter Four

Once the masque's overture began, I forgot to be nervous, and so did the rest of our cast. This is not to say we spoke every word as we should, or danced with perfect grace, or even that we did not collide or tangle our plumed headdresses. But no expense had been considered too great to bolster our performance, and once our efforts were combined with the pomp and majesty of the settings and music and costumes, our errors paled to merest insignificance.

It was helpful, too, that our audience was indulgent to the point of doting, just as Monmouth had predicted, and not the rowdy, orange-tossing critics of, say, the Theatre Royal in Bridge Street. Two tiers of chairs had been needed to accommodate everyone from the court, plus specially invited guests, and doubtless there were many more in London who would have freely offered a pretty penny in exchange for admission.

In the center, of course, sat the king himself, a pair of his favorite spaniels draped over his knees and the queen at his side. The Duke and Duchess of York held the next precedent for seats, with everyone else arranged accordingly by rank as if it were the grandest banquet. But they were a cheerful crowd and took their cue from His Majesty, clapping and shouting with great heartiness, though doubtless the wine and fresh olives that were served throughout the night also fed their enthusiastic response.

I was especially pleased by my costume. While Margaret Blagge—who played Diana—and I were the only two in the cast not nobly born, we'd still been lavished with the same finery as the princesses. My Mercury glittered in shot silver velvet and brocade, with a cunning helmet graced by feathered wings, and in place of skirts I had short, full breeches that daringly displayed my legs in pale blue silk hose with silver garters. Around my throat and wrists I wore gold chains spangled with pearls and sapphires, loaned to me for the occasion by the Duchess of York, and altogether I felt as fine as any true god or goddess.

Yet even as I postured before the rows of oil lamps and torches that made the Great Hall as bright as day, my thoughts were still too jumbled for me to truly enjoy myself. Just as I was Mercury, Lady Anne played the nymph whom Mercury desired, and while this might seem a pretty conceit between friends, it also taxed me mightily. Anne had accused me of preferring John Churchill to her, and as I declared Mercury's undying passion, I did indeed think of him, even as I smiled into her adoring face. As I took her plump little hand to lead her through our dance, I couldn't swear which partner's hand I imagined in my own: Mercury's nymph, or Lady Anne, or the handsome young colonel. The confusion taxed me so that by the last time the blue, crimson, and white silk curtains were drawn and we all took our bows, my head ached abominably, and all I longed for was to be alone.

But of course I was expected to stay for the dancing afterwards, as much a part of our performance as what we'd done on the stage. I danced with many gentlemen, and heard just as many awkward paeans to the charms that my costume had revealed. Only once did I glimpse John Churchill at a distance, and though I couldn't see his partner's face, her dark copper hair could belong to no other but his mistress Lady Castlemaine.

I looked away, blinking back angry tears for my own folly. I was no better than any other foolish innocent, confused and hurt without a real reason. Hadn't I learned anything in these past two years? Didn't I know not to trust the idle interest of gentlemen who sought to intrigue for sport alone? Fiercely I told myself that John Churchill was no different from any other man, and deserved no more, either. I could not possibly have fallen into love at first sight, the way the poets claimed true lovers did; surely my heart was stronger than that!

But despite such brave assurances, I dreaded that he'd see me in return, or worse, try to speak to me with Lady Castlemaine on his arm. All I wished was to escape the ball, and I was nearly to the doorway when Mary Beatrice beckoned me to join her. I had no choice but to hide my misery and obey my mistress, and pray she'd send me on some little errand that would take me from the room.

"I had great pleasure in your performance, Miss Jennings," she told me, and kissed me twice, on each cheek. She was slender and elegant in bright blue satin, but the girlish merriment that I remembered so well from when I'd first come into her household was nearly gone, worn away by disappointment and sorrow.

"Thank you, Your Grace," I said, making a bow instead of a curtsey in my silver breeches. "I am glad you enjoyed it."

She laughed at my peculiar bow. "I most liked you and Lady Anne."

"It was most natural for us, Your Grace," I said, trying to put aside my earlier misgivings. "We are so often together."

"I could tell it was so." She nodded and motioned with her fan for me to come closer so that others would not overhear. "I have not said this before, I know, but I would also thank you for all your rare kindness to the princess, Miss Jennings. She is not an easy lady for friendships."

I nodded, understanding far more than she'd said. When Mary Beatrice had wed, she'd gained two stepdaughters as well as the duke. She had liked Lady Mary at once, the way most people did: at thirteen, Mary was quick and fair, with clear, rosy cheeks and thick black curls, and she laughed often and with ease. In the masque tonight, she'd happily taken the title role of Calisto, and had basked in the attention like a bright flower turning towards the morning sun.

But my poor dear Anne had proved more difficult, as she always did, having none of her older sister's graces or charm. It was too easy to mistake Anne's shyness for a dull wit, and her reserve for the brooding discontent of a heavy, plain girl with an angry squint. Yes, she could be selfish, and she could be demanding, but once her trust was won, there was no more true or loyal creature under heaven. I would indeed have been both thick-witted and cruel to turn my back on such devotion, or not to consider how one day the worth of a princess's friendship might prove more valuable than gold.

"Lady Anne is still young, Your Grace," I said, soothing. "In time, she'll grow more at ease in company at court."

But the duchess did not wish to be placated, and tapped the folded blades of her fan against her cheek. "Lady Anne does not have the luxury of that time, Miss Jennings. She is a princess. She has responsibilities."

"Lady Anne knows that, Your Grace," I said, thinking how many of Anne's difficulties came from the weight of those responsibilities. "She needs to find her place, that is all."

Mary Beatrice's smile turned brittle. "Lady Anne knows that already, Miss Jennings. Her place is three removes from the throne."

I didn't nod so much as bow my head. With no male heirs, the crown would pass from Charles to James, then to Mary and finally to Anne, the one who'd want it the least.

"That is what so many of you English desire, isn't it?" she continued bitterly, taking my silence as encouragement. "To be ruled by another Protestant? Even the king, my brother Charles, bends to the will of his impertinent people. To put his own soul at eternal risk for their sake is lamentable enough, but to insist that Lady Mary and Lady Anne must be raised falsely as Anglicans, yes, and even my own little Catherine, is a terrible sin."

"I am sorry you are troubled, Your Grace," I said, all I'd dare. I had worked hard to earn her confidence and trust since I'd come to court, but there were times I heard more than I wished to know. "I am sorry."

"It is not your sorrow, Miss Jennings." The duchess's eyes were bright with unshed tears as she touched the gold crucifix she wore tucked in her bodice for comfort. "But what if there are no princes, from the queen or from me? What if my poor daughters must risk their place in heaven for the whim of these misguided English?"

"It won't happen that way, Your Grace," I said quickly. "You're young and healthy, and sure to be blessed with many sons."

"If God wills it, yes." Her eyes were filled with melancholy. She had borne one daughter already and miscarried another, yet only a son would keep her from being a failure at the role she'd been born to play. "But my husband is a good man, and he will make a good and just ruler for the people of England. He will lead them back to the true faith of Rome, the one rightful faith, and all will find peace."

"Yes, Your Grace," I said, and nothing more.

Truly, how else could I answer? Mary Beatrice had come from Modena with instructions to sway the English duke back to the pope, and on that I would always differ with her—or would, if it were my place to speak freely. With sadness and foreboding in my heart, I thought again of how much depended on the birth of a single male baby, a Protestant prince who would live and grow to lead England.

John Churchill had asked me where I'd place my loyalty if pressed: with the Duke and Duchess of York, or with my faith and my country. With that troubling question in my thoughts, I glanced back across the dancers, hoping for another stolen glimpse of him. Instead I spied him standing against the far wall, watching me in turn so boldly that I caught my breath.

"So it is true, Miss Jennings." Mary Beatrice's voice betrayed her curiosity. "I had heard others talking tonight, but did not credit it, not about you. You have noticed Colonel Churchill, and he you."

Purposefully I turned my back, not wishing to give him any encouragement. "Colonel Churchill will have no lasting interest in any woman without fortune or influence, Your Grace."

But the duchess only smiled. "A brave and handsome gentleman can find other ways to make his fortune than a favorable marriage. Colonel Churchill has served both His Majesty and His Grace with much distinction, and he has already achieved a rank in the army higher than many men twice his age. I know His Grace favors him over every other young gentleman in our household, and speaks nothing but praise for his bravery and diplomacy, too. Who can say what other glories lie ahead for the colonel?"

I thought again of what the colonel had said to me, and wondered if it was easier for a soldier who had followed different armies and served different kings to shift loyalties. What would *he* do? I wondered. Would he follow his master the Duke of York, or his country, or would he decide not from loyalty at all, but from which would bring the greatest benefit to himself? And were my own loyalties any more pure, or less ambitious?

"You could do far worse for yourself than Colonel Churchill, Miss Jennings." Turning thoughtful, she again tapped her folded fan against her cheek. "All things are possible in this world."

All things are possible in this world. I realized later that she was only matchmaking, and that she wished me not to let my heart be ruled by my lack of a fortune. But instead when I heard her words, I thought only of the possibility—the likelihood—that if her husband became king, then this world would be an altogether different place.

And not for the better.

Those who have never been to court will often speak of how the life of a palace is nothing but intrigue and secrets. In truth it's exactly the opposite: not even the deepest secret of state has any chance of survival at court, where even the king himself must bathe and dress before a score of noble witnesses. Nothing is hidden, nothing kept private. Was it any wonder, then, that before the next day's sun had risen, my own little secret was as common as a prayer book?

As I should have expected, Lady Ainsworth was the first to pounce. "So tell me all, Miss Jennings," she said. "I wish to know *everything* about your evening. Is it true you've set your heart on John Churchill?"

She'd found me in the lodgings I shared with the other maids of honor, not far from Her Grace's rooms. I'd already traded my costume for my night rail and a dressing gown, my borrowed jewels carefully counted and put away to be returned to Mary Beatrice in the morning. Bent over a washbowl, I was laboring to scrub the last of the paint from my face, which at least gave me an extra moment or two to compose my reply.

"I've not set my heart on anyone, my lady," I said as the maidservant blotted the almond milk from my face with a linen cloth. "I fear you must be sadly mistaken."

"Oh, but I'm not," Lady Ainsworth purred, leaning closer. She must have come directly from the Great Hall, for she was still dressed for the ball, the jewels in her hair twinkling by the candlestick's light and her black cloak sliding from her shoulders. "You needn't even confess your affections yourself, you know. The colonel has already betrayed his interest in you."

"He *has*?" I asked too quickly, betraying myself, too. It wasn't so much that I wanted to deny that I'd felt drawn to John Churchill, but more that I'd hoped to hold the secret of it close for just a bit longer. I was still not yet fifteen, and all this was like magic to me.

I wanted to remember his dark eyes full of interest and desire, and how the heat had flowed between us when our hands had touched, the glow of our shared delight something rare and wondrous indeed. I wanted to hear more of Tangier, and I wanted to discover exactly where those scars of honor were placed upon his body. He'd been different from all the other gentlemen I'd ever met, just as—I hoped—I'd been different from other ladies, as he'd claimed.

But of course Lady Ainsworth would understand none of that.

"Oh, the colonel has already tipped his cards, and every one was a heart." Her eyes widened as she warmed to her telling. "Yes, yes. He was observed to pay particular attention to the masque whenever you were on the stage, his admiration there on his face for all the world to remark."

"That signifies nothing, my lady," I said, ashamed that I felt a bit disappointed. The maidservant placed her hands on my shoulders and gently pushed me down to sit on the dressing bench as she began unpinning and brushing out my hair for the night. "Especially with gentlemen."

"Then why would he ask for you at the ball, plaintively demanding of everyone he met if they'd seen the fair Miss Jennings?"

"He did not!" I protested. "He *would* not, my lady. He's not so foolish as that!"

"Every man's a fool in love," she said coyly. "Or in lust. And oh, how he's smitten with you, my dear."

"But he scarce knows me, my lady. Even today we spoke but a handful of words, that was all."

"Sometimes that is more than enough." She sighed happily, arranging her bracelets over her wrist as if ordering my life to sit as neatly beside Colonel Churchill's. "It won't be easy, of course. Castlemaine won't wish to give him up."

I didn't know Lady Castlemaine to speak to, and she'd never lower herself to acknowledge me. But I certainly recognized her: the fiery hair that matched her temperament, the lush, voluptuous body laced so tightly that her breasts always seemed barely contained by her bodice, the imperious voice that could coax and wheedle one minute and demand like an empress the next. She'd grown immensely rich in the king's bed, but she'd also grown old: she must have been thirty if she was a day, near twice my own age. Through the coldhearted eyes of my youth, I could see how loose those much-vaunted breasts had become. The famous chestnut hair was now improved with henna, and when she rode or walked in the park, the sunlight showed the deep-carved lines in her face that the Whitehall candles still softened by night.

Perhaps it *was* time for her to part with John Churchill. Perhaps he'd thought that, too.

And perhaps—*perhaps*—I agreed.

I raised my chin as the maidservant pulled the brush through my hair, sleeking it down my spine to my hips before she began plaiting it for the night. "I am not afraid of the Duchess of Cleveland, my lady."

Lady Ainsworth rounded her mouth in an oval of feigned surprise. "You should be, Miss Jennings. She was born a Villiers, and they make the worst possible enemies. Lord, child, but you have beautiful hair!"

"Thank you, my lady." My hair was thick and shining and as golden as the honey-water I still washed it with each day. What need had I of henna or the false flattery of candlelight?

"I'll grant that you *are* lovely enough to win him away," Lady Ainsworth said, considering me with rare thoughtfulness, "and clever enough to amuse him for more than a single night. And of course you'll have to play him along with great care and cunning, to make him value the prize all the more. But, lah! To think that John Churchill will be the one to claim the most coveted maidenhead in St. James's!"

"He won't," I said, "not if all he wishes is a dalliance."

She tipped back her head and laughed, as if this were the greatest jest in the world.

"A dalliance *will* be all he wishes, my dear," she said. "Colonel Churchill is one of the most charming, most desired bachelors at court, and determined to stay that way. He has seen much of the world and taken his pleasure with many of the women in it. Do you really believe a man like that would let himself be trapped into marriage by a little mite like you?"

I smiled with the brazen confidence of my age. "There'll be no trapping, my lady, not by him nor by me. All we must do is please one another sufficiently. I have yet to meet another gentleman I liked better than Colonel Churchill, or who would suit me more. What other reason need there be?"

"Because he is poor as a country parson, you pretty little fool," she said, her contempt as sharp as a saber's blade. "Everyone knows that his father has near buried him with the family's debts, the sorriest legacy possible for an eldest son. He could never begin to afford a wife like you, without a marriage portion or family influence."

I thought of how he'd called me ambitious, and how he'd smiled when I'd called him the same in return. But we'd understood one another, and young as I was, I realized that such an understanding could be far more lasting than how my heart had quickened when he'd taken my hand.

"Being poor makes no difference to me, my lady," I said. "He and I shall simply have to make our own way, and work together to improve our fortunes and our stations."

But though I was certain John Churchill would understand, Lady Ainsworth did not.

"You are a fool if you believe that, Miss Jennings," she said curtly. "Colonel Churchill is not some blacksmith's apprentice, toiling at his anvil to become a journeyman. You cannot improve your station at court through hard work. In this life, gold and influence are the only sure paths to success and power, and the sooner your impudent little head can be made to understand that, the better."

The maid had finished braiding my hair, and as I rose, I flipped the long, fat plait over my shoulder.

"Thank you for explaining that to me, my lady," I said, making my voice purposefully bland as I dipped my curtsey in my dressing gown. "I shall mark your words, and learn from your wisdom."

I wasn't sure she believed me, for her only reply was more an impatient growl than any real word as she dismissed me with a quick wave of her hand.

I didn't care. I turned away from her, and I smiled. She was my senior in age, and my superior in rank, but I—I knew better.

It was a warm evening the following June, and Mary Beatrice's parlor was close with her dutiful guests. The last notes of the harpsichord faded, and the singer swept so low a curtsey that the yellow plumes in her black hair brushed the floor. I clapped politely with everyone else, the way Mary Beatrice expected. The duchess was very fond of music, and particularly favored the Italian singers who reminded her of her old home, no matter how tedious they might seem to the rest of us. As the harpsichordist now rose to take his bows, I left my tabouret and began to slip through the other chairs towards the door.

"Miss Jennings!" called Mary Beatrice, leaving me no choice but to stop and turn back towards her high-backed armchair.

"Yes, Your Grace?" I asked, hoping she wouldn't make me linger. It was half past nine, and I was already late.

She took my hand, clasping it with great fondness. "You aren't leaving, are you?" she asked. "You will stay to hear the next group of songs? Ahh, Signora de Rosella's voice is worthy of the angels in heaven."

I smiled with wistful regret and pressed my free hand to my forehead. "Forgive me, Your Grace, but I must beg to be excused. Perhaps it is the heat, or the turtle soup, but my head aches abominably."

"My poor girl," she said, her concern so genuine that guilt almost made me confess my falsehood. "Of course you have my leave to go. I'll send one of my maids with a special potion of mine to ease your pain."

"Thank you, Your Grace," I said quickly, "but I'll be well enough with sleep."

She let me go, and I made my escape as quickly as I dared. Near the door, Lady Ainsworth caught my eye, and with one silently raised brow, she told me she knew exactly where I was going, and it wasn't my own bed.

I didn't care. I rushed through the halls of the palace, walking so fast that I was just short of running, my petticoats flying around my ankles and the ribbons streaming from my hair. I paused at the end of the hall, near the way to the Banqueting House, making certain that I was not followed nor noticed. Then I slipped through the last arched door, down the twisting stone steps, and into the palace's privy garden.

In the distance I could still hear Mary Beatrice's singer, and from the other direction came the lazy trill of a nightingale. I held my breath as if afraid to break some sort of spell, seeing nothing beyond the pale marble statues, copied from the ancients, that filled each square in the garden's formal grid.

"Are you there?" I finally asked, a whispered call far softer than the nightingale's. "Are you—"

"Here, sweet," John said, sliding from the shadows behind me. He circled his arm around my waist, taking advantage of my surprise to kiss me. I let him, but only for a moment before I pushed myself free, laughing, and skipped away from him.

Of course he came after me. "Where have you been, Sarah? Have you any notion of how long I've been waiting for you, or are you too cruel to care?"

I walked backwards, facing him, my heels crunching on the stone path. "The duchess wished me to stay to listen to her latest signora. Arias from Monteverdi."

"Saints deliver us," he said, reaching his hand out for my arm. "They should have delivered you to me instead."

I skipped free, looking back at him over my shoulder. He was impossibly handsome in the moonlight, his smile white and his long hair tossing in the breeze over his shoulders. Like most soldiers who didn't want the bother of a wig in battle, he still wore his own hair, thick and curling, and I loved that he did.

"The duke was sitting beside the duchess," I said. "He's your master, just as she is mine. You should have been there with him."

"I was waiting here for you instead."

"That is no fault of mine, Colonel," I said, though of course it was. Even if I hadn't been delayed by the singers, I'd meant to keep him waiting at least a quarter hour past the time we'd agreed. I'd learned that little trick made him more eager, more ardent, and held him on edge, all of which were to my advantage. "I never asked you to wait."

"You never asked, but what other choice did I have if I wanted to see you?" He caught my hand and pulled me back into his arms, into the shadows of one of the statues. "Why do you torment me so, Sarah? Don't you know I think of you night and day and night again, until you've crowded every other thought from my pitiful head?"

I smiled up at him through my lashes and drew the little nosegay of pinks from the hollow between my breasts, teasing the feathery flowers lightly across his jaw. I was fifteen now. I'd learned my share of ways to beguile a gentleman. But when John held me like this, his arms around my waist and his chest close to mine, I was always conscious of how much larger and stronger he was than I, and how perilous the game I was playing with him could become if I pushed too far.

I would be the one at fault, too. I'd already observed in such circumstances that the gentleman was considered to have been somehow tempted beyond reason, while the lady, however virtuous before, would be dismissed as the sorriest slut in Christendom. The poets might promise a better side of honor and true love, but the reality at court was far more complicated, and dangerous.

But John Churchill—ah, he was worth any risk.

He took my hand and raised it to his lips. "Come with me tonight, Sarah," he said in a rough whisper. "My lodgings aren't far, only in Jermyn Street. I'll have you back to St. James's before you're missed. Her Grace will never know."

"I can't, John," I answered softly, tucking the nosegay into the top buttonhole of his coat. "You know that."

"Yet you claim you love me." He turned my hand over in his, his mouth moist as he first kissed my palm, then nipped it lightly with his teeth in the way he knew made me catch my breath. "If you did, then you wouldn't refuse me."

"I do love you," I said, and I meant it. "Yet how can I give you what you wish when you ask me to share your heart with another?"

He sighed mightily, my hand still in his. "You mean Barbara."

"I do," I said, trying to put as much suffering into my voice as I could. "Lady Castlemaine has always been there between us."

"She has been a great friend to me, Sarah," he said. "I cannot cast her off like some old unmatched glove."

I took my hand back, clasping it with its mate. "Nor do you wish to."

"Sarah, Sarah." He sighed again, more breeze than I wished to hear. "There is no love between Barbara and me, and never was. Affection and regard and desire, but not love. Not what I have found with you. You should not be jealous."

"You are still seen with her."

"Only in passing," he said, "not by arrangement. You know how difficult it is to avoid anyone in this place."

I bowed my head with a show of contrition, avoiding his eye as I wondered if that passing still included visits in her bedchamber. Even those who despised Lady Castlemaine admitted that she knew more ways to pleasure a man than there were days in the year; why else would His Majesty, who could have nearly any woman he wished, remain bewitched by her for so long? Lord knows she'd had other men besides the king, including my John, yet her power over His Majesty was so great that he always indulgently forgave her indiscretions and returned to her bed.

"Then tell me, John," I said, almost a whisper. "When will you break with her for good?"

He didn't answer, and I feared I'd gone too far. No matter what he claimed, there was much that Lady Castlemaine had given him that I could not: five thousand pounds for his favors, to buy his first commission and an annuity with it, influence to help ease his way through the court, an illegitimate daughter who she'd let the king believe was his own . . .

"Soon," he said at last, and I realized then I'd been holding my breath. "Soon. That is all I can promise. By the end of this year."

I looked up again, my smile radiant. "I am *glad*."

"Then show me." He caught me in his arms and pressed me back against the base of the statue, the back of my skirts snagging on the bricks. "If you love me, then show me."

"You know I love you, John, more than anything," I cried, trying to wriggle free. But I already knew where this was headed. In the short weeks since we'd been together, we'd had this conversation more times than I could recall, and it never became any easier, or more pleasant. He would not consider marriage because he claimed he was too poor, while for that same reason, I would not consent to becoming his mistress. "But I want you forever, not just for tonight."

"Tonight may be all we have, Sarah." His hands moved restlessly over the curves of my hips, and even with so many layers of clothing between us, I could still feel the heat of his desire for me. "I must leave for France in the morning."

"You're leaving?" I asked, unable to keep the little flutter of panic from my voice. "You're going away?"

"On a matter for His Grace. I can tell you no more than that."

I knew that John had been sent before on certain diplomatic missions for the king as well as the duke, missions where his courage and intelligence were as important as his familiarity with foreign countries and languages. With all Europe uneasy and King Charles desirous to keep England at peace, John's talents and ambition were much in demand, and, I suspected, well rewarded. This was good; the more he prospered, the sooner he'd be able to consider marriage. But he'd never confided the details to me, and I knew better than to ask.

"How long will you be gone?" I asked, slipping my hand free of his so I could lay it upon his chest. I'd grown so fond of him that I could not imagine my life at court without him in it.

"Only long enough to do what I must." He slid one hand higher, gliding over my waist to where my breast pressed high above my stays, and curved his hand over the soft bared flesh. I shuddered, but didn't pull away, nor did I wish to.

"Oh, my dearest." I turned my face up towards his, wanting to remember every detail of his face. "Have you any notion of how much I'll miss you?"

"No more than I'll miss you, Sarah," he said, and kissed me with fervor and passion enough to steal my very soul away. This was how he paid me back for my coquettishness, for he knew exactly how to tease and torment my inexperienced body, how to kiss me until my head spun round with pleasure and my blood raced so fast through my veins that I turned weak with it. It was like finally tasting the richest of dishes after only reading the cookery receipt, and with John as the chef, I was as greedy as any starving beggar.

Yet deep down I knew the price of temptation, just as I knew the value of denial, and with a gasp of regret I broke away from his mouth, and from him.

"Please, Sarah," he said, reaching for me again. "Stay with me."

I shook my head and backed away, knowing that if I went back I'd be too weak to refuse him again. "I cannot, John," I said, not hiding my misery. "I cannot."

"I told you you were cruel," he said, but there was no malice in his voice, only a raw, dark regret. He took my nosegay from his buttonhole and held it to his cheek. "How do I know you won't find another lover while I'm away?"

"Trust me," I said, still breathless from his kiss. Yet what would I do if he were the one to find another? What would I do if I'd played this wrong, and he returned with some beautiful French lady as his wife, or worse, returned to Lady Castlemaine? As clever as I knew I was, I had no answers to such questions, nor an answer to how I'd fallen so completely in love with him, and he, I prayed, with me.

"If you love me, John," I said softly, my heart aching with the pain of parting, "then you must trust me without doubt."

"Be true," he said, almost an order, "and I will."

"I will, too," I said, his face and wide shoulders blurring through my tears. "God help me, I will."

Chapter Five

If I were a sailor tossing on a distant sea, or a colonist alone in the wilderness forests of Virginia, or any poor soul spinning out her life in Scotland or Ireland, then the life I followed at the Stuart court might seem by comparison full of splendor and excitement. But in truth the court can grow as tedious as any other place, especially for one as young as I.

New scandals replaced old disgraces. A certain dance would become a two-week madness, as quickly forgotten as it had been learned. A mantua-maker arrived from Paris and decreed a new fashion for looped-up petticoats and narrow lace tippets, and as slavish as conies over a cliff, we ladies would rush to follow. The king designed a new racquet for playing the game of tennis, and the whole court dutifully sat on cushioned benches in the gallery to watch His Majesty play, and win every match. Even the greatest peers were born, wed, took sick, and died, much like their humbler fellows.

Neither Queen Catherine nor Mary Beatrice had given birth to a son and heir to the throne.

In the seven months since I'd parted with John Churchill in the garden, I'd grown taller, the angles of my body rounding into more womanly curves. I was nearly sixteen. Mary Beatrice continued to be pleased with me, and increased my income, and presented me with a handsome fine necklace of pearls and coral beads. My friendship with Lady Anne flourished and grew over countless games of whist and ombre.

And oh, yes, when John finally returned from Paris in time for Twelfth

Night, he came first to me. Not to Lady Castlemaine, or some phantom, foreign wife, or to any other woman in London.

To *me*.

While the Duke and Duchess of York considered St. James's Palace as their own home, especially in the summer, they also kept rooms across the park in Whitehall Palace, near the king's. When the winter snows came, it was easier not to have to cross the park for the celebrations of the Christmas season, and though Twelfth Night was now past, the Yorks' household had yet to return to the other palace.

Like every good maid of honor, I'd been quick to learn my way through Whitehall's confusion of back stairs and half halls, the better to serve my mistress. Whitehall was also far more crowded, filled with petitioners from every corner of the realm, each determined to catch a minute of His Majesty's time. Because Mary Beatrice shared her faith with Charles's Portuguese queen, I was often sent to carry messages between them, and my path would take me from one set of royal apartments to another, and through the crowds who gossiped openly and without shame. If in the process I overheard conversations or saw things that proved interesting or useful, well then, that, too, was part of my education as a courtier.

On this particular January afternoon, I was hurrying from Queen Catherine's quarters to Mary Beatrice's. My pink silk petticoat, quilted with an elaborate pattern of tulips and vines, swung heavy as a cast bell around my legs as I walked, but the palace was cold, and quilted petticoats and bodices, woolen shawls, and gloves were necessities, even beside the fire. Skipping down the staircase, my breath showed, and I kept my hands tucked into the pockets in my skirts to warm my fingers.

Her Grace had sent me for another skein of blue silk for the pillowbier she was embroidering while keeping company with the queen, and she didn't want to waste a moment of the precious winter daylight for her needlework. Mary Beatrice trusted me to match the proper color without tangling the other threads, the same way she'd come to trust me in so many things, and the guards who stood before the Yorks' apartments let me pass without question.

The rooms were quiet, empty of their usual bustle, and I quickly found Mary Beatrice's workbox beside her bed, where she'd told me it was. The workbox would have been difficult for anyone to miss: an elaborate creation of rosewood with inlaid angels of mother-of-pearl that the duchess brought with her from Modena, and one of her most treasured possessions. With great care I opened the lid and bent over to search inside for the proper silks for her embroidery.

"Miss Jennings, isn't it?"

I turned around at once, hideously conscious of how I'd just presented my nether quarters so ungracefully to my master the Duke of York.

"Your Grace," I said, making my curtsey into a hasty apology. "Forgive me, but I did not hear you behind me."

"Oh, no harm, no harm," he said, waving his hand in airy dismissal. The tall, mounded curls of his wig rose up from his forehead much like a sculpted haystack, while the lacy collar of his shirt was so stiff and unwieldy that it seemed almost to support his chin. "No harm at all."

"Thank you, Your Grace." It was strange to hear those words from him, the same he'd used the only other time he'd come across me alone, soon after I'd come to court. For a man who professed such devotion to both his church and his wife, he had no qualms about indulging his insatiable desires whenever a woman presented herself. He'd nearly trapped me before, and I wouldn't let it happen again, no matter the unfortunate position in which he had discovered me.

"Her Grace sent me for a length of blue silk," I said, holding the skein out in my palm as proof. "She is stitching close work beside the window in Her Majesty's chambers, and she wishes to make the best use of the light. If you'll excuse me, Your Grace, I shall return to her now."

I made to move towards the door, but he neatly blocked my path. "I recall your sister," he said. "Frances, wasn't it?"

"Yes, Your Grace." The bedchamber door was still ajar, and I could make an inelegant dash around him. But to do so would make me a laughingstock in this worldly place, and I'd also risk the displeasure of my master and his wife, a chance I could ill afford to take.

"My sister is happily wed now," I said, "with two children."

"A pretty lass," he said, his gaze roaming over me with growing interest, and freedom, too. "Not the true beauty that you are, to be sure, but pretty enough."

The way he spoke made me wonder uneasily how much of his regard he'd lavished upon my sister when she'd been a part of his household. Frances wouldn't have told me, she was that private, and I that much younger. But the duke had long been in the habit of choosing his mistresses from among his wife's maids of honor, so much so that behind Her Grace's back, our quarters were called the duke's private brothel.

I glanced again at the door, then back to the duke. There were many ladies who would have given much to be in this place. To catch James's eye, to secure a place in his favors, to earn the rewards that fell to a royal mistress—a great prize, true, but not one I wished, not at all.

"If you recall Frances so well, Your Grace," I said, choosing my words with care, "then you also recall how virtuous she is. In that way, we are much alike, Your Grace."

"Is that so?" He was clearly paying little heed as he inched closer to me, his thoughts on other parts of me than my words. It was the fashion then for tight lacing and low bodices without the decencies of a kerchief even on a day as chilly as this, and the duke was making such a thorough study of my newly plumped breasts that it took all my will not to cover myself with my hands. There were some gentlemen who found such shows of modesty doubly titillating, and the last thing I wished was to excite the duke further.

"Frances was uncommonly virtuous?" he continued. "I don't recall that of your sister."

"You should, Your Grace," I said, determined to outwit him. "She was held in much regard for it. A most admirable quality in a lady, Your Grace."

He glanced up from my breasts with a knowing leer. "I'll wager that's not what Churchill fancies about you, is it?"

I hadn't expected that, not even from him. "I am sorry, Your Grace," I said, my voice trembling with the anger I dare not show, "but such a discussion must remain private between Colonel Churchill and me."

"Don't be coy, Miss Jennings," he said. "You both belong to my household, my family. There's nothing to hide between us, is there? I know how you two wish to make a match of it, but because the poor fellow hasn't two farthings to rub together, you won't give him what he wants."

I felt the angry flush warm my cheeks. Most likely the whole court did know my dilemma with John, but I hated to hear it made light of by the duke, as if our lives were no more than another bawdy jest.

"Colonel Churchill and I shall find our own way, Your Grace," I said, striving hard to keep my temper. "I thank you for your interest, Your Grace, but I—"

"Does Churchill give you pleasure, Miss Jennings?" he asked, his voice low and suggestive. "Is that the real reason behind your reluctance? Hasn't he showed you the tricks he must have learned from that great whore Castlemaine?"

If John were with me to hear this, I was certain he would have knocked His Grace to the floor, and ruined his own prospects forever. No matter what happened next, I knew I could never tell John any of this, and bitterly I realized what a perfect courtier I had become.

I swallowed hard. "Your Grace, I do not believe that I—"

"Don't believe anything, Miss Jennings, until you listen to me." With greedy freedom, he reached out to run his hand up the length of my arm towards my breast. "You and Churchill and I could come to an agreement, yes? Or maybe he doesn't need to know. Maybe we keep it just between us. A settlement, a house, whatever will be agreeable to you both, in exchange for—"

"For me, Your Grace?" I felt sickened with disgust, at the duke and myself as well.

"You always were a clever lass, Miss Jennings, and now you've grown into a beautiful one, too." He touched the long curled lovelock I wore falling over one shoulder. "You have the hair of an angel, my lamb. Like golden guineas, eh?"

"Thank you, Your Grace." I eased myself away from his touch, carefully, so as not to offend him. "But beauty of the flesh is fleeting, and does not last. The only lasting value for a woman comes through her virtue, and her modesty."

"Oh, of course, of course." He was too preoccupied with sidling closer to me again to listen.

I stepped away from him again, as if following a dance, and continued.

"Virtue and modesty, Your Grace," I said firmly, and paused to give emphasis to my next words. "In that my little friend Lady Anne and I are in absolute agreement."

He frowned abruptly, like a man shaken from sleep. "Lady Anne? What of my daughter?"

"Lady Anne is my dearest friend here at court, Your Grace," I said blithely, "and I hers. We confide everything to one another, you know. I wonder that she hasn't told you that herself."

"Everything?" I saw the doubt flicker through his eyes, and I knew, once again, I was safe. "I've seen you together often enough, yes, that's true, but still. You say you tell my daughter everything?"

"Oh, yes," I said. "She is closer to me than my own sister."

He gnawed on the inside of his lower lip. "You tell my daughter everything."

"I do," I said, and smiled. "We are such close friends that I cannot imagine doing otherwise. Now if you'll excuse me, Your Grace, I must return to the duchess. Good day, Your Grace."

I backed from the room, as was proper before a royal duke, but also wise with a gentleman whose lust had been thwarted. Then I fled as fast as I could, the skein of silk clutched so tightly in my hand that the dye bled and turned my fingers blue.

And as I ran, I thought again of how at court, no attachment or connection was ever too slight to be of some usefulness, not even a friendship with a lonely eleven-year-old princess.

Chapter Six

"Barbara is now gone not only from my life, Sarah, but also from England," John said, his smile a shade too smug for my liking. "She has packed up her household, and left this morning for Paris."

"She has?" Skeptical, I looked up at him sideways, beneath my lashes and beneath the wide, flat brim of my lace hat. We were trailing at the end of the crowd of other courtiers following after the king as he walked the Horse Guards Parade through the park behind Whitehall. Charles did this every day, so long as the weather was fair, and John and I had taken to walking together then, too. And if some mornings—and this was one such—we failed to keep pace with His Majesty's long legs, and thus fell behind where we'd be alone together with more privacy, why, so it happened. "Why have I not heard of Lady Castlemaine's leaving?"

"You are hearing of it now, Sarah," he said, his smile widening. "I'm telling you, so you'd be first to know."

"After you, that is," I said, suspecting that Lady Castlemaine would have insisted upon the fondest of farewells. "What I have heard is that she was miffed at having lost her position as Lady of the Bedchamber for refusing to swear her oaths, and would go to France for the sake of her faith. Perhaps you take too much credit for yourself as the reason."

Just as the immoral and dissembling Duke of York considered himself among his family to be a model papist and Christian, so Lady Castlemaine, too, made a great show of following the Catholic priests.

Gossip said she had traded the honest Anglican faith of her parents for that of Rome in the hope of acquiring more influence among the French and Spanish ambassadors at court. If that was true, then she'd been bitten by her own ambition, and justly punished for betraying her beliefs for gain.

To curb the power of Catholics within the government and at court, Parliament had passed a Test Act, requiring all holders of public office to swear to certain Anglican tenets, or resign. The Duke of York had refused, and lost his place as first minister of the Admiralty. Lady Castlemaine had done likewise, and been forced to resign all her plum posts in the queen's household. It was all common enough knowledge, yet as I glanced up at John, I wished he'd admit to it as well.

But instead he swept his hand through the air, as if to sweep away my suspicions with a single grand gesture. "I told you before I'd broken with the lady, and now you'll have nothing whatsoever left to fear."

"Until the duke or the king should send you to Paris on some trumpery that will permit you to call upon her there." I sighed irritably, brushing aside a stray lock of hair that the breeze had blown over my face. It wasn't an idle objection, either. In this last half year, John's mysterious, secret acts of diplomacy continued to take him from London—and from me—for weeks at a time. "Why should I believe you?"

He stopped walking, drumming his fingers impatiently on the filigree hilt of his dress sword. His red coat with its gold braid cut a brilliant slash across the path in the sunlight, the plume on his wide-brimmed black hat tossing in the breeze.

"Because I love you, Sarah," he said, as if that explained everything. "Because you are dearer to me than all the world. Why must you always plague me by pretending otherwise?"

I did not stop with him, but took three more steps away before finally I turned around to face him.

"I'm not pretending, John," I said. "But after so long, I cannot quite believe that Lady Castlemaine is finally gone."

"Then believe me." He stepped forward and took my hand, lifting it to his lips. "I've done as you asked, Sarah, and I've given you my heart and my devotion as well. For God's sake, what else must I do to prove my love?"

I held the little posy of white carnations he'd brought to me beneath my nose, twisting the ribbons around my finger. "You love me, John, and I love you, more than I've any right or reason to. But you know that isn't enough, not for either of us."

"And I say it is." He circled his arm around my waist and drew me back into the shadows beneath the row of elms along the west wall.

To be fair, I went willingly, for this was a favorite place of ours, and when he kissed me, I kissed him back with my lips parted and welcoming, as hungry for him as he was for me. We'd played this little game a hundred times before, and I never wearied of how he could make the blood thrum through my veins with desire. But I knew the danger of the game, too, and the perils I ran even here in the park with so many others around us, and with a reluctant sigh I pushed away from him.

Purposefully I looked away, back towards the cluster of courtiers around the king in the distance. "It's time we rejoined the others, John."

"The devil we should." He took my hand, blocking my path. "Why won't you give me what we both want, Sarah?"

I pulled my hand away, nearly leaving my pale grey glove behind. "Because if you love me as you claim, then you'll want the same as I do."

"Sarah, Sarah." He groaned and shook his head. "You know that is not possible, not for either of us. The circumstances—"

"A pox on the circumstances!" I cried. "I *know* by the standards of court that I am poor and you are poor, and I do *not* need to hear it from you again. But—*if*—if you loved me as you say, then you'd find a way to make us both happy!"

This was the only card I had to play, and I knew it grew more tattered and worn each time I set it before him. And each time he refused to take it up, he rejected me as well, and each time the pain struck me a little harder.

I turned and left him, the lacquer heels of my shoes crunching the graveled path in a furious staccato that matched my black humor. He had made a bold show by sending Lady Castlemaine away, but it wasn't enough, not by half.

Hadn't I turned down the Earl of Lindsey only last fall, and he a peer? I was nearly seventeen. Each year I remained a spinster at court would make me more familiar, less desirable, and I despaired over my folly at having followed my heart instead of my head for the sake of John Churchill.

"Sarah." He fell into step beside me, though he didn't dare take my hand again, nor did I look his way.

"The deer are most lively today," I said, pointing towards the tame deer that Charles kept here in the park, along with a small herd of curious long-horned piebald goats that had been a gift from some Eastern pasha or another. "I suppose they must enjoy the warmth of the morning sun, too."

"The deer," he said grimly. "So that is what you wish to speak of? The damned deer?"

"We can speak of whatever you please, John," I said, as pleasant as could be. I *would* speak of anything—anything, that is, except skipping up the back stairs of his bachelor lodgings like any other of his strumpets.

He made a deep, disgruntled sound in his throat. "Then let us speak of the king."

"The king?" I looked ahead to where Charles towered above the others—he was very tall, a head above most of his male subjects in height—the elaborate silver lacing along the cocked brim of his black beaver hat almost like another kind of crown. "What have you to say of the king?"

"They say beneath his periwig he is as bald as a goose egg now, and that his beard is nearly white."

This seemed a trifle odd from John, but not so very different from my venture with the deer. "I'll grant that His Majesty's no longer a young man, but most would say he's still in his prime, not even fifty."

"Perhaps," John said. "Perhaps. But the trials of his youth have left their mark."

Now I did turn to him, my concern genuine. "Is the king unwell, John? Have you heard something that I should know?"

He shrugged elaborately, his broad shoulders rolling beneath the scarlet coat. "Nothing of any certainty, no."

"No?" I knew him well enough that I was sure more would follow, and it did.

"It's said that there's a palsy to the king's left hand when he wearies," he said, lowering his voice though there were none around us to overhear. "A shaking that he labors to hide. The lid of his left eye will droop, too, and when it does he turns his head away from company so none will take notice."

"Such signs could mean nothing, John," I said, praying I was right.

"The surgeons fear an apoplexy," he said, "though you must swear not to tell anyone."

I nodded, sorry for Charles, but glad that John had confided in me. At least we would not quarrel over that. Because of our places in the duke's household, there was much we could discuss with one another and no one else. And who knew when or how such knowledge might prove important?

"There has been no other king in our lifetime," I said, once again taking his hand. "I can't picture court without him. Can you fathom how the people will grieve when he dies?"

He linked his fingers more closely into mine, as if he feared I'd pull away again. "What would they do, I wonder, if they ever knew of the 'gifts' Charles receives from his cousin King Louis?"

"They would not believe it," I said firmly, "no more than do I. All that gossip about the French messengers bringing gold to the king's bedchamber by the same hidden staircase that his mistresses use—why, that is preposterous."

"It's true." The way he said it left no doubt. "Do not ask me the details, sweetheart, for I cannot tell, not even you. But suffice to say that Louis remembers his poorer cousin Charles, and regularly. The ties between France and Rome and England are more tangled than any of us can guess."

"Indeed." I glanced again at King Charles, his deep, distinctive laughter rolling over the heads of those around him. "How could he do that to England?"

"He does what he must, Sarah," John said firmly, and there was a ruthlessness to his voice that I'd not heard before. "Our king can keep more trinkets in the air than the master juggler at Southwark Fair. He keeps everything in balance—Louis and his brother and Parliament and the Dutch—and all for the sake of England's peace."

"But what becomes of a juggler with a palsied hand?" I shivered, despite the warmth of the sun. "If only Queen Catherine had borne a son, then none of this would matter, would it?"

"A Protestant son," John said. "One without any doubts or clouds around his birth, like our friend Monmouth. How different all this would be if only Charles had long ago wed Monmouth's mother instead of the queen!"

"Mary Beatrice is with child again," I began, trying to find some brightness in so much gloom. "If it proves to be a boy, and he is raised as an Anglican, like his sisters have been, why, then—"

"He'll be of no importance whatsoever," John said, dismissing the child before it had even drawn its first breath, "because the crown must first pass through his father the duke."

I sighed unhappily. "And all the juggler's trinkets will tumble to the ground, and us with them."

"Listen to me, Sarah." With both hands on my shoulders, John held me so I couldn't turn away even if I'd wished it. "Nothing is certain. No one knows what will happen, not tomorrow or next year. All we may have is today. I know you're weary of being a maid of honor. Let me protect you, and keep you safe."

I stared at him, shocked, and forgot everything else. "*Protect* me?"

"I can, Sarah," he said, warming to his disreputable pledge. "That much I can do. No grand house, I fear, but we'll be together, and you'll be safe away from court."

"You want me to become your mistress because you love me," I said, wanting to be sure. "Oh, John, not again!"

"I'm offering what I can, Sarah," he said, as if there truly were any honor in such an offer. "I will, because I love you so much. Say yes, sweetheart, and all we desire will be ours."

"*No*," I said, practically spitting the word. "Because I love you, too,

John, I will never settle for being your whore. And if you love me as you claim, you will never speak of it to me again."

All of us who served the duke and duchess had long known that James had abandoned the Church of England and converted to Catholicism, much to the joy of his wife and the sorrow of his brother the king. John and I spoke of it between us, with worry and concern, as did nearly every other in the Yorks' household, but little was said aloud beyond the palace walls—until Easter came that year, and the rest of the world learned the truth.

"Where is Father, Miss Jennings?" Anne whispered beside me. We were together in the royal chapel, the sunlight through the stained glass windows making cheerful colored patches on the stone floor. Before us the two dark oak armchairs reserved for the Duke and Duchess of York sat pointedly empty, with only one other—the high-backed one with the red plush cushions—waiting for the king. "Why hasn't he come?"

I twisted around in my straight-backed chair, peering back towards the door. At Anne's special request for this morning, I had been permitted to sit beside her here in the second row, both to keep her company and to ease her nerves. She was to be confirmed by Dr. Compton, the Bishop of London and the religious tutor to both her and Lady Mary, and for the first time Anne would be permitted to take Holy Communion with the rest of us for Easter. It had been a constant thorn to James that his daughters had been baptized and raised as Anglicans by the sensible order of the king. By choosing to follow Rome, James had traded away control of their education and upbringing.

"His Grace your father will come soon, my lady, I'm sure of it," I whispered in return. "He knows what this morning means to you."

But she only frowned and gave her head a small shake of resignation inside her white lace hood, recognizing her father's stubbornness better than I. She clutched her new Book of Common Prayer in both hands, her fingers moving restlessly over the gold-embossed leather, and I placed my hand over hers, both to comfort her and to still her fingers. Distraught though she might be, the small chapel was crowded with courtiers who would watch for such small signs of distress from her, eager to report them to others.

"Father's not coming," Anne said. "He'll stay with the duchess instead, and worship with her."

"His Grace wouldn't dare stay away." Here I'd been worrying over Anne betraying her uneasiness in tiny ways, while her father was risking the greatest of scandals. "Doubtless there's been some small mishap that's delayed him, that is all."

"Father is never late." With her hands quieted, Anne had begun tapping her feet, the pointed toes of her white slippers jostling from beneath her skirts. "Not unless he wishes to be."

Her sister Mary turned in her chair and glared, her glossy black curls swinging against her cheeks.

"Hush, Anne." Her whisper was so loud everyone must have heard. "And be *still!*"

The door to the vestry opened, and Bishop Compton entered and genuflected before the altar, his vestments rich with gold and silk embroidery to mark this holiest of holy days, and the end of Lent. The rest of us rose with a *shush* of silk skirts and lace cuffs, and in well-practiced unison, we turned towards the door to wait for the arrival of the king. I nodded to John, standing to the back with the other Gentlemen of the Bedchamber.

We did not wait long. Charles swept briskly through the door and up the aisle, his long coat of clipped blue velvet swinging around his legs as he passed among us, bowing and curtseying with our eyes lowered. He genuflected, as even a king must do, then paused to stare at the two empty chairs beside his.

"My brother has not joined us," he said to the bishop, an observation that everyone else in the chapel had already made. But the displeasure in Charles's voice gave it an awful new weight, and made the significance of James's absence obvious to everyone. "Dr. Compton, we shall proceed without him."

Beside me Anne made a little gasp of distress and disappointment, and once again I slipped my hand around hers. If the Duke of York had stood at the top of London Bridge and professed his faith in the Roman Catholic church across the rooftops of London and to heaven above, he could not have made his choice more widely known. For now, those of us in the chapel knew for certain that the heir to the throne of England was a confirmed papist.

By sunrise tomorrow, everyone in the city would as well.

And what would become of us all—and of England—after that was anyone's guess.

Chapter Seven

To my surprise, one evening the Duke of Monmouth sought me out in the duchess's drawing room. I could scarce object; I'd been losing at whist, anyway, and because Monmouth had been much in France, and away from London, I'd not seen him for many months. He'd taken to wearing a tall, full, black periwig in place of his own hair, I suppose to increase the resemblance to his father, but to my eye it only served to make him look older than he was.

"Miss Jennings," he said as he singled me out from the other ladies at the table. "A word alone with you, if you please."

"As you wish, Your Grace." I put down my hand of cards to follow him into the antechamber. There had been a time when I would have offered any excuse not to be alone with him. But since I was now so often in John's company, Monmouth had finally relinquished the field or at least the siege, and for the sake of his comrade, he'd ceased to view me with anything but the general regard of an old friend.

"I didn't know you'd returned to London, Your Grace." I paused before the window bench, sweeping my skirts to one side as I prepared to sit for this conversation, the way we might have in the past. "How grand it is to see you safely back among us."

But his expression was far from friendly, without a speck of his usual warmth.

"You needn't sit, Miss Jennings," he said curtly. "What I must say will not take long. I want you to release Colonel Churchill."

"Release him?" I asked, stunned he'd ask such a thing. John was away again for his master the Duke of York, but his letters to me had remained ardent and full of protestations of love. "How can I release him, Your Grace, when I hold him to no obligation?"

"Don't lie to me," Monmouth said with such sharpness that I drew back. "You lead him about as if you were queen yourself, making him grovel like a beggar. He may be too besotted to put you in your proper place, madam, but I am not. For the sake of his future, I must ask you to end it with him at once."

I could feel the angry patches of heat on my cheeks. "Forgive me, Your Grace, but I do not see how my acquaintance with Colonel Churchill is any affair of yours."

"Because he is my friend, Miss Jennings," he said, "as you so clearly are not."

"How *dare* you say that to me, Your Grace?" I demanded, my temper making me forget myself. "No one can care more for Colonel Churchill than do I."

"Then tell me, madam," he said, thumping his fist against the paneled wall beside him, "tell me why you have chosen to dissuade him from taking the next step in his career."

I shook my head, as much from anger as denial. "You make no sense, Your Grace, none at all!"

His expression darkened further, near as black as his wig. "Colonel Churchill was offered the chance to put his talents to an admirable use through an appointment sought by many, yet he refused. He *refused*, madam, though many, including myself, spoke his praises. He could have been the lieutenant colonel of the Royal English regiment, earning glory and promotion on the battlefield. But he *refused*, Miss Jennings, because of you."

"Because of *me*?" I could scarce believe that John would make such a sacrifice for my sake, nor would I ever want him to. His courage, his assurance, his bravery, even the dash with which he tied his sash over his coat—each was so much a part of John that I could not conceive of him without them. "*Me?*"

"You, Miss Jennings," he said, the words laden with accusation. "He claims that too much is unsettled between you for him to leave you to risk his life in battle. He would rather keep fluttering back to you like a trained pigeon, to calm his fears that you'll abandon him for another. Even the French ambassador is repeating how Churchill is no more than a dishonorable English carpet-knight, a lackabout who'd rather serve his mistress than his king."

"But that is not fair!" I cried furiously. I did love John for the man that he was, but I was also relying upon his continuing success in the army and at court. "How *dare* they say such things about John. It's not true, none of it."

"The only part that isn't true, Miss Jennings, is the one that calls you his mistress," he said, his words as cutting as the sword at his waist. "You forced him to break with Lady Castlemaine this summer, but at least that lady put both her gold and her person at his disposal."

"You know as well as I, Your Grace, that Lady Castlemaine left London for Paris because she wouldn't swear her oaths, and lost her place as Lady of the Bedchamber," I said warmly. "Besides, Colonel Churchill wearied of her long ago."

"What Colonel Churchill wearied of was your shrewish rants against her and any other lady you perceive as your rival," he said. "You demand everything from him, Miss Jennings, and give nothing in return."

"He has my love," I protested, "just as I have his."

"He has nothing," the duke said. "He can never prosper so long as you hold him back. Even his father says he's squandering his future on you. You have no fortune, no connections, no influence to aid him. If you love Colonel Churchill as you claim, then you must set him free, or else suffer knowing you were his ruin."

"You are wrong, Your Grace," I said, my hands knotted into tight fists at my sides. "You are wrong about everything!"

But he didn't answer, and he didn't say farewell beyond a quick bow. All I was left with was the fear that he'd been right, and that I might have ruined the best man I'd ever met, at court or anywhere else, and ruined myself with him.

Three weeks later, John returned from France, his business there for the duke done at last. He came to me in my closet before he'd even had the chance to change from his traveling clothes, his long coat and high riding boots thick with dust from the road, and his face lined with weariness. I was having my hair dressed for the evening, but he did not wait for me to dismiss my waiting woman before he pulled me from the bench of my dressing table and into his arms.

"Tell me your last letters were false, Sarah," he demanded. "Tell me you did not intend the pain you brought me with each word."

"John, please, one moment," I said breathlessly, twisting around in his embrace to nod over my shoulder to my waiting woman. "You may go, Elizabeth."

Her eyes round as tea-dishes and her fingers bristling with my tortoiseshell hairpins, the woman backed through the open door and fled.

"You frightened her, John," I said, but he only pulled me closer, the dust from his coat drifting over my skirts like fine grey snow.

"You frightened me." He circled one arm around my waist to keep me close, and slid his other hand along my jaw until he reached the long, thick lock of my hair that Elizabeth had not yet pinned in place, and that still hung loose over my shoulder. Slowly he coiled the hair around his fingers like a golden ribbon, holding me fast so I could not turn my head to look away.

"How many times have I told you that you are my world," he said roughly, "that I love you more than any other man ever could? Yet in place of the love you once showed me, you now write only to question my courage as a soldier, and my devotion to you."

"John, please, I—"

"No, Sarah, please *me*," he demanded. "Please me, and be truthful. Why did you write me letters that were so cold and without heart, as if you cared not whether I returned to you?"

"What else can I do, John?" I wanted to be strong, to state my case with reason and measure, yet my senses were betraying me. He smelled of the wild places he'd ridden through, of wind and oaks and the streams he'd crossed, of his horse and leather and wool and steel, and all of it so male I could have closed my eyes and swooned from the pleasure the scents alone gave me. "When your friends come to me with tales I must believe, and when they—"

"What friends?" he demanded. "Tell me, Sarah. What tales?"

"Monmouth," I whispered. "He claimed I'd swayed you from accepting a command in his regiment."

"I didn't take it because I chose not to," he said. "To fight for the French, even in an English regiment, would not be wise now."

"You know I would never want to hold you back," I said, confused. "But Monmouth said I was being selfish, putting myself ahead of you."

"How could you?" he asked, incredulous. "You knew none of my reasons for refusing, nor any of the politics behind it. And I know you, Sarah. I know you'd never expect that of me."

"But Monmouth—"

"Monmouth can think of only one path to glory, and that with a sword in his hand. He doesn't understand how diplomacy can accomplish just as much, if not more. I'm not going to be held back by anyone, Sarah, not even you."

I nodded, reassured that he was still the man I'd want to share my own life's fortunes, but with one last doubt. "He said your father swore I'd be your ruin."

His face tensed, and I knew I'd struck a tender spot with him. "My father wishes me to marry some great heiress, just as your mother would wish you to wed a lord with a fine estate. That should be no news to you."

I nodded, for it wasn't. "Monmouth told me the gossips at the French court said I'd made you over into a mere carpet-knight, and that if I truly loved you, I would set you free."

"And you listened to him?" He stared at me with disbelief, and now I could see the pain my words had caused him. "You let him tell you I'd be better without you? Is that why you wrote such cruel letters to me, Sarah?"

"You weren't here to ask." I was sorry to have wounded him like this, especially when he'd been so far from home. But what other resource did I have as a woman? Perhaps I was gambling with my love and my future as my stake, but what else could I use to defend myself and my heart than my pen?

I reached up and laid my hand on his cheek, rough with the stubbled beard that he hadn't stopped to shave away.

"You weren't here in London to ask, John," I said, as sorrowfully as I could. "Monmouth had seen you in France, since I had. How was I to know what was true and what wasn't?"

"Because of this." He took my hand in his and placed it on the front of his coat, over his heart. "Never doubt me again, Sarah, not for a single moment."

He kissed me hard and deep, as if to mark his possession in a way that words could not. He could be the tenderest and most agreeable gentleman imaginable, but now there was too much desperation and urgency and anger, too, roiling between us for that. He didn't have to say more; I knew it already, as much with my soul as with my heart.

He pulled his hand free of my hair, the tightly wrapped lock uncoiling like a flicking snake against my cheek, and pressed me against the wall. I slipped my hands inside his coat and around his waist, and with a groan that vibrated between our mouths he ground his body against mine. I arched my head back, relishing the familiar feel of him, and he pressed his lips to my throat.

"Now, Sarah." His breath was hot upon my skin as he grabbed a fistful of my petticoats and pulled them upwards. "Tonight, here."

"No, John, *no*," I said, my whispered protest so ragged that it might well have been permission. "You know why we cannot—"

"Damnation, Sarah, don't you know how you torture me?" he muttered, his hand warm on my bare thigh, above the flowered ribbon of my garter. "Don't you know how I've missed you?"

"I cannot risk it, and neither can you, not unless you are willing to—"

"How will that change what I feel for you?" He twisted me around so I faced the wall, and jerked my bare bottom against his shaft, hard and demanding beneath the wool of his breeches. He moved against me, mimicking the act that I still refused, holding me tight with one hand while with the other he worked his fingers against me with such cunning skill that I shuddered from it. The more I fought him to escape, the more aroused we both became, and though I knew all too well the dangers of such a game, I had missed him, missed him sorely.

"How will marriage make me love you more?" he demanded, his words hot on the nape of my neck. "How can marriage be better than this?"

I gasped as my knees buckled with delight, leaning into him to keep from falling to the floor as he stroked me harder, his other hand reaching into my bodice to fill his palm with my now-bared breast.

"I—I swear it would be," I managed to stammer as I finally twisted around to face him, slipping to my knees as I fumbled with the laces and buttons on his breeches. To keep that last scrap of my virtue, I'd learned to give him the French pleasure, and to delight in it from him. "With me as your wife, it would be."

"I cannot wait to discover how," he said, his voice more of a growl as finally I freed his staff from his breeches. I knew how to touch him, too, and to give him the most delectable of kisses. "Oh, sweetheart, like that again."

Some, I know, would call this a vile corruption of what God had intended for husband and wife, a terrible defilement of honest English passion by French instruction because I let his seed fall on barren ground instead of into my ripe womb. Perhaps it was, and that was why we would be punished later.

But while I'll never be shamed by how I loved John, I will admit that my young life had been molded by what I'd seen at court. By then I'd lived among so many women who were free with their favors and even more giving with their experiences and advice that I was far more knowledgeable in worldly matters than most other girls my age, or even most modest married women, if it came to that. I didn't see what John and I did as wrong, but right, and necessary, too, if I was to keep him.

In silence we sat together afterwards before the fire in my tiny hearth, he with his arms around me and I lying back against his chest, watching the log turn grey with ash and the embers beneath hiss and pop.

"You will always be mine, Sarah," he said with unshakable conviction. "No matter what else may happen, no matter where my fortunes take me, I'll never love another woman as much as I love you."

"And so I love you, too, John," I said, unwilling to make any greater promise than that. I sighed and closed my eyes as I curled myself against his chest. What else could I say and keep to the truth? Once again I'd gambled, and again I'd won, and for now I would not wonder how long my luck would need to hold before he'd marry me.

* * *

My affairs with John were not my only trial at this time, and though this next is not easy to write, it, too, must be included.

One night I was returning to my quarters alone, having already met and parted with John for the evening. Though the hour was late, the palace was as usual still merry, filled with courtiers laughing and chatting in the halls and chambers. Lost in my own thoughts, I paid little heed to those around me as I hurried along, until someone seized my arm at the elbow and pulled me aside into a small bend in the hall.

"Mother!" I cried, for it was she. "Whatever are you doing here, at such an hour?"

"To see you, Sarah, of course." Though her dress was neat, her linen widow's coif pressed, the old madness burned from her eyes, and her fingers curled tightly into my arm to keep me with her. "Where have you been, daughter?"

"I answer now to Her Grace the duchess, Mother, not to you," I said warmly. Lately she'd taken to waylaying me like this in the park or in St. James's itself, playing the meek widow on a false errand to cozen her way past the porters. I'd dutifully continued to send her money, of course, but nothing had changed between us. "You've no right to be here now, as you know well enough."

"I've every right to see how my own daughter fares in this wolf's brothel," she said, "and I can see the truth plain as the day. Your face is flushed with wickedness, Sarah, your mouth ripe with it. You've been playing the whore with that John Churchill again, haven't you?"

"I owe you no answer to such a question." I struggled to break free of her hand, but she held me fast, pulling me closer as if I were still a child.

"You owe me that and more." Rage turned her voice shrill. "I let you come to court to find a decent gentleman—a lord!—for a husband, not to have your belly filled by a base scoundrel like Churchill."

"Be quiet, Mother," I ordered sharply, praying that no one else would hear her shameful raving. "You know not what you say."

"Don't I, daughter?" She jerked me closer, her other hand groping at me through my petticoats. "Come, let me know my bastard grandchild!"

"No!" At last I pulled free and backed away before she could catch me again. "I owe you nothing more, Mother. *Nothing.*"

Then I turned and ran, my heart pounding in my breast as her empty accusations rang in my ears. Not only did she unsettle and threaten me, this mother of mine, but I also feared what she could do to my prospects with John. What gentleman would wish such a woman for his mother-in-law, so full of venom and bile? What man wouldn't look at such a wretched old witch and think twice of what his future might be in such a family?

There was but one course for me to take, and next morning I spoke in private to Mary Beatrice.

"You are certain of this, Miss Jennings?" she asked gently, perplexed and worried by my request. "You speak of your own mother."

I didn't hesitate. My mother was the unnatural one, not I. "I fear that I am, Your Grace."

The duchess frowned with concern. "You truly believe yourself at risk?"

Myself, and my prospects, too, though I did not say so.

"Yes, Your Grace," I said, and it took only a little art to put the tremor of fear into my words. "My mother is in every way a madwoman, her actions so wild and unpredictable that she is a danger not only to me, but to all among my acquaintance."

"That is not to be tolerated," the duchess said firmly. "I won't have you so distressed, not while you are in my household."

"No, Your Grace," I murmured, a sweet tear of gratitude on my cheek. "You are always most kind."

She smiled and patted my hand. "Be easy, Miss Jennings. The order will be posted this night, with special notice given to all servants and guards. Your mother Mrs. Jennings is banned from this court and will be charged if she dare venture near you again."

"Thank you, Your Grace." I smiled with relief, and with satisfaction, too, for thus I was rid at last of my intemperate, inconvenient mother. "I thank you with all my heart."

The Yorks' next ball in St. James's was a small one, mostly their followers and a few visitors from the French court as well, and because we all knew one another, spirits were high and the laughter and giddiness often threatened to drown out the little orchestra's music. It was, after all, less than a month until Christmas. The smoky scent of roast geese and beef already came from the sideboard in the next room, and mingled with the steamy, spicy fragrance of the mulled wine. Scores of candles lit the room bright as day, with the richly colored velvets and satins of the guests reflected over and over in the tall looking glasses that Mary Beatrice had had brought specially from Venice.

"Why don't you dance, Miss Jennings?" Mary Beatrice asked, joining me where I stood alone by the window. "I know it's not for want of a partner, for many gentlemen have asked for you this evening."

"Thank you, Your Grace, but I prefer not to," I said as I watched the other dancers. "I am well enough as I am."

"Perhaps a glass of wine will improve your humor, yes?" the duchess asked, ready to beckon to a footman for my sake. "I cannot bear to see one of my prettiest young maids here alone like this."

I made myself smile. "Forgive me, Your Grace, but tonight I prefer my own company."

"If that is what you wish, my dear," she said with her usual kindness. But before the duchess moved away to her other guests, she glanced from me to the nearest pair of dancers and back again. Her kindness shifted to purest pity, and once again I felt the burning knot of unhappiness well up in my throat.

Half of the couple was the duchess's newest maid of honor, a dreadful creature named Catherine Sedley. She was no beauty, with dark hair and skin pale as death, and so gaunt that her breastbones showed above her bodice. Her nose was long and her mouth as wide as the river—and every bit as foul, as everyone knew who came within hearing. Yet despite all of these deficiencies, she was vastly desired because she was the only heir to her father, Sir Charles Sedley, and as such reputed to possess a portion of ten thousand pounds. This may not sound so very grand today, but in that time, when most titled families could live quite lavishly in London and in the country on an income of five hundred a year, and a squire's family on half that, it was no real wonder that all the bachelors at court were scrapping over Catherine Sedley and her ten thousand pounds like dogs with a mutton bone.

Every bachelor, it seemed, including Colonel John Churchill.

He was smiling as he led her through the steps of a hornpipe, a dance not commonly ventured by ladies. But Catherine would do anything, no matter how improper, and she hopped and capered gracelessly along with the gentlemen, holding her skirts so high that all could see her bright green stockings and the gold buckles on her red garters. She laughed with John, her mouth gaping wide as a crocodile's to show all her teeth, and dipped down low, displaying how not even the tightest lacing could make a show of her pitifully small dugs.

"Do you still love Colonel Churchill, Miss Jennings?"

Hurriedly I composed my face as best I could before I turned to curtsey to the Lady Anne, standing beside me. She was here among us tonight as a special treat, dressed in a green-gold velvet gown with the pearl bracelets that her cousin King Louis had given her for her birthday.

"Good evening, my lady," I said. "How handsome you look tonight."

She gave her shoulders a restless small shrug, uneasy with any compliments to her appearance, and squinted back at the dancers. "You haven't answered me, Miss Jennings. Do you still love Colonel Churchill as once you did?"

I didn't answer at first. How could I, when before me John could not look away from the dreadful creature on his arm as she hopped like a leashed monkey beside him?

"So you do," Anne said, her voice touchingly earnest. She was nearly twelve, and eager to decipher the mysteries of love—mysteries, of course, that as a princess she'd never have for herself. "Even I can see it. I cannot fault you, for he is as perfect a gentleman as any at court. But you do love him, just as everyone says."

"Everyone can say what they please, my lady," I said, my own words brittle as ice. Anne had been right to call John handsome, for he'd never looked more so than in his scarlet coat and golden sash, his dark eyes full of merriment. He danced as well as he did nigh everything else, with a fine, manly grace. I hated to see him squander himself on Catherine Sedley, laughing and teasing her the way he once had done with me, yet still I could not make myself look away, as if such suffering were some sort of dreadful penance that I'd contrived for myself. "The truth, my lady, lies only between Colonel Churchill and me."

"Ahh." Anne sighed and peered down at her thumb, scratching at a scrap of skin beside the nail. "Then I should not tell you."

I could no more not ask than look away from the dancers. "Tell me, my lady? Tell me what?"

She looked up at me dolefully, without lifting her chin. "I heard the duchess speak to Father today of a letter she'd received about Miss Sedley."

"Miss Sedley, Miss Sedley!" I cried with frustration. "Why does all the world care so much for that awful creature?"

"It wasn't all the world today," she said. "It was only Sir Winston Churchill. Your handsome colonel's father."

That made me pause, my chest tight. "I know perfectly well who Sir Winston is, my lady."

"Then you must also know perfectly well that Sir Winston's letter asked the duchess's permission for his son to court Miss Sedley, as one of her maids of honor."

"Miss Sedley?" I repeated, too appalled to say more. "To *court* Miss Sedley?"

"Sir Winston feels it would be a good match for them both, and Father and Mary Beatrice agreed." She fidgeted with the clasp on her bracelet, looking away from the shock that must have shown on my face. "I suppose that when it comes to marriage, Sir Winston values Miss Sedley's fortune more than all the love in creation."

"You are certain you didn't mishear, my lady?" I demanded, part of me wondering, quite meanly, if this was no more than one of Anne's inventions to draw more attention to herself. "It wasn't another gentleman?"

"Sir Winston Churchill, Colonel John Churchill, Miss Catherine Sedley." She sniffed and rubbed at the weepy corner of her eye. "I have no weakness of the ears, Miss Jennings. I heard the names perfectly well."

I shook my head, desperate for another explanation. Perhaps John's father had written this letter without consulting him. Surely John himself could know none of this. Hadn't he told me I'd always be his, and never to doubt him?

But hadn't he also said that no one would hold him back, not even me? What was love beside ten thousand pounds?

"It cannot be true, my lady," I said, as much to convince myself as her. "It *cannot*."

"I am sorry, Miss Jennings, but it is." She sighed mightily. "They said that Sir Winston had already spoken with Sir Charles Sedley, who has given his blessing as well. I shouldn't have told you, and now you're cross with me."

"Of course you should have told me," I said. "It's better I should know than not. And I am not cross with you, my lady, not in the least."

"I'm sorry, Miss Jennings," she said again, though now I wasn't sure what she was apologizing for. Self-consciously she tucked her hand into mine, taking care that no one else would notice behind the folds of our skirts. "I am. But no matter what happens, you shall always have me as your friend."

My first response was to tell her I didn't care, she didn't matter, that no mere friend could ever replace what I had with John. But then I remembered that she was a princess, and a princess as a friend was something very different indeed. If John was bound to make his way however he could, then so would I.

I took a deep breath to steady myself, then squeezed my fingers around hers. "Thank you, my lady," I said. "I thank you with all my heart."

The dance ended, and Catherine turned her sweaty face up to be kissed. At once I closed my eyes tight, both to keep out the dreadful sight of her with him, and to keep in the angry tears that threatened to spill over.

"Sarah."

I opened my eyes with a start to find that Lady Anne had vanished, and John was there instead before me. "Colonel Churchill."

"I've missed you, sweetheart," he said, his voice low and coaxing sweet, the way I heard it in my dreams. "How beautiful you look tonight, like an angel of gold in that ivory gown."

"Don't, John," I warned. If my jealousy would give me strength for this, then deadly sin or not, I would use it. "Please. Don't begin."

But he only stepped closer, closer than he'd any right now to be. "Why are you being so cruel to me, Sarah?"

"Cruel!" I cried, so loud that others turned to gawk, then quickly lowered my voice. "*Cruel?* I have not been the cruel one, John! How can you say that to me when you have been so faithless with that—with Miss Sedley."

Sadness filled his eyes. "You know it's not my choice, Sarah."

"Oh, yes, then who else has chosen to laugh and smile and scrape before her, as if she were the greatest prize imaginable?"

"Sarah, please," he said, coaxing. "You don't understand. It's you I still love more than ever. You're the one in my heart, Sarah, and always will be."

"Where does that leave Catherine, pray? The ugly one in your marriage bed?" I demanded, my hurting pride adding tinder to my temper. "You pretend you have a great passion for me, John, when in reality there is no such thing—none."

"How can you say that to me, Sarah?" he said, almost pleading. "Once you swore you loved me better than any other man."

I would not give in, no matter if he fell to his knees before me. I would *not*. "Your father has given his blessing to the match, and hers with it. You can't deny that, can you? I wish you well of her fortune, John, for that is the only comfort you'll find with—"

"John, my darling, come, come!" Possessively Catherine slipped her arm around his waist, her monstrous mouth grinning up at me with triumph. "Ah, Miss Jennings. I should ask you why you don't dance, too, but I suppose all the gentlemen must have already made their choices."

"Yes," I said, taking one last look at John. "Yes, Miss Sedley, it would seem that they have."

And as I crossed the floor, I held my head high, and did not care who saw the tears that streamed down my cheeks.

Chapter Eight

The afternoon my sister Frances, Lady Hamilton, returned to St. James's Palace was marked by a chill, heavy rain that flattened the first green shoots of spring, much as the cold hand of fate had worked to flatten my sister's hopes.

I should first say that our lives had long ago grown apart, and I had not seen much of her since her wedding ten years before. If the page had not announced her before she came to me in the duchess's drawing room, I'm not certain I would have recognized her, she'd become so changed. Though still a beauty, her round face was lined with woe, her bright gold hair seemed dulled, and the deep mourning she wore for Lord Hamilton, killed in the battle of Ziebernstern, seemed heavy enough to drag her to the ground.

"You must help me, Sarah," she said as soon as we'd embraced. "I have no one else."

I sat on the bench beside her and poured her a dish of tea from the pot that the duchess had thoughtfully sent. "I cannot believe that Lord Hamilton did not provide for you and the children."

"What George provided, Sarah, was his debts." She drew out a black-bordered handkerchief and pressed it to her red-rimmed eyes. "He was perfection as a husband and father while he lived, but he had suffered certain—certain reverses, and now the children and I have less than nothing. Oh, Sarah, you must help me!"

"Mother sent you to me, didn't she?" I asked warily, already sure that she had. Though I dutifully sent my mother part of my income—more, really, than she deserved—she'd made it abundantly clear through her hateful letters that she continued to think me the worst sort of jade, refusing to make a decent match from spite and stupidity. Considering how badly I'd misjudged John, though, perhaps my mother was right.

"Mother said you could help me, yes," Frances said. "She said you were a favorite, with influence."

"Have you gone to Ralph?" I asked, dodging the request I knew was coming. If I had grown apart from Frances, then I was another world away from our bachelor brother who was older still, living alone on what remained of our family's lands in Hertfordshire.

She shook her head and sighed. "Ralph claims to have trials of his own, and no sympathy to spare."

I doubted she wished sympathy alone. I poured my tea from the cup into the dish to cool, watching the steam rise in a fragrant cloud as I thought of how much my sister's predicament was repeating the woes that had plagued our mother. "You know I would help you if I could, Fan, but my situation is not much better than your own."

"But it is!" She seized my hand in her black glove, her gaze seeing a lie in my yellow damask gown with the elegant knots of silk ribbon, and the loops of gold and pearls that hung from my ears. "Everyone has heard of you, Sarah. You are a great favorite here, much admired. Surely you have had your share of offers."

At once I thought of John, and how hopeless matters were with him. Over these last months since the ball, I had watched his reputation grow at court, his star rising with the speed and brilliance I'd always expected from him. He wrote to me, wrote to me often, but I seldom answered. I avoided him in company, the course I knew was wisest for me, and I'd begun encouraging the attentions of other gentlemen. Yet still there had been no match announced between John and Catherine Sedley, and still, too, I could not quite banish him from my heart to make room for another.

I drew my hand away from my sister's, and fanned it over my tea. "There is nothing definite, Frances."

"No?" Frances tipped her head to look at me, a shadow of her old coyness returning. "That's not what I've heard. I've heard the Earl of Lindsey has paid you court again, and that you've also caught the eye of the Duke of Monmouth *and* the Duke of York. Those are prime fish in your net, sister."

"They are not in my 'net,' as you call it, " I said sharply, "nor do I wish them to be."

While Frances couldn't know that Monmouth's friendship had cooled towards me over John, she surely understood what the rest of England did: that despite his ever-growing devotion to Rome, the Duke of York remained next in line to the throne after his brother Charles. Not that such a sorry ascendancy would matter to me, for I would no more be kept by a king than I would by a duke.

Frances made an impatient *tut-tut* sound. "Gentlemen do not wait forever, Sarah. You must make the most of your beauty and youth while you can. Either duke would be most generous to—"

"They are both married, Frances," I said, "and so, too, I should like myself to be one day."

"I know they each have wives, Sarah, but in your situation, you must consider every possibility." She gave my knee a little pat of misguided encouragement. "It might not be such a bad thing to be mistress to a great lord. I see that now. A house, a living, a carriage and servants, influence, even a title of your own in time—these are not to be scorned."

"Why not tell me to open my bodice and spread my legs, and ply my trade between the empty stalls at Covent Garden at midnight?" I did not bother to hide my bitterness. "The only difference would be what I earned, not how I did it."

"Oh, Sarah, don't turn righteous with me," she scoffed, echoing our mother in both her unpleasant demands and her scorn. "The Duke of York is a handsome and vigorous gentleman who would please any lady."

"If you are so enamored of the duke, then why don't *you* become his mistress?"

"Because I am thirty, Sarah," she said, her voice suddenly turning hard as steel, "and you are seventeen, and this court has no use for any lady over twenty years."

I rose, too agitated to remain beside her. "You followed your heart and wed for love. Why am I not permitted to do the same?"

"Because now I know that love will not last, or feed my children, or keep us from the almshouse," she said, her once-beautiful face heavy with the burden of such knowledge. "Love is an indulgence women in our position can ill afford. You must make the most of your beauty while it still has value, Sarah, and seize as much for yourself as you can."

The icy rain rattled against the window like small stones thrown against the glass.

"I'll speak to Her Grace about your situation, Frances, and ask her to help ease your distress since you once served in this same household," I said, hating everything about this conversation. "You are still remembered at court. The duchess is a most generous lady and will pity you if I ask. Be certain you tell Mother I did so, too."

I heard the rustle of my sister's skirts as she rose behind me. "I cannot thank you enough, Sarah, and if there is ever any way that I might be of help to you, why, then I promise I—"

"Never advise me again on how I can better myself by playing the whore," I said sharply, without turning. "I'm sure you remember the way out, Frances. It hasn't changed. And neither, thank God, shall I."

It was October, in 1677, when Prince William of Orange first deigned to come to the English court and finally meet the two princesses who were his Stuart cousins.

Now to Prince William, as well as to the common folk who crowded into the corners of the Banqueting House for special feasts to watch the king and his relatives dine, the lives of these royal princesses must have seemed grand indeed. To wear jewels and sit upon velvet cushions stuffed with swansdown, to have their every whim met by servants, to have soft beds to lie upon and more food each day than they could ever eat—what could be better? Yet because I was constantly with Lady Anne and Lady Mary, I saw things differently, and I wouldn't trade my lot for theirs for my weight in golden guineas.

To most Englishmen as well as to Dutch William, the sisters were the royal princesses. To me, they were dear companions and friends, as well as mistresses. But to King Charles and to Parliament, they were stakes for bargaining, and England's only chance to preserve a Protestant succession.

Of course the princesses themselves realized this. How could they not, when from the cradle they had been raised as Anglicans, against their father's will? But though they knew their duty would be to marry as they were told, they were young girls still, harboring dreams of love and a handsome, charming bridegroom—dreams that the rest of us knew were sadly ill founded.

"I do not care if he is a distant cousin," Anne said as we stood side by side in the duchess's drawing room, whispering behind our fans as the gentlemen finally joined us. "He is Dutch, and unspeakably ugly. He could play the part of Caliban to perfection."

I frowned, knowing how such uncharitable words could carry to the wrong ears. "Hush, my lady, hush, or he'll hear you."

Anne wrinkled her nose with disdain. "It won't be anything he's not heard before."

Likely she was right. William, the Prince of Orange, had come from Holland on some matter of diplomacy with the king, and while the gentlemen praised the prince's sagacity, we ladies could find scarcely a wisp of merit to him. His nose was large and hooked, his eyes hooded and baleful, and when he spoke he wheezed with every word. He wore his own lank hair instead of a periwig, and dressed day after day in the same drab black suit. Worst of all, he was so short that Lady Mary had declared him to be a dwarf, and even if he'd wished to dance—which he never did—no one would have wanted him for a partner, for fear of seeming too large and ungainly beside him.

In all this I agreed with Lady Anne. But she had overlooked the two most important qualities of the Prince of Orange: he was Protestant, and he was eager—most eager—for a wife of the same faith.

And he did not leave England without one.

Before a month had passed, we were gathered in Lady Mary's apartments for her marriage to Prince William, late on a Sunday night. For a royal wedding, our number was small, mostly family and the closest members of the Yorks' household. It was the groom's twenty-seventh birthday, and if he was happy with the match, he kept his sentiments to himself. There was no such reticence from fifteen-year-old Lady Mary; she had wept ceaselessly since her father had told her only days before, and she wept still, her lovely eyes so swollen from weeping she could scarcely see.

Perhaps that was a blessing. Mary had inherited the Stuart height and was nearly six feet tall, while at her side William barely came to her shoulder, his Dutch accent so thick we could scarce make out his responses. To one side stood James, who had hoped to see his daughter wed to a prince who was both French and Catholic, and did not bother to hide his unhappiness with this groom. Mary Beatrice wept, too, inconsolable over losing her favorite stepdaughter, and not caring how her tears fell onto the great swell of her once-again pregnant belly. Queen Catherine's face had a melancholy cast, her head bowed as she doubtless was recalling her own wedding journey to a foreign place and unknown husband. Even Bishop Compton was grimly solemn for a wedding, likely aware of the importance of a strongly Protestant union in such threatening times.

The only one of us with the proper merriment for a wedding was Charles, full of such raillery as he gave away his niece that I wondered if he'd needed strong drink to do it. But why shouldn't he be merry? The king continued to be the master juggler, tossing this sad little Protestant wedding against the growing suspicion and dislike of James among the people. It was a bold trick, yes, but one that did not please me to watch.

Lady Anne was not there, having felt feverish with an aching head and kept to her bed. In a way, this was likely for the best. She would herself be married soon to some other Protestant prince whom the king chose for her, and sent away to live among strangers at another court. If I were wed myself by then, there'd be a chance I would be chosen to go with her as a lady-in-waiting. If not, I would be left behind with Mary Beatrice. Though Anne and I shared little in temper or interests, we'd spent much time as young girls together in the adult world of the court, and we'd a special fondness for one another. I would miss my little Anne horribly when she wed and was sent from me, and as I watched Mary's wedding,

I couldn't keep the unhappy prospect of Anne's to come from my thoughts.

But there was more to distract me, too, for standing across the room from me where I could not miss him was John Churchill. His long absences overseas these last months made sense now, for it was widely accepted that he'd had much to do with persuading William to accept the king's offer of his niece's hand. John must have been rewarded well; his presence here at the ceremony was proof of that. Our eyes met, and he didn't smile, but his slight, solemn bow was more than enough to make me flush.

Purposefully I looked away, concentrating instead on the details of the service to tell Anne later. When the bishop reached the point in the ceremony for William to promise to endow Lady Mary with his worldly goods, William followed tradition and dropped a handful of coins into the opened pages of the bishop's prayer book.

"Gather it up, niece!" called Charles, as if he were at the playhouse instead of a royal wedding. "Gather it up and put it in your pocket, for 'tis all clear gain!"

A few of the company laughed, more from nervousness or because it was the king's jest than from true amusement. I did not. All I could see were the golden coins sitting atop the promises to love and honor, and I thought with sad regret of how it had been the coins that kept me from John. Not love, not honor, not respect, not affection, but gold—and when I glanced back at him, his face perfectly composed like the good soldier and diplomat that he was, I wondered if he thought it, too.

Poor Mary's mood only worsened during the supper that followed, and when she was led away by the duchess and the queen to be undressed for the bedding, one would have thought her preparing for her death instead of her bridegroom. Finally we all traipsed back into the bedchamber one last time where the new couple sat against the lace-trimmed pillow-biers in the bed, side by side as husband and wife, but still too shy to touch. Mary's long dark hair had been brushed out over her shoulders like a glossy black cape, and though she'd finally managed to stop weeping, I saw how her hands trembled with fearful dread as she took the cup of fortifying hot posset from William, as was the custom.

Nor did the king make it any more agreeable for her. As the rest of us filed from the room, Charles stayed last for the privilege of pulling the heavy damask curtains closed around the bed, stopping short of commanding the poor newlyweds to perform for his amusement. As it was, he'd likely be first at their bedside in the morning, too, gleefully prepared to inspect the sheets for the sordid proof of Mary's shattered maidenhead and William's dutiful seed.

"Now, nephew, to your work!" he called for all of us to hear, the brass rings of the bed-curtains scraping over the rails. "Hey, hey! St. George for England!"

Poor unhappy princess! I was thankful that Anne was not here as a witness, and that she was spared being part of her sister's humiliating ordeal.

But as soon as word of the wedding spread, London and the rest of the country rejoiced with wild celebrations and pealing church bells, with every tavern and alehouse filled with those drinking toasts to the Prince and Princess of Orange and making wagers over how soon they'd produce a babe. Even this tiny possibility of a Protestant heir was enough to inspire relief and delight in a populace growing more and more uneasy with James's oppressive Catholicism—exactly as Charles had known it would.

The next night, I joined the rest of the court standing along the rooftops and balconies of Whitehall to drink spiced wine and watch the bonfires and fireworks that lit the city. Despite the cold, the streets below us were full of people cheering and singing with delirious joy. Bright sparks from the open fires drifted through the chill air, while the sky-rockets overhead danced with their own reflection in the river.

Snug inside my black velvet hood, I turned my face up, following the next rack of fireworks as it burst into extravagant stars overhead, and sighed with delight.

"How happy you look, Sarah!" John said as he joined me. "I always like to see you smile."

At once my smile wilted into wariness. We were standing apart from the others, just far enough for him to speak as freely as he wished, and I cursed the coincidence that had left me so vulnerable to his attentions.

"I've not had much reason to smile lately," I said, my hands tightly clasped inside my muff.

At once his face grew solemn. "Forgive me my thoughtlessness, Sarah. I was sorry to learn of your brother's death."

I was surprised that he knew of it—Ralph had been as good as a hermit, never once in his life venturing to London—and surprised, too, that he still cared enough for me to offer his solicitude.

"I thank you, John," I said softly. "I had not seen my brother for many years, so I cannot claim my grief is deep. His estate is not without debts, but it will provide some comfort to my sister and her children to balance what Mary Beatrice has given to them."

"And comfort for you, too, I trust?"

"It's not ten thousand pounds, if that is your meaning," I said, unable to keep the unworthy thought to myself. "No one shall mistake me for a great heiress."

He smiled. "No one will ever mistake you for anything other than yourself, Sarah."

"I would not wish it otherwise." If anything he'd grown more handsome over time, the last sweetness of the boy he'd been finally gone from his face. "But then you have Miss Sedley to amuse you now, don't you? How often she speaks your name among the other maids!"

He grunted, the white plume in his wide-brimmed hat rippling in the breeze. "Speaking my name doesn't make me hers."

"Tell that to her, not me." Because I knew I'd nothing left to lose, I let my disappointment spill over. "They say there should be no secrets between a man and wife."

"She's not my wife, Sarah, nor will she be," he said with grim finality. "Her temperament vexes me beyond measure or reason."

"You would go against your father's wishes?"

"I would," he said, surprising me again. "No matter how much you refuse to believe me, you're still the only woman I've ever truly loved or wanted."

I steeled myself against his compliments, staring out over the river so I wouldn't be charmed into folly. "And what version of this tale have you told Miss Sedley?"

"I've told her only the truth, Sarah," he said. "I've told her that as much as I might try to esteem her, my love would always belong to another."

I let out my breath, not realizing I'd been holding it until I saw the puff in the icy air before me. "You truly said that to her?"

"She didn't care, Sarah," he said, "for she claims to love another, too."

"She does?" I asked, incredulous. Because I knew his value, his worth, I could not believe a low, vulgar creature like Catherine Sedley would dare scorn him. "She can't."

"Oh, yes," John said, his expression purposefully blank. "And she claims His Grace the Duke of York returns her ardor."

I gasped, stunned, for though I kept my ears open wide for news within the Yorks' household, I'd not heard of this. "His Grace? She desires His Grace?"

"Yes," he said curtly, and that was all. What need had he to say more? John's sister Arabella had borne a handful of bastards by the duke while she'd been his mistress, and I'd never forgotten the ugly scene I'd witnessed between them long ago. When the duke had tried to press himself upon me, I had refused him for the sake of John, and now the lady whom John had wooed—albeit halfheartedly—preferred the duke. Could there be any more squalid, slippery stew than this little sampling of our lives at court?

I looked up at the sky again, pretending to watch the fireworks as I let this rare news settle between us. "So pray, John, tell me," I said at last. "Was it the wedding last night that has turned your thoughts this way?"

"That wedding put me to mind of many things." He held his open hand out before him, as if to grasp the entire celebrating city before us. "If London rejoices like this for Lady Mary's wedding, what will it do when her father takes the throne instead? Charles believes he's outwitted his people again, but all he's done is raise false hopes. And if Mary Beatrice is delivered of a boy, why, the crash of those hopes from this height will be worse than the king ever dreamed."

"Her Grace has only borne one child that has lived beyond the cradle, and that a girl."

"Her Grace is not yet twenty years of age, a young woman in her breeding prime," he said. "She's proven she's not barren like the queen. She could well produce a half-dozen sons before she's through."

He was right, of course, as he so often was. "What should His Majesty do?"

"What, if I were king?" That made him smile, though his answer was blunt and humorless. "I'd send James away. To Scotland, or Wales, or even Holland with William. Exile him and his wife and their nest of Romish priests with them, and steady the confidence of his people."

I nodded, considering. John was not the first to venture this notion of exile. Though the duke trusted his brother too much—and perhaps too foolishly—to consider such a possibility, I'd seen how it worried the duchess and made her pray all the more. "Where would that leave us, John?"

"I would follow the duke," he said with conviction. "Regardless of His Grace's faith, that would be where my loyalty must lie."

I looked up at him, his face lit by the scattered glow of another sky-rocket. "For now?" I asked. "Or forever?"

"For what would seem the wisest course," he replied sagely.

"The wisest course for you?" I asked, thinking of what an adroit courtier he had become. "Or for the country?"

"One follows the other, Sarah," he said, so much the perfect ambassador's answer that I nearly laughed with delight. No wonder that idle creature Sedley hadn't appreciated him.

"But what of you, Sarah?" he asked. "Would you repay Her Grace's kindness towards you and follow her into exile?"

"The duchess is my mistress," I said promptly, my own answer as ready as his, "and she has shown me much favor since I've been part of her household. But if I were forced to choose—this night, this moment—I would follow the Lady Anne."

"The remaining Protestant princess."

I nodded. "Because she is shy, others misjudge her as doltish. But she listens to everything that's said around her, and she remembers it to sift and consider later. Most of all, she has little use for her father and Mary Beatrice, and less for their priests. She's still only a girl, I know, but she won't let them push her aside. She tests everyone as allies, or enemies."

His dark green eyes were full of the old admiration he'd shown me in the past, that mutual appreciation that had been so much of what we'd shared. "She considers you an ally?"

"Oh, yes." I smiled, remembering how Anne had decided that on the first day we'd met. "She favors you, too, John, and trusts you even though you are in her father's camp."

"Because she trusts you."

"Most likely," I said. "But she also likes you because you're more handsome than any other gentleman at court, certainly more than any mealy prince she'll be wedded to."

"So you would say the wisest course for us both would be to follow not James, or Mary Beatrice, but Lady Anne." To my surprise, I could tell from his face that he was considering it. "We could do worse, far worse. Clever Sarah! What a head you have!"

I shrugged at that bit of foolishness, determined to show how little I cared. "It's the head I was born with, and it does occupy my neck."

"It does far more than that." He pulled off one glove and reached into my hood, cradling my jaw in his hand. His palm was warm against my night-chilled skin, the grasp of his fingers at once so intimate and possessive that I jerked away.

His smile was slow and knowing, too confident. "Do you know how much I've missed you, Sarah?"

"Lah, however would I have guessed?" It was a flaw, I know, but I clung fast to my jealousy. "You've found others enough to ease your suffering."

"But not like you," he said. "Not with your fire."

"My fire, you say?" I narrowed my eyes, daring him. He wanted me, I knew, and God help me, I wanted him, the way it always had been between us, pulling us together like wild creatures. "Then take care, Colonel Churchill, lest you be burned."

"Too late for such warnings, pet." He swept his hat from his head with self-mocking grace. "Miss Jennings, may I have your permission to call upon Her Grace to ask for you?"

I caught my breath, never dreaming he'd dare me back like this. "Nothing has changed, John."

"Nothing, and everything." He reached into my muff and drew out my hand, lifting it to his lips. "We deserve one another, Sarah."

Too stunned by the suddenness of his offer, I could only shake my head. "Why now, John? After everything else, why now?"

"I'm not certain." He smiled crookedly, enough to melt my heart. "It must have been hearing the words spoken over the prince and princess, and realizing how much I wished them to be said over us. I cannot offer you much more than the stars in this sky, my love, but I pray still that you'll honor me and be my wife."

Nothing had changed, but still I didn't hesitate with my answer.

"Yes, John," I said, and the thing was done. "*Yes.*"

Three days later, the Duchess of York gave birth to a lusty son. Her labor was quick, and the boy was strong and promising. He was given the name of Charles, Duke of Cambridge, the same ill-fated name and title granted to his three half brothers who had died as infants, and though many thought this to be a woeful omen, no one dared say so in the presence of the overjoyed duke. And like a snuffer dousing a candle's flame, the birth put out all the hope and rejoicing of the Protestant wedding.

The sour little Prince of Orange viewed the new male heir as a personal betrayal, his reaction so venomous that I wondered what ill-founded promises the king had made as part of the marriage pact. John wouldn't tell me more, only that the prince had no care for making friends among the English. In his wheezing wrath, William announced that he and Mary must leave England's insalubrious climate and return to his home at once. He made no effort to hide his distaste for Charles's court, which he judged vain and dissolute, and his growing impatience with his fifteen-year-old bride.

They stayed in London only long enough to attend the ball in honor of Queen Catherine's birthday. To try to please William, Mary wore the splendid suite of pearls and the ruby ring that he'd given her as his wedding gift. He danced with her only once. The day after that, in a fresh wave of tears and with remarkably little ceremony, Mary was carried off from us by her husband to the icy Dutch port of Rotterdam. Most cruel of all, William forbade Mary to say farewell to Anne, fearing her fever would be transmitted between sisters to him.

Anne would never forgive him. From that time onward, she refused to use William's given name, calling him instead Caliban—or worse, in her letters, "the Dutch Abortion."

But William had been wise to keep Mary clear of her sister. Soon after they had sailed, the first tiny pimples appeared on Lady Anne's cheeks, a gentle scattering that turned to angry pustules in the course of a single night: the desperate roses of smallpox.

Chapter Nine

I was born in 1660, in the year of the Plague, and for all my life people would speak of that time in hushed dread and reverence for how swiftly death had cut through London without heed of rank or beauty, youth or wealth. Yet when the Great Fire came, the flames that savaged the city also ate away the disease to nothingness, never to return among us.

Smallpox has no such tidy conclusion. While the Plague's power was soon spent, smallpox never ceases, destroying even the youngest and most promising without warning or reprieve, as I was to learn to my endless grief. For those blessed few who do survive, the price—blindness, baldness, a loathsome face so pitted and carved that not even velvet patches can fully mask the damage—is often never paid until the grave.

Everything possible was done to ease Lady Anne's suffering. The windows of her bedchamber were sealed shut to build the fever, the walls draped with red cloths to help draw out the poisons, and she was bled rigorously, upon waking in the morning and at dusk. Her father James decided the shock of Mary's hasty departure would be too much for her to bear in such a perilous state, and none of those attending her were permitted to mention it.

Yet as ill as my poor Anne was, religion still warred over her sickbed. Only those who'd had smallpox and survived were allowed in her rooms, and Bishop Compton himself was furious that the nurse in charge of Anne's case was an ardent Catholic, determined to steal her very soul for the pope if, near death, Anne faltered from the Anglican faith. England had already given away one of its Protestant princesses to the Dutch; to lose the second one now to death was unthinkable.

Sickened, too, was Lady Frances Villiers, who had served as the governess to both Lady Mary and Lady Anne since they'd been in the nursery at Richmond Palace, and refused to leave Anne's side even now. Alas, this dear, wise Protestant lady was not so strong as the princess, and the smallpox filled her lungs and claimed her life almost at once, a solemn warning to the rest of us.

For my part, I sat alone in Mary Beatrice's sitting room for what seemed endless hours, waiting for any news of Anne as I tried to play cards, or read, or even to pray. Except for visits from John, I was alone, the other ladies and maids preferring to sit with Mary Beatrice in her bedchamber and coo and prattle over the tiny new Duke of Cambridge. How could I have the heart for such merry idleness, when Anne lay suffering?

"You'll have to chose new loyalties if Anne dies, Sarah," John said, ever pragmatic when we were alone. "It won't be an easy choice."

"Hush, John, don't say such things!" I said, refusing to accept such a dreadful possibility. "She's my lady and my friend, and she's too stubborn by half to die so soon."

Anne was, too. Finally word came to us that the princess's fever had broken and her pox had scabbed over. I was waiting when at last the physicians declared her safe to return to company, and she came to join us in her stepmother's rooms.

"Welcome back to us, my lady!" I said as she embraced me in turn. She was much changed: she'd lost so much flesh that her gown hung limp from her shoulders and her steps seemed weak and halting. But worst of all were her face and breast, as purplish red as if she'd been boiled, and still covered with the remnants of the pox. I knew these last crusting scabs were a sign of healing and would soon fall away, but each one would leave a pitted scar to mar her complexion. Though she had never been as attractive a child as her sister Mary, any hope of her blossoming late into a beauty was now destroyed.

Yet still she smiled, her eyes bright with tears of mingled joy and sorrow. "Oh, Miss Jennings, I am so happy to be back here, too! Now where is my new brother? Where is the little darling? I cannot wait to see him!"

Mary Beatrice came forward, the baby in her arms swallowed up by his elegant, trailing linens and ruffled cap, most fitting for a future king. Clinging to her skirts was her only other surviving child, the silver-haired Lady Isabella, scarcely a year old and the third princess in the succession. Her first daughter, Catherine, had died of a putrid quinsy the winter before, princesses being as sadly fragile as other children.

"Here he is, Anne," she said proudly, "and so eager he is to meet his sister, too! Oh, yes, my darling little fellow, isn't that true?"

With a sigh of happiness and infinite care, Anne took the baby from Mary Beatrice's arms, holding him close as fresh tears started in her eyes. John could never fathom how either Anne or Mary could be so fond of the children born to their father and Mary Beatrice, especially the boys who took their sisters' places in the succession. But I understood. Although Anne could never let herself trust Mary Beatrice as a replacement for her own mother or forgive her father for marrying again, she was still so desperate for family that she gave herself over to these innocents, the only ones free of complication or intrigue. Regardless of what wickedness their elders did, she was bound to these children by their shared Stuart blood. How could she not coo over the new brother in her arms, or give him her pinkie to grasp in his own tiny fingers, or at last dare to brush her kiss across his forehead?

"Where's Mary?" she asked, looking up from the baby in her arms. "Why isn't she here?"

Mary Beatrice smiled with forced cheer. "Why, she has already left with her husband for Rotterdam. His Highness the prince had business that could not wait any longer."

Anne frowned down at the baby, her mouth drawing into a tight knot of disappointment. Given William's temperament and the difficulty of travel, it was entirely possible that the sisters might never see one another again.

"She wanted to say good-bye," Mary Beatrice said quickly, clasping and unclasping her hands. "Truly she did, Anne. But because you were ill, and His Highness wished to return to—"

"He wouldn't let her see me, would he?" Anne said. "He thought I'd make *him* sick, didn't he, the selfish little Caliban."

The baby gave a slow, lonely wail, to my mind more of sympathy than discomfort, but Mary Beatrice snatched him from Anne's arms. "There, Anne, see how you've upset him! Hush, hush, sweet, I'll keep you safe."

She swept the baby away from Anne and carried him like a prize back into her bedchamber, her ladies following and clucking like broody hens to soothe the baby and his mother, too. I stayed behind; I would have been both cruel and foolish to abandon my lady now.

Anne stood alone in the center of the room, her arms hanging empty and forlorn at her sides. "I never meant to frighten him, Miss Jennings," she said plaintively. "You know that of me, don't you?"

"Of course you didn't, my lady." I slipped my arm around her shoulder for a moment, wanting to comfort her just as the others had gone to assist Mary Beatrice and the baby. "His Grace is like every other babe, ready to squawk at everything and nothing."

She closed her eyes, hugging her arms around herself, and didn't answer. I let her be quiet, knowing how her tempers needed time to settle.

"Mary should have come to me," she grumbled, but with little heart. "I wasn't so ill as that, not at the wedding."

"Her Highness is married now, my lady," I said softly. "She has no choice but to obey her husband's will."

She gave her head a small shake, as if settling some question in her head, and opened her eyes.

"I shall take Mary's rooms for my own," she announced. "They're mine by rights now, and much nicer than my old ones."

"Yes, my lady," I said, the only suitable answer. If seizing Mary's bedchamber for her own, like battlefield plunder, eased the loss of her sister, then so be it.

"They're mine now," she repeated, and squarely met my gaze as if she'd thought I'd disagree. "My sister will have no need of them."

Then abruptly her shoulders sagged again, and the stern set of her mouth wobbled. "Lady Frances died, and they did not tell me, and Mary left me without saying good-bye. You won't leave me, too, Miss Jennings, will you? You'll promise to stay with me?"

"Oh, my dear lady!" I opened my arms to her and she came to me, resting her ravaged cheek against my shoulder with a shuddering sigh. In her short life, she'd already lost so many who had been dear to her—three brothers, two half sisters, her mother, her grandmother, her aunt, and now her governess—that it was no great wonder to me that she'd dread losing more.

Yet still I could not forget how John and I had discussed exactly this same question, and how my answer would determine our future even more so than Anne's.

And no one, I think, would fault me for keeping to myself the news that I'd accepted John's offer to wed.

"My place is here with you, my lady," I said softly, putting aside protocol long enough to fold my arms protectively around her. "As long as Her Grace will have me, I shall be here as your friend. However can I do more?"

She raised her head from my shoulder to study me, her eyes so close to mine that I could see the grey flecks deep inside hers, like chips of steel. Lightly she touched her fingers to my cheek, a simple gesture that could have been from affection, but instead felt more as if she were marking me, claiming me as her own.

"Keep your word to me, Miss Jennings," she whispered. "If you will be loyal to me, then that is what you must do. Always keep your word, and you will stay my friend."

Less than a week after that, the Duke of Cambridge woke in his cradle, crying inconsolably in the dark night. Nothing would comfort him, and as the desperate nurses stripped away his sweat-soaked gown to lave his tiny body with damp cloths, his mother Mary Beatrice noticed the first sore in the sweet hollow beneath his arm.

Within the fortnight, the month-old duke was dead of smallpox, and the court went deep into mourning, once again bereft and troubled without a male heir to the throne.

It was no idle whim that made John ask Mary Beatrice for my hand instead of my mother. First, of course, it was proper, as Mary Beatrice was my mistress, and responsible for me in a way that my mother had long ceased to be. Of even more importance were the favors that the duchess could grant us: not only did she give me permission to remain as a maid of honor and continue receiving my living—which John and I would sorely need—but from kindness she also granted me enough of a dowry to pay off the debts that had encumbered my inheritance from my brother.

We were wed late one evening in her apartments. To keep my place as a maid of honor—for by the rules of the position, all maids were to be virgins, even if few in truth were—our marriage needed to be secret from the rest of the court. Thus there was nothing that would draw attention or curiosity: no rich new wedding clothes or jewels, no music or flowers, no family or other guests to share our joy, especially not in that sad household, still black with grieving. At the duchess's insistence, not even Anne was invited, from fear she'd tell her other attendants. James, Mary Beatrice, and two others of her ladies served for witnesses as we said our vows directly to one another in the old fashion of the countryfolk, without even the nicety of a cleric to offer his blessing. Yet when we were done, I felt as bound to John as if I'd sworn to love him in St. Paul's before a thousand witnesses, and from the way he gazed at me, I know he felt it, too.

We had no bedding ceremony, either, no drunken guests to cheer us raucously through the marriage act, or worse still, no leering courtiers determined to observe us for the sake of preserving a royal dynasty. There were, after all, advantages to being common-born.

For years now I had resisted John's invitation to his bachelor apartments on Jermyn Street, not far from the palace. Now as I followed him at last up the winding wooden stairs to his rooms, I couldn't quite believe that I'd finally gotten the prize I'd wanted for so long.

"You're not frightened, dear soul, are you?" John asked as he turned the key in the latch.

"No," I said at once, even though my heart was racing with excitement. "How could I ever be frightened of you?"

He laughed, as much from joy, I think, as from amusement. "That's because you're never frightened of anything, Sarah."

"I'm not." I lifted his hand to my mouth and gave him not the kiss he expected, but a fierce little nip to the fleshy part of his palm.

"Vixen." He grabbed my arm and deftly twisted me around, trapping me against the wall with his body. "Would you draw my blood already?"

"I would if I came upon you with another woman," I said, and I meant it, too. "I'm yours now, John, and you're mine, and nothing will ever change that."

"Fight at my side, then, not against me," he said. "I should take you into battle with me."

I laughed, daring him, even as he pressed so closely against me that I could feel the hard muscles of his horseman's thighs, pushing between my legs. "Give me a sword, and I'll lash up my skirts and clamber over the ramparts beside you."

"You would, too, and be worth a score of Frenchmen," he said, his voice dark and low. "No wonder you're the perfect wife for me, Mrs. Churchill."

"Don't let anyone hear you say that," I scolded, but I didn't really care. I liked the sound of that "Mrs. Churchill," even though it must be our secret for now. I liked it just fine, and I slipped my arms around his shoulders and turned my face up to kiss him.

"Not here," he said, taking my wrists away from his shoulders. "I've had my fill of skulking in passageways with you. You're my wife now, and I mean to have you that way."

He pushed the door to his rooms open, holding it there for me to enter first. *Rooms* sounds far grander than his apartments here deserved, as I soon saw when he lit a single candle. Never one to squander money on his own comforts, John had one small room that served as parlor and office, his sword and armor hung on pegs along the wall. Beyond that I could glimpse a tiny dressing room, and at last his bedchamber. The furnishings were few and spartan, more fitting for an officer's field tent than a courtier's lodgings. But the sparseness pleased me, for I knew how much it reflected my new husband's well-ordered self, free of extraneous luxuries or show.

"This way." He reached around to unhook my cloak, then tossed it onto the back of the nearby chair. "No dawdling, now."

" 'Dawdling,' hah," I said, gathering up my petticoats in my hands as I ran, away from him but back towards the bedchamber. "I'll not be the one who dawdles, John Churchill!"

I was fast, but so was he, and truth be told, I did wish to be caught. He grabbed me around the waist just before I reached the doorway to the bedchamber, lifting me up into his arms with no more effort than if I'd been a child's plaything.

"I'm supposed to carry my bride over the threshold," he said as I laughed and wriggled in his arms, "and until we have a proper house, this will have to do. There, wife, consider yourself mine!"

He set me down again, and at once I pulled towards the bed, the curtains already drawn and the coverlet drawn back in unabashed invitation. There was a fire in the hearth, too, making the room cozily warm for a winter eve, which made me guess that he'd left instructions for his landlady to make things ready.

But as immodestly eager a bride as I was, John was the one who held me back.

"Hold now, Sarah," he said softly, coming to stand before me. "There's no need for haste, not tonight. I would see you first in all your beauty, and learn how rare a prize my wife is."

" 'All my beauty'?" I repeated, smiling because it was John, not because I understood what he wished from me. "I do not see what—"

"Then I'll show you, sweetheart." He stepped behind me, unfastening the knot at the back of my bodice to draw the corded lacing through the eyelets, one by one by one, until the heavy boned silk slipped forward. Impatiently I shrugged my arms free of the sleeves, tugging at the heavy lace cuffs while he unfastened the waist of my petticoats. I shook my hips to twitch the heavy skirts downward, and hopped free to stand before him in my smock and stays, my stockings, garters, and high-heeled shoes.

"Your turn, husband," I ordered, my breath coming fast enough to make my stays feel tight around my ribs. Most likely it was knowing that tonight we would not stop, that there'd be no frantic reminders from me. Tonight we were not simply amusing ourselves, but consummating our marriage, perhaps even conceiving our first child, and the finality of that was at once solemn and exhilarating.

"Very well, wife," John said, already discarding his coat, and his waistcoat after that. But he never looked away from me, locking his gaze with mine. With his usual economy, he stripped away his breeches and his stockings until he stood before me in only his shirt, the old-style tails hanging clear to his knees.

He smiled and held his hands out to his sides with a conjurer's flourish. "As you please, Mrs. Churchill."

"I thank you, sir," I said, determined to match his humor. Hadn't I just declared I feared nothing? I raised my chin and smiled back, and hooked my thumb into the strap of my stays to try to wriggle from them. But I'd had a maidservant of my own to help me dress since I'd come to court, and I'd forgotten how difficult it was to unlace stays unassisted, especially when my fingers were clumsy with ardor and anticipation. The harder I tried to free myself, the more impossible that task became, and as I struggled, I could not miss the way John's smile twitched at my expense.

"Don't laugh at me," I said crossly, "or I shall turn about and walk from that door and never return."

"You won't," he said, coming to stand behind me. "You can't. You're my wife, and you must do as I say."

"I should like to see you make me do anything against my will," I said darkly. "You'd learn what manner of sorrow that would earn you."

"Or what amusement," he said, unlacing my stays with such ease that I did not wish to consider how he'd acquired this familiarity with ladies' dress. He slipped the stays from my body, letting them fall to the floor as he bent and brushed his lips across the nape of my neck. I closed my eyes and let my head fall back as he began to pull the pins from my hair until the heavy knot spun apart and the heavy waves tumbled down my back. I gave my head an extra shake so the firelight would play across my hair, for I knew how it had always fascinated John.

"Sarah, Sarah." His voice was ragged with desire, his breath warm over my ear, as he slid his hands around my waist, pulling my back against his chest. The fine linen hid nothing on either of us, our bodies pressed so tightly together that it served as no more than a fair-thee-well between us. "Do you know how long I've wanted you?"

"Forever," I said, so forcefully as to leave no doubt. That was how long I'd wanted him, and I wouldn't allow that he'd wanted me any less. I twisted in his arms to face him and slid my palms up the front of his chest, his skin hot beneath my palms. "You're mine, John, just as I am yours, the way that fate intended us to be."

But at that moment, he was giving far less thought to fate than to me. He pulled my smock up, blinding me in a brief cloud of white linen as it went over my face, and his shirt soon followed. As much as we'd dallied before, I'd never stood thus with him, and I caught my breath at the newness of it. Not that I was shamed or shy: though at seventeen my form was still slight in comparison to the fleshly voluptuousness that the king's mistresses had made the fashion, I knew that John found me wickedly desirable. And more, because I'd brought him no gain or advancement, I knew he'd wanted me for what I was.

I looked at him with my own delight, for as God had made him, John Churchill was a paragon of manly beauty, as handsome as any ancient's Adonis. Already his staff stood proud and ready for me. It was no wonder that he'd caught the eye of every lady, high and low, at court, but I— I was the only one who'd captured him for my husband.

Lightly I traced my fingertips along the scars that crisscrossed his body. Some had come from fighting in Tangier, others against the Dutch, and two more, I'd heard, from duels of honor in St. James's Park. All were proof that my husband was no idle, mincing courtier, but a man of rare strength and courage. I'd chosen well. Now that strength and courage belonged to me, the pair of us as one. With pride and satisfaction I smiled up at him, and he caught me about the waist.

"Now who's the dawdler, Sarah, I ask you?" he asked, his patience finally no more than a slave to his passion as he guided me backwards towards the bed. "Who's squandering our wedding night?"

I laughed as I fell wantonly on the bed, sinking deep into the feather-stuffed mattress with my arms looped around his shoulders, drawing him down atop me.

"I *would* fight beside you, Colonel Churchill," I whispered fiercely, threading my fingers through his long hair to hold his face over mine. "Your battles are mine now, and I will never fail you in anything."

"Then prove it, Sarah," he said, kissing me hard enough to steal the breath from my body. "Prove it now."

And I did. I thought I'd known what to expect from my husband's lovemaking, but oh, I'd no notion at all of the wondrous ways he had to coax pleasure from my body. Over and over he raised my passions so high that my desperate cries begged for release, but each time he did no more than soothe me, calm me, only to send me soaring once again. When at last he claimed my maidenhead, I wept not with a virgin's pain, but with a lover's tears of purest rapture.

Afterwards I lay curled beside him, exhausted, and gladsome of his arm protectively around my waist. Beneath the coverlet our skin was still slick with sweat, the air of the small bedchamber thick with the musky scent of our passion. As much smaller as I was than he, I'd matched him when we'd come together, fierce as any tigress with her mate. Now I sighed with contentment, more happy than I'd ever been in my short life.

"Tell me your thoughts, Sarah," he whispered, kissing my throat below my ear. "Tell me, love."

I took his hand and slid it from my waist to low on my belly, holding it there in my own. "I was thinking how the midwives say a man must give his wife satisfaction and joy for her to be fertile and conceive. If that's so, John, then we've gotten our first son this very night."

"Only the first of our brood," he said, pulling me closer as he spread his fingers possessively across the cradle of my hips. "Ah, Sarah, Sarah. How blessed I am to have you for my wife!"

"This is only the beginning, John," I whispered. "As long as we're together, what can't we do?"

Again I smiled in the dark, my hand over his as I thought of how our future together surely must glitter with the brightest promise. Yet as vast as my dreams might be, I'd no notion then of how far and fast we'd rise, John Churchill and I—nor how far we'd tumble, too, like angels cast down from heaven itself.

I continued in my old place as a maid of honor through the following spring, serving both the duchess and Lady Anne, and keeping my old name as well. Most who knew me well also knew I was John's wife, but in a court with so many other secrets, mine seemed only a trifle. I went freely between St. James's Palace and John's rooms in the west end of

Jermyn Street, our little newlywed nest, and anticipated the day when we'd have funds enough for a proper house.

Although Anne was unhappy to have missed my wedding to John, she was delighted to have me as a secretly married friend. She was thirteen now, and like most girls her age, so much given to dreaming of love and sentiment that she found our clandestine marriage the most romantic possible. She'd always liked John, and now she simply extended my friendship with her to include him, too, another champion to take her side against the iniquities she constantly perceived around her.

But ah, how my dear husband did prosper! In February, he was gazetted a full colonel in a new infantry regiment, a great honor for so young a military gentleman. I rejoiced with him, and in my giddy delight I agreed to journey with him to meet his parents in Minternie, in Dorset. I did resolve to be my most agreeable. But I could not forget that while these two aged persons had sired my husband, they had also made their dislike for me abundantly apparent before our wedding, dismissing me as a greedy, conniving chit and doubtless far worse. I do not take such ill usage lightly, and never have. But with John between us, the oil poured on troubled waters, we kept a pretense of genteel behavior, though I did embark on more long walks across the Dorset countryside than ever I did the rest of my life.

There was one other small solace to be found in that time, too. From my friends at court, I learned that Catherine Sedley, John's parents' choice for his bride, was now not only flaunting her position as the Duke of York's new mistress, but also parading about her belly, already swelling with James's bastard. How satisfying it was to share that particular news with Madam Churchill!

So matters went, until in April a courier brought urgent orders from the duke, calling John at once to London. He was then to proceed to Brussels with his good friend Sidney Godolphin, and in the company of Prince William, the three of them were to begin negotiations for a new alliance between England and France. Godolphin was a thoughtful, homely man from Cornwall, clever with reckonings and other such puzzles, and he and John had been close since they'd both long ago been pages at court.

Of course I congratulated John for receiving such a diplomatic plum, a reward for his skills and talents, and one that was sure to bring him more success and honor. Besides, I told him playfully, after all the practice he'd had negotiating between his odious, hateful mother and me, what surprises could any mere Frenchmen offer?

But the jest twisted round to bite me like a serpent in my hand. Because of the delicacy of John's mission, it had been determined that I not return to court alone, but remain in Dorset with his parents until he returned from Brussels.

Of the bitterness of my situation beneath the thumb of his gloating mother; of my tears of misery and loneliness, and disappointment that I'd yet to conceive a child; of my fear for John's safety as talk spread not of peace, but of war; of the resentment that I let chill the pages of my letters to John during those months apart—of those I'll speak nothing more. Any new bride who has been forced by circumstance into such solitary proximity to her husband's mother has surely felt the same.

But as grievous as my own trials were to me, there were others far larger and more perilous tearing at England. By the time John returned home in October of 1678 and fetched me back to London, a new madness had seized the country, and our lives together would begin a course from which there'd be no return.

Chapter Ten

"I enjoyed that immensely, John." I smiled as I leaned my head against his shoulder, closing my eyes as the hired carriage rolled over the cobbled streets. We seldom went anywhere outside of Whitehall or St. James's Palace—not only did our affairs keep us occupied there day and night, but we also did not choose to squander what money we had on idle amusements—but tonight John had surprised me with tickets to a play presented by the Duke's Company at Dorset Garden. "We should go more often."

"If it pleased you so, sweetheart, then we shall," he said, giving my knee a small fond squeeze. "Soon enough you won't wish to go anywhere."

I laughed softly. I was scarcely a month gone with our first child, and as delighted as I was to be in that enviable state, I'd underestimated how poorly I'd feel in these early weeks after I'd first missed my courses. But I was determined to relish this time before I became too unwieldy and was forced to retire from company for my confinement.

"I'll go anywhere, John, so long as it's with you," I said, reaching up to kiss his cheek. "Not that I should have to tell you such."

"And not that I tire of hearing it," he said. It was late, nearly midnight, and I could just make out his smile in the murky shadows of the carriage. What little light filtered in through the windows seemed to settle and glint on the gold lace and buttons of his uniform; there was a great deal more of it to glint now since he'd been promoted again, to brigadier of foot, in honor of his success with the French treaty.

Yet so much lace came with a price. "Tell me, John. What was the hero's name in tonight's play?"

"The hero?" He frowned a bit, as if he truly would be able to recall it. "The fellow that was the captain?"

"He was an admiral," I said. "I don't suppose you can recall the poor heroine, either?"

He sighed ruefully, knowing he could fool me no longer. "Was I so very obvious?"

"Oh, I doubt the players noticed on the stage," I said, twisting to face him. "But I know your humors too well, John. What is it that so occupies you tonight?"

"What doesn't?" He leaned his head back against the leather squabs. "The peace, the king, the duke. You, of course. Our child."

"Our *son*," I said firmly. Even so soon, I was sure of that: a son to follow after John, to carry his name, to inherit all we were working towards. "And you needn't worry over us. *We* can look after ourselves perfectly well."

He chuckled, a sound I never wearied of hearing. "True, Sarah, true. I should save my worries for those who need it more. Monmouth, for one."

"Monmouth?" Last summer, while I'd been stranded in Minternie, a mad parson named Titus Oates had stirred the country with a wild mix of lies and half-truths about a popish plot to murder the king. No sane person believed him, but enough of the rest did to blind the senses of those who should have known better. The Romish church became the symbol of more evil than the Devil himself, and the hysteria sent several of the land's highest Catholics first to the Tower for treason, and then to the gallows—a dirty, wicked business. Catholics of every rank were abused and beaten, their churches burned, with loyalty to the crown as the shameful excuse.

But it did not end there. Certain members of Parliament had tried to change the laws of succession, removing Catholic James and legitimizing the king's son Monmouth—a bastard, yes, but a Protestant one—so he could rightfully claim the throne instead. The king had refused, and in January had dissolved Parliament by way of punishing them, only creating more discontent among his subjects.

"If even the king won't acknowledge Monmouth as his heir," I continued, "then what hope can he have left?"

"More than he should, if he'd any wits," John said grimly. "He listens too much to those around him, so much so that now he does believe the throne should by rights be his. When I last saw him, at the tennis courts, he could speak of nothing else."

"I'm sorry for that," I said, thinking back to happier days for us all. "But he's never been a clever fellow, and too pretty and petted for his own good."

"Monmouth's as brave and loyal as any man under fire, but he's always been easily led, instead of leading for himself." John looked away from me, out the carriage window, and I knew his thoughts were on the past as well. "It won't end well, Sarah. It can't."

I curled my fingers around his, understanding the rest that he'd left unsaid. James had never been more despised by the people, or more at risk. The people were right, too, since I'd never known a greater pious hypocrite than this Duke of York. Yet for the present, John and I were bound to him both by loyalty and for our livelihoods, making our place as Anglicans serving in the first Catholic household in the land an uneasy one at best.

"As foolish as Monmouth can be, John," I said, "I do believe I'd rather have him for a king than James. You know as well I do that the minute Charles dies, he'll try to make us all Catholics, and deliver us up to the French if not to Rome—"

"Hush, Sarah," John ordered curtly, his hand raised to warn for silence if his words failed. He was still turned to the glass, but now he was taut with readiness, listening for something I could not yet hear.

"What is it?" I whispered. I noticed now that his hand had come to rest on the hilt of his sword, his fingers tightening in anticipation. "What do—"

"*Listen*," he said. "Can't you hear it?"

I couldn't, not yet, but then he was opening the window to the carriage, thrusting his head and shoulders through to call to the driver, and I could hear it, too: angry, raised voices, shouting back and forth and echoing off the walls of the buildings on either side. The carriage was slowing, and I fumbled at the latch of the second window, determined to rise beside John to see for myself.

"Damnation, Sarah, sit!" With his free hand, he tried to push me back inside. "Show some sense!"

I frowned, not liking to have my sense questioned, even by John. Now I could see the bobbing shadows along the walls of the houses, coming closer to us, and I could smell a tarry smoke, too. There was no room in the narrow street for the driver to turn the horses about, and so at John's insistence the man guided us lurching to one side of the street, as close to the building as could be managed.

Suddenly a black tide of men coursed around the corner and into the street, their hats pulled low and dark scarves pulled up over their faces, their raucous chants and catcalls filling the air. Lit by the bobbing torches were two crudely fashioned straw effigies on long poles, one with a long wig of raveled rope and a turnip for a nose, the other with a nodding pasteboard miter, their wrists bound together with red ribbons like makeshift manacles. Pinned to their straw chests were placards to proclaim their identities:

JAMES STUART, ENEMY TO ENGLAND
THE CATHOLICK POPE, FRIEND TO FRANCE

I stood frozen at the window, unwilling to leave John's side or to look away as the mob surged closer to the carriage. I was Brigadier Churchill's wife, and determined to be every bit as brave as he—yet seeing a distant bonfire from the safety of the palace was far different from being near enough to see the hatred in these men's faces. My heart raced within my breast, and furtively I touched my gloved hand to John's back.

Our horses balked, white-eyed with fear and whinnying at the smoking torches while the driver fought to keep them from bolting. The men in the crowd stared boldly up at us, their contempt palpable as they passed us by. They bumped and jostled the carriage, some daring to strike their fists at the sides as they shouted the vilest obscenities about both James and the pope, and I thanked God for the anonymous hired carriage that hid our identities.

At last they passed away from us and down the street, and I realized I'd been holding my breath. I let it out in a long, shuddering sigh, and John slipped his arm around my waist.

"I'm sorry you had to see that," he said grimly, still watching the last of the crowd. "But at least you know now what James is facing. The grandsires of these men overthrew one king. It won't take much provocation before this lot does the same to another."

"Where do you think they're headed?" I asked, uneasiness giving my voice an uncharacteristic squeak.

"Likely as near to St. James's as they can get. You've seen other fires yourself."

I pressed closer against him, needing reassurance. "But the palace guards will keep them at a safe distance."

"Tonight they will." He shook his head, the tension in his body remaining though the effigies were long out of sight. "But I'd ready my belongings for a journey. My guess is that the king will soon send his brother away, and us with him."

I nodded, not surprised. "I'll speak to Lady Anne's servants, and make sure she's prepared as well."

"Lady Anne won't be going with us," John said. "Nor will her sister Lady Isabella. His Majesty's already determined that. The Protestant heirs must remain here in London for safekeeping."

"To be separated from their parents—that's cruel, John."

"Cruel or not, that's how it must be," he said. "And it certainly hasn't made His Grace their father change his behavior or beliefs one whit. The princesses have no more say in this than do we."

I tried to consider this and put aside my own worries. "Where will we be sent, John? Paris? Dublin? The Hague? Edinburgh?"

"Wherever His Majesty decides, Sarah," he said, his voice hard and practical, no comfort at all. "So long as we are loyal ourselves, then we have no choice. All we can do is obey."

Chapter Eleven

"I'll shower you with chocolate sweetmeats!" Lady Anne said to her half sister Lady Isabella, swinging the tiny girl, giggling, up into the air before her. "If you promise to be good with me, Bella, then I'll make certain you get to eat your fill. Won't I, Mrs. Churchill?"

"If Her Grace Lady Isabella's mother agrees to it, my lady," I said, mindful of how closely the duchess watched over the delicate constitution of the youngest princess.

But in the time that Lady Anne and I had been apart, I here in Brussels with her parents and she only now permitted to visit us with her three-year-old half sister, the differences between us had grown and tried our friendship. I was nineteen, no longer a maid of honor but a married woman expecting a child, while she'd remained a spoiled girl of fourteen. I'd forgotten how strong-willed she could be, and how quick she'd be to remind me of it, too.

"If I wish to give chocolate sweetmeats to Bella, Mrs. Churchill, then I shall," she said, imperious as any other Stuart. "I'll order a mountain of chocolate, piled high on a salver for us alone!"

Lady Isabella squealed and clapped her little hands with delight, while I could not keep silent, as I should.

"Forgive me for speaking plain, my lady," I said, "but Her Grace is most strict about what the Lady Isabella is permitted."

Lady Anne raised her chin, the better to look down her nose at me. "You are impertinent, Mrs. Churchill. I shall do as *I* wish, not what you or the duchess desire. If I want a mountain of chocolate, so I shall have it."

"As you please, my lady," I said, biting back my temper. I was four months within my reckoning now, the babe quick within my belly, and though my humors had settled as I'd progressed, the mere thought of a mountain of chocolate sweetmeats, the greasy sweet gloss of them and the heavy scent, made for queasy contemplation for me on this warm summer afternoon. "You may ask Her Grace at tea, my lady."

"I'm not ready to go inside yet," Anne said, turning away from me. "We shall walk about the courtyard one more time."

"Yes, my lady," I said, biting back the retort I'd prefer to make, and dutifully I set my steps with the three other English ladies—Lady Peterborough, Lady Bellasis, and my own sister Frances, recently remarried to Lieutenant Colonel Richard Talbot, James's Groom of the Bedchamber, making Frances a part of the Yorks' household—attending the princesses' exercise.

"You shouldn't let Lady Anne irritate you so," Frances whispered as we walked side by side in pairs. "She'll tell her parents."

"No, she won't," I said, too vexed to bother whispering. "Before dinner she'll come to me and weep over my hands and beg my forgiveness. You'll see. It is always the same between us. But that's no excuse for her to treat me so ill now."

"It's her age, that is all. She means no real harm."

"She wishes for a friend in private, and a lackey among others," I fumed. "She's old enough to know that, too."

"Sarah, don't," Frances warned with her usual gentleness. "Better for you and the babe to think generous thoughts, and admire the beauty of this place."

"Beauty, hah," I grumbled, but I knew she was right in regards to the babe. I wanted John's son to grow strong and straight, not crabbed by my spleen and ill humor. I took a deep breath and tried to find the beauty that Frances praised. We were staying in the Hotel des Hornes, also called the Haureanum, the same house where the king had resided during his own exile a generation ago. For exiles, our quarters were agreeable, if not lavish, with all of us ladies living within two large chambers that had been roughly partitioned into tiny closets for a measure of privacy. Behind the Haureanum lay a large garden, enclosed on all sides, in which we were walking now, and beyond these walls we could see any number of curious turrets and rooftops.

Thus most would judge Brussels a pleasant enough city, but to me the taint of Catholicism hung over the entire place, from the Romish tips of the overproud church spires to the humblest market stall, and cast over everything an unhealthy pall of superstition and deceit which I found impossible to overlook. I missed London sorely, and I missed the freedom to be found there even more.

Following the princesses, we turned back towards the door, and as we did I saw His Grace the duke and several of his men coming forward to meet us. Alas, my John was not among them, still engaged on yet one more of His Grace's desperate, pointless errands.

The duke smiled as he came closer, as proud and doting of his daughters as any other father when it suited him to appear so. The bright summer sun betrayed the new lines carved into his face, put there by the strain of his exile, and though his sorrows were of his own prideful doing, I still couldn't help but pity him as I watched the cold way that Lady Anne greeted him. Even at fourteen, she took her role as an Anglican heir most seriously. She faulted her father for much of the turmoil that was roiling through England, as well as for the exile that had split their family. Now she did not return his smile, offering her cheek in the chilliest fashion to receive his kiss without venturing one of her own.

"I trust you've amused yourself today, Anne," he said with a hearty show of interest. "Mary Beatrice told me you went with her to the shops."

Anne's face was set, stubborn and determined, a cast I knew from experience was hard to break or alter. "We did go, Father, but I cannot say I was amused."

"No?" he asked, surprised. "I'd heard you made a number of pretty purchases."

"What do ribbons or laces matter when weighed against the false beliefs of the shopkeeps, Father?" she said with more forthrightness than I'd ever expected from her. "Every window had its picture of a weeping saint or bleeding Savior, and around every throat is a gruesome crucifix. I'd never seen the like, Father, nor do I wish to again."

The duke's smile vanished. "Consider what you say, Anne. These people have been more kind to us than the barbarous English."

At once Anne's entire posture changed, her shoulders hunching and stiffening in defense as her expression retreated into her more customary sullen blankness. She'd been well schooled to question her father's faith, but to do so as freely as she had just done took great daring—more, perhaps, than she truly possessed.

"We *are* English, Father," Lady Anne protested as Isabella scurried back to the safer arms of Lady Bellasis. "We are not of this place."

"You may choose to link yourself to the common Englishmen, Anne," the duke said, his anger clear to us all, "but the longer I am kept away from them, the more foul and odious a people they become."

"They are not like that, Father," Anne said faintly, her rare rebellion fading away with her voice. "Not the Anglican ones."

"The ones who choose to ignore the true faith, you mean," he said, his face livid and his hatred so violent as to sicken me. "But they shall understand their error, Anne, no matter how you've been trained to take their unholy side."

Torn by the conflict between father and faith, Anne's cheeks had paled and her lips trembled, and I thought of how dangerously wrongheaded the duke was to treat her thus, and how unfortunate it was for England that he was destined to be our next king.

"But Father," she began one last time, "I do not see how—"

"You *will* see, Anne, and so shall they!" he declared. "One day I will return to rule them, and by God, I mean to discipline the Protestant wickedness from their souls."

I heard the door behind me open and saw my husband rush from it, and towards our party. To my surprise, he did not so much as look my way, but instead he hurried to the duke, bowing deeply before him to catch His Grace's eye.

"The English will learn that I've not forgotten them while they've turned their back on me," the duke continued to rail, "and how they will be made to suffer for— What is it, Churchill? What do you want now?"

"Pray forgive me, Your Grace," John said with such gravity that my heart filled with dread for what would come next. "But a messenger has just arrived from London with the most unhappy of news. His Majesty your brother is dying."

Chapter Twelve

Although the king had expressly forbidden the duke to return to England, His Grace, John, and Lord Peterborough left almost immediately for London with two footmen. Not only did the duke wish to return for a final meeting with his dying brother—a natural enough desire—but also because he feared the consequences to his own future if he were out of the country when the king died. Monmouth's popularity had risen just as the duke's had dropped. The Whigs were currently in control of Parliament, a good thing for Monmouth and, to my mind, for England.

While I made my living at court, I'd never forget my common roots, nor my attachment to the Whiggish cause. As a political party, the Whigs had much to recommend them. They wished to limit the kind of absolute royal power favored by King Louis in France, and they supported toleration for dissenters and others with differing opinions from their own. Most importantly, they were the party of choice for common-born folk such as soldiers and sailors, merchants and farmers, who believed the Whigs reflected their desires better than the Tories, the other party, who were largely noble-born and landed, and favored a strong monarchy.

It was no wonder, then, that the Whig Parliament had already voted to refuse any further moneys to James for his expenses, and to refuse the king as well for supporting his brother's cause against their will. James had every reason to hasten home to protect his interests.

Yet as John told me later, it seemed as if the very winds must be Whig as well. Though the duke and his small party had ridden hard to Calais, their crossing was slow and tedious, over nineteen hours before they landed at Dover. There they were recognized at once by the master of the post, despite their disguises as ordinary gentlemen. But the man didn't dare try to stop them, and onward they pressed to Windsor, John and the duke outriding the others. At seven in the morning—an inconceivable hour at court—they finally arrived at His Majesty's chambers, and at once the weeping duke dropped to his knees beside his brother's bed.

But even on his supposed deathbed, the king who was called "the Merry Monarch" for his playfulness managed to toy with us yet again. For while the physicians had given him up and prayers were sent heavenward from every Anglican church in the land, His Majesty tricked the world, and did not die. By the time his brother and John had arrived, he was already sitting up in his bed, eating partridges with his newest mistress Louise de Keroualle, and glad to forgive the duke for his disobedience with a brief reprieve from his banishment.

While this reconciliation brought much unhappiness to Monmouth and his Whig supporters, I rejoiced when the news reached us. Our little exiled court in Brussels was now free to return to England, too, and eagerly I oversaw the packing of my few belongings. With my time fast approaching, the duchess would soon excuse me from my duties. Now I could be sure our child would be born in England, in our own quarters in Jermyn Street, and not in a foreign Romish place like Brussels.

Before I had returned with the duchess, Lady Anne, and the others, John was again sent away on secret missions, this time to Paris. His goal was to try to persuade King Louis to support James's Catholic cause, and to subsidize him financially as well. Louis's support could be the duke's last hope. Charles had tried his best to preserve his brother's claim to the throne, remaining loyal to him against every advice to the contrary, but a newly elected Parliament was even more determined to see James ousted from the succession.

But while my good husband was as persuasive as ever, the French king was not to be convinced to support the duke, and dismissed James's case as a lost cause, unworthy of further investment. Besides, Louis had still not forgiven James for not standing firm for the Catholic faith, but rather permitting his daughter Mary's marriage to the Protestant

William of Orange. To no one's genuine surprise, Louis sent John home empty-handed.

"Why won't His Grace realize his folly?" I asked as we sat together over supper. I'd made modest small improvements to John's bachelor quarters, plush cushions and new candlesticks and such, but the best attribute of our home was that it was the one place we could speak freely. "The more stubborn he becomes, the more difficult he makes it both for his brother and the country."

"I know," John said wearily, pouring himself more wine. He'd dismissed the servants earlier so we could be alone. "And if it's ever learned that he turned to Louis for help, the people will hate him even more."

"Or the people shall rejoice, knowing that for once Louis showed admirable good sense." I pushed my chair back from the table to give myself more room. With only a few weeks left, I felt as thick and slow as an ox, and yet as awkward as I was, I was restless, too, and impatient with everything. "But James will only see it as one more outrage against him, one more wrong that he'll be determined to set right. He will make a disastrous king."

John drank deeply of the wine. "Then we must hope that he'll mellow with the crown finally on his head."

"You know as well as I that that won't happen," I scoffed. "Before his brother's even cold in the grave, he'll begin settling old scores and making new enemies."

He set the glass down, frowning absently at it. "Charles says James won't last three years upon the throne."

"He did?" Such candor—and perspicacity—from the king surprised me. "I would agree, of course, but I cannot believe Charles would speak it aloud."

"Oh, he made a jest of it, as is his way, but none of us doubted he spoke from his heart." John sighed, tapping his fingers lightly on the rim of the empty plate. "His Majesty's a melancholy man these days, and who can fault him for it? God knows he's loyal to his brother, but to see how that same brother is so determined to destroy everything Charles has believed and done—"

"*I* should become queen instead," I said, hoping to make him smile. "I would make an infinitely better queen than James will a king."

"You would, Sarah," he agreed, but to my sorrow he didn't smile as I'd hoped. "You understand more of the temper of this country and its people than James ever could, and you know how to coax others to your will, so sweetly that they scarce realize it."

"I've had the best masters to teach me," I said, which was the truth, both for bad and good.

"Then you've learned well, sweetheart," he said. "Mary Beatrice tells everyone how she misses your company, you've made yourself that much a part of her life."

"That's from coming to court so young," I said ruefully. "I cannot keep from striving to please my betters for gain."

"In many ways we both came to this wicked world too young." He turned his chair from the table and patted his thigh. "Come. Sit on my throne, Queen Sarah."

I smiled again and came as he'd bid, settling on his leg with his arm familiarly around my waist, or where my waist once was. I kissed him feather-light upon his forehead, there directly above his brow, and at last he smiled.

"If you were to choose another country to rule, Your Majesty," he asked, curling a lock of my hair around his finger, "what would it be?"

My smile fell, for this was no idle riddle. "Not France. Nor Brussels again, if you please."

"Then for now we'll settle on St. Albans." My father's old house, called Holywell House, lay near the town of St. Albans, in Hertfordshire, and my sister and I had inherited the property from our brother. John and I hoped one day to save enough to buy Frances's share from her, and make it our country home, far from London and the court. We had each been raised in families plagued by the impoverishment and the uncertainty of Cromwell's wars; was it any surprise that we wanted more security for our own children?

"Queen of St. Albans has a fair sound to it," I said, happy to imagine us there beneath the willows at the pond, surrounded by a brood of children. "I'd be more than content."

"What would please me most is to share this little kingdom here with you." He rested his hand on the huge swell of my belly, holding it still until he felt the kick of his child within. I could see the movement myself: I'd long ago given up wearing stays and bodices, instead wearing only one of John's old flannel waistcoats tied over my smock and petticoats.

"We'd be the most loyal of subjects," he said softly. For a soldier, he was a man of rare gentle kindness at home, one of the reasons I loved him so dear. "A populace of two for you to rule."

"Your son," I said, covering his hand with my own.

"Or daughter," he countered. "You know I care not whichever you give me."

"A general needs sons," I said, determined that it would be so.

"And a queen needs daughters." He raised my hand, turning it gently to kiss my palm. "What would you say to serving the Princess of Orange?"

"Mary?" My fingers curled shut. The Hague was Protestant, true, and neither Brussels nor Paris, but it wasn't London, either. "She doesn't care for me, John, any more than I care for her. She's never favored me nearly as much as Anne."

"You could win the other princess, too, in time," he said. "Be as you are with her sister, and she'll soon love you as well."

"Would William love you, too?"

"He's noticed my merits, aye."

"As the lone Protestant still trusted by the duke, and the most useful to William."

"The prince may lack charm, Sarah," he said evenly, "but he's also a shrewd judge of a man's character and convictions."

"Including yours, of course," I said. "He knows how the duke favors you nearly as much as the son he doesn't have. Yet if you turn coats and go to William's side, he'll accept your knowledge and the soldiers who will follow you, but he'll never trust you. He'll remember how you abandoned James, and wonder when you'll do the same to him."

"Then I would have to do my best to keep William from remembering," he said. "It would not be so very hard, Sarah."

I shook my head, troubled. In the wrong ears, such talk would be enough to convict John of treason. But in such unsettled times, what else could either of us do? The wars on the Continent had ended for now, taking with them not only all of John's chances of pay and promotions as an officer, but also the opportunity for him to demonstrate his gifts for strategy and leading men in battle. Dependent as we were on the favor of the Yorks for our livings, our choices would be even fewer if James should fail as king.

He saw my unease and kissed my hand again to reassure me. "Charles may survive another score of years to outfox James, and make all such worries moot. For now, I remain bound to the duke and no other."

"And I to Her Grace, and the Lady Anne." There was a terrible irony here: we were at home in palaces, renowned as the favorites of royalty, and yet our lives always danced in precarious balance, with less freedom than any humble country miller and his wife. "I cannot see that changing soon."

"Nor I." He pulled me closer to his chest, sliding his hand higher to cradle one of my breasts, already heavy with milk. "You're beautiful like this, Sarah, so warm and ripe with our child."

"More rightly so clumsy and fat," I said, but I kissed him the same. For husband and wife, we'd been parted often, and we'd spent so little time together since we'd married that I'd learned to cherish whatever we had. He deepened the kiss, and I chuckled with contentment. As I was, most pleasures of the flesh were beyond my reach, but to kiss John Churchill— ah, that would ever be my rarest joy.

"Sarah, my Sarah," he murmured against my throat. "How much I shall miss you this time!"

I pulled back with dismay. "But you are here, John, where you cannot miss me even if you wished to."

By the fire's light, I could see the sorrow in his eyes. "Tonight, yes. But for the peace of the country, Charles has ordered James and his family from London again, this time to Edinburgh, and I must go, too."

"To Edinburgh?" I'd wanted John here at my side for the birth, not banished to dreary, distant Scotland. "Oh, John, *Edinburgh?*"

"At least this time Charles cannot be accused of favoritism," he said, purposefully misreading my unhappiness. "He's ordered Monmouth to The Hague."

I'd no disappointment to squander on Monmouth. "I thought you'd be here with me," I cried forlornly. "I thought we'd be together when— when the baby came."

"When the king orders it, Sarah, I must go," he said as gently as he could. "You know that as well as I. But I swear I'll do my best to return to you by the date the midwife reckoned."

He could do no more, and I did know it. Wouldn't I, too, be expected back in Her Grace's household as soon after this birth as I could travel and my child be left with a country nurse? Yet still I felt my eyes burn with tears, unable to deny the unfairness of John's leaving. Babies were not clockwork, and seldom appeared on the midwife's predicted day. Besides, a thousand hazards could delay him on the icy winter road from the north, while just as many perils could waylay me in childbed. I could as easily die as not, and the thought that this might be the last time I kissed my husband in this life was beyond bearing.

"I will come back as soon as I can, Sarah," he said. "I give you my word, and my love."

"As soon as you can, John," I whispered miserably. "As soon as ever you can."

"You must bear down, Mrs. Churchill," the midwife ordered. "The child is crowning, and you must help it!"

I gasped another breath, clutching hard on Frances's hand. I felt myself split and torn in two, the pain that knifed through me worse than any I'd felt in my life.

"You're almost done, Sarah," my sister said, her whisper urgent beside my cheek. "Courage, and another push, and you'll have John's child in your arms."

John's child: with my last scrap of will I ordered myself to think of that instead of the pain. He had not come in time, kept away by the duke, but I still found strength in his memory. With my knees drawn high, I curled myself tight the way the midwife had explained, squeezed my eyes shut, and pushed with all my might.

"There it is!" cried Frances. "Oh, Sarah, she's perfect!"

"Such a pretty lass, Mrs. Churchill, and mark that lusty cry," the midwife agreed. "Praise God for the safe delivery of you and your daughter."

My daughter? The pain that had clouded my thoughts was gone, but the confusion remained. This should have been John's son, not my daughter. Exhausted and shaking, I struggled to raise my head to look just as the midwife laid the squalling, thrashing infant in my arms. I looked into her tiny wizened face, still daubed with blood and sticky muck, while she stared back at me, perplexed and cross at the gross indignity of being born, and at once it no longer mattered that she was no son, but a daughter. I tumbled headlong into instant love.

"She has your strawberry hair, mistress," the midwife said, rubbing the baby clean as I cradled her against my chest. "What a thatch for such a mite!"

"Harriot," I croaked, recalling the name that John had chosen. "Her name is Harriot."

Rejoicing in my new love, I soon recovered. But little Harriot had not my strength to thrive, no matter how much I cosseted her and whispered my endless devotion into the tiny pink shells of her ears. One rainy late night in March, while I held her in my arms, her sweet soul slipped free of her small, suffering body to rise to heaven.

I had never suffered such a loss, such grief, my eyes nigh swollen shut from weeping tears torn straight from my heart. Those who sought to console me said that it was God's will, that I was young and healthy, that I would bear many more children in my life, but all I cared for now was the one I'd lost.

I paid the gravediggers extra for the fire to burn away the winter frost in the churchyard's ground, so my daughter could be properly buried. I walked alone behind her tiny casket, my head bowed and the ground hard and barren beneath my feet.

A fortnight later, John finally returned from Edinburgh, delayed by the demands of his master the duke. Because of His Grace, John had come too late for his daughter's birth, too late to learn the delicacy of her fingers or the coppery gold tendrils upon her head or the happy small sighs she'd make when she suckled.

And far, far too late for her death, and my broken heart.

Chapter Thirteen

While the Duke and Duchess of York had made their latest journey into exile in Edinburgh, they'd stopped often along the way to visit friends and supporters of their faith, and they'd taken thirty-five days to cover the six hundred miles between London and that bleak city to the north. With no such distractions of my own upon the road, I'd reached Edinburgh in nearly half that time, but when at last my coach drew up before the door of Holyrood Palace, every bone in my body was battered and aching from my jolting passage across so many bad roads in ill weather.

"Good day, Mrs. Churchill," the butler said as he handed me, stiff and sore, from the coach. "Her Grace has been expecting you. She asks that you join her in her rooms before supper."

I nodded, but my thoughts weren't for the duchess.

"Tell Colonel Churchill that his wife has arrived," I said. I had been living with my sister in Jermyn Street for the better part of the last year, away from the court and its follies. John hadn't been home since July, when he'd come for our second daughter Henrietta's birth and christening, and I could scarce wait to see him again.

The butler bowed slightly, acknowledging my request, but made no move to fulfill it. I didn't recognize him, nor he me; the only certainty in this house was that the man was Romish. "Colonel Churchill is with His Grace, ma'am, and cannot be disturbed."

I frowned, disappointed. "Surely you can pass word to the colonel."

"I have my orders, ma'am," he answered with stern disapproval, as if such a request were the most barbarous sin imaginable. "His Grace and his gentlemen are hunting in the park."

As much as I disliked playing second to killing grouse and stags, it wasn't excuse enough for me to question the duke's orders. Hadn't I just left my infant daughter in the care of others hundreds of miles away simply because the duchess had demanded I join her? For John and for me, the word of the Yorks was as good as law, and I'd no choice now but to follow the footman up the staircase to my new quarters, close by the duchess's.

A sprawling, chilly pile of yellow stone and turrets, the palace was worn and gloomy, like much of Scotland itself. I thought of how this same place had been like a prison to the tragic Queen Mary of the Scots, and I caught myself praying for considerably better for us.

"Have my trunks and boxes brought up at once." The rooms I'd been given to share with John were large, but musty with damp from the nearby sea. "And build up that fire, too. Colonel Churchill will expect its warmth when he returns from hunting."

I busied myself with unpacking, directing my maid and the footmen. I'd brought few clothes for myself—I was still thick-waisted from Henrietta's birth, and even with tight lacing, most of my gowns hadn't fit—but many things that John had requested from London. Edinburgh was primitive and notoriously short of common necessities, and coffee, India tea, writing paper, and wax lights had made the journey with me.

"Take care with that chest," I chided two footmen who were wrestling clumsily with the chest holding my smaller tea service. "If you break so much as—"

"*Sarah.*"

I turned swiftly, and there stood John in the doorway. His face was ruddy from hard riding, his buff leather hunting coat bloodied by some unfortunate beast, and he looked as wild and rough as the land he'd just left. If I had not seen him in two months, I had not lain with him for three more beyond that on account of Henrietta's birth, and a wicked, feverish lust for him now burned hot in my veins.

Without looking away from him, I clapped my hands once, to make the servants attend. "Leave us at once. All of you, now."

With heads bent, footmen and maid alike bowed their way past John and from the room, the last closing the door. In three long strides, the rowels of his spurs clinking, John shoved me onto my back upon the bed. He twisted aside my heavy skirts and took me then, still in his boots, riding me hard as he had his horse to the hunt. I writhed beneath him, relishing his rough possession as he marked me for his own, and the guttural cries pulled from my throat were more animal than lady, my nails carving frenzied half-moons into the leather of his coat.

We lay tangled together for a long time afterwards, before John remembered finally to kiss me in welcome.

"My own dear soul," he said, smoothing my tangled hair back from my brow. "I truly did miss you, you know."

"I do know." I smiled up at him, more at my ease than I'd been for months. "You proved it most fiercely."

"You, too, madam." He laughed rich and deep with satisfaction. "How is my other lady?"

"Henrietta was most well when I left her last." My smile grew clouded; I couldn't help it. Our second daughter was strong and flourishing where Harriot had been delicate, already a dark-eyed beauty with glossy black curls and her father's charm. But the life of even the healthiest babe was a fragile wisp in the winds of fate, and I worried fearfully for her each day we were parted. "She's growing so fast, we'll hardly know her when we see her again."

"Of course we will, Sarah," he said, understanding. "But you're needed here. Have you seen the duchess or the Lady Anne yet?"

"You ask as if there's something to be noticed when I do." I sat upright on the bed, tucking my skirts over my legs. Despite the fire, the room was cold, and I dreaded what it would be in winter. "Tell me, John. Tell me all."

He rolled onto his back, stuffing a pillow beneath his head. "Except for this bed, you won't find Holyrood a happy place, or a safe one. Trust no one, especially those new to you. You must guard yourself at all times, and mind every word you say."

"Which is how we lived at St. James's," I said. "Is this so very different?"

"It is, Sarah." He lowered his voice, careful in his frankness even in our own rooms. "The duke has become so strident and vengeful in his hatreds that it's close to madness. He is cultivating the army, employing the Highlanders—a savage pack, but the only papists among them—to quell those in the Lowlands. Already the best of the Scottish peers have fled the country, looking for a Protestant champion."

That was easy enough to guess. "To William in the Netherlands," I said softly. "Oh, John, it only grows worse, doesn't it?"

John nodded. "James should take notice, but he doesn't. He's too occupied by making every lowly Presbyterian an enemy to be vanquished. To him they're all dissenters—sinners to be tortured into conversion, or executed as traitors to the crown."

"He is *torturing* them?"

"Thumbscrews, nailed boots, even cutting off the hands of the worst offenders," John said grimly. "The Scots have a penchant for such activities, and the duke embraces it."

"But in the name of his wretched religion!" I was horrified, but not surprised, having witnessed the duke's cruel rages. Nor was I surprised that John hadn't written of such outrages to me in his letters. Though like everyone in high places we were careful to use false names and ciphers in our correspondence, assuming our letters could and would be intercepted and read, there were still some topics too sensitive—and hazardous—to commit to paper. "I've heard none of this in London. The king cannot know, can he?"

"I'm certain he does, but chooses to ignore it, so long as James causes him no trouble in England." He sighed and shook his head. "I must warn you, sweetheart. You may be expected to watch the executions. He has forced both the duchess and Lady Anne to do so, for the sake of their mortal souls, and I cannot imagine your being excused."

When I looked at the dark brown stains on his coat now, I thought not of the blood of wild game, but of men. "How do you fare with the duke, John? Are you still in favor, and not in danger?"

His smile was anything but reassuring. "It's a fine rope to dance, Sarah, but I see no cause for alarm yet. The duke has known me for so long that he trusts me to be there always without question. So long as I keep myself clear of matters of his faith, he need not consider mine."

I leaned closer, my hands clasped anxiously in my lap. "He has not tried to make you swear allegiance to Rome, John, has he?"

"If he did, I would resign his service, and leave." He reached out to take my hand in his. "The duchess means to surprise you, but I'll whisper it now, to show you how safe our place is here. You're to be made Her Grace's Groom of the Stole. That's four hundred pounds a year, Sarah."

"Truly?" I smiled because he did, though it was hard to rejoice in the middle of such a conversation. But four hundred pounds a year was not to be sniffed at for our growing family, especially not when added to the pension I already earned as a former maid of honor, and I was grateful, too, for the confidence the appointment represented.

"Truly," he said. "There's little for you to do in return for it, too."

"Except to watch the heads of dissenters tumble to the ground," I said warmly.

"It would not be wise for Anglicans like us to refuse, Sarah."

"To make these folk die for their faith is to make martyrs of them," I said, hating the duke's hypocrisy. "Whenever will His Grace understand? How much better for him—for us all!—if he concentrated only on the state of his own mortal soul, and left the rest of us to worship as we pleased."

"Sarah, don't," John warned. "If you speak as rashly as that outside this room, then I'll soon see *your* head on a pike as a warning to others, too."

"Oh, I know, John, I know," I said, unhappiness making my voice tart. "I'll only speak so free to you. But having given birth to new life twice, it will be much harder to watch another's taken away by one man's cruel impulse."

"It's not easy for any of us." He pulled me gently down atop his chest, our faces close and my breasts spilling from my bodice. "I'm not the only one glad that you're here, sweetheart. It's no secret that the Lady Anne is lonely."

"How could she not be, still grieving for little Isabella?" The four-year-old princess had died not long before at St. James's Palace while her parents and half sister were in exile here—a great cruelty to everyone—leaving James and Mary Beatrice once again childless. "Everyone she cares for leaves her, or dies."

"Not everyone," he said. "She claims she's found Edinburgh tedious without your company."

"To make it less so will be the greatest challenge imaginable." I traced my fingertip lightly along the straight bridge of his nose. "I cannot exactly amuse her in the same way I do you."

He grunted beneath me, entertained by that thought as he worked his hand beneath my skirts, along the backs of my thighs. My breath quickened, and I felt his cock swelling beneath me, a gladsome thing for a wife after so long a separation from her husband.

"You've always been clever, Sarah, particularly with Anne," he said, his hands sliding higher over my bare flesh. "I've faith you'll find some manner of diversion for the princess."

"I've not seen her for over a year," I said. "Is she much changed?"

"You can judge for yourself," he said, rolling me beneath him. "Later."

Mary Beatrice, Lady Anne, and the other ladies, as well as the duke's gentlemen and the rest of our exiled court, were ordered to attend the executions, by way of instruction to us and example to the Scots. I sat not with John, but with Anne, and beside me she was as pale and stiff as a wax doll. She wouldn't forget what she saw; none of us would, or could. The executions were not every day, or week, or even every month, but came without warning, and they never grew any easier to bear.

Dissenters, Presbyterians, Covenanters—their common sin was any faith the duke deemed immoderate and dangerously unlike his own. Regardless of their rank, those sentenced to die were not even granted a gentleman's death by the axe, but hung from a gibbet like the most common thief. Some were dragged to the noose, their feet crushed to bloody stumps by the boot's torture. Others had had their eyes pressed and gouged into empty, gore-filled sockets, or their fingers twisted and ripped from their blood-blackened hands. One man who'd tried to greet his Maker with a sacred hymn upon his lips had his tongue sliced from his mouth while we watched.

While we *watched,* as if we were lined in tall-backed chairs for a play: the drop of the plank door, the jerking, twitching dance of the feet as they struggled in vain for purchase, the crack of neck bones as they broke and one by one pulled apart. We watched how the eyes bulged and the tongues thrust from swelling lips, and the final ignominy of death, when the bowels released their foul soil.

We watched, and were forbidden to look away. I tried to set my thoughts to anywhere else, to blur my eyes until they would not see, to steel my ears with prayers or creeds of my own faith for courage against the choking gurgles of the dying. But still I saw, and heard, and felt the shame of being party through my silence to such unforgivable abominations.

And for the sake of all our souls, I wept, and prayed this hateful winter in exile would soon pass.

It was not until summer that the king finally relented. His brother's banishment had served its purpose, and James's unreasonable intolerance had been sufficiently forgotten by the English that he could leave Scotland and return to the court. In London, it seemed, no one gave much care or thought to the horrible persecutions the duke had committed in exile. But no matter what His Grace's welcome proved to be in London, it could never compare to the rejoicing that followed his departure from Edinburgh.

Chapter Fourteen

"There he is, Mrs. Churchill!" Anne's voice rippled with excitement as she peered across the dancers, squinting to see better. "The dark man, there, in the green coat. John Sheffield, Earl of Mulgrave. I ask you, have you ever seen a more perfect figure of a gentleman?"

I looked to where she pointed with her fan, wishing with all my heart she'd meant another. Lord Mulgrave was a close friend of Lord Rochester's, which instantly marked him as untrustworthy with women; one glance at his dark, sullen face, and the arrogance with which he regarded the world, told the rest of his ugly tale as far as I was concerned.

But not for the princess. She was seventeen, bored, and eager for a sweetheart like the other ladies at court—all three explanations for fancying herself in love with this most dreadful specimen, but none an acceptable excuse.

"His Lordship is a most worldly gentleman, my lady." I was wary of treading too heavily and driving her into Mulgrave's arms, but also fearful of saying too little and weakening my warning. I was only twenty-two myself, and unsure of playing this role as a wise older woman. "There's not a soul at court who'd say otherwise."

She sighed happily, clutching her fan in both hands to her breast. "Of course he is worldly, Mrs. Churchill. He has been fortunate to live *in* the world, and not be locked away as I was in Edinburgh for these last two years."

"He is also nearly double your age, my lady," I said. "He's as wily as any old fox who's outraced the hunt. A maiden lady such as yourself should be on her guard with him."

"Oh, a pox on my guard," Anne scoffed gaily. "What lady wouldn't wish Lord Mulgrave for an admirer? Quiet now, he comes this way!"

In my complicated position as chaperone as well as friend, it saddened me no end to watch the princess lifting her chin with a tiny preening shake, smoothing her hair with her palms, and blushing with delight as Mulgrave came through the crowd towards her. Anne wasn't the kind of great beauty who turned heads, but she was young and fresh, with a sweet, shy smile and doe's eyes that were the banner of her innocence. Now I regretted that I'd advised her on which gown flattered her most, because she was as handsome a lady as any in the room.

"My lady," the earl was saying to Anne now, bowing so low over her hand that the curls of his wig brushed the floor. "How honored I am to be once again in the bright circle of your presence."

"Rise, please do, Lord Mulgrave," Anne said breathlessly, her cheeks pinking with pleasure. At least she was mindful of how foolish she must look with him groveling about her hem. "I beg you, please stand, before others take note."

It was far too late for that, not that Mulgrave cared.

"Let them, my fairest Lady Anne," he said, one hand over his breast and the other imprisoning Anne's fingers. "Let them all see how I worship thee, oh, my princess."

"What they see, my lord, is your impertinence." I reached out with the blades of my closed fan and struck his wrist to make him release the princess's hand. "Recall yourself, my lord."

"Don't, Mrs. Churchill, I beg you," Anne cried with dismay.

"Mrs. Churchill and I are well known to one another, my lady," Mulgrave said, though his expression was anything but friendly. "Her husband and I both served together as striplings in Tangier."

"The difference, my lord, being that Colonel Churchill served with bravery and distinction," I said. "Come, my lady. His Grace your father is summoning us."

"Father never summons me," Anne protested as I hustled her away. "You only wished me to part with Lord Mulgrave."

"True enough, my lady." Swiftly I led her through the crowded room and into a small window alcove where I could speak to her more privately. "His Lordship's attentions are flattering, I know, but he is a notorious rake, and not fit company for you."

"He is not!" Anne's face puckered with stubbornness, more wounded than angry. "Lord Mulgrave is a gentleman and a poet."

I sighed, wishing I could make her understand. "Whatever Lord Mulgrave may be, my lady, you are a royal princess, and you cannot let yourself become the plaything of a man such as that."

"He's far too honorable for that."

"Oh, yes, His Lordship's honorable," I said, my temper getting the better of my judgment. "That's why his friends are calling him 'King John,' because he boasts so often of his intimacy with you."

"And what is wrong with that?" she asked, though I heard the sad tremble of doubt. "Why can't I be admired, too?"

"Because if Lord Mulgrave or another like him ruins you, my lady, then you will never marry," I said with grim certainty. "You know as well as I that no prince will have you, and you will be a disgrace to England."

Her face crumpled, her nose red. "You have Colonel Churchill. Father has Mary Beatrice and Mary has William, while I'm not permitted to have anyone."

"You will, my lady," I said, keeping my doubts to myself. Most princesses were wed at fourteen or younger—particularly Protestant ones who would make for one more alliance against France. "I'm sure His Majesty is arranging a suitable match."

Her tears slid unevenly down her pockmarked cheeks. "I'm seventeen, Mrs. Churchill, and I—I still have no one."

"You have me, my lady," I said gently, laying my hand on her arm. How could I not pity her? Motherless, her only sister far away, she was cursed with an intolerant, unpredictable tyrant for a father, her life long devoid of love or even affection. "You'll always have me."

"I know." She bowed her head, covered her eyes with her hands. "Where would I be without you? What would I do? Oh, Mrs. Churchill, I am so—so wretched!"

With a racking sob, she pressed her face against my shoulder and let her tears flow. I put aside our rank, and I slipped my arm around her quaking shoulders to hold her close. We were both so young to have learned that the great, cruel world was neither fair nor just. How could I guess then that the lesson had only begun?

My chance to put an end to the princess's sorry mischief with Mulgrave finally came in November, when I gave John the letter I'd found beside Lady Anne's bed, clearly mislaid there beneath a discarded petticoat. He read it quickly, his frown deepening with each false endearment writ in Mulgrave's hand.

"I know Her Grace makes light of this—this matter, so long as Lady Anne is happy and agreeable," I said, "and I know the duke is too occupied with his own wickedness to pay any notice at all to his daughter's flirtations, not unless Mulgrave converts to Presbyterianism. But there comes a point when willful ignorance is dangerous."

"Where Mulgrave is concerned, that's most certainly true," John agreed, shaking his head. "I know the man professes himself to be a poet, but that rubbish about kissing his dove's sweet nest while she flutters with joy—there's no decent way to consider that."

I smiled at his indignation. "Spoken like the father of a daughter."

"Spoken like a man whose wife's responsibility is to watch over the virtue of the princess," he said. "Doubtless Mulgrave himself is behind the rumors that he's already seduced the princess."

I paced restlessly across the bedchamber, torn between loyalty to the princess, what I knew was best for her future, and my own ambitions. I could not decide my course. I was with child again, a state that always left me woefully indecisive.

"The duchess has given Anne far too much freedom with the man," I said, thinking aloud. "Riding together in Windsor Park, long walks to gather flowers in the gardens—*flowers,* for all love!—permitting him to attend her singing lessons! If Mulgrave hasn't compromised her yet, then it's not from lack of opportunity."

"I thought you were sure she was still a virgin. No royal prince would settle for Mulgrave's leavings."

"I am sure," I said, remembering the giddiness of Anne's constant babbling praise for so unworthy a man. "She couldn't keep that a secret. Is there anything so foolish as a lovesick girl?"

"I'd rather have her foolish and lovesick than swelling with Mulgrave's bastard." Absently he rubbed the back of his neck, thinking as well. "Though if that happened and she were ruined for a royal marriage, then James would have prevented another Protestant alliance, and won more favor with France."

"John, he is her father!"

"He also values his church and his vengeance more than his daughter." He folded the letter once again, pressing the creases sharp between his fingers. "But not even the duke can overlook a letter such as this. You must show it to him or the duchess at once."

"You and I and Anne," I said. "Our fates are so tangled together."

"By our choice," he said firmly. "Our fates, and our futures, and those of our children, too."

I took the letter from him, letting it lie in my palm gingerly, like the weapon it was. "To have Mulgrave banished from court will be grievous hard on Lady Anne, John. Recall how distraught she was last month when Her Grace dismissed Mrs. Cornwallis from her service."

"Yes, and recall the true reasons for the dismissal, too," he said with a shrug. "You among all others must acknowledge that our Lady Anne suffers from a surfeit of passions. When young girls like the princess kiss and embrace and call one another *husband* as an endearment—"

"Oh, hush, John, don't repeat idle scandal." The tales had been outrageous, that the older lady had let her fondness for Lady Anne twist and grow unnaturally, until it had threatened to corrupt the princess's innocence. The scandal had not been the rumored attachment itself— among the maids of honor, there had been several ladies whose friendship had blossomed into lovers' passion, and in that jaded court, with so much of the French and Italian flavor to it, no one had given much thought to these little sapphic romances—but that Mrs. Cornwallis had been so much the senior, corrupting the young royal lady in her care. "This intrigue with Mulgrave is far more dangerous than that."

"Then go to the duchess now, Sarah," he said softly. "There's nothing to be gained by dawdling like this. You might even be rewarded for your loyalty at once with Mrs. Cornwallis's post."

"Don't tempt fate by speaking so, John." It was widely known that I wished to become the princess's Lady of the Bedchamber, for its power and influence as well as the income, and I knew I was Lady Anne's first choice. I was already such a favorite that there'd even been unkind whispers about how I'd plotted Mrs. Cornwallis's downfall. I hadn't, of course; it hadn't been necessary, not when Mrs. Cornwallis had so obligingly ruined herself. "Now I'll have to be sure that Anne puts in her best words for me with her father."

"You know she will," John said. "She loves you better than any other lady at court."

"Which is often too much to be borne," I said, rubbing my temple with my fingertips.

"Not for the princess."

"I meant *me*, John," I said sharply, then sighed. "Oh, I know she means me no harm, but there are times I feel imprisoned by her devotion, as if there were leg-irons and manacles binding me to her. No real friend would expect so much."

"My own dear, weary soul," he said, slipping his arm around my waist and pulling me close. "God knows I don't wish to be apart from you any more than you are already from me. But Lady Anne is no common friend."

I rested my hands on his chest to feel the steady beat of his heart. He *was* steady, my John, and free of the impatience and quick temper that always plagued me.

"Of course she's different," I said. "She's Lady Anne of York. But I vow she's grown so accustomed to me that I don't believe she can fathom her life without me beside her."

"She will once His Majesty finds her a husband," he said, soothing me as only he could. "And for now she'll never suspect you of finding Mulgrave's letter. She'll think it was a maidservant, and blame her instead of you."

I sighed again, but with more content. "Why are you so wickedly wise, Colonel Churchill?"

"Because I married you, Mrs. Churchill." He chucked me beneath my chin and kissed me lightly. "Now go, my love. Take the letter. It's your duty not only to the princess, but to the Church of England as well. You know you must."

I did. That afternoon, I gave the letter to Mary Beatrice, who in turn showed it to His Grace. Three days later, Lord Mulgrave had not only been dismissed from court—"for writing to the Lady Anne" was the given reason—but was on his way back to Tangier, purposefully sent away to his new post by the duke in an ancient, leaking frigate.

Soon after that, I was appointed the princess's new Lady of the Bedchamber. Lady Anne was overjoyed, telling me again and again that I was the only true friend she had, the only attendant she could ever trust, and all the time I spent with her was still never enough. In my company, Lord Mulgrave was soon forgotten, as was Mrs. Cornwallis, exactly as John had predicted.

John's loyalty was rewarded as well, with a Scottish peerage granted by the duke. Side by side John and I greeted the new year of 1683, watching the fireworks over the Thames as Baron and Baroness Churchill of Aymouth. We had at last been able to buy my family's old place at St. Albans, near the River Ver, and though the house needed considerable work, we spent as much time there with Henrietta as we could steal away from London and the court. We were, I'd venture, as happy as we'd ever be.

And when our next daughter was born in February, John and I instantly agreed upon her name, just as there was no question of who should stand as her godmother for her christening.

Anne.

Chapter Fifteen

If John and I were common folk, then all I should write of here would be the common triumphs and woes: how the undertaker we'd hired to make repairs at Holywell refused to work as quickly we wished, or when the plums would be ripe for plucking in the orchard, or how Henrietta had tumbled down the stairs chasing a kitten, or when baby Anne would cut her first tooth.

But through design and by luck, John and I weren't common folk, but Lord and Lady Churchill, and while those private concerns were of great interest to us, we were also swept up in the greater events of the nation at that time, and not always for the better, either.

Just as the violent sentiment against popery had waned enough for James to be able to return to court, so, too, had the feelings against the Whigs grown, like a swing pushed one way that has no choice but to return the other. Now the Tories were in full flower, preaching moderation and support for the monarchy as it was, flaws and all. The Whiggish support for Monmouth's cause faded, and those who had cried out for James to be removed from the succession at any cost were now labeled as dangerous radicals bent on destroying the monarchy.

Worst of all, a spurious plot to assassinate the king and his brother was uncovered, and the so-called leaders, among them Lord Russell, were imprisoned and later executed for their beliefs. Monmouth and his ambitious mistress Lady Wentworth fled to Prince William in The Hague while James's popularity rose. My sister Frances's place at court had grown, too, for her husband Lieutenant Colonel Richard Talbot, a prominent Catholic, had found great favor with the duke for his outspoken views against the Protestants in Scotland and Ireland, which in turn had strained my relations with Frances. Because she was nearly fourteen years older than I, we had never been particularly close as sisters, but now, because of her husband's politics and religion, I no longer trusted her, either.

And although John's interests now ran counter to my own support of Whigs, and instead lay firmly among the Tories—his days of blustering camaraderie with Monmouth were long past—he had as little patience with the Tories' violence towards those accused of involvement with Lord Russell as he'd had with the Whigs' hysteria during the popish plot. In disgust, and with fewer obligations to His Grace, John—newly made a brigadier general—devoted more time to his regiments, while I remained at Lady Anne's side wherever the court took us, from Whitehall to Windsor Castle to Tunbridge.

A Lady of the Bedchamber has many responsibilities. I oversaw the princess's dress and assisted her at table as she dined. Anyone who wished to converse with her was required to ask permission of me first, and I in turn introduced others to Her Ladyship. My role was both to oblige the princess in every way, and to keep my silence where my own politics and personal opinions were concerned.

Alas, as my life would show, I was by nature far better suited to the one than the other.

I stood to one side of the princess, smoothing the silk rosettes at her elbows as she studied her reflection in the looking glass before we joined my husband, her family, the prince she was to marry, and the others in the receiving room.

"You're beautiful, my lady," I said softly. "His Highness Prince George is sure to be impressed."

"I don't know, I don't know." Anne tugged at the front of her gown, her mouth twisted so tight with uneasiness her lips had almost disappeared. "Does this color silk truly suit me? You don't believe it makes me sallow, do you?"

"His Highness will see only your grace and charm, my lady," I murmured, smiling into the glass. "You've never looked more lovely."

She was tall and sturdy, like all the Stuarts, and though I was twenty-three to her eighteen, she was much the larger woman. My face and form would always be more fair, yet this July morning Anne was truly regal in sapphire blue silk sewn with tiny pearls, with the rich fabric gathered and draped into a graceful train behind her. Deep cuffs of Venetian lace made every gesture more graceful, and the rubies that hung from her ears gave color to her cheeks.

But still Anne's gaze remained far too doleful for any bride. We both knew the truth, of course—that Prince George of Denmark would do as he'd been ordered by his brother the Danish king, just as Anne would obey the wishes of her uncle King Charles. What else could such an alliance between Protestant royalty be? George would declare Lady Anne to be a paragon of beauty. He would dutifully fall in love with her and she with him in the three weeks allotted to them, and then the two would wed.

Yet because love had always been in short supply in Anne's life, I did wish for her to find it now with her prince. I motioned for the hairdresser and other maids to leave us, and when Anne and I were alone, I put my arm around her shoulder with the kindness of an older sister.

"Lord Churchill has written to me that His Highness is a good and honorable gentleman, my lady, and that he will make the best husband imaginable." John had escorted the prince from Denmark, and so had met him before the rest of us. He'd also noted that the prince was the dullest gentleman he'd ever met, whose notion of a well-spent day was to stand gazing at the same window by the hour, but I saw no reason to tell that to Anne.

"Lord Churchill says the prince is tall and handsome, too," I continued with an optimist's cheer, "and that he possesses the most agreeable temper. He's everything you deserve, my lady, but what will he think if he sees your eyes red with weeping?"

"What if he finds *me* lacking?" she asked tremulously, staring at her miserable reflection. "What if I'm not as Lord Churchill described?"

"His Highness is *not* the Hanover prince, my lady," I said severely. Earlier another Protestant prince, George of Hanover, had come to consider Anne as a bride, and to everyone's shock and the princess's shame and mortification, he had returned to the Palatine without asking for her hand. "Lord Churchill says His Highness already speaks of you as his sweetheart, and his bride."

"He could still have a change of heart." Anne's eyes were growing redder by the moment. "He could meet me, and not—not like me. Oh, Lady Churchill, why couldn't I have been born as fair and clever as you, so he *would* love me?"

She threw her arms around my neck to weep against my shoulder, the way she had before more times than I could count, and I rested my palm on her back to comfort her as I usually did as well, my poor, dear princess.

But this time as she wept she turned her face towards mine, so close that the starched lace of her headdress brushed my forehead and her tears fell onto my cheeks.

"You love me, don't you?" she said between sobs. "You—you love me as I am?"

"Of course I do, my lady," I whispered, smoothing back one of her formal curls, stiff with sugar-water. "Haven't I always?"

"You have." She ran her hand along my jaw, her fingers trailing over the pulse of my throat as she held my face before hers. She leaned closer, I thought to study me, and in turn I saw the pain in her golden brown eyes, longing for the happiness she'd never find. Her breath was sweet with the honey drops she favored, and as she tipped her head the sunlight danced through the ruby in her ear, casting a score of bloodred stars into my eyes.

Dazzled, I felt her lips brush over my skin, kissing away the tears she'd shed upon my cheek. The rare intimacy of such gentleness made me catch my breath, yet I did not pull back, not even when her mouth came over my own, fluttering and settling there as if to draw away my life in a kiss I'd never sought. With great daring, her tongue parted my lips and slipped within, and discovered my own tongue in a flicking caress that left me stunned.

"My own lady," she said when at last she lifted her mouth away. "You do love me!"

Her smile was so full of devotion and wonder that I'd not the will to cross her, and truly, how could I? I remembered what was said of Mrs. Cornwallis and Anne, and a score of other hinted tales with other ladies. Sapphic love was but one of the erotic amusements practiced at our decadent court, and I'd known several of Her Grace's maids of honor who had openly practiced tribadism, preferring one another's embrace to any man's. I would not judge what these ladies did, no more than I'd concern myself over His Majesty's delight in keeping several ladies at a time together in his bed, but I'd never considered engaging in any such pleasures myself, either. Until now: now my head spun with new possibilities and my heart raced with confusion, my breath coming so quick I could scarce speak the only words permitted to me.

"Yes, my lady," I whispered through my bewilderment. "Yes, my lady, I do love you."

"*Yes.*" A flush of excitement—or was it guilt?—now stained her cheeks. "No matter what may happen, my dearest friend, I shall always have you."

"Yes, my lady," I said, feeling the heat in my face as well. "If you please, my lady, we should join His Highness and the others."

I stepped aside to let her pass, my head bowed beneath the weight of my loyalty, and she swept by without another word, her skirts brushing against mine. I let her go ahead, taking another few moments to compose myself before I followed.

She had me, yes. How could it be otherwise? She was my princess, my mistress, my friend. But ah, no matter what might happen, I would have her as well.

"They make a fine pair," John said as we watched the new Princess of Denmark dance with her bridegroom. Though married a week now, they'd worn their wedding clothes to this ball in their honor, and the gold threads in the white silk of their matching dress winked beneath the candlelight of the palace's Banqueting House. "Marriage has made Her Highness almost passably fair."

"Don't be cruel, John. She's far more than 'passably fair.'" I stood so close to him that our words would be lost to others in the music and rendered as confidential as any in a crowded hall. Weighed down as I was by the heavy silk brocade of my gown, I kept the ivory blades of my fan moving at a quick pace before me. Not only was the room almost unbearably close, but the heat of the evening combined with the pomp and excitement of the past week to make me feel as brittle inside as a twig of tinder.

"All brides are fair, John," I continued, "and Her Highness is no exception."

"Then that, my wife, must explain why you're the most beautiful lady in the kingdom." His hand curled around my whalebone-narrowed waist, pulling me so close that I felt his breath warm upon the nape of my neck. "I swear you grow more ravishing each day, Sarah."

"And surely you, my lord colonel, must speak more pretty nonsense than any other gentleman in the realm." I smiled as I turned to face him; because of the princess's demands, I'd seen little of my husband in private this month, and I'd missed him sorely. "I can think of far better ways to put that silver tongue of yours to use. Perhaps I should have you counsel the prince, so he can better please his bride."

"Her Highness has confided that to you?" he asked with surprise.

"Oh, no." What the princess had told me was far more damning: that as pleased as she was with her new husband, she would never love him with the same fervor as she loved me. Prince George struck me as agreeable enough, but impossibly dull and devoid of wit, and though he was tall, blond, and portly, his wheezing bouts of asthma were worryingly similar to those of the princess's brother-in-law, William the Prince of Orange. "Her Highness is thoroughly pleased with the prince."

"Pleased *with* him is not the same as being pleased *by* him," John said dryly. "But as much as I wish the princess joy, all the prince must do is play the village bull and sire a Protestant heir."

"How can it be otherwise?" I said sadly. The Stuart curse had fallen, too, on the Prince and Princess of Orange, and after five years together, their marriage was still barren of children. All hopes for an heir had shifted to my dear friend, and as I watched her smile shyly at her new husband, I prayed they'd be blessed with a whole brood of healthy sons.

"I'll grant this prince is a handsome enough fellow, far more so than the Prince of Orange." John chuckled, for he knew the rivalry between the royal sisters as well as I. "I'm sure Her Highness has so informed the Princess of Orange, too."

"She has," I said. "I wrote the letter for her because she said her eyes pained her too grievously to stare at the paper."

"So now you're her secretary as well as her advisor on new husbands," he teased. "Is there anything you don't do for Her Highness, Sarah?"

But though I knew he meant this only in jest, I could find no humor in it. Without realizing it, he'd pricked my conscience regarding the princess, and the wound stung.

"I do whatever she asks of me, John," I said, more tartly than I'd intended, "just as you obey her father's wishes, no matter how odious his beliefs or actions may be to you."

John's smile vanished. "Where is the relevance of what the duke believes or does? His daughter is as innocent of her father's sins as any woman can be, and if I obey his desires, why, it is to keep ourselves balanced between the two for our own betterment."

I flushed, caught in my own tangle. I'd thought often of how, when I'd first come to court, the duke had tried to seduce me, and how resolutely I'd resisted him. Now I was a married woman with daughters of my own, yet when the princess had kissed me, I'd not shown any of that earlier fortitude, but instead been meek and accepting. I'd foolishly ignored the fate of the unfortunate Mrs. Cornwallis, who rumor whispered had also shared the princess's kisses, and been banished for it. And more: I'd come to welcome such proof of the princess's devotion, even encouraged and sought it, despite her courtship with the prince.

I looked away from my husband, to the couples now separating before us as their dance finished. Was I being false to my vows as a wife, or true to the path John and I had sworn to follow through life together?

"I don't know why you're questioning me about the princess," I said, my temper set to smolder by his doubt. "We've always agreed to do what was necessary to advance our fortunes for the sake of our family."

"We have, Sarah," John said, "and we've prospered because of it. But I don't understand—"

"Colonel Lord Churchill!" My old acquaintance Lady Ainsworth glided towards us, her cheeks flushed with drink and lewdness. She had long ago given up her place serving Mary Beatrice, but she was still often at court with her husband. "And Lady Churchill, too. How are you, my dear?"

She asked the question of me, but her gaze lingered on my husband in his red coat of the King's Regiment, her heavy-lidded eyes as hungry as a tigress's.

"I am well, Lady Ainsworth," I said curtly. "Is not Lord Ainsworth here, too, or have you mislaid him?"

"Oh, he's about somewhere." She smiled up at John, not me. "Ah, they're calling for a saraband! Do you dance, my lord colonel?"

"Yes, Lady Ainsworth." My hand tightened possessively around John's arm to lead him away. "He dances with me."

"If you'd wished to dance, Sarah, you'd only to ask me," he said as I pulled him towards the others gathering in the center of the room. "There was no cause for you to be rude to Lady Ainsworth."

"Oh, yes, just as there was no cause for her to devour you alive." I took my place at the end of the ladies' line, while he stood across from me. "Or is that how you amuse yourself while I am dutifully occupied with the princess?"

The music began before he could answer. I curtseyed and he bowed to begin the set, gliding back, then side to side, but soon enough the dance brought us close again.

"You are the only woman in my life, and in my heart, Sarah." More pretty words, true, but now each one was clipped black with an anger that matched my own. "The *only* one."

Knowing I could not say the same made me defensive. "You should tell that to Lady Ainsworth, not me."

The music separated us and gave us other partners, a cruel mockery of our quarrel, then brought us back together. John's jaw gleamed with sweat above his linen neckcloth, his eyes so intent upon me that it seemed his gaze alone could sear my flesh.

"You are my wife, Sarah," he said. "By now you should know the love and esteem I have for you."

"What I know and what I believe are two different matters, husband," I said warmly, giving a disdainful twitch to the heavy skirts around my ankles. "Perhaps you'd do better to demonstrate your love, rather than declaring it with empty words."

His mouth set with fury, he did not answer, but instead grabbed my hand and jerked me, stumbling, from the line of dancers.

"What madness is this?" I demanded, my cheeks flushed as I heard the ladies around me gasp and twitter. "Stop now, John, *now!*"

But he didn't stop, half dragging me through the crowd with the same fearsome determination he must show on the battlefield. My heel caught in my train, the rich fabric rending as I pitched towards him. He caught my arm, steadying me, but only long enough to begin again, from the Banqueting House and past the idlers outside. They watched with curiosity, even world-weary amusement: Colonel Lord Churchill off to discipline his headstrong wife, as was his undeniable right by law and by God.

But not, I vowed, by me.

"You *are* mad, John," I said furiously, still trying to pull free as he turned down the twisting hall that led to the king's private chambers. "What demon has possessed you that you would—"

"*You're* my demon, Sarah!" He wheeled around to face me, pushing me back against the oak-paneled wall and trapping me there with his body. "How dare you question my devotion to you? You know I've never been false to you, not once. You know I love you more than any man. You *know.*"

He kissed me hard before I could answer, his mouth grinding down upon mine: a kiss of possession, not love. I understood the difference, and my temper burst like an ugly boil, spilling poison and bile.

"*Love!*" I cried, near spitting the word. I grasped his shoulders and shoved with all my strength. "Don't talk to me of love, John, not when you treat me like this!"

"What choice do you leave me, Sarah?" he demanded hoarsely. "Tell me!"

I raised my hand against him, and he caught my wrist and held it tightly over my head. I yowled my helplessness with wordless frustration, but still he held me fast, his body pressed so close against mine that the domed gilt buttons of his long waistcoat jabbed into my belly, the silver scabbard of his dress sword flat against my thigh.

"What choice, Sarah?" His breathing was ragged, a match for my own.

"There are no choices, John, not when—"

"That is true," he said. "There are none. You are my wife, my partner, my love, the mother of my children. My love, and no other. In all those things, you have no choice. No choice, Sarah, mind?"

My wife, my partner, my love, the mother of my children. The words fell onto my anger like cooling drops of water. His face close over mine, he shifted just enough that the moonlight from the passage window slanted over him, so I could see not only the anger that remained in his eyes, but the pain I'd brought to him as well.

"Oh, husband." I licked my lips, my breath still coming in fierce gulps. The music and laughter from the ball could have been a hundred miles away instead of only a hundred paces. "Why else would I fight for you, John?"

Slowly he lessened the grip on my hand, lowering it to kiss my fingertips. "I would rather fight with you, Sarah, than against you."

Remorse swept over me, and tears of misery stung my eyes for what I'd wrought. Why had my mother's temper come to me as this awful legacy, cursing me to pain the ones I loved most?

"I am yours, my own love," I whispered, reaching up to pull his mouth back to mine. "My heart belongs to no other."

"My own dear Sarah." He kissed me now with the hunger of a man deprived of all sustenance and succor, and so I kissed him in return, desperate and hungry for what he could give me.

"You're mine, Sarah," he said, his voice thick with desire. "No other man will ever have you."

No other man. My conscience stilled my eager hand, troubled. "There will never be another man, John, but I must—"

"The princess." He sighed and smiled wearily. "Is she the source of all this tonight?"

"How did you know?" I asked swiftly. "I've told no one."

"You didn't have to." He let my skirts drop. "She betrays herself in a thousand little ways around you, so clear I couldn't mistake it."

I should have known better than to keep such a secret from John, the one person in this life who could see into my soul.

"It's far more than that," I said, the truth now spilling out. "She—she wants all of me, John. She claims she cannot be happy without me, even for a day, and when we are apart—when I'm with you—she writes me endless letters pledging her devotion and begging me to return."

His expression didn't change. "Serving a princess is not always easy, sweetheart, but you know as well as I that the rewards can be just as great."

I shook my head, though I'd no real choice but to agree. "Whatever I do, I do for us, for you and our daughters."

"I know," he said softly, "just as I know how much the princess needs your love and kindness, in whatever manner it takes. Poor lady! There are precious few she can trust in this palace or her father's house, God preserve her."

"You have learned something new?" I asked, startled. Though James still trusted him with absolute confidence, John had begun to withdraw from the household of the Duke and Duchess of York, spending less time there and more with George and with Anne, the Prince and new Princess of Denmark. "Is there a fresh danger you've not told me?"

"Hush, hush, it's only the old concerns," he said, smoothing a stray strand of my hair back around my ear. "So long as James insists on his mulish path with Rome, you and I will do better to follow Anne, and the Anglican Church. For us, and England."

"She needs friends who will be loyal, John," I insisted. "Friends like us who will support both her wishes and her faith. And with Mary barren, Anne could well become queen."

"She could indeed, and raise these same loyal friends up with her."

"And the children of those same friends, too," I said. "Pray recall our Henrietta and Anne, and the others we may have."

I couldn't help but compare the perils and uncertainties of my own childhood to the lives of our two small girls, plump and cosseted by their nursemaid in the country. What wouldn't I do to keep them there, safe and secure and far, far from this wicked court?

But if I were honest, there was more that I'd be loath to put aside. I liked the power that came from being Baroness Churchill. I liked my place as Lady of the Bedchamber, and how others must come to me first before they could address the princess. And I liked how John and I now owned all of the house in Jermyn Street, and that we kept a dozen servants of our own, their livery trimmed with gold lace.

And if I truly would be honest with myself, then I'd admit that my greatest uneasiness with the princess's fervid attentions had been that John would protest or grow angry. Now that he'd absolved me of such worry, I could admit that Anne's kiss, though far different from my husband's, was neither vastly unpleasant nor intolerable, especially not in light of the betterment that came with it.

"You always put our little ladies first," John said, mercifully unaware of my less worthy thoughts. "And I know you'll hold true to what we both cherish most."

"Which is to serve the princess however we can."

"Dear, clever wife." He cupped my cheek in the palm of his hand, tipping my face so he could smile at me. "No wonder the princess loves you so."

"I believe she always has," I said, remembering how we'd met as girls when I'd first come to court. Anne had needed me then, and she needed me still: I must take care not to forget that. "And with a little more of my—my kindness, I believe she always will."

"As she should." He spread his hand over the elaborate drape of my mantua and pulled my hips close against his, so there was no mistaking his desire and affection for me, nor the strong reminder of what he could give me that no lady ever could. "So long as I keep the first place in your heart."

"Always, John." I smiled, sinuously curving my body to fit with his. "My heart will never belong to any but you."

For all that George the Prince of Denmark seemed a pleasantly empty-headed fellow, he was devoted to the princess, and to his sole reason for coming to England to wed her. Unlike Mary, whose husband the Prince of Orange had required her to return to Holland with him, the Prince of Denmark had agreed to live his married life in his new wife's country, and clearly the English climate agreed with him. A month after their wedding, Anne was already retching over the chamber pot I held for her, and by December her first pregnancy was announced to an England delighted by this prospect of a Protestant heir. Though James was pleased for his daughter's sake, his priests and Catholic supporters grumbled ominously in his ear, reminding him of his own lack of a son. And William of Orange, too, greeted the news of Anne's pregnancy with hostile jealousy, even daring to suggest that he'd been intentionally offered the barren Princess Mary for his wife.

But no matter. The princess was blissfully happy and her husband devotedly attentive, which lessened the demands upon my own time. Although she swore to write to me each day, I was able to slip away to St. Albans and spend rare time with my own family at Holywell House— which John and I had finally purchased as our own—and by the end of the year, I, too, was again with child. I was certain this one would be a son to carry my husband's name and glory. As we made improvements to Holywell, adding a summer parlor and a new roof, I imagined a small, forthright version of John paddling about in the newly dredged fishpond outside our bedchamber.

Alas, in some miserable ways the princess and I shared too much in common, after the fashion of close sisters and friends. In May of 1684, she was brought to bed of a stillborn girl, much to poor Anne's devastation. The cause of the infant's death was determined to be Anne's incautious fall from a horse early in her pregnancy, and though such an outcome was sorrowful, there now was proof that the princess could conceive with ease, and carry a child to her time.

But I did not. One afternoon soon after my own child had quickened, I was driving my chaise home myself from a brief errand at the mercer's shop in St. Albans. The afternoon clouds threatened to spill and I was eager to be home before they did, yet the horses turned stubborn, unwilling to hasten as I wished. My irritation grew, and with no other recourse I applied the whip to their idle backs so smartly that I grew winded from the exertion. I drank three tumblers of lemon-water to refresh myself when I reached home, and thought no more of it.

That night I woke with grievous pains in my belly, and before the midwife could come, I had miscarried of my first son. I was as grief-stricken as I'd been at Harriot's death, perhaps even more so, since this had been the boy I'd so wanted to give to John.

My dear husband comforted me as best he could, never faulting me for our loss, and instead saying that we were young—I was but twenty-four, a young woman by any measure—and sure to be blessed again with other children. It was his notion that I return to the princess as soon as I'd recovered, so that we could ease one another's sorrow. He himself was leaving Holywell soon, too, bound on another mission of the king's to Paris, and there was no real choice open to me.

That summer I joined the princess and her stepmother Mary Beatrice at Tunbridge Wells, where both had gone to take the waters to increase their fertility in the hopes of bearing sons—one praying for a Protestant prince, one for a Catholic. I went with them, because I knew I must, not because I'd yet the heart for it. I went, bringing endless joy to Anne by my return. I went, feeling no joy myself at leaving my daughters, and even less that my two poppets were so accustomed to parting with me and to my long absences at court that they shed not a tear between them as my carriage drew away from Holywell.

And by the end of 1684, the princess was most happily with child again, while I, living away from my husband so I might wait upon her—I most sadly was not.

Chapter Sixteen

"Have you ever seen anything more beautiful, Lady Churchill?" Swaddled in rich furs brought from New Amsterdam, Anne leaned back against the sleigh's leather cushions and sighed with happy wonder. "It's as if London were made of spun sugar and diamonds, it sparkles so!"

"It's London swallowed up in ice, Your Highness," I said, my words coming out in clipped little clouds before my face. This was the coldest winter in anyone's memory, cold enough that the Channel itself was frozen two miles out from the coast. Even wrapped in my fur-lined cloak with my feet propped up on a tin box full of hot coals beneath my quilted petticoat, I still felt the chill clear to my bones. "We're no better than poor beasts fallen into a pond and trapped within the ice."

"But it *is* beautiful, Lady Churchill," Anne persisted. Above her woolen scarves and veils, her nose was as red as a cherry and her weak eyes watered with the cold, and she wiped them clumsily with her thick-gloved hand. "Who would dream the Thames would freeze as solid as this?"

"This once is enough for my lifetime, Your Highness," I said, handing her a fresh handkerchief before my fingers dove swiftly back into warm hiding inside my ribbon-trimmed muff. And yet she was right: who would have thought it would ever be possible to drive across the Thames like this—a Thames frozen thick enough to support with ease a sleigh and two horses and our mounted escorts as well?

Nor were we alone on the river this day. Crowds of Londoners of every rank had made their way over the banks, through the rougher ice and broken rushes that covered the marshes or down the slippery river-steps, to enjoy this rare novelty, and while some brave souls glided by on Dutch skates strapped to their shoes, most slipped and slid across the ice. There were other sleighs on the ice, too, and young blades in bright capes and plumed hats who'd had their horses reshod with spiked iron shoes cantered briskly across the white ice, as pretty a show as one could ever view.

With so many people, enterprising shopkeepers had declared a Frost Fair and set up huts and booths from which to sell their wares—gimcrack toys, long-stemmed clay pipes and twists of Virginia tobacco, hot cider and steamed chocolate. A printer had even hauled his press down upon the ice, and for a halfpenny he'd set the type to print anyone's name. With the Thames's usual foul scent for once subdued, the air was fragrant from roasted chestnuts tossed on braziers full of coals until their glossy skins burst. The ice had gripped so hard that bonfires could be lit upon its surface without fear of melting, their flames burning bright late into the night.

"God bless you, Your Highness!" shouted a man as our sleigh passed by, and the children beside him hopped up and down with excitement when Anne waved back.

"I wonder that they recognize me wrapped up like this," she said. The king had long ago set the fashion for going out among his people, and though the princess was too shy to enjoy such attention the way her uncle did, she understood the good in it and had resolved to show herself, too. "And how kind of them to wish me well."

"Every Englishman and his wife who worship each Sabbath in an Anglican church would do the same, Your Highness," I said. "You are much loved."

She flushed, and beneath the fur she drew off her glove and slipped her bare hand beside mine in my muff.

"To be loved by so many is a fine thing, true," she said, looking straight ahead. "But I should prefer the love of the one dearest to me, over the thousand I could not name."

I turned towards her, the fur lining my hood brushing against my cheek, and let our hands lie together. I'd been expecting this moment since I'd rejoined her in Tunbridge, and I was ready with my answers.

"You have that love, Your Highness, a husband who loves you with the greatest devotion."

"Yes," she said slowly, as if this were a new notion for her to consider. "Yes, he does."

The tiny bells on the sleigh's harnesses jingled, a merry sound in the clear, sharp air.

"You are not cold, are you, Your Highness?" I reached across to pull the furs higher, tucking them more closely around her as if she were a favorite child ready for sleep. "Perhaps we should return to the palace. You must not risk a chill, not for you or the babe."

"I've ordered the driver to turn back at the bridge. I'm fine until then, and so is my child." She smiled with such tenderness that I feared she'd weep. "You see how it is between us, Lady Churchill. You care for me as no other can or could."

"I care for you as my princess, Your Highness," I said, "and I care for you, too, as my dearest friend."

Inside the muff, where no others could see, her fingers curled around mine.

"You are my dearest friend, too," she said, her voice breaking on the word *friend*.

More touched than I'd want to admit, I squeezed her fingers in return. "It's as it should be, Your Highness."

She nodded eagerly. "You do like your new quarters, don't you?"

"How could I not, Your Highness?" That was true, too. As a wedding present, the king had not only granted the prince and princess an allowance of four thousand pounds a year, but also had given them a splendid set of rooms in Whitehall—pointedly apart from those of James and Mary Beatrice in St. James's Palace—in a part of the palace known as the Cockpit. Though the rooms dated back to King Henry's time, and had in fact centered about a pit for fighting cocks, they had all been newly refurbished in the latest fashion. There were plasterwork ceilings, oak paneling on the walls, and gilded looking glasses everywhere, with new furnishings of oak and mahogany and new damask hangings on the bedsteads and windows.

The princess was generous with her new lodgings. While I had been with her at Tunbridge, she'd ordered a new set of rooms for my husband and me, situated directly below her own, surprising me when we'd returned.

"You are certain the apartments are to your wishes?" Anne asked, ever anxious to please. "We can always call back the carpenters or the undertakers if not."

"I've never had a more generous gift, Your Highness," I said, my smile genuine. Even in my position as the princess's Lady of the Bedchamber, such convenient and spacious rooms were a great show of favor indeed at court, and one provoking much enjoyable envy among the other ladies and gentlemen, too. "And to be placed so near to you and your rooms— ah, could there be any better situation in the entire palace?"

"Near *me*." She smiled shyly, as if amazed by her own good fortune.

"Near you," I said softly. "I'll never be far, Your Highness."

"That was my wish, Lady Churchill." She glanced down at the muff that hid our linked fingers. "That, and to make you happy, which is why—why your quarters are for both you and Colonel Lord Churchill."

"I know, Your Highness, and I cannot be more grateful for your generosity to us," I said. "Though Colonel Lord Churchill is so often from the country on orders from His Grace and His Majesty that I fear he'll make little use of your kindness."

"A soldier's life is not an easy one, for him or for you." She flushed again and impatiently tugged her woolen scarf away from her mouth to speak. "But because of that, and other things, I hope you'll turn to me, Lady Churchill. I know how much you love your husband and that is right, just as I love His Highness. But you and I are friends, dear friends, and I dare hope—I pray!—that there might be one tiny corner of your heart left with a place in it for—for me."

My first thought was how pitifully wrong she was: how the arranged marriage she shared with her prince could never be the same as mine with John, fashioned only by us with true love, esteem, and respect. My entire heart belonged to him and always would, and my soul with it. Anne was my dear friend and my mistress, but she'd never have a share of what I gave so freely to John.

Then I thought of the new apartments in the Cockpit, how I alone among the princess's ladies had been asked to ride beside her in this sleigh, and how tenderly she now held my hand in hers. I thought of our house at Holywell, my daughters, my husband, and the hopes we dared have for an uncertain future, and miraculously I discovered an empty place in my breast—if not precisely in my heart, then close enough.

I bowed my head with becoming meekness. "You need not ask for such a favor, Your Highness. You've already had my love long in your possession, the gift of one true friend to another."

"Ah!" she cried out, the sound echoing in the cold air, and if not for the others around us, I felt sure she'd have kissed me again. "Ah, my dearest! If only I could make you as happy as you make me!"

I raised my eyes to meet her gaze, my smile as sweet as I could contrive it to be.

"But you *will* make me happy, Your Highness," I whispered, my voice low between us as, inside the muff, my fingertip traced a tiny heart in the center of her palm. "In every way possible, I am certain you will."

A week later I woke abruptly, torn from my sleep by what sounded like an entire regiment of fusiliers, all firing at once. Disoriented, I shoved aside the curtains around my bed while the thunderous cracks continued to drown every other sound. I clambered from the bed and stumbled barefoot across the chilly floor to the window, wishing desperately that John were here to explain whatever was happening.

Frantically I breathed against the pane to melt the frost, then wiped it away with the sleeve of my smock and peered through the cleared glass. Yet there were no soldiers, no armed attack by Frenchmen, the park before me empty and still in the silvery moonlight of the last hour before winter dawn. Sheepishly I realized the sound must be the ice in the river breaking up at last, cracking and splitting and popping as the water beneath it came sluggishly back to life. I smiled at my own foolishness, as panicky as a stewing hen newly parted from her head, but before I could return to the warmth of my bed, I heard a woman at my door, tapping and calling my name. Her obvious desperation made me hurry to answer, crossing my arms for modesty over my linen smock and cold-stiffened nipples.

"Oh, Lady Churchill!" Lady Sunderland's face hung ghostly pale on the other side of her candlestick, the ruffles on her nightcap trembling with agitation. "We must go to Her Highness's bedchamber and wake her at once!"

I smiled. "Forgive me, my lady, but there's no need to disturb the princess. It's the ice on the river breaking, nothing more."

"But it *is* more, Lady Churchill, much more!" she cried, and now I could see the tears in her eyes. "Her Highness must be wakened, and told! His Majesty's been struck by a violent apoplexy in his bed and the physicians despair of his life, may God save him!"

Of course I woke the princess with the somber news, and soon all London knew as well. This time, no amount of Protestant prayer could save the king, and over the next week, minute by painful minute, he slipped away from this life to the next. On the night he sensed would be his last, Charles bid farewell to the sobbing queen, his brother, and each of his children by so many different mothers. Exhausted by this final bit of ceremony, he asked that the curtains be opened wide so he might watch the sun rise from his bed, and died.

It was Anne's twentieth birthday.

Charles had been only fifty-four, a shockingly young age to die for so robust a constitution. While some accepted that his death had come from constant indulgence in carnal pleasures, the princess and I and many, many others believed that Charles had been poisoned by papal agents. While such a crime was never proved, there was no doubt that James and the Duchess of Portsmouth, Charles's last, French-born mistress, had smuggled in a priest to convert the dying king to Rome—an unforgivable crime against those who wished the best for England, yet only the first of many that were to come.

In my lifetime, England had known no other king, and I could scarce imagine either the country or the court without Charles's benevolent presence to oversee them. But I would learn the difference soon enough. James was crowned the new king, free at last to rule as he pleased, and life for all of us would never again be the same.

Though word of Charles's death flew through Europe, the formalities of royalty still must be obeyed, and John, as James's most trusted emissary, was sent to King Louis in Paris to announce one English king's death and the crowning of the next. There was, of course, another purpose to John's visit: to try to persuade Louis, as the wealthiest of the Catholic monarchs, to show his support with a handsome secret allowance to James, the poorest. But besides being the richer royal cousin, Louis was also far more crafty, and before John could make his plea, Louis made an unsolicited gift to James of a half million gold livres—less than James could have wished, but so much that to ask for more would have been unspeakably rude, even among cousins. Ruefully John turned back towards England— and to a far different role in James's reign.

Encouraged by the Earl of Argyll, a handful of malcontent Whig noblemen, and a mistress who wished to be queen, the Duke of Monmouth had foolishly declared himself the rightful heir to his father's throne. Not only did he claim that his parents had in fact lawfully wed, neatly erasing his own bastardy, but he accused James of setting the Great Fire twenty years before, poisoning Charles, and bringing the pope himself from Rome to London. No person with half a wit would believe such tales, but Monmouth's cause found many supporters among poor tradesmen and farmers, and the Protestant Scots who'd already suffered under James.

When Monmouth—"King Monmouth" to his followers—landed with a small force in Lyme on June eleventh, the king at once determined to quell the rebellion. Now cast as a soldier instead of a diplomat, John was soon marching towards Lyme with five companies of foot and eight troops of horse guards and dragoons. Yet as daunting as such a force must have been, more and more men threw their lot in with Monmouth, until he was reputed to have as many as ten thousand followers. It was easy for me to imagine him, as handsome as the day on horseback, a younger version of his father ready to draw the poor and disenchanted to his cause and promise them everything that James couldn't.

But the awful truth was that these makeshift soldiers were often armed with no more than pikes or scythes, and woefully unfit to meet my husband's experienced force. In late June, the two sides met near Bath; the casualties were light on both sides, but the reality of battle made large numbers of Monmouth's force desert and melt away as surely as dew before the morning sun. The end came in the drained marshes of Sedgemoor, where my husband's men put a bloody end forever to Monmouth's hopes of the throne.

The rebellion was done, but not the rebels. By way of example, prisoners were hung from trees and their bodies left to sway and rot as warnings. John and his troops returned before the king's real retribution began, hundreds of rebels being hung, drawn, and quartered at what became known as "the Bloody Assize." The rights of hundreds more prisoners were distributed as favors among James's friends, with the unfortunates to be transported to the West Indian sugar plantations and sold as slaves for a handsome profit. Among these were a group of young girls from Taunton, whose only misdeed had been to stitch Monmouth's banners; though there was much lascivious amusement at court imagining the treatment these toothsome young slaves deserved, and would receive, at the hands of their new overseers, I was sickened by the whole sorry business, and would listen to none of it.

Nor did their leaders receive any better. The Earl of Argyll was executed at Edinburgh, his head stuck on an iron spike at the Tollbooth until the crows had picked the bulging eyes clean from the sockets and the flesh had rotted away from the skull. Monmouth himself was ignominiously taken prisoner where he'd hidden in a ditch, dressed as a common laborer, as sorry an end as could be to the long-ago friendship between the duke and my husband. Monmouth was brought back to the Tower, and though he groveled and wept for mercy in shameless display, the king's heart was as hard as marble.

At James's insistence, we attended the execution. Though Monmouth had paid the axeman extra to be swift about his task, the man faltered so badly that after seven misfired strikes of the axe, he was forced to draw his knife to finish severing Monmouth's handsome head from his traitorous body.

Putting aside all the merry days of our youth, Anne said her bastard cousin had gotten what he'd deserved, and spoke no more of it. But I could not forget how prettily Monmouth once had danced in his father's favorite masques, dressed as Mercury in a suit of silver cloth; how easily he'd laughed and teased every lady at court; and the horrified look frozen in his eyes as the executioner had at last held his dripping, ravaged head high for all to witness.

For James, the thwarted rebellion was a chance to glory in his power, and again ignore the desires of the people he ruled. He increased the size of the standing army, put more Catholic officers in command, and reviewed his troops accompanied by his priests and a trundling portable chapel drawn by horses.

The night John returned from putting down the rebellion, he took me at once to our bed and made violent love to me, full of passion and fire, until dawn, when he had no choice but to return to Whitehall. For his ruthlessness at Sedgemoor, he was granted an English barony to match his Irish one, Baron Churchill of Sandridge, and made major general.

And of the battle and Monmouth's capture, of blood and death, of trees strung with rebel corpses, and the tears of English mothers begging mercy for their sons—of these things he said nothing to me, and never did.

It was already clear enough to each of us that the price of certain honors in this world was very dear indeed.

Chapter Seventeen

"I think the rash is improved, Lady Churchill, don't you?" Anxiously Anne studied the face of her infant daughter Mary, held up in the nursemaid's arms for approval. "Does it not seem less pronounced across her cheeks this morning?"

I considered little Mary's woeful face inside her heavy beribboned bonnet. She was nearly three months old now, a weak and fretful child who had yet to learn the knack of thriving. Not only were her cheeks blotched over with some manner of red, peeling rash, but her eyes watered and squinted much like her mother's, her tight little fists flailing with unfocused impotence.

"Yes, Your Highness, I believe there is some improvement," I said, wanting to ease the princess's concern. "Besides, the old country wives swear an early rash like this only improves a child's complexion later in her life."

Anne's eyes lit with hope. "Truly? I can see the sense in that. The rash would serve rather like a purge."

As if to fault my well-meant lie, Lady Mary gave a mournful, bleating cry, twisting her blighted face into the side of her bonnet, away from our scrutiny.

At once the nursemaid began to pet and soothe her, making gentle *cluck-cluck* noises and rubbing the baby's back as she pressed her to her breast. "She's weary, Your Highness, that is all."

Anne's face puckered in sympathy, or maybe only with wordless sorrow that she understood so little of her own child's wants or needs—the sad lot of most royal mothers. "Yes, yes, then do put her back in her cradle to sleep. That would be wisest, wouldn't it? To let her sleep?"

"Yes, Your Highness, that's wisest," the nursemaid said, managing to make her curtsey and back nimbly from the room while holding the squalling baby. "As you wish, Your Highness."

"Sleep well, my own angel!" Anne called after them, waving her fingers, then bowed her head over her empty arms so forlornly that I patted her shoulder by way of reassurance.

"All my girl needed was a little nap, Lady Churchill," she said. "You heard her nurse. She's weary, that is all."

"It's all that ails most crying children, Your Highness."

"Yes, yes." Anne sniffed and made herself smile. "Where's that book of fables, Lady Churchill? I would have you read more to me while my daughter sleeps, to amuse me."

"I can fetch the book directly, Your Highness," I said. "It's in my bedchamber."

She turned, her expression achingly insecure. "You will return to me, won't you? You won't stay away?"

"Of course I'll return, Your Highness, as quickly as I can." I curtseyed and hurried down the hall and the staircase that led to my rooms. To my surprise, my sister Frances was waiting on the bench outside my door.

"Sarah, at last!" she exclaimed, her hands outstretched to greet me. "I've been waiting here at least an hour to talk with you."

"Then I regret that you must wait longer still, Frances," I said as I opened my door. "I'm only here to retrieve a book, and then I must return to Her Highness the princess at once."

"Only a moment, Sarah," Frances pleaded, coming to stand beside me, her silk skirts *shushing* against mine. "She can spare that. Aren't I your only sister in this world?"

I sighed impatiently. Anne had used Mary's birth as an excuse to keep herself from her father's court. We knew her apartments in the Cockpit were watched, and I suspected the king had planted spies among the lower servants. But beyond Anne's daily attendance at Anglican services in Whitehall's Chapel Royal—she was the only member of the royal family to do so now—she was seldom seen in Whitehall, and I gladly followed her lead, encouraging her to keep apart further. She feared her father would force her to convert; her letters to her sister Mary were full of her worries. Neither Anne nor I wanted any part of James's new regime of high Masses and Catholic graces said at state meals, or old friends stripped of titles and lands for the sin of being Anglican, while fawning Catholics like my sister's husband were raised to the peerage.

"You've had little enough to do with me of late," I said. "You've made your choices in life, Frances, and now you must abide by the consequences. If you cannot sleep at night because of what hateful, intolerant things your husband has said or done—why, that's of no account to me."

"I must abide by my husband's choices, Sarah, the same as any other wife," she said, covering my hand on the latch with her own. "Even you. Oh, Sarah, please, I ask only a few minutes of your time."

I sighed again, disgruntled, for she was indeed my sister.

"Very well, Frances, but mind you, I cannot keep the princess waiting for long." I held the door to my rooms open to let her pass and join me, noting the French lace pinned around her shoulders, the pearls around her throat, the gold rings on her fingers. "At least this time you won't be begging for money."

"Not for mere silver or gold, no," her husband said, suddenly appearing to push his way after Frances into my rooms. "The Christian soul of the Princess of Denmark is worth far more than any worldly price."

"I mean to speak to Frances, my lord, not you," I said, furious that he'd hide behind my poor sister—such a piddling trick. Whatever quality had she seen in such a man to marry him? "Now leave here peaceably, or I'll call a footman."

"No need for that, dear sister." Lord Tyrconnel was a blustering, bullying Irishman, his chest like a rum barrel, and his smile as he closed the door so smug I longed to slap it from his face. "Not until we speak of your undue influence over Her Highness."

"It is by Her Highness's choice that I am in her household, my lord," I said warmly. "It is no affair of yours."

"It is when your interference with the princess disturbs the balance of the country," he said, leaning so close to me that I could see myself reflected in his bulging eyes. "It is when you betray Her Highness's trust by whispering the foulest of blasphemies into her ear, leading her from the true church to certain damnation."

"The only blasphemies come from such as you, not me," I said, refusing to be intimidated. "The princess's faith is shared by the majority of the people of this country. We are in England, my lord, not Rome or France."

"You forget yourself, Lady Churchill." The menace in his voice was unmistakable, as black as the stiff curls of his periwig.

"Rather I recall who I am, my lord," I said with perhaps more truth than wisdom, "which I advise you to do as well. For while you may believe yourself now to be such a fine fellow—tra-lah, His Lordship the Earl of Tyrconnel!—to me and most others you will never be more than Lying Dick Talbot, an officer no English soldier would ever trust on the field of battle."

Behind me I heard my sister gasp. "Oh, Sarah, please don't!"

"Please what, Frances?" I asked without looking, for I knew better than to turn my back on her husband. "What? Would you rather have me betray the princess and my own faith than tell your husband how little use I have for his low, conniving tricks?"

"Don't concern yourself, Frances," Lord Tyrconnel said. "She's doubtless only parroting the falsehoods she's heard from Churchill himself."

"Why should my husband concoct any such lies, when the entire court knows the truth of your cowardice in battle?" I said. "Colonel Lord Churchill would never sully his honor by repeating the sordid tales that cling to your coattails."

His expression darkened. "You see it is just as I said, Frances," he said. "Your sister is unable to tell truth from lies, testimony to her own willfulness."

"Willfulness, hah." With no desire to continue such a conversation, I reached for the latch, but instead Tyrconnel shoved his oversized body between the door and me. "Stand from my path, my lord. I must return to Her Highness. Stand away at once!"

"What, because you order it, Lady Churchill?" His laugh rumbled with mockery. "Perhaps such orders hold weight in the Cockpit among the other hens, but not with me."

"You would dare call Her Highness a—a *hen!*"

"I would dare a great many things, Lady Churchill, especially when there are no cocks to be found for your cause," he said ominously. "You are already in peril, countering His Majesty's wishes by encouraging Her Highness's infatuation with Protestant beliefs. You have not only come between a father and daughter, but a king and a princess. You have kept her from attending Mass and receiving instruction from the priests sent to enlighten her in her darkness."

My fingers knotted in tight fists at my sides. "Her Highness is my mistress, my lord, and because I serve *her,* I obey *her* wishes in all things, including her faith."

"Her wishes, or yours?" He snorted with bemused disgust. "Everyone knows the princess is a weak woman, who follows you in all things. If you were to suggest to her the correct path of worship—"

"Which she has already followed from birth!"

"Sarah, please, listen to Richard!" My sister rushed forward, looping her hand in the crook of her villainous husband's arm with such sheepish devotion that it nigh made me ill. "He has the king's ear, and in turn is privy to His Majesty's deepest thoughts. Oh, please, Sarah, for John, for the sake of your little girls at Holywell, please consider what he says!"

"What of your own thoughts, Frances?" I demanded. "You were baptized and confirmed in the Anglican church, the same as everyone else in our family. Have you cast your beliefs aside and converted for the sake of preferment and gain?"

She glanced up at her husband for reassurance, her hand tightening around his sleeve. "I have—I've chosen to follow the true faith for the sake of my immortal soul, and to insure my place with the saints in heaven."

"Rubbish," I said roundly. "You did it because this wretch of a husband has forced you."

"I've heard enough, Lady Churchill," Tyrconnel ordered sharply. "And if you're wise, you'll listen to what I've told you. This king has no use for traitors at his court. If you value not only your own place with the princess, but also your husband's commission and titles, you will do what His Majesty asks, and soon."

I said nothing by way of farewell as they left my rooms, or to show that Richard's threatening words had made any impression upon me whatsoever. But I did slam the door after them with a resounding *thump*, loud enough to rattle the very hinges, and rouse my lady's maid Mrs. Mowdie from where she'd surely been eavesdropping in the next chamber, to drop a drowsy curtsey before me.

"Her Highness has asked again for the book of fables I was reading to her last night, and I must take it to her at once. At once, do you understand?" Her sleepy eyes seemed sure proof that she'd been napping while she should have been tending to my belongings, and I clapped my hands sharply together to make her move faster. "I left it last on this table. At once!"

With my hands at my waist, I watched her scurry about searching for my mislaid book like a confused mouse in a hayrick.

John and I couldn't really be in peril, could we? No one was invulnerable in this court, not even the king himself, but I'd been sure after Sedgemoor that John was soundly in James's favor, while I was balancing my side of our affairs well enough with the princess. Yet if I were perceived, however falsely, as the sole stumbling block before Anne's conversion, then so long as the princess and I remained within the king's reach here at Whitehall, then indeed the danger was real. My brother-in-law wasn't clever enough to have invented such a scheme himself, or to call me a traitor, either. Likely that honor belonged to other men with more power and more opportunity to use it against me, or John.

Unlike Charles, James believed that the king answered to no authority, especially not to Parliament or the people he ruled. I'd already seen others who dared challenge him pay dearly for their convictions. Would I be next for helping Anne worship the way she wished? Was everything that John and I had toiled so hard to achieve in jeopardy if I didn't act now, *now*?

"Haven't you found that book yet?" I demanded. "The princess hates to be kept waiting, Mowdie, and that is exactly what you are doing to her."

"No, my lady," the maid mumbled, on her hands and knees as she groped beneath my desk. "Yes, my lady."

Unable to bear such ineptitude, I turned away from her hapless figure and spied the missing book in plain sight upon the table. I seized the book in both hands and raised it above my head, and as hard as I could I hurled it to strike the wall above Mowdie's head, the pages fluttering like pale wings before it crashed to the floor.

"*There* is the book Her Highness desires," I declared, "plain as the dawn for those clever enough to use the sight God gave them!"

Carefully Mowdie retrieved the book from the floor, smoothing the bent pages between her fingers as she brought the book to me. I snatched it from her, and with my skirts flying around my shoes, I ran up the staircase. By the time I reached the princess's rooms, the anger had drained from me, and I was solemn and composed as I swept my curtsey before the princess's chair. Everything seemed clear to me now, every word waiting for me to speak.

"Oh, you did find the book, Lady Churchill," she said with unabashed relief, "and you came back to read to me!"

"Yes, Your Highness," I said gently, holding the book close to my breast so she wouldn't see the crumpled pages. "But first I fear we must speak of other matters. For the sake of all we hold dear, Your Highness, you must leave Whitehall as soon as it can be arranged."

Chapter Eighteen

I closed the playing cards in my hand and tossed them onto the table. "I've enough play for today, Your Highness. This afternoon's so warm, that with the wine we drank at dinner, my head's too muddled for anything taxing."

In truth it was the sorry level of Anne's play that made me wish to quit, not the summer day. She loved every sort of card game with a passion, but though she'd played since childhood, she had no more luck or skill than a gnat. She almost always lost, and just as predictably was surprised and wounded to see that one more game had gone against her. At my insistence we played for the tiniest of sums, but the others at court were not so kind. The Prince and Princess of Denmark were reputed to have lost nearly all of the princess's income of thirty thousand pounds, forcing Anne to dip deep into the pocket of her father the king to make up the difference. This was a time when an English family of the middling sort could live with comfort on forty-five pounds a year; Anne could wager and lose ten times that on a single hand.

"One more game, Lady Churchill?" Anne pleaded. "Just one?"

I shook my head, covering my mouth as I yawned. "If I should try, Your Highness, I'm certain I'll fall asleep right here with my head on the table."

"It's the new babe in your belly," she said sagely. "I know I'm always so weary in the first months I can scarce move."

The princess would know, I thought, for in the five years since she'd wed, she'd suffered through five confinements, having last been brought to bed of a girl in May. At least now fate seemed to be treating her with more kindness: unlike the unhappy results of Anne's earlier pregnancies, Lady Mary was nearly one and learning to walk, and Lady Anne Sophia, though no more than a frail wisp born before her time, was doing better than any expected. For myself, I was simply thankful to be with child again, and willing to endure the discomforts that came with that happy state. It was past time I bore another child, anyway: Henrietta was nearly five, and Anne three.

"I know it's so, Your Highness," I admitted. "I'm always thus before the child quickens, though I've never had the toothache as wickedly as I've had this time."

"Toothache's a sure sign it's a boy." Next to cards, there was nothing Anne liked more than to discuss breeding.

"I pray you're right." I stifled another yawn. "Forgive me, Your Highness, for being such poor company."

"You never are to me, Lady Churchill." She came around the table and took my hand to raise me. "If not cards, then, what would it please you to do?"

If she truly wished to please *me,* I'd be in a carriage bound for home at Holywell. But this question, though asked by the princess, was more for her pleasure than mine, and so I tried to consider a proper reply. What *were* we to do?

What, indeed. Windsor or Richmond, or Hampton Court or Tunbridge: it mattered not to which royal place we journeyed, for as long as Anne and I were removed from the Cockpit and Whitehall, the answer was always the same. Because of her weak eyes, the princess did not read, and her mind was shallow and uninformed. Because she was shy, she did not enjoy company, particularly if it was clever or outspoken. Because she had few opinions of her own, she had no conversation. Because her father had placed so many spies around her, she trusted few, and could not abide to have her servants or other ladies with her more than was absolutely required. Because she was so often pregnant and unwell, she seldom wished to walk or hunt or even to go out in a carriage.

There was, in short, only one thing in this life that always pleased her, and that was to be alone with me—as possessive and pitifully jealous of my person as the most demanding husband in the world, no matter how hard I tried to please her.

"Come, come," she said, "let us sit here by the windows while you consider. It's cooler here, too."

She led me to sit on the wide bench, first pushing away the three long-eared spaniels sprawled across the dark green cushions. We were not in the castle itself, but in the Denmarks' own house in Little Park, more of a true home than a formal state residence. The tall windows were thrown open wide, and spread before us the geometry of the castle's gardens contrasted with the curving silver band of the Thames. The air was heavy with the *thrum* of fat bees drawn to the flowers in the garden below, and with the musky-sweet scent of new hay in the summer's sun.

"How wise you are, Your Highness," I said, relishing the way the breeze from the open windows grazed over my face. "It's much more agreeable here."

"It is." She sat beside me on the very edge of the bench, suddenly ill at ease. "Yes. I would make a suggestion to you, dear friend. When we are alone like this, or when we write one another, I've found—I've discovered—that the rank due me seems unnatural between us, unnatural and odious."

I frowned and looked askance, not sure where this peculiar reasoning would take us. "Yes, Your Highness."

"That is precisely what I mean!" she cried excitedly, sliding closer to me. "That title sits like a barrier between us, a stone wall that I would tear down. Rather I would have you as my equal, the way that common women can be with one another. I've even chosen the two names by which we shall address one another: Mrs. Morley and Mrs. Freeman."

The notion struck me as so preposterous that I twisted around to face her. Titles and rank existed to exalt royalty; it was *intended* as that stone wall between them and the rest of the world. Even as a child, I'd known the importance of calling the princess by her proper title, and to do away with protocol now on a whim seemed beyond scandalous.

And yet, and yet—could there be any greater proof of her attachment to me, or better way to keep it? "You are sure of this, Your Highness? You are certain?"

"Quite." She waited, breathless, as if such a seditious scheme depended entirely upon my acceptance. "I want you to treat me not as your princess, but as your equal, honest with me in all matters. So shall you be Freeman, or Morley?"

"Mrs. Freeman, if you please." I laughed softly, as much with disbelief as anything. "With my temperament, who else could I be?"

"My dear, dear Mrs. Freeman." Her cheeks were flushed with happiness, so much so that I wondered how long she'd been planning this. "You see how well that sounds! Now when we must be apart, our letters can be without restraints. We can call our husbands Mr. Morley and Mr. Freeman, too, and no one shall be the wiser."

John would be amused by such a conceit, though I wondered if the prince would be as entertained; like all men with little real power, he clung to the trappings and show of his rank with an ironclad grasp.

"Dear, dear Mrs. Morley." I smiled wryly as for the first time my mouth formed the name that would become so common between us. "Do you still fancy the sound of it?"

"I do, Mrs. Freeman, and always will, so long as it comes from your lips," she said, her hand on my jaw to raise my face towards her. "The dearest, sweetest lips to me in all creation."

She kissed me then, tender and expectant and still redolent with the sweet wine from dinner. She did not kiss nor taste like John, and she'd never replace him in my heart, or my bed. No woman would. But as a diversion, another way of proving my devotion to her and hers to me, I'd come to view it as a pleasing passion, particularly on a warm summer afternoon such as this.

"Oh, Mrs. Morley, please!" I whispered. "How you delight me!"

"Mrs. Freeman, Mrs. Freeman." She slipped her hand inside the loose silk wrapper I wore over my smock, and I sighed as she found my breast, full and ripe with the coming baby, for I was always more wanton when with child.

"Mrs. Morley, Mrs. Morley," I answered in husky echo, though I could imagine precious few of the common goodwives she wished us to be engaged in such abandonment.

I twisted around, easing her back along the cushions so that I might have freer access to her person, and she to mine, my breasts now swaying like lush fruit over her. I eased my hand beneath her skirts, along the soft skin of her leg and higher, above the silk ribbon of her garter, to let her moan with anticipated joy. I'd learned she liked me atop, for it made her feel somehow more delicate, a dainty fragile creature to be ravished instead of the large, square woman she was, and she liked to be teased, perhaps because as a princess she'd always been granted every wish: oh, yes, I'd learned many, many things about her.

Frantically she pulled at my own clothes, our hair coming unpinned around our shoulders and the pearls swinging from our ears. Her flesh was pale and soft as doeskin, revealed to me as our skirts tangled around our limbs. Our actions made the warm afternoon even warmer, until at last I gave her what she sought, my fingers nimble across her nest to discover and play the honeyed jewel within. She arched against me, panting and blowing as she clung to me so hard that I couldn't have escaped even if I'd wished it. She followed her satisfaction by seeing to mine soon after, and we lay together afterwards, pressed thigh to thigh in drowsy contentment as she combed her fingers through my tangled hair.

"Oh, love," she murmured happily. "I shall never tire of you, my darling Mrs. Freeman."

I smiled, and kissed her cheek, and prayed in silence that what she said was true. I was her closest attendant, her advisor, her own Mrs. Freeman, and her dearest friend in this life, enough to secure my place in her favor. Yet I was also my mistress's mistress, and I'd seen enough at court to understand that the power of any royal mistress was as fragile as spun glass.

But I—I would be strong. For John, for our daughters, for the sake of the Protestant faith, for dear Mrs. Morley, and oh, yes, for myself, too, I would be strong.

And through the force of my will, I would not break.

Chapter Nineteen

I was slow to open my eyes in the big bed, relishing the luxury of waking at my own pace and not at another's summons. Inside the square of the walnut posts and heavy drawn curtains, I'd my own little island of peace and warmth, and I sighed with contentment, happily unaware of whether it was night or day beyond my bedchamber's windows. After each of my daughters' births in London, my lying-in had been little more than a hurried fortnight, made brief by our household's economy and my responsibilities at court. But this time, here at Holywell, I intended to savor my entire month of being cosseted and looked after, far away from the princess and the court, and free to enjoy the special pleasure of my new babe.

And this time, too, my joy at a safe delivery seemed a hundredfold greater, because this time, at last, I'd been delivered of a fine, squalling son. As was proper, he'd been named for John, though from the first we'd dubbed him Jack, and I smiled as I thought of his round, rosy cheeks, his thatch of unruly dark hair. Not even a month old, Jack already struck all who saw him as a most promising boy, alert and quick, and his nurse had proclaimed that she'd never seen so vigorous a kick whenever she changed his swaddling bands.

I heard the door to the room open, and then the bed's curtains were pushed aside, the iron rings scraping over the rods. I blinked as my eyes grew accustomed to brightness: it was in fact day, and though the curtains were still drawn over the windows, I could see the sun upon the snowbanks outside glow about the curtain's edges. I felt the chill of that snow, too, despite the fire in the fireplace, and I drew the coverlet up higher over my linen bed gown.

"Good morning, my love," John said, leaning forward to kiss me. He wore a long yellow brocade dressing gown over his shirt and breeches, the bright silk fanning about him like some Indian potentate's. "Though it's precious close to afternoon."

"Hah, and what if it is?" I asked, grinning as I lounged back against the feather-stuffed bolsters. Though he'd not been at Holywell in time for the birth, he had been able to come down from London for Jack's christening; I'd been especially glad that my little fellow had had his father with him at the font beside his godparents, seeing as I, having not yet been churched since the birth, could not attend. "You but wish you were still abed!"

"Only if I had you beside me, and beneath me, and around me in every other posture we could contrive," he said. "It's been a long time, Sarah."

"Another week, that is all," I said, my voice low with promise as I reached up to kiss him again. It *had* been a long time, but after I'd lost my last son early, John and I had been most careful. "I have to regain my strength for you, you know. All you must do is stay here, and not trot back to London."

"With this snow, I'll have all the excuse I need." He climbed onto the bed beside me, settling comfortably into his usual spot. "I can't recall the roads being closed as often as they have this month."

"Let it snow until June, if it keeps us here together." He'd left off his periwig, and I reached up to run my palm across the bristle of his close-cropped head. I missed his long hair, as thick and full of curls as any woman's, but I could understand why gentlemen found the wigs less of a bother. "Should I send for coffee or chocolate?"

"I've brought you something else." He reached inside the dressing gown and brought out a thick stack of letters. "These came earlier. I've no notion how long ago they were written, considering the snow."

At once I recognized Anne's spidery handwriting, and sighed. Here, in these letters, was the end of my peace and solitude.

"If you don't wish them, I can take them away to the parlor," he said, seeing my reluctance. "But considering how she regards your friendship, to write so many letters to you—"

"Oh, I know, I know, I must read them, and answer them, too." I took the letters, setting them on the dip in the coverlet between my legs. "But doubtless they will all be tediously alike: how dull her life is without me, how she fears I won't return, how no one else can do anything as I can."

"Likely her life *is* dull without you," John said, curling a lock of my hair around his finger. "I know mine is, when you're away from me."

"But she agreed to let me have my confinement here at Holywell, John."

"Agreeing doesn't mean she won't miss you," he said gently. "You consider her a friend, Sarah, as she does you. You can scarce fault her for that."

"No, I suppose I cannot." I heaved another sigh, and with the first letter in my hand, I nestled my head against his shoulder. "Mind you, however, that in all this scribbling, the greatest news will be how one of her dogs chewed one of the prince's stockings."

I slid my finger beneath the wax seal, unfolded the page, and began to read.

"Oh, no, not again!" I cried as I finished the first page. "She has miscarried again, John. That's at least the third time. Oh, how awful it must have been for her to read my letter about Jack's birth, and how happy we are!"

He curled his arms around me, drawing me closer against his chest. "It can't be helped, sweetheart, nor can you be blamed for her loss. Poor lady!"

But with a haste born of dread, I'd already begun the next letter in the pile. I read, and I gasped, and read again to be sure.

"Has the princess's health worsened, Sarah?" John demanded, and unable to tell him myself, I pushed the second letter into his hand and turned to the third, then the others as fast as I could read them.

His Highness the prince had felt unwell soon after Anne had miscarried, and he, too, had taken to his bed. Four days later, his fever had worsened, and the first signs of smallpox were unmistakable. Weak as poor

Anne had been from her miscarriage, she'd still dragged herself to his bedside, refusing to leave him, until the horrifying news had come from the palace nursery: their older daughter, Lady Mary, was now gripped by the smallpox, too.

By the next letter, tiny Lady Anne Sophia had been stricken as well.

Terrified and unwell herself, the princess went from one sickbed to the next, dreading the worst. She begged me for my prayers, asking God for the miracle that would deliver her family and spare them just as she herself had once been preserved.

Frantically I ripped open the last letter. Anne had written only a handful of sentences, all she'd needed, and all she could bear to write. My eyes swam with tears as I read, blurring the grim words that couldn't begin to carry the weight of my Anne's suffering.

The prince was out of danger and recovering. But all of Anne's prayers had been unable to save Lady Anne Sophia in her cradle. Three days later, Lady Mary had followed her sister to heaven, and God's embrace.

I thrust the last letter into John's hand, pushing myself clear of him. "I must go to her," I said, throwing back the coverlet. "She needs me, John. I must go to her at once!"

"You will not," he said, grabbing me gently by the arm. "You'll stay here at Holywell for your full time as was arranged."

"But Anne—"

"Let Anne turn to her husband, Sarah," he said. "Such a grievous tragedy should be shared between them."

I struggled to pull free. "But how can I deny her now, when she needs me most?"

"Then *I* will, Sarah, if you won't," he said firmly. "I refuse to let you put yourself at risk by going where there's been smallpox. Give thought to your own children. What would become of them if you were taken next?"

I went limp against him, my cheeks wet with grieving and frustration. Like all lying-in women, I felt everything with raw intensity, both joy and pain infinitely keener. In sharing Anne's burden, I could not help but recall my own Harriot's death and the other son I'd miscarried as if they were fresh new sorrows.

"In a fortnight, then." I struck my fists on my knees with determination, even as my voice quavered with my tears. "I *will* go to her, John. I will do whatever she wants, whatever she needs. I won't fail her when she needs me most."

"Ah, Sarah, Sarah," John said. "I never dreamed you would."

Although I went to the princess at Richmond Palace as soon as I was able, by March we were planning to move again. Now I stood on the opposite side of the open traveling trunk, watching as sharp as any hawk as the two maidservants brought the princess's blue brocade mantua, wrapped in a length of linen to protect the delicate silk.

"Take care, now," I cautioned. "Mind you keep the sleeves clear of the sides, else you snag the silk."

Overseeing the packing of Anne's belongings for journeys was another of my duties, especially since we seemed to always be going one place or another. This time we were bound not to another English palace, but a Dutch one: the king had granted permission for the prince to visit his family in Denmark, while Anne would stay with her sister Mary in The Hague. Of course I would go with her. We all were eager to leave Richmond and its melancholy ghosts: the nursery was dark and empty now, the fouled bedding of the two dead children burned and the tiny gowns and bonnets and rattling corals locked away against the hope of future babies.

No wonder the princess longed to escape, even for a month or two. Grief had slowed her recovery from her last miscarriage, and her doctors had warned that she'd not conceive again until she could clear the melancholy from her body as well as her spirit. Easy advice to give, I'd thought, but nearly impossible for the poor princess to obey. Not only had she lost her two daughters, dearest to her in all the world, but she had also failed the Protestant faith and her country by not producing an heir to the throne.

Bitterness mingled with grief, and now Anne and her barren sister Mary together shared their outrage over James's attempts against their faith with unabashed vehemence in their letters. For Anne's health, I hoped her visit to her sister would bring her comfort and peace, but I suspected instead that her ever-growing resentment for her father and his beliefs would be fanned into outright hatred by Mary and her husband Prince William of Orange.

Yet while Anne's constitution might not be prepared for such an impassioned union, having the sisters and their resentments joined in this would not be the worst eventuality for England. When John and I discussed these possibilities—of course with the greatest care not to be overheard, for James had placed more and more spies about his daughter's household, particularly around me—we gravely agreed that the next year would test and try our loyalties, and decide our futures, too. I'd told John, then Anne, of the threats made by my sister Frances and her husband. Both had reacted the same way: that the threats must be taken seriously because they most likely had come with James's knowledge, if not his encouragement, and that I should remain wary of any further contact with my sister. Thus I, too, was eager to leave England, if only for The Hague.

I was determined to learn what I could as well. John believed that the Prince of Orange was not only Protestant, but also an ambitious, clever man, one who watched England with more patience and understanding than James ever did.

For John and for me, the best course seemed to be for me to stay linked with the princess while John continued in the king's service, but also kept in correspondence with William, linking both of us to the Protestant cause. But where such decisions would finally take our fortunes—and how close that distant storm would come to us and our little family at Holywell—was still too hazy to guess.

I looked again at the maidservants lowering the princess's gown into the trunk. The stiff, boned gown bore the shape of a headless woman, the linen wrapped around it like a winding sheet and the open trunk like a yawning coffin. Abruptly I pressed my hand over my mouth to stifle my gasp and turned away, fearful that what I'd just glimpsed would somehow presage my own fate.

Yet as I did, I heard footsteps in the hall and the princess's voice, sharp with anger. I'd only a second to compose myself before she charged into the room. Her usually pale face was flushed, a sure sign not so much of wrath, but that she'd been crossed in some way that did not please her.

"Go, all of you except Lady Churchill," Anne ordered imperiously, scattering the curtseying servants. "At once, I say. Go!"

She swept past them as if they'd ceased to exist, coming to stand at my side. "Do you know what *he* has done? Do you know what *he* has dared to tell me?"

I didn't have to ask who this *he* might be. Since I'd returned to the princess's service after Jack's birth, Anne had stopped referring to the king as *Father*. Instead, to her James was now *His Majesty*, or *the king*, or most often and most venomously, simply *he*.

She slammed the lid of the trunk closed. "*He* has forbidden me to leave the country! *He* has told me it's too hazardous for me to travel to Holland. *He* has dared order me to stay here in England, away from my own sister, his own daughter!"

"But His Majesty has already given you leave to go."

"Oh, but that—*that* was last week," she said. "Since then others have clearly spoken to him, and warned him that for me to see Mary would put the country into such peril that it cannot happen."

She dropped onto the lid of the trunk, her shoulders bowed and her arms dangling disconsolately at her sides. She had aged much since her daughters' deaths, her constant expression one of pain and suffering, with bluish shadows that refused to fade beneath her eyes.

"I know it is the priests and those false ministers of his who have persuaded him to this decision," she said, her voice still taut with anger and frustration, and the old wounds, too, caused by such a father. "I know they fear that Mary and I will collude, and plot their downfall, and that I will refuse to return. I would rather believe that if such a decision had been left to *him*, that *he* would never treat me with such rash disrespect. But oh, Mrs. Freeman! To be charged without having sinned, to be humiliated with so public a refusal!"

I perched beside her on the trunk, slipping my arm around her waist to comfort her as best I could. "Perhaps in a day or so, it will be possible to persuade His Majesty to reconsider."

"*He* will not," she said with unquestionable finality. "*He* is far too stubborn, and will not be challenged."

I thought how the same could be said of her as well, though I was wise enough to keep that judgment to myself, even if she had ordered honesty between us. "If perhaps Her Highness the Princess of Orange wrote to His Majesty, then—"

"No," she said, closing one hand over the other in her lap, her spine stiff beneath my arm. "It will not happen that way. I've resolved to act upon my own. If I don't, then soon England will become no better than France, driving out every good Protestant of conscience."

I nodded, sharing this same fear. When King Louis had revoked the Edict of Nantes and stolen away the rights of his Protestant subjects, forcing them to flee for their lives, James had publicly applauded his cousin's so-called wisdom. While I thought the two kings made a fine pair of asses for such intolerance, I also shared Anne's concern that worse could come for Anglicans as well.

"Yes, I *am* resolved," she continued. "I've had quite enough. My sister informed me that Mr. Freeman is familiar with a certain Dutch gentleman, recently sent to England by her husband. My sister said if *he* caused me any difficulties, that I was to turn to this gentleman and rely upon him for counsel. Very well, then. *He* has, and I should like the gentleman to come to me as soon as Mr. Freeman can fetch him."

I kept the surprise from my face, never suspecting such resolution from her. Of course I knew of this Dutch gentleman. His name was Everard van Weede van Dijkvelt—the usual clumsy Dutch mouthful of a name—and he had been sent to England by William to speak discreetly with numerous peers and discern the level of support there would be for a Protestant rule. It was the first tenuous step towards overthrowing the king; we all understood, though no one would yet dare speak it aloud. John had been one of van Dijkvelt's first contacts, and one of the most important. Not only was my husband known to possess the king's trust, but he was also party to the growing number of secret alliances within the army and the navy, groups of concerned Protestant officers already planning how to preserve their rights against the king.

"Such a meeting would be . . . ah . . . a momentous step for you to take, sweet," I said with great care. "If Her Highness has told you of the Dutch gentleman, then I pray she has likewise explained his reasons for being here in England."

"I know it," she said, almost haughty. "I wonder that you should question if I do."

"But if you should—"

"If *he* will not grant me permission to visit Holland," she said, raising her long Stuart nose with disdain, "then I see no earthly reason why I should not converse with a Dutchman here on English soil, so that he might convey my concerns directly to my sister and her husband."

I nodded, striving to sound encouraging instead of critical. "I only wish that you realize fully the significance of this gentleman's visit to—"

"I know that *he* would consider any Englishman receiving this Dutch gentleman a traitor," she said. "I know that *he* would be most unhappy if *he* were ever to learn of my meeting such a gentleman. But the only ones who would know would be my sister, and Mr. Freeman, and you."

John and me. So she understood the concept of treason, but not the enormous risk she was so blithely asking us to bear on her behalf. What princess would?

"Mr. Freeman can arrange this meeting, can't he?" she asked with her more usual uncertainty, misinterpreting my silence. "My sister assured me that—"

"No, no, you may have every confidence in Mr. Freeman." I smiled. As hazardous as it was, what Anne was proposing would bolster the Protestant cause no end, and, if she were properly guided, make her more useful. "But thus far in his time here in England, I do not believe that this Dutch gentleman has met with any ladies, let alone any ladies of royal blood like yourself."

"No?" Her mouth puckered with anxiety. "You mean it would not be proper for me to meet this gentleman?"

"I might suggest a letter to begin," I said, knowing how shy she could be with strangers. "Only to spare yourself any inconvenience or indelicacy."

"Ahh." She frowned, considering as if the idea had been hers to begin with. "That might be wisest. You would help me compose such a letter? Mr. Freeman could advise you as to the wording, couldn't he? I know less than nothing of how such business is conducted."

"You know far more than you realize, Mrs. Morley," I said, pressing my hand over hers. "You know your conscience and your heart, and in matters such as these, those are most important of all. For you, and for England."

"For England," she echoed breathlessly, her eyes shining. "And for you, my dear Mrs. Freeman."

My smile was tender as I kissed her, my affection for her genuine. How could it not be? I'd worked hard to merit such confidence and trust from her. To have it so freely given, in so important a decision, was not to be taken lightly, and I could scarce wait to tell John. Of course I would guide her, and help her compose her letters, and support her in every way she desired.

What else, I ask you, would a true friend do?

Chapter Twenty

"You saw Mrs. Morley's last letters?" John asked as we walked side by side in step, my hand tucked in the crook of his elbow, his arm around my waist. "You know their content?"

"I know, because I wrote them for her." I pressed against John's side, thankful for his warmth. It was a chill night for autumn, the sky overhead low and heavy and without stars or moon, yet I couldn't help but recall another evening, long ago in this same privy garden behind the palace. Then, too, John was leaving for the Continent, but we'd been no more than lovers, and the only uncertainty we faced was when I would finally tumble into his bed. And now—now I was twenty-seven and heavy again with child, and he was thirty-six. We'd been man and wife for nearly ten years, and as we walked with our heads bent together, we spoke not of love or seduction, but of treason.

"Did she write the same as the other letters to her sister?" he asked. "More of her true feelings?"

"More, and more beyond that." Uneasily I glanced over my shoulder. Surrounded by bare paths in the center of the garden, we could be overheard by no one save the white marble gods and goddesses, yet still I could not relax. "She used the usual names in code, of course, but her determination and fury against her father grow by the day."

"Would she feel the same if he were put into the Tower and tried?"

"Don't be coy, John," I said impatiently. "What you mean is would she protest if she were part of the reason her father was convicted and executed? You wish to know if she could bear the guilt of having brought about her father's death, and I say yes, yes, she could, her wrath against him is that righteous."

He grunted. "Doubtless fed by you, my sweet little wife."

"There's never been a need," I said. "And I fear for her like this, John. It's as if she's been seized with a rare madness, and her passions are not her own."

"More likely it's the child in her belly," he said. "When she's safe delivered, she'll show more sense."

"But it's that selfsame babe that drives her so, you see! She fears that she'll perish in childbed, before she's had the chance to see 'England set to rights.' That's what she calls it, John: 'England set to rights.'"

"That's as fine a way to call it as any, though not even William himself believes it will happen by year's end. The time must be right."

"Of course it must." Mary was the logical choice to replace her father on the throne, with William as her able consort. She was next in the legal succession, she was Protestant, and she had her husband William's military forces to support her claim. The only question for us was whether England was unhappy enough under James's rule to overthrow its second Stuart king in fifty years. "There won't be a second chance, not for any of us."

"William is a cautious man," John said. "He's well aware of the dangers, as well as the rewards, and he understands England far better than James ever has."

"William will come, won't he?" I still remembered the unpleasant, stunted Dutchman who'd coughed and wheezed through his wedding to Lady Mary, not the thoughtful leader John claimed the Prince of Orange to be. "He'll not falter now? We'll all be 'set to rights' soon, won't we?"

"Oh, he won't falter," he said softly. "He wants to challenge Louis next. That's his true holy crusade, to reinforce the League of Augsburg against the French, and he can't do that without having England and her navy in his pocket first."

"Hah," I said bitterly. "That's the gist of it, isn't it? I'll save your faith, if you'll fight my war."

He tapped his forefinger on the end of my nose. "What a pretty cynic you've become, wife."

"I see things as they are, John," I said, "the same as do you."

"Then what I see is that William wishes both to be the savior of English Protestants," he said, "and to make war upon the French. It pleases him no end that your Mrs. Morley has sworn that not even her life is worth more than her faith. And I've told him, too, that none of the honors and titles that the king has granted us matter more than being true to our religion, and the chance to restore old England back to her glory."

"Nothing goes backwards, John," I said, too practical to be lulled into such poetical dreams. "Not even because you order it. Better we should consider the sort of rulers Mary and William would make for England, instead of romanticizing the country into some creaking Covent Garden slattern, down on her luck."

He laughed. "I've said before that you would make the bravest queen. You're the only one of the entire lot at court with enough cunning for the task."

"Oh, John, be serious." I stopped and stepped back, pulling my cloak more tightly around me as I searched his face. "We know the king already suspects me of having far too much influence over his daughter. But what if he should come to mistrust you, too?"

He tipped my face up towards his. "I have always been worthy of His Majesty's trust, Sarah, and he knows it," he said softly. "Just as he knows I'll not grovel before his priests and convert like Sunderland did, just to please him. I'll continue to serve the king with absolute loyalty in everything except his religion, and what it may wreak upon the country."

"At least my service to Mrs. Morley is to a fellow Anglican." I slipped my hands inside his coat to rest my palms on his chest and feel the steady, comforting rhythm of his heart. "Come back as soon as you can, John. Don't stay away an hour longer than you must. We've come this far together, love, and I mean to see it done with you, too."

"Now you're a tigress, too," he said, kissing me. He reached inside my coat, spreading his open hand low across my belly and the slight swell that was all that yet marked our next child. "You know I'll be back before this one's born."

"You'd better be back in England before March, my lord general." My fingers brushed across a flat, rustling packet tucked inside his waistcoat. "What is this, then? More secret letters?"

"Ah, how could I forget?" He pulled the letters out, holding them as if they were the most precious things imaginable. "I've brought these to you from the girls at Holywell."

I smiled, thinking of how like John it was to carry our daughters' letters himself when he'd so much else of worldly importance to attend to.

"I see Henrietta's made no progress controlling her pen." I tipped the topmost letter towards the fading light, squinting at our daughter's misshapen, blotted efforts. "By her age, she should be developing a genteel hand, not this sort of wretched scribble."

"She's only six, Sarah," he said easily. "She'll learn in time."

"What time will be better than the present?" I shook my head at how willing John was to indulge his girls. Because of the princess's demands upon me, he saw far more of our children than did I, and though I could hardly begrudge their strong affection for him, I did wish he'd be more forceful as a father, and not so quick to excuse and forgive.

"Henrietta's trying her best," he said. "She'll improve."

I tapped the letters on his arm with growing impatience. "I should not have to tell you of the expectations the world—especially *our* world—places on ladies. Henrietta's a nobleman's daughter, not some wild gypsy creature in the forest with torn petticoats and twigs in her hair. Though to judge by these letters, there's scarce little difference."

"Perhaps you should judge *what* she writes instead of how it's written," John said. "She wept after she read your last letter to her, you'd found so much fault."

"Then Henrietta was being far too sensitive," I said, more sharply than perhaps I should. "As I recall, she'd just mislaid her third pair of gloves in a month, and I'd chided her for her carelessness. Or would you prefer I let that pass unremarked, too?"

"They're only gloves, Sarah," he said, growing testy in return. "We can afford it."

I forced myself to take a deep breath, and another after that.

"They're only gloves, yes, and I refuse to quarrel over something so foolish before you must leave." I tucked the letters into my pocket to read later, and linked my arms around his shoulders. "Now come, my dearest husband. Let me tell you how vastly much I shall miss you, and how even more I love you."

"You know I love you, too," he said, settling his hands at my waist. "There should never be any doubt of that. It's only that I wish you would show more . . . kindness to others, that is all."

"I *am* kind, John!" I protested, wounded that he'd dare say such a thing to me. "Surpassing kind!"

"Then a fraction more will be no challenge at all," he said. "Even a queen must be kind."

"Don't talk to me in riddles, John," I said. "I'm too weary for that now."

"No riddles," he said, his face close over mine to kiss me. "I'm speaking as plain as I can. Be more kind, Sarah, that is all. Beginning now."

To the sorrow of many, but the surprise of few, Princess Anne was delivered of another stillborn child, a son, in October, two months before her time. The royal physicians attending her said the child had lain dead within her for some time, and that the birth of a moldering little corpse, when at last it came, was the best and safest outcome for the princess.

But royal physicians are heartless men, wise perhaps in their learning and skills, but arrogant and ignorant in how much more the heart and soul of a woman suffers than her mere earthly body following the grievous loss of a child. This time at least I was there at Anne's bedside to offer what solace I could, though I knew my own ripening body was a cruel if unintentional reminder to the poor princess of what she herself had lost.

Yet soon after came news of another pregnancy with far more significance than my own. To the amazement of the entire country, James solemnly announced that his wife Mary Beatrice was once again with child, after years and years of no issue. What should have been cause for rejoicing became one of endless controversy: the Romish supporters called the coming birth a blessing by God upon the true faith, while

Protestants questioned the convenience of the pregnancy, as well as the queen's refusal to let any but her Catholic ladies see her undressed.

There were already mean-spirited cartoons showing Mary Beatrice pinning a cushion beneath her skirts, and others, more hateful still, that showed her as a bare-breasted wanton, cuckolding the king with Father Petre, his own priest and confessor, and gleefully placing her illegitimate child on the English throne.

For Anne, this news was doubly bitter. Not only had she lost yet another baby, but she had also failed the Protestant faith. If Mary Beatrice's child proved to be a boy, then England was virtually guaranteed a Catholic succession, while the Protestant hopes linked to Mary and Anne weakened perilously.

Was it any wonder, then, that Anne was among the loudest who dared call the queen's pregnancy a papist contrivance, a hoax against England? Bitterness mingled with grief, and jealousy, too—a most poisonous brew, and the one I'd meant when I'd told John I feared for Anne's sanity.

In February, I retreated once again to Holywell to give birth. John's duties kept him away, and I missed him sorely when I was brought to bed of another daughter, baptized Elizabeth. She was large for a girl, strong and lusty, yet she cried so incessantly for no reason that I kept her little in the bed with me during my lying-in, instead handing her to the nursery-maids so I might sleep and recover my health before I must return to court. My darling one-year-old Jack felt much as I did about Elizabeth, that she made too much noise. He was clearly put out to have been replaced so soon by another baby, yet glad to discover he remained first in my heart.

While Jack was with me, Henrietta, now six, and Anne, five, were in turn delighted with Elizabeth, and lavished their little sister with the cloying attention most girls saved for their doll babies. In this fashion, I suppose everyone was as pleased as possible at Holywell, and when the carriage took me away to London in March, I wept, true, but I was also soon able to turn my attentions to the princess.

Anne needed it, too. In my absence, she had turned more to her sister Mary, and in their letters back and forth across the Channel they had shared their outrage over their coming stepsibling with unabashed vehemence. The resentment against their father now flared into full-flowered hatred against "Mansell"—their code name for the king—and his pregnant wife.

They were far from alone. Monmouth's rebellion, which had seemed so idle and foolish at the time, now was interpreted as a harbinger of genuine discontent. Dissatisfaction with the king and his policies rumbled through the countryside like a summer storm gathering in the distance, from the soldiers in the army resentful of the Catholic officers placed over them, to the farmers at market unhappy with new policies with France that lowered the value of their crops, to the great Protestant lords who now pointedly chose to remain at their country estates rather than take part in a court that included Catholic Masses and blessings said by priests at every meal.

James was failing other Protestants as well. The French had seized William's principality of Orange in the south of France, and Louis had sent his dragoons to torture and kill all Protestant refugees found there. On behalf of William and her fellow Protestants, Mary asked her father to protest both the invasion and the persecution, but James ignored her, blatantly taking Louis's side against the Prince and Princess of Orange. Once again he failed to realize how such actions increased William's support and soured his own.

But the king's final misstep came in early summer, shortly before the queen was due to give birth. Against all advice, James issued a new Declaration of Indulgence relaxing every English law and restriction against papists, and then insisted that it be not only obeyed, but also read aloud from the pulpits of every Anglican church in the country. The Archbishop of Canterbury and six other bishops bravely refused, along with scores of lesser clergymen in countless parishes. On behalf of English Anglicans, the bishops presented their petition to James, who responded in the worst possible way. In a furious rage, he ordered the bishops arrested and imprisoned in the Tower, charged with seditious libel.

The news swept through London, and John and I hurried to watch from the roof of the palace. The barge carrying the bishops to the Tower moved slowly against the current, or perhaps the men at the oars understood the symbolism of these outspoken leaders in their care. As far as we could see, the banks of the river and the streets along it were thronged with hundreds of Londoners, and more crowded in every window and along every rooftop. Some even waded into the river as the barge passed, their arms raised as they begged for a blessing from these holy men. The cheers from so many throats rose into one giant roar of support, and of defiance as well.

Our own small group here on Whitehall's roof—only a handful of courtiers had dared to gather for such a sight—was nearly silent, subdued by more knowledge than most common Londoners could possess.

"They won't be convicted," I whispered to John. "They couldn't be. Not even James is foolish enough to make them martyrs."

John's face was like a mask beneath the broad brim of his hat, all his emotions hidden deep inside. "His Majesty will try his best to have his way."

"But John, to arrest the Archbishop of Canterbury, the leader of our church!" I shook my head, refusing to believe that such a shameful crime could happen in England. "That even His Majesty would dare brand such courageous gentlemen as traitors is beyond bearing."

"I said His Majesty will try for conviction." John's gaze remained fixed on the barge with its somberly clad passengers below us. "He won't get it. Soon, Sarah. Soon."

He said no more, nor did I. But even on this sunny spring afternoon, I shivered, and pulled my trailing lace scarf more closely over my shoulders. I thought of our children playing merrily beneath the willow trees at Holywell, our youngest daughter Elizabeth not yet three months old. For their sakes I tried not to see the scene before me, but to picture instead an England free of intolerant hate and prejudice, the England John and I were toiling to restore.

On the second Sunday in June, the queen gave birth to a large, healthy son. He was baptized as a Roman Catholic: James Francis Edward, Prince of Wales. Most Englishmen believed as did the princess, that the pregnancy had been false and this child, an imposter, had been smuggled into the queen's bedchamber.

Certainly the only celebrations for his birth were the ones James ordered himself. Instead, effigies of the pope and the king were burned in huge bonfires within sight of the palace. In the west, where the reprisals against Monmouth's followers had been most brutal, straw figures of the hated baby heir were likewise tossed into the bonfires. The queen wept, and would not let her son from her sight.

That dark, distant storm of rebellion was gathering, drawing closer and closer, and nothing now would stop it.

Chapter Twenty-one

"Well, *that* is done." Anne tossed her fan onto the table, and her gloves after it. "I've finished my duty, and none can say otherwise. The queen now has no reason at all to complain of my neglect."

"No one can complain of your behavior in any of this," I said, opening the window to freshen the air. While the Denmarks had been again in Tunbridge Wells for the princess's health, hoping that a round of taking the waters would improve her chances of bearing a healthy child, the princess had ordered improvements made to her quarters and mine below, and the rooms still smelled foully of fresh paint. "You called on Her Majesty as soon as you returned."

"Yes, I did." She dropped into her favorite armchair, taking up a tumbler of sweet lemon-water. "Her and that wretched little wart in the cradle. What a fuss she and her ladies make over it, cooing as if it weren't a nasty dark creature!"

"He doesn't seem a promising child at first glance, no." The baby *was* dark complected, following both after his d'Este ancestors and his late uncle King Charles. But even though I understood Anne's reasons for despising the prince, the vehemence of her hatred still took me by surprise. Today she had refused to hold or kiss the babe, and referred to him only as *it*, never by name or relation to herself. I'd stood behind Anne's chair, as was my place, while she and Mary Beatrice took tea, and I'd heard the contemptuous way in which the princess had addressed the queen. Anne's incivility was so complete that I almost pitied the queen, poor lady. Whether the swarthy little babe was truly her son or not, she did seem to love him as if he were, and the princess's ill-meant asides must have cut her to the quick of her mother's heart.

"It's as ugly as original sin," Anne said with relish, "and I cannot wait to write about it to my sister. And as for *him* wishing me to state publicly that it is his—why, he'd do better to whistle to the moon."

"His Majesty's gathering witnesses to persuade you," I warned. "My sister's one of them, and she told me she'd been asked to swear to the truth, along with every other lady and gentleman who attended the birth, and the royal physicians, too. His Majesty realizes how much your opinions are valued by the people, and he'd rather have you on his side in this matter than against him."

"Your sister Lady Tyrconnel says that?" Anne asked suspiciously. "But she's a papist herself, isn't she? I know her husband, a black Irishman if ever there was one. Why should I believe any oath of hers?"

I sighed. "I'm not asking you to believe Frances because she's my sister. I'm telling you what His Majesty is planning to do, so that you will be prepared when he orders the Privy Council to present you with their evidence."

"The Privy Council may present whatever fool's evidence they please, but it won't change what I know to be true." Anne shrugged. She chose a stuffed sugared date from the plate beside her, and first licked the sugar from its wrinkled surface before she popped it into her mouth. "But that's all old news, isn't it? Come, come, and tell me what you have heard from Mr. Freeman today!"

I moved my tabouret as close as was possible beside her chair, lowering my voice to a whisper. News came to the Cockpit in fits and starts, through scribbled notes in code and servant's gossip. Though we were alone and the door to her chamber was locked, we could not be too careful.

"His Majesty's army is fair melting away," I began. Earlier in the month, the king had determined to make a show of his power by joining his troops in the field, and to be ready beside them to quell his contentious country if necessary. "They say each night scores more are deserting from the ranks, and their Romish officers are helpless to stop them."

"Romish, except for our two." The princess nodded sagely. Both my husband and hers were with the king now, their loyalty on display if not in their hearts. "How wise of Mr. Morley not to accept a commission when it was pressed upon him, and thus be forced to rally his men in the name of so wicked a commander."

"Indeed," I murmured, the safest course. While the Prince of Denmark was an amiable enough gentleman, he lacked fire behind his bland, colorless face, and he was happiest when left to spend his days staring out into space—or making certain the poor princess was constantly with child. It was impossible for me to imagine him rallying anyone to do anything, let alone a regiment of determinedly independent English soldiers. Refusing the offer of a commission from the king was likely the most forceful action the prince had made in his entire life.

"Mr. Morley turned the commission down outright," Anne repeated with satisfaction. "His reason to them was that he lacked experience, but to me he confided that the officers would be the ones in the gravest danger, and he'd no wish to be among them. Excluding Mr. Freeman, of course. Mr. Morley says he's so loved by his men that they'd follow him quite anywhere."

"So Mr. Freeman tells me, too," I said, with more hope than conviction. While John assured me that he still had the king's trust, the specter of a court-martial for him and a trial for high treason for me hovered among my worries. As much as the princess loved me, there would be a limit to her protection if the king decided to punish John and me for real or imagined crimes.

With such thoughts clouding my head, it was not easy to smile, yet because Anne did, so did I. "Yet no matter how many soldiers desert the king's army, Mr. Freeman says His Majesty refuses to believe that the Dutch fleet is any more than a rumor."

"Rumor, hah." Anne's laugh was almost gleeful. "What would he say if he learned it was true?"

"By now everyone in London must know William has sixty warships sailing for England, each one bristling with guns. They say he'll command a force of fifteen thousand men."

" 'I will maintain the Protestant Religion, and the Liberties of England,'" Anne said, reciting the slogan embroidered upon William's banners, which Mary had proudly written that she'd helped stitch. "That sounds very well as a declaration, doesn't it? 'The Liberties of England.' How could *he* deny that, I ask you?"

"His Majesty may not be denying it as much as you believe," I cautioned. "I heard today from one of Her Majesty's ladies that plans were in place to send you, the queen, and the prince to Portsmouth for safekeeping, and to be able to send you quickly to France if it came to that."

Anne gasped, panic flooding her face. "I will not go," she declared, clutching the arms of her chair as if she were being taken even now. "I won't go with them, not to France. They wouldn't dare force me! My place is in England, among English people, and nowhere else."

"They shouldn't misjudge your resolve, or your courage," I said firmly. "You won't be anyone's pawn."

"I won't, will I?" She nodded, agreeing with herself as she jabbed her fingertip into the almond filling of another date. "*He* believes he can push me about however he pleases, but he can't. He *can't*."

"That's because our cause is a just and honorable one, following the desire of the people for the freedom to worship however they please."

How many times had John and I said these same words to ourselves? Yet still we'd made our wills anew with fresh provisions for our children's welfare, and secured our fortune and properties against an uncertain future. The desire of the people could change on a whim; nothing, nothing was certain in our lives at present except the dangers ahead.

Outside the open window, the last dry leaves on the mulberry bushes rattled sadly on their branches in the breeze. Though this afternoon was warm for September, the fading sunlight mellow as golden guineas across the new-painted wall, winter would come before another summer. What season would favor us? I wondered.

"Each day I pray that we are right," Anne was saying with the fervency of the only Stuart left in the palace's Chapel Royal. "I pray that God in his magnificence will shine his favor upon us, and bless the choice that we have made."

I covered her hand with mine, and at once she turned hers so our palms touched and our fingers curled together, her ruby ring gathering the last light into a crimson glow. Despite her bravado with me, among others she was still a shy and timid woman, and I didn't want her so hard-pushed that she faltered.

"Let your prayers give you courage, sweet, and comfort as well," I said gently. "Once the Prince of Orange has landed, then we must trust that others will follow their consciences to take the right course and swear their loyalty to him."

She nodded. "I must be sure to pray for those lowly soldiers, too."

"Don't forget their leaders with them." I pulled my hand free of hers to count off the names of the men who John was confident would go to William. "Among them your cousin Lord Cornbury, Colonel Berkeley, the Duke of Grafton, your husband and mine, and scores of others in the army and the navy, too, who've sworn to follow their consciences. For England's sake, they must all quit His Majesty at the same time, and bring as many men with them as they can."

"They will," Anne said. "They *must*."

"To have the king's army simply fall away before they must fight will accomplish far more than any battle between them and William's forces. That is the goal." I lowered my hand, tapping my fingers on the edge of the table. "And if that does happen, then His Majesty will be . . . devastated."

"*He* will." Her expression was fixed and fierce, without a scrap of filial sympathy. "To be betrayed by those he trusts most could kill him."

"No one truly wishes for that," I said quickly, and not for the first time I marveled at the rancor she nursed so consistently against her father. I'd never known another woman who would remember ill usage and slights like the princess, and once her tender heart had turned against another, it became as hard and unyielding as the great stones in a seaside jetty. "Death would only serve to make the king a martyr, or worse, a papist saint."

"Of course it would." She nodded eagerly, without an ounce of re-morse or regret for how her own defection might wound her father. "We cannot afford to give the papists even that morsel of advantage."

"The best eventuality would be either for the king to concede his faults, and vow to change," I said, "or for him to turn tail and flee to France, and Louis."

"*He* would flee."

"For the sake of the queen and their son, that might be safest."

"*He* would flee, because *he* is a mean-spirited coward who would hide behind his queen's petticoats. No wonder my courage comes entirely from you, Mrs. Freeman, for there's little enough in my own blood." She placed her hand on my cheek and smiled, doting upon me, with tiny brown flecks of sugared date clinging to her front teeth. "Entirely!"

I smiled and drew her hand forward so I could brush my lips across the back of her fingers, that combination of affection and fealty that was so precious to her.

"You have your own share of mettle, my dear Morley," I said, "else you wouldn't have come this far. We'll need it, too, when our turn comes to flee London, and follow our husbands to the Orange camp."

"For freedom." Her eyes were bright with excitement. "For England, for our faith, for ourselves and—and our children."

A simple enough declaration, true, yet I felt uneasiness ripple through me. For the first time in our acquaintance, Anne and I were both with child, and due the same month in the late spring. There was so much uncertain about my life at that time, yet this coincidence was what struck me as most unfortunate, even ominous. I was convinced the princess's grievous history would somehow transfer to me. I feared this child I carried would be tainted, stillborn as so many of Anne's had been, or be so weak at birth that death soon follow.

"Wouldn't that be a pretty dream?" Anne asked, her hand over her belly, her voice pleading both for me to agree, and for the dream itself to be made real. "Our two little babies together as playmates in a better England?"

I forced myself to forget my superstitions, and nodded, making my smile as warm as I could. What better way could I hope to provide for this child and the rest of my brood at Holywell than to continue in the princess's favor?

"May these two be as dear friends to one another as we are," I said, reaching out to place my hand over hers, and over her unborn child. "May their lives be long and sweet and full of joy, in the England their parents did strive to protect."

At once her eyes filled with tears and her mouth twisted. "All I pray for is that this baby will be given to me to keep," she sobbed, "that he'll be spared, that—"

"Hush now, hush," I said. "Don't distress yourself. It's unwise for the child, and for you."

She gulped back her tears, struggling for control. "Stay—stay with me," she begged. "Don't leave me alone. You are so brave and I am not, and I need you to keep me safe from the papists and the queen and—and my father's soldiers, and—and—"

"I'm here, I'm here," I said, smoothing her hair away from her teary, scarred cheeks, the way I always did. "I'm here, and only your order would ever make me leave."

With a shuddering sigh, she nested her head in the familiar hollow of my shoulder. "My own friend," she whispered wearily. "You will be rewarded, in this life and the next. You *will*."

"Yes, Mrs. Morley," I said, and smiled against her cheek. "*Yes*."

When at last the word came in November that the Prince of Orange had landed and John and the Prince of Denmark had defected from the king's camp and gone to join William at Axminster, I was ready. In the manner of such grave events, the news had been garbled, and I'd learned of it not by a messenger from John, as we'd planned, but through the young officer from the king who'd come to arrest me. I'd talked my way free long enough to warn the princess, and put this next part of our escape into motion as quickly as we could.

With the hood of my cloak drawn low to shadow my face and my head bowed for good measure, I hurried across the empty park towards the Cockpit's side door. There would be guards posted at the front of the palace, but seldom here, and I was counting on being unchallenged tonight.

It must have been close to midnight by now, the new moon offering only fleeting light as clouds drifted across its face, and in the stillness of the hour, I heard every sound magnified a hundredfold, whether the beating of my heart, the crunch of a stone beneath my shoe, or the sleepy bark of some dog roused from its rest. John had told me that this was the way of things the night before a battle: everything too still, and yet too noisy, as if the waiting itself were somehow filling the air. This night would be as close as I'd ever come to such an experience, God willing, yet my life was as much at risk as John's had ever been on the battlefield.

Now I could see that the windows in the princess's bedchamber were dark, exactly as they should be. We'd made our plan so hastily this afternoon that I hadn't been sure until now that she'd follow it. But there was no time left to us for second-guessing: the orders had been sent to arrest me for treasonous conspiracy and to seize our property. Only the influence of Mary Beatrice, remembering me kindly from the old days as her maid of honor, had staved off my immediate arrest. If the princess and I did not flee tonight, then the king's soldiers would come for me by dawn.

My quarters on the ground floor, below the princess's, had a convenient door to the park. I flipped back my cloak, drew the key from the chain around my waist, and opened the door as quietly as I could. With one final glance over my shoulder to make certain I'd not been observed, I slipped inside. I lit the lantern on the table, closing it so only a glimmer of light peeped through, and rushed across the room to the closet in the corner. Inside was a hidden staircase, part of the recent renovations that John had helped plan, and with my skirts bunched to one side, I ran up these steps and scratched on the door to the princess's bedchamber.

At once the door flew open, Anne's face as pale as the moon itself in the half-light. "Lady Churchill! Oh, it *is* you!"

"Hush, hush, Your Highness, for all love." I pressed my gloved hand lightly over her mouth. "Do you want to raise the guards?"

She pulled my hand away, her eyes round with fear, and behind her now I could glimpse the other two women who were trustworthy enough to flee with us: Lady Fitzharding, another Lady of the Bedchamber, and a maidservant.

"Did you see soldiers?" she asked. "Oh, please God that they haven't discovered us!"

"No," I whispered fiercely, "but that's not to say His Majesty's soldiers are all snoring in some rum shop. Are you ready?"

She held out her hands to show me her gloves and muff; what I saw was how they trembled with fear.

"I did exactly as you said," she whispered contritely. "I told my ladies I wished to sleep and locked the door to my bedchamber. Then I scattered my clothes about, to make it look as if I'd been carried off against my will."

"You've brought nothing with you?"

"Only what I wear."

"Then let's be gone." I went first, holding the lantern high to guide the others. Anne came last, picking each step as timidly as if she were some ancient, unsure crone clutching at the balustrade instead of a young woman of twenty-three.

"You've seen these stairs a hundred times by day, Your Highness," I said impatiently. I knew she was more fearful because she was with child again, but then so was I, and for the sake of that unborn son or daughter, I was more determined than ever to keep from imprisonment. "Nothing's changed now at all except the hour."

"I'm coming as fast I can," she said, her voice tremulous as she felt for the last step with her toe. "I can't help not being so brave as you."

I seized her by the arm, half dragging her along with me. "If you're brave enough to turn against your father, why, then you're brave enough to walk across an empty room in the dark."

She made an odd gulping sound, of nervousness, I guessed. "I'd rather jump from my window than face *him* again."

"Then make haste," I said, "for he and his army are drawing closer with every minute we squander."

To my relief, the park still seemed empty. We needed to go only as far as Charing Cross, where the hired carriage would be waiting. Yet it might have been across a vast inhospitable wilderness as far as Anne was concerned, she'd grown so unaccustomed to walking from the ill health of her near-constant pregnancies. I took her by one arm to support her, while Lady Fitzharding took the other.

"It's not far, Your Highness," I said. "The others are already waiting to carry us away."

"Who—who are they?" she asked, already breathless.

"Friends, Your Highness," I said, mindful of the dangers we all shared. "Let it stand as that for now, and no more."

"Friends," she repeated. "Meaning that you fear we'll be captured, and wish to protect me from being forced to confess."

"You'll know them soon enough, Your Highness." She was right, of course. Neither of us had forgotten the undue pleasure that the king had shown long ago at the torturous interrogations of the Scottish dissenters.

"Then will you tell me if you've heard from your husband, or mine?" she asked, her whispered voice pinched with anxious dread.

"No." The single word hung between us; we each knew what that signified, too.

"Nothing from a servant?" she persisted, praying for more. "No note?"

"No, Your Highness," I said, and Anne's hand found mine to offer solace.

All I knew was what the soldiers had told me earlier in the day: that John and the prince had deserted the king's camp by night, and gone over to Prince William in Axminster, and that they were both now considered traitors. But I'd no word of this from John, no letter or other reassurance that such was true. Likely Anne's husband, being of royal blood, was well, wherever he was, but the same could not be said of John. He could already be dead, or grievously wounded and dying, or being tortured, or otherwise brutalized in captivity.

And if I were taken, too, the same fate would await me.

"Come, Your Highness, come," I urged her as we began across Pall Mall. I could see the dark bulk of the carriage ahead of us, waiting at Charing Cross. "The sooner we leave here, the sooner we'll learn what has happened."

But even in November, the ground had yet to harden with a killing frost, and the sticky mud of Pall Mall slowed us, dirtying our hems and sucking at our feet.

"My shoe!" the princess cried, twisting around. "I've lost my shoe!"

The maid dropped back, hunting for the lost shoe in the mud, but I pushed onward. "I'm sorry, Your Highness, but we cannot stop. The carriage is right there."

"I see it, too," she said, then, to my surprise, she laughed, almost giddy. "I can feel the mud through my stocking—between my toes!"

"Your Highness!" A large man with a shock of white hair had clambered from the carriage to take the princess's arm. "Your Highness, are you hurt?"

"Bishop Compton!" she cried happily, for she'd likely no greater champion in this rebellion than the Bishop of London—one of the same bishops who'd been imprisoned and tried by her father earlier in the summer, and acquitted to great rejoicing from the people. "I've only lost my shoe, but you—you've come to save us!"

"I'm your servant, Your Highness," he said gravely, "but as for saving you, we must make every haste."

As the Earl of Dorset—for he was a member of our little party, too—helped the other ladies into the carriage, the bishop stopped me. A great lion of a man, he had served with honor in Charles I's army before entering holy orders, and because he'd always seemed less a bishop and more a soldier, like my own John, I trusted him like no other. Even now he wore armor over a buff leather tunic, a sword, and a brace of pistols at his waist.

"You've done well, Lady Churchill," he said, his polished breastplate gleaming in the half-light. "You've secured Her Highness's safety with your brave action this night, and helped our cause no end. Her Highness is fortunate in her friendship with you."

I was thankful that the night hid my flush. The bishop was more of this world than the next, true, but I'd no notion whether he understood the true depth of my friendship with the princess; most clergymen would regard it as a barbarous sin. "Her Highness is most dear to me."

"She is most dear to us all," he said, betraying nothing. "Your husband will be proud of your efforts here tonight."

"You have heard from General Lord Churchill?" I asked eagerly. "You have word from him?"

"Not from him, but of him," the bishop said with great satisfaction. "Two nights ago, he and His Highness Prince George left the king, and are now safe with the Prince of Orange. Four hundred men left with them, and once word had spread that General Lord Churchill had gone, many others deserted as well. God is on our side, my lady. There's no doubt of that."

Relief swept over me, so palpable that I felt faint from it, and had to grasp the bishop's arm to stop myself from falling. "Then we are succeeding?"

"We are, my lady," he said, handing me gallantly into the carriage, "though the danger is still great. The sooner we leave this place, the better for us all."

We drove to the bishop's house in the City, and stopped there to dine and to rest until just before dawn. With armed guards atop the carriage, we then resumed our journey, traveling from London through Epping Forest to Lord Dorset's house, Copt Hall. Because we'd no notion of how close the king's soldiers might be, we kept a furious pace, changing horses often at private houses instead of public inns. At each stop, the bishop asked for news, and reported to us what he'd heard: a troop of dragoons hard after us, a thousand infantrymen, a vast reward for anyone who could capture the missing princess and return her to her father, rumor piled on rumor. Nothing was certain. The bishop watched over us like a militant guardian angel, leading us next to Castle Ashby, home to his nephew, the Earl of Northampton, and then, finally, to roost in Nottingham, a stronghold against the king.

Our coach was greeted with crowds of cheering supporters, and the surrounding Protestant nobles—the Earls of Scarsdale, Devonshire, Nottingham, and Chesterfield—rallied around the princess with a force of six thousand horsemen and militia to protect her. We were feted with banquets and celebrations, which pleased and flattered the princess no end. Here at last was the proof that her lonely course against her father's papist court had not been in vain, that nineteen out of twenty Englishmen truly did believe as she did.

James and his dwindling army decided not to face William and his forces, but to retreat to London. There would, it seemed, be no battle between them, or even a skirmish. The country was now in open rebellion, with city after city choosing to repudiate him as their king. The captains of the navy, under Lord Byng, had given their allegiance to William. Great lords offered up their counties and their loyalty, and prayers of celebration and thanksgiving were read in every Anglican church.

After less than a week, with all around him deserting and his power in ruins, James finally abandoned his troops and disappeared into the country-side with his last trusted supporters.

The day after we'd learned the king had left London, the princess and her party entered Oxford to be reunited with her husband the Prince of Denmark. All the secrecy of our earlier flight was gone, its purpose no longer necessary. Now was the time of pomp and splendor, a great show for the crowds who gathered to greet us. Despite the cold, Anne chose to ride in an open carriage, as much to see the parade as to let the others see her. As her sole lady-in-waiting, I sat facing her, the two of us thankful for our fur-lined cloaks and the little tin boxes of coals on which we rested our feet, tucked beneath our quilted petticoats.

In a purple cloak, Bishop Compton rode before us with his sword drawn, at the head of the troop of noble gentlemen, while we were followed by the Earl of Northampton and five hundred horse. After them came the local militia, and flocks of children waving homemade flags.

"Is this not the most glorious show?" the princess asked, her cheeks red from the cold but her eyes as round and glowing with excitement as a child watching ropedancers at a fair. "Oh, Lady Churchill, what a splendid day!"

The splendid days continued. By December eighteenth, William was in London and in control of the government, and on the following day, we were once again in the Cockpit as if we'd never left, the princess receiving well-wishers by the score.

Best of all for me, in London I was finally reunited with John. He found me in a crowded drawing room, and with an exultant cry, I forgot my place and rank and flung my arms around my husband. He laughed, and those around us laughed, too, and cheered John as a hero as I followed him from the room and into the hallway.

"Why did you not tell me you'd be here, John?" I whispered, breathless from the pure joy of having him safe. "Why didn't you warn me?"

"What, and deprive myself of the rare chance to surprise you?" He pulled me close and kissed me with passionate abandon, heedless of those around us.

"You're wicked, John." I chuckled with pleasure, happier than I could ever express. "But because you're here, I forgive you."

"You should," he said, and though his smile remained, the expression in his eyes turned serious. "We won, Sarah. We gambled, and we won."

"For a free England, and the Anglican church." I smiled again, threading my fingers into his hair. "But most of all, for us."

But while John and I knew we'd won, the prize still felt strangely uncertain, never more so than three nights later, when the princess hosted a small party to celebrate her father's flight.

"Sit with me, Lady Churchill," she ordered, pointing to the velvet-covered tabouret placed beside her chair. "You've been so faithful to me that I cannot fathom being parted from you for even a night."

She smiled with fond eagerness as I sat, arranging my skirts about my legs. Not that such arrangement would make much difference in the comeliness of this particular gown: to show our support for William, Anne had ordered all ladies this night to dress in orange, a hideous, unbecoming color ill suited both to silk and to the complexions of women with child.

"How well you look in your new gown!" Anne said, beaming at me. "But then, orange becomes us all, doesn't it?"

"Yes, Your Highness, it does," I agreed crossly, leaning towards her so none but she would hear, "especially if one is a fat summer gourd ripening upon the vine."

"Then I suppose we shall be two gourds on this single vine, eh?" She laughed with her face close to mine, and applauded her own nonsensical wit, her gloved palms patting softly together.

I took the glass of wine the footman offered. This child wasn't due until the summer, yet already I did feel fat and unwieldy on my low stool—a sign, I was told, that I carried another daughter. "You're a merry one tonight."

"Why shouldn't we be, my dear?" Anne asked, undeterred. "We've every reason in the world for merriment."

She laughed again, while I glanced about, trying to hunt for John without her noticing. William had kept him so occupied that I'd scarce seen him at all, either by day or night. He'd promised he'd try to join me here tonight, though by now I knew better than to hold him to it.

But at last I spotted him, there at the door. I smiled, and waved to catch his eye, but his expression was solemn as he made his way across the room to the princess and me.

"Your Highness," he said, bowing deep to her. "I've most serious news."

The princess narrowed her eyes at him, as if she thought him teasing. "Yes, General Lord Churchill?" she asked archly. "What can be so serious that you'd interrupt our evening?"

I knew that such a flippant question must displease John, but he kept his expression as solemn as before. The other guests fell silent around us, jockeying closer so they could eavesdrop without shame.

"Prince William thought you'd wish to hear it, Your Highness," he said. "We have learned this night that His Highness your father has finally departed the country for France with the queen and their son."

"*He* is gone?" she asked, her voice rising high with excitement. "*He* has left England?"

"Yes, Your Highness," John said gently. "Now that he has made that decision, it is unlikely he'll return."

Some of us gasped, most waiting to see the princess's response first. Would she pale from such news, even faint? Would she weep at having lost her father? Or would she show remorse, or guilt at the part she'd played in driving him from his throne? Our king and queen might be gone, but we were still all of us courtiers.

"So *he* has gone." The princess nodded. "To France?"

"To France," said John. "Both His and Her Majesty will find a safe haven with King Louis."

"Louis is welcome to him." She smiled as if that were the greatest jest imaginable: no grief, no remorse, not even a seemly show of regret. Instead she was as merry as she'd been before, perhaps even more so.

"Come, Lady Churchill, come!" She rose to her feet, pulling me upright with her, and making every other lady in the room stand, too. "I'm feeling most wickedly lucky tonight. Who else shall join me at the tables for a game of basset?"

Thus were we all at the end of 1688, and the beginning of the next year: wickedly lucky. We'd witnessed a complete and noble victory of the Anglican faith, a glorious uprising by great England over the Roman tyrant, a triumph for justice and freedom, wrought without bloodshed or death. No wonder the bells rang from joy in every Protestant steeple, and people laughed and danced in the snowy streets as if it were May instead of December.

If in the course of these celebrations, Catholic chapels were attacked and burned, if the mobs in London looted the homes of noted papists, if the waves of refugees now flowed from England to France, if my sister Frances was forced to retreat with her husband to his estates in Ireland because he'd bound himself too close with James—well, that was the price that freedom demanded, wasn't it?

Why shouldn't we feel lucky? We weren't James in exile. It was only later that John heard the truth of the old king's last days in England: how the desertions by the three he held dearest—his two daughters, and the man he'd loved almost as a son—had broken his heart, and his spirit with it. He'd left the country dressed in a disguise he hadn't needed, for he'd become so aged and bent in one month's time that none would recognize him.

And later I learned that my own clever ruse, pretending that the princess was kidnapped, had been so successful that a furious mob had stormed the palace, threatening to murder the terrified queen in retaliation. Mary Beatrice and her little son had barely escaped unharmed, only to be forced to flee for their lives again to France, never to return to English soil.

Now if Mary Beatrice had not gone against her husband's will and asked the guards to stay my arrest—if she'd not let me steal away in the night with the princess, and help make Anne a glorious symbol for the Protestant cause—if she'd not thought of happier times in the past—if, in short, the queen had not shown me such rare kindness, then who knows what might have happened to me, or to England?

All I can vow for certain is this: that I never again in this life saw Mary Beatrice nor James Stuart, and that John and I were soon granted the titles of Earl and Countess of Marlborough, in honor of our services to the new regime. John was named a Privy Councilor and a Gentleman of the King's Bedchamber. Of more importance and interest to him, he was also given the enormous responsibility of reconstructing the English army.

We had gambled, yes, but we had won. Surely luck—grand, glorious, wicked luck—was now tucked deep in my pocket, and I meant to do everything in my power to keep it there.

But luck, I learned, had notions of its own.

Chapter Twenty-two

Anne thumped her fist so hard on the table beside her chair that the silver candlesticks jumped. "I do not care what he says! William is a mean, grasping little toad, and I will *not* bow down to him the way my sister does, not in this or anything else."

Standing before her, John paused, clearly considering another course of argument. The princess had already resisted appeals from her uncle Lord Clarendon and several bishops, and John himself hadn't wanted to be here at all, preferring to keep himself disentangled from the thorny question of succession. He'd already managed to be away at Holywell during the discussion on the subject in Parliament, avoiding making any public comment. But now, with Anne's stubbornness in full flower, I'd begged him to come try his best. Anne had always liked John, and on occasion would take his counsel over mine; if anyone could alter her mind now, he could.

He smiled, his hands open before her in charming appeal. "For the sake of the country, Your Highness—"

"Oh, 'the sake of the country, the sake of the country'!" she fumed. "Haven't we already caused enough mischief for the sake of the country?"

She scowled down at the orange and green ribbon she had pinned to her bodice, a show of support for the House of Orange that we all were wearing, and tore it away as if it were some vile beetle newly landed there. She wadded it into a ball and hurled it over the andirons and into the open fire, watching it hiss and curl into a black wisp.

I folded my arms, the deep lace of my cuffs falling over my belly. "You would not have your father back, would you? One way or another, the country must settle on a ruler."

She sniffed disdainfully. "The country will have a perfectly useful one in my sister, with her husband to advise her if she needs it."

John shook his head. "His Highness the prince does not believe that wise."

"I have heard what my brother William says, that he will never settle for being his wife's gentleman-usher." She sighed restlessly, waving at the tabouret beside her. "Here, Mrs. Freeman, come sit by me and comfort me."

I sat on the tabouret, resting my hand over hers on the arm of her chair. I hoped she hadn't heard what else William was saying, that he and Mary wouldn't be governed by the Churchills the way the Prince and Princess of Denmark were.

"The prince doesn't believe a woman can rule," I said. "That's the nub of it."

"The nub, Sarah, is a question of succession," John said, "not capability. If the Prince and Princess of Orange share the throne and the princess should die first, then His Highness will continue to rule until his own death, in which case Princess Anne and her children will succeed him."

Anne sniffed again, dabbing at her nose with her habitual handkerchief. "William's claim comes only through my sister, and through his grandfather, while my own lineage is direct. By every right, I have the precedent. All he wishes is a chance to play at politics, and keep me below him."

"I'll grant that the prince is not an easy gentleman for company," John admitted.

"He is most barbarously rude," Anne declared. "I've watched him when we dine. He won't speak to you or any of the other English gentlemen, only those vile Dutchmen of his."

"His Highness's conversation is not in question," John said. "Rather, given his persistent weakness in the lungs, it is commonly ventured that both you and your sister will long outlive him."

"And my children." She curved her arm around her belly, her smile too smug, I thought, for a lady who'd suffered so many losses. "William hasn't been able to sire a single one, you know."

When John wisely had no answer to that, she sighed, her fingers twisting absently beneath my hand.

"You believe I should concede this, don't you, Mr. Freeman?" she asked finally. "You believe I'm being a foolish, stubborn woman, don't you?"

"I believe nothing of the sort, Your Highness," John said with the precise degree of gentleness to make her smile in return. "You are well advised to be cautious. Yet in this, you'd accomplish nothing by refusing, but you'll win much favor from the people and from Parliament if you accept."

"My father refused to care what his people wanted," she said with surprising shrewdness. "I would never wish to follow him in that."

John smiled. "There will be other battles more worthy of you, Your Highness."

She glanced up at me. "I should trust Mr. Freeman's judgment, shouldn't I?"

"I'll not tell you what to do, my dear," I said, though of course in a roundabout fashion I was doing exactly that. "You must decide for yourself."

"Then I will sign William's precious agreement," she said, squeezing my hand fondly, "because it will be my child, and not his, that will at last sit on the English throne."

"Ah, Mrs. Morley," I said, reaching up to kiss her on the cheek. "I ask you, who's the old politician now?"

The coronation took place in April, in Westminster Abbey. This was the first coronation in England's history in which a king and a queen were crowned together, to share the throne equally. But it was also the first time an English monarch had shamefully abandoned his throne and run from the country, thereby abdicating his rule and his responsibilities to his people. Was it any wonder, then, that despite the magnificence of this day, we all sensed the undercurrent of uncertainty bubbling beneath the splendor and pomp, the piping boys' choir and the silver trumpets' fanfares, the peers and peeresses gathered from every corner of the kingdom and dressed in gold and lace and furs?

Or perhaps it was only that I knew what most here did not: that Anne and Mary had each received letters early this morning from their father in exile, cursing them in the most bitter and hateful words imaginable. I knew, because after Anne had read the ill-fated letter, she handed it to me without comment or emotion, as if it were no more than a new receipt for lavender-water.

"*Look* at my sister," Anne whispered loudly at my side. "She has let them jam that crown upon her head at such a peculiar angle that it's sure to topple off before she's gone back down the aisle! Wouldn't that make for a sight, eh? All the dukes and princes scurrying about on their hands and knees to find the queen's crown beneath a pew?"

"That would never happen," I whispered in return. Somewhere below us in the great abbey was John, too, though I'd yet to spot him from our perch. "Not to an English queen, even if she is your sister."

Because of our pregnancies, we'd been spared active roles in the coronation ceremonies, and instead had been given a special private box from which to watch. Not only was I grateful in my present state not to be made to stand by the hour in heavy robes, but I was also glad that only I could hear the usually taciturn princess's commentary on the events below us.

"Have you ever seen a more ludicrous couple than my sister and her husband?" She leaned forward, the better to see. "Why, he must be nearly a foot shorter than she, the perfect crouching Caliban at her side."

It had been like this all the day, with her picking and jabbing at the new king and queen to a wearisome degree. From the moment that Anne had shown Mary to her new quarters in Whitehall, they had been at odds over every matter, large and small. Anne thought Mary behaved with unseemly glee as she'd inspected the royal chambers, still filled with many of Mary Beatrice's belongings, left behind when she'd fled. Anne believed the old queen's personal furnishings should be returned to her, but Mary claimed them all with vengeful greed, most especially a cabinet of silver filigree that had been a special gift to Mary Beatrice from her mother the Dowager Duchess of Modena.

"She looks stout to me," Anne continued with a hiss of satisfaction. "I can see her lacing from here, yet still her bodice fits her ill."

Mary had her share of complaints as well. She resented how Anne had openly challenged William's place in the succession, and how her sister ridiculed William's appearance, accent, and demeanor at every opportunity. Worst of all in Mary's eyes had been the arrangement of Anne's income. Instead of paying her a fair annual allowance, or better yet, releasing Anne's income from her father's estates, William had wished to play the parsimonious Dutchman, offering her fifty thousand pounds and payment of all outstanding debts if she would not carry the matter before Parliament.

Now I had always maintained my own fortune and funds, with the perfect sympathy of my husband, and I realized the difficulties that could arise for the princess were she to be so personally indebted to William. It was clear as the dawn to me that William held little use for women and believed this an easy way to keep Anne in his control.

Instead I'd urged her to strive for an income independent of him, and present her case to Parliament. In her interest I had begun to seek support for her among my acquaintance, which angered William no end. The question had not yet come up for discussion in Parliament, but neither William nor Mary would forget what I had done nor forgive the princess for following my advice. While I didn't regret my actions on Anne's behalf, I realized that I'd declared my loyalty to Anne over Mary for the entire world to remark.

"I vow that even the crown does nothing to improve Caliban's ugly face," Anne was saying. "He looks so like a beast, I marvel that he can form a man's words."

"Take care with His Majesty, my dear," I cautioned. "He makes a fair copy of an ape in a periwig, yes, but he might well be the cleverest man in this entire crowd. And now he is king."

To show what she thought of my comment, she drew up her nose and puckered her mouth as if tasting a bitter draught. I feared for her welfare if she continued on this path, for the new king would make for an uneasy enemy at best.

Yet at heart the princess knew better. Later that night, we all attended the great drawing room—a kind of open reception where guests paid their respects and conversed with one another—held in the palace as part of the coronation ceremonies. As large as the room was, the number of well-wishers made it crowded indeed, a huge heated crush beneath the hundreds of candles and the smoky coal fires that the queen, always chilled, had insisted upon. Preening in new finery and old jewels, courtiers and country visitors alike were forced to stand and wait their turn to kneel and kiss the hands of the new king and queen, and swear their loyalty. Wearing the famous necklace that William had given her as a wedding present—each pearl the size of a pigeon's egg—Mary fair glowed beneath the attention, while beside her William wheezed and gasped from the closeness of the crowd, and spoke scarce two words to those who'd waited for the privilege.

Yet it was the demeanor of the princess that drew the most comment. Although she'd been excused from the rigors of the coronation, Anne had attended the banquet that followed, and now would take part in the drawing room, sitting to one side of her sister as a show of unity within the royal family. For Anne, it was a show of her fecundity, too, for she was even more swollen with this child than was usual for her. Her head bowed demurely, she walked at a stately pace to the front of the room, leaning upon her husband's arm.

He tried to guide her to the cushioned tabouret beside her sister's chair, but Anne demurred. Loudly, so everyone could hear—and because everyone was taking care to listen, everyone did—she protested that the stool had been incorrectly placed beneath the shadow of the canopy of state. Refusing to sit until the tabouret was moved the proper distance from her sister's state chair, she was applauded both for her respect and for her knowledge of such official niceties.

To most in attendance this was a pretty scene, the younger sister deferring to the older. But as soon as Anne had settled herself on the tabouret and I had knelt to help arrange her skirts, she smiled shyly down at me, like a child eager for approval. I gave her the slightest possible nod in return, wanting to reassure her.

But over her shoulder I caught Mary's gaze, as hard and hateful as stone itself for having lost the crowd's attention to Anne, and to me.

And there was nothing, nothing, pretty about that.

Chapter Twenty-three

Soon after, the princess retired to Hampton Court to await the birth of her child, preferring the healthier country air to that of the foulness of London. Likewise it provided a useful excuse to escape the intrigues of Mary and the rest of the new court, which in their way likely plagued the princess's health as mightily as did the London air.

I, too, was now excused, and gratefully retired to Holywell until my own child was born. The house was at last as John and I wished it to be, with a summer parlor opening to the gardens and rooms sufficient both for our family, and to display the many treasures—paintings, plate, porcelains—that John had acquired over time on his many journeys. It was a fine, small country house for a gentlemen, with five sashed windows across the front, three floors of open, airy rooms, and a handsome entry with columns and a curving drive before it. I spent that spring and summer often in the garden, as fat and content as could be, and glad of a respite from my duties.

While my daughters were in the care of their governess, making lamentable progress towards becoming the young ladies they'd been born to be, little Jack was my constant joy. Only two, he'd yet to be breeched and still trotted about in petticoats, but already he showed more spirit than three girls put together. He chattered away at my side, showing me toads and worms and other fine boyish treasures, and as soon as he could toddle about he was riding upon his stick horse, waving his wooden sword and crowing in the perfect image of John. I might despair of my daughters, but never of Jack. He was the future of our line, the next Earl of Marlborough, and whenever my burdens at court weighed upon me, I'd only to recall his bright, brave chirp to have my hopes restored.

Thus with great delight I learned that the princess was safe delivered in late July of a son of her own. Unlike his unhappy predecessors, this child appeared full of vigorous life. He was soon christened William Henry by Bishop Compton, and made Duke of Gloucester by his godfather the king—the first male Protestant heir to the throne in many, many years. I rejoiced with my friend, though my own news, when it came, was not quite as splendid: instead of a brother for Jack, I was brought to bed of yet another daughter, Mary, with the queen graciously standing as her godmother.

Once again, John was away for another of our children's births. As he'd predicted, William had wasted no time in making war upon France, through a coalition of several countries: Spain, Prussia, Sweden, Holland, Austria, and Germany all sent men, with the English troops under my husband's command. By reputation the English were held in slight regard by the other armies, but John had insisted on discipline and respect within his ranks, and his men surprised the others in the coalition with their bravery.

But though John was praised for his leadership and ability, he still felt underappreciated by William, and I could sense his discontent in every letter I had from him. For William to underemploy a general of John's abilities was, to me, a most grievous disgrace, both to the country and my husband, and I urged John to remain steadfast. While my lying-in days were dwindling and my return to court was imminent, I tried to encourage him from afar; given William's ambitions, there were bound to be other wars, and other chances for glory.

Chapter Twenty-four

I found Anne alone in her cabinet, her small walnut desk covered with papers like drifts of old snow. She held her pen over the sheets, clearly unsure when or how to attack them.

"Oh, my dear, you startled me!" She twisted her chair around towards me, covering as much of the papers as she could with her hands and arms—as guilty a pose as ever I'd seen. Her eyes were red-rimmed, either from her usual strain from reading, or from weeping, or perhaps both.

"Is there some way that I might help?" Since I often wrote her letters for her, it was unusual that she hadn't asked me earlier to tend to this correspondence.

But she only shook her head, then pressed her hand over her mouth to stifle a sob. "Oh, no—no one can help me outside the king, and he—he's far too hard-hearted against me."

"What are you saying, sweet?" At once I came to put my arm around her shoulder, already suspecting the worst since it involved William. "Whatever do you mean?"

"I mean that my little family has nothing to live upon!" She shoved the papers with her hand, sheets scattering to the floor. "Until Parliament decides upon an income for me, I have nothing. *That* is what William says these papers mean—by his reckoning I am worse than a penniless woman in the street."

I glanced swiftly over the pages left on the desk: rows and columns of figures in the tiny, overtidy hands of a legion of scriveners and clerks, made purposefully incomprehensible for someone like poor Anne. "This came from His Majesty?"

"From his offices, yes. He sent them to me, for my review, and for me to see how little I have to my name." She pressed her palms to her forehead and squeezed her eyes shut. "Oh, what am I to *do*?"

"You may wail if you wish," I said, "but that will solve nothing. Now come, tell me these troubles, and I'll do my best to relieve them."

She fumbled for her handkerchief in her pocket. "You know how William refused me Richmond, even after I begged for it on behalf of my boy?"

"Because the Villiers pack had their greedy claws in it." Anne had desperately wanted a home in the country for her infant son, whose health could not bear the rigors of London. Who with any heart would fail to understand such a desire? She'd asked William to grant her the palace at Richmond, where she'd spent much of her own childhood. But instead William claimed members of the Villiers family already held the rights to the palace, and he'd refused her with his typically blunt ill feeling.

"Then you recall how I've been forced instead to make do, and rent Lord Craven's house, near Kensington," Anne said, squeezing the handkerchief into a tight ball in her palm. "The costs of that property are very dear—very dear. And now these mean letters tell me I've nothing left to pay them, or for the support for my husband or my child!"

I remembered how often King James had paid his daughter's gaming debts, substantial sums that would no longer be forthcoming. "Do you owe that much from the tables?" I asked gently. "Any outstanding sums from gaming?"

"No!" she cried, with the indignation of the truly guilty. "That is, no more than any other lady!"

I let that pass. William didn't play, and he'd disapprove of any gaming debt, whether it was five pounds or ten thousand. "I know that Parliament is dawdling over deciding your income—"

"They *are*," she said, seizing on that excuse. "But even worse is how William refuses to discuss my share of my father's fortune!"

Now this was news, and not of a good kind, either. When James had fled, his properties as a private individual should have reverted to Mary and to Anne. "Why won't His Majesty discuss it? The rest of England does. I've heard the income from your father's Irish lands alone was close to one hundred twenty thousand pounds a year. Your sister can grant her half to His Highness if she wishes, but by rights you are entitled to half— *your* half."

"He says it's his to manage, not mine."

"Then His Majesty is barbarously mistaken," I said, my temper warming on her behalf. "If he feels you cannot manage such matters yourself, then surely your husband might do it for you."

"He has nothing but contempt for the prince," she said, rightly wounded. "His Majesty says even less to my husband than to me."

"Surely if you went to Her Majesty—"

"My sister will only obey her husband," Anne said tartly, "in this and in all other things. She will never take my side against her wretched Caliban. She's every bit as furious as he is that I went to Parliament about my income."

"What, instead of groveling at his feet with a begging bowl, grateful for any scraps he tosses your way?" I swept my hand across the piled papers, scattering them to the floor. "Sending this rubbish is only one more way he can show his contempt of you, and the prince, too. Likely these papers were designed to be so willfully confusing that they'd make no more sense to the Lord of the Exchequer than to us."

She scowled down at the papers around her feet, her lower lip jutting out with frustration. "But what can I do? What recourse do I have when the king himself is cheating me of what is mine?"

"You have the gentlemen of Parliament," I said firmly. "That's why Lord Marlborough and I urged you to turn to them. While at present I can't fathom a lawful way to pry your money from His Majesty's greedy fists—at least not yet—I can urge Parliament to make more haste with their decision regarding your income."

"You can?" she asked, her face twisted with doubt. "You would do that?"

"I would, sweet," I said, running my fingertips lightly over her face to smooth away her uncertainty. "You know me. You know I would, and I will."

She opened her hand, the crumpled handkerchief unfurling in her palm like a linen flower. "But to challenge the king for my sake—"

"For you, dear Mrs. Morley." I smiled. I welcomed the opportunity to serve my princess, and though it might not have been the wisest course for my career, I couldn't help but relish the chance to be the irritant burr beneath the king's saddle for treating her so ill. "For you, I'd do that, and infinitely, infinitely more."

Soon after, I received a most surprising visitor in Jermyn Street, but one whom of course I welcomed.

"Lord Shrewsbury, I am honored." I swept my curtsey to the duke, my smile gracious as I motioned for him to sit across from me. It was not every day that I received a secretary of state in my parlor, nor was I in the habit of inviting gentleman as handsome as Lord Shrewsbury to call upon me alone. "Might I offer you refreshment?"

"Thank you, no, Lady Marlborough." He waited with showy gallantry for me to sit first, then drew his own chair closer to mine. He smiled warmly, the way men do when they are confident in their power and their appearance; there were reasons aplenty for Shrewsbury to be called "the King of Hearts," and so many ladies in his life that at thirty he'd still not settled upon one for his duchess. "At least I flatter myself that you've not asked me here solely to pour me a dish of tea."

I smiled in return, for we both understood the rules of this little game. On his account, I'd taken great care with my toilette and was dressed with elegant nonchalance in a dark red gown, simply cut but tight-laced, and beguilingly low in the bodice. "Forgive me for speaking plain, my lord, but it was you who wished to address me."

"Ahh, that's right," he said, tapping his forehead as if to shake the memory free. "You declined to call upon me, preferring that I come here to you."

"It was more seemly this way, my lord."

"Oh, of course," he said, shifting his weight in his chair so it would appear his arm brushed my hand by accident. "And of course Lord Marlborough knows I am here this morning."

"He does," I said, though John didn't, being so occupied with his duties with the army that he was seldom in London. "We trust one another implicitly, you see, as husbands and wives should."

The duke nodded, his hand now brushing across mine. "Lord Marlborough is most fortunate to have the trust of such a beautiful wife."

"He is," I said. "But I believe, my lord, that you came to discuss not my husband, but Her Highness the Princess of Denmark."

"Then tell me, Lady Marlborough." He nodded absently, his dark eyes beneath straight black brows shifting from my face to my breasts. "Does Her Highness trust you with the same freedom as does your husband?"

"She does, my lord."

His lips twitched with interest. "Such . . . *freedom* between two ladies is a rare and glorious thing."

"It is indeed, my lord." I drew my hand away from his, folding it with its mate in my lap. Why was it, I wondered wearily, that gentlemen found the devoted friendship I shared with the princess to be so titillating? "Her Highness regards me with every confidence, which is why she has entrusted me to discuss her affairs with you now."

He smiled again, more slyly, I thought. "Then perhaps you can advise her to cease her foolish appeal to Parliament for an income, and instead accept what His Majesty has so generously offered."

I smiled, too, though with none of his smugness. "How can I advise her to accept anything that is not in her best interests?"

"But it is, Lady Marlborough," he said. "For how better to please the princess than by pleasing His Majesty?"

"My first loyalty is to Her Highness."

He chuckled softly. "His Majesty believes that in your zeal to serve the princess, you have misled her away from the natural protection of His Majesty, as her kind and lawful brother by marriage."

"A kind brother of any sort would see that his sister was not left without funds," I said, "which is exactly what the king has repeatedly done to Her Highness and her family. If she accepted his offer of an income now, then what guarantee would she have in the future that he would not perhaps 'forget' his payment to her again?"

"While His Majesty's word of honor is sufficient for me, I can understand the princess's uneasiness," the duke said, laying his hand over his heart. "Thus I'll offer my own honor as well. If the king should ever break his word to the princess, then I shall resign my office."

"And what good, pray, would come of that, my lord?" I widened my eyes with incredulity. "What hope could she possibly have of her funds if you are no longer in office? Forgive me, my lord, but I can certainly offer her more useful guidance than to accept an offer as rotten as that one."

"You are frank in your judgement, Lady Marlborough."

"I am when it serves Her Highness."

"You would prefer that Her Highness be used for the political gain of others?" he asked, his tone growing sharper. "This appeal to the Commons for an independent income will only result in making her vulnerable, a figurehead for those who will seek to separate her from the king."

"Her Highness is the heir, and her son after that," I said, my tone still as pleasant as can be. I'd expected this sort of lecture, and I was determined not to tumble if he baited me, or to lose my temper. "I pray that His Majesty has not forgotten that Her Highness signed away her imminent right to the throne to let His Majesty be crowned first. Perhaps for the sake of the country as well as the princess herself, a show of independence from Her Highness is not such a great evil."

Impatiently he drummed his fingers on the paw-shaped arm of his chair. "His Majesty is aware of how you have personally solicited the support of certain members of Parliament on behalf of the princess. He is also aware of how you have sought to divide the princess from her sister the queen, and how you hope to better your own position through this interfering mischief."

I tipped my head to one side, my pearl earring swinging gently against the side of my throat. "Is that why you have called, my lord? To order me to cease my 'interfering mischief'?"

"My advice, Lady Marlborough, is to recall that the proper sphere for a woman's interests does not include politics," he said, rising. "Countering His Majesty's wishes for your own sport is a dangerous amusement, both to you and to the princess you pretend to serve."

I stood as well, my smile still in place. "I thank you for your kind advice, my lord," I said cheerfully, holding my hand out to him. "Though as a woman, it may not be within my sphere to act upon it."

His expression darkened, all gallantry gone. "Then I'll trouble you no more, Lady Marlborough, beyond wishing you the fate you deserve."

I curtseyed, the hems of my skirts whispering over the floor. "Good day to you, too, my lord," I called after him as he left, "and might I wish the same for you!"

Soon after, the Commons did what we had prayed and hoped, and voted Anne an independent income of fifty thousand pounds a year. This was ironically the same amount that William had offered, but the fact that the grant would come from Parliament instead of the king's ever-tight pockets was cause enough for rejoicing in the Cockpit. With the most humble thanks, Anne raised my own salary from four hundred pounds to a thousand pounds a year, then begged that it never be mentioned between us as friends again.

But the resolution made the king and queen look grasping and greedy with the princess, while the princess, who already had a greater popularity among the people than her sister, was seen as being forced to turn to the Commons as a desperate move. A family disagreement had swelled to a public disgrace. William tried his best to move forward, but Mary refused to forget the shame she believed her sister had brought to the crown.

It was my belief that the sisters would have quarreled without this provocation. Each was as different from the other as possible, with Anne shy and stubborn, while Mary was given to vivacity and constant chatter. Each irritated the other no end, and combined with the fact that they had lived apart, in different countries and circumstances, for the past ten years, there was little common between them save their blood.

But most of all, Mary blamed everything ill that happened between her and her sister upon me.

The entire court knew it, too, after a small supper during Christmas week. The Banqueting House was decorated with greenery for the season, and the musicians in the gallery were playing the merry old songs from the days of Queen Elizabeth.

I was with child again and so weary I could scarce keep open my eyes, but still I stood behind the princess's chair at the high table, my place until the end of the long meal. From there I could see the usual inequities piled upon my friend. I watched how the queen purposefully made silly jests and conversations that excluded her sister, and instead left her to sit in shy, uncomfortable silence, staring at her plate. I saw how the king, too, showed her little regard, plucking the choicest fruit from the bowl for himself and his wife, while dropping only a bruised pear and a bedraggled bunch of grapes onto Anne's plate.

At last the queen rose, signaling that Anne and the other ladies should withdraw with her. I helped Anne from her chair and began to accompany her, as was my duty.

"Lady Marlborough," the queen said. "You will remain."

Stunned, I stepped back and bowed my head in silent acquiescence. What choice, truly, did I have?

But now it was Anne who surprised me. "Lady Marlborough attends me, Your Majesty."

All around us conversation stopped and the clink of forks against plates stilled, with every head craning to see and hear what came next.

The queen stared down at her sister, giving an imperious twitch to her skirts. "Lady Marlborough is not to join us."

Anne's chin wobbled. "Lady Marlborough is *my lady,* and my friend."

"Your *friend?*" Mary's voice rose, capped with a short, scornful bark of a laugh. "Who are your friends, but the king and I?"

Anne's eyes were growing watery, and I prayed for her sake she'd not shed her tears before her sister. "If Lady Marlborough is not permitted to attend me, then I will not come, either."

"You would refuse me, Princess?" asked Mary, incredulous, as disbelieving that Anne would dare challenge her as by the challenge itself. "You would counter my wish?"

Anne flushed with misery. "I—I am unwell, Your Majesty. Pray excuse me for this night."

Mary's dark eyes filled with disgust as she looked from her sister to me and back again.

"Then go," she ordered. "Leave me. *Now.*"

As soon as we were in the hall and out of sight of the others, Anne grabbed my hand, squeezing it reverently to her breast as the tears now slipped down her cheeks.

"Oh, that she would try to order you apart from me!" she cried. "That she would send you *away*."

"Hush, hush," I said softly, troubled for other reasons. I'd not soon forget the rancor in the queen's eyes when she'd looked back to me. "It was brave of you to do that, yes, but you needn't have crossed Her Majesty like that, not over me."

"Her—her *meanness* left me no choice but to defend you." She shook her head, scattering tears over my hand. "My own Mrs. Freeman! You have done so much for me, that surely I must do this little thing for you!"

"Yet I would not come between you and your sister," I warned. "It's not a wise place for either of us."

"My sister and her obstinancy have put you there, not I." She frowned, all fierce determination, while her fingers tightened around mine with the desperate strength of a foundering woman. "I won't let her treat you ill. Know that, my dearest. Look into my heart, and know that nothing will ever induce me to part with you."

Chapter Twenty-five

The summer night had clung to the heat of the day, with a sky the velvety deep blue that never comes to London. The air was soft and ripe with the scent of the honeysuckle that twined over the old stone walls around our house, and I let my shawl drop into the crooks of my elbows as I made my way across the lawns. My loose linen smock fluttered around my bare legs as I walked slowly, my breath short and my too-full breasts aching beneath their bindings. My second son Charles had been born only five days before, and if I'd any sense I'd have still been in my lying-in bed.

I avoided the long splash of lantern light from the stable's open doors, instead slipping inside through the shadows. Spread out over the floor were John's pistols and swords, his powder horn and tinderbox and fresh lead for casting balls, his armor—new-polished bright as sterling—and spurs and even the heavy saddle and harness his horse wore into battle. John always put off packing until the last night, and now he and his two menservants were checking everything one final time before it was loaded into the trunks for the wagon to take in the morning.

"Lady Marlborough!" The younger servant spied me first, doubling over into an ungainly bow that was echoed by the second man. John hurried towards me, offering his arm for support.

"Sarah, Sarah, what are you doing here?" He flipped a blanket open over a bench, guiding me to it. "You belong in bed."

"I came to find you." I tried not to wince as I sat on the hard bench. "Are you almost done?"

He looked past me out at the moon to gauge the hour, and sighed. "To be honest, I'll likely be toiling here until dawn."

"Then I'll keep you company." I tried to smile, as if both my body and my heart didn't ache. He stood with his sleeves rolled up over his forearms and the collar open at the throat, his shadow stretching out long behind him into the night as if half gone from home already.

"Do you think that wise, Sarah?" he said, frowning with concern. "You'd be more at ease in bed."

"I'd be more at ease if you were in bed beside me," I said. "I'll have time enough to rest tomorrow."

He sighed, knowing better than to try to persuade me. He nodded to dismiss the servants, and we were left alone with only the sleepy, snuffling breathing of the horses in their stalls behind us.

"You should have those men pack for you, John," I said as they left. "What's the use in keeping servants if you let them be idle?"

"Because I'm the one going to fight in Ireland, not the servants." He crouched down and drew his sword from the scabbard with a screech of steel, then critically studied the blade. "If something's mislaid or left behind, then I'll suffer on the battlefield, not some plump fellow here on the Holywell staff."

"Don't make jests like that to tempt the fates." I twisted my hands in the corners of my shawl. "You know I fear for you each time you must go to war."

"And you know I always come back to you, dear soul." He smiled at me over the sword's blade, his face dimly reflected in the steel. "I worry for you, too, each time you're brought to bed of another child, yet you always survive and prosper, more beautiful than before."

"That's rubbish, John," I scoffed, though he was right about the dangers we each faced. I'd made my will anew before Charles's birth, and John had done the same this week, before he left for war. "Next you'll claim I drop your children in the straw like an old broodmare, here in the stable."

He winked slyly, the same way he'd done when we'd met fifteen years before. "But you *are* beautiful, dear wife."

"More rubbish," I said, though foolishly pleased that he'd still call me beautiful when I so clearly wasn't. "I'm fat and soft as dough left too long to rise, with my hair plaited like a farmer's wife's."

"Still my beauty." He laughed, though his smile didn't last. "You knew I was a soldier when you wed me, love. It's my duty to go to that wretched island, though God knows I wish the king had realized that earlier, too."

"You're going soon enough." While John had been away fighting the French as part of the coalition, James had assembled an army of supporters in France and sailed for Ireland as a toehold to Britain. He'd been greeted warmly there, his Jacobite forces swelling with recruits, and William himself had headed the English troops to put down this rebellion. But William had pointedly left John from his group of leaders, instead making Dutchmen with half John's experience into generals. Only now, months into the campaign, had John finally been called to join them. "There'll be plenty of glory left for you."

"No glory in this," he said with disgust. "At least not for anyone besides William."

There *was* much ignoble about this war. It was Monmouth's rebellion all over again, placing John across the field from old friends and acquaintances changed into new enemies. Among them would be my sister's husband Richard, now made Duke of Tyrconnel and a general for James's cause. Frances had curtly written to inform me early in the summer, then written no more, our sisterly relations broken by our separate loyalties to our husbands and our faiths.

Nor was John's lot any more felicitous. The English army had become a hodgepodge of different nationalities under William, with the disgruntled Englishmen he purported to rule passed over for honors and advancement. Most shocking to me was the bounty the Jacobites were offering for John, captured or dead, as one of the most notorious traitors to the old king.

"What William should do," I said, "is give you the independent command you deserve. Only you among all those pinchbeck generals will have the wit and courage to do what is necessary."

"But William doesn't listen to you, sweetheart." John thrust the sword back into the scabbard. "I could drive Louis himself clear into the sea, and William would still never trust me with any real responsibility. He was quick enough to take my support when he sailed to England, and just as quick to forget it when the crown was on his head."

"I've tried my best to be your advocate at court, and not succeeded at all," I said with regret. "You know my tale. The queen despises me, and the king refuses to acknowledge my presence, let alone hear my pleas on your behalf. The only one who listens is the princess, and she has no real power, not yet, nor in such matters."

"Ahh, would that Anne were queen instead of Mary."

"Anne trusts you as no other man, John. She may love her husband, but she trusts you."

"That's because she trusts you more than any other mortal, woman or man." He came to sit beside me on the bench, looping his arm around my waist to pull me close. "Though for the princess's sake, I'd hardly wish the throne upon her. Poor lady, she's enough misfortune in her life to bear without the weight of the crown, too."

I rested my head on John's shoulder, my hand curled upon his thigh, and watched the white-winged moths that dove and danced through the lantern light. Anne had miscarried yet another baby shortly before I'd left court; she'd suffered through so many such tragedies, grieving year after year, that even as her friend I could scarce recall them all. Yet in the house behind us, our new son slept in his cradle, our other five children snug and content in their beds.

Fortune had smiled on me in so many ways. Would it smile still, and bring John back safe from Ireland? Or would he perish for the sake of some Dutchman's ill-timed orders, and leave me a loveless widow and our children weeping for their father?

"Tell me, Sarah," he said, his voice low with idle reflection. "Do you ever question whether we erred by trading James for William?"

"Whatever are you saying?" I whispered sharply, twisting away from his shoulder. "Do you know what would become of us if anyone heard you speak so?"

"And if I cannot speak in the stable of my own house where only my wife and my horses can hear me, what is the use of being a free Englishman?"

"Then consider what you say, as much as where you say it!"

"I have," he said slowly, "nor am I done with my considering. We risked everything for William's cause, Sarah, even our lives. I thought we'd find favor, yet he has repaid us with contempt and distrust."

"He has also made you an earl and a general and Gentleman of the Bedchamber." I sat upright so I could face him square, with no chance for dissembling between us. "What of our faith, John, our consciences? What of vowing to remain Anglicans, instead of being forced into James Stuart's Romish ways?"

He frowned, avoiding my gaze as he ran one fingertip across the strand of coral beads around my wrist. "To worship as one chooses is a fine thing. But God has blessed me with many gifts, Sarah, and to be forbidden to employ them in a useful way seems, to me, a great and wasteful sin."

"That's a slippery path you're ambling down, John Churchill," I warned, "and all I can see at the bottom of it is mud and muck."

He smiled, though his eyes were far too humorless for my liking. "You always do see things plain, don't you?"

"I see them as they are," I said firmly. "One of us must. Have you forgotten that James put foreign officers over Englishmen, too, French papists who in turn put Louis first? Is that so much better than William's Dutchmen?"

He shook his head as if to agree, but I knew already he wouldn't hear me. If I was the one who saw things plain, then John was the dreamer, and ever had been. He was brave and daring and full of imagination, qualities that made him a leader trusted by his men as well as an unparalleled tactician in the field. But I also knew that with John, recklessness lay only half a step beyond daring, and that the same imagination which could conceive of great triumphs could just as easily turn a blind eye towards any disasters or failures.

"Sarah, all I wish is the chance to serve England," he said gently, "and to do my best for you and our children. That's never changed, and never will."

"But these doubts, these regrets," I said, my uneasiness growing. "Why didn't you speak to me of them before? Why wait until this night, before you must leave?"

He shrugged with maddening nonchalance. "I didn't wish to trouble you so close to your time."

"*Trouble!*" My frustration—and my fears—bubbled over, and with my fist I struck his shoulder as hard as I could. "How *dare* you condescend to me like this! Haven't I always been your partner as well as your wife? Haven't I always been the one you can trust above all others? Yet you would not *trouble* me?"

"Sarah, Sarah." He caught my hand and held it tight, his fingers swallowing mine. "Sarah, please. You know I love you too much for this nonsense."

I tried to jerk my hand free, my breathing coming fast and hard. "What I know is that you're a madman!"

"And you, sweet, are my own dear madwoman," he said with a patience that infuriated me more. "I didn't intend to plague you so, Sarah, or to—"

"Do you mean to go over to James, and abandon William?" I demanded bluntly. "Is that what this is? That you will turn tail and run?"

He took a deep breath, puffing out the wind before he answered.

"What this *is*, Sarah, are my idle ponderings, and no more," he said at last. "I will follow my duty to my king and my country. For you, for the children, for Princess Anne, too. You have my word, sweetheart. And if I do turn tail and run, it will be to your arms."

"If you do, I'll turn you right back." I wanted desperately to believe him, and with my emotions still so raw from childbed, I felt tears sting my eyes. "A pox on you for doing this to me. You know you couldn't if I didn't love you so much."

"I must be blessed." He smiled and pulled me into his arms, and God forgive me, I curled against him. "I love you like no other, Sarah, and I always will. No matter what else may happen, remember that, and know it's true."

He kissed me then, as I knew he would: a pledge, an apology, a farewell. He did love me, and I him. I never doubted that, not once in all the years we were wed.

Yet over his shoulder, I watched a moth flutter before the lantern's flame. His wings beat so fast I could scarce see them as he flew closer to court the brilliance of the wavering candle, closer and closer still. Then with a sudden hiss and sputter, the white wings glowed bright and turned to ash and cinder, a crumbled scrap of ambition and death.

Chapter Twenty-six

Living at court, we were among the first to hear the freshest news from Ireland, and that summer and autumn the news was nothing but splendid for the king's forces. The Jacobite army, swelled with a hundred thousand Frenchmen, still crumbled in such disarray at the River Boyne, north of Dublin, that James himself retreated back to the safety of France.

My sister's husband was among those driven back at the Boyne. Struggling to rally his retreating troops, the Duke of Tyrconnel suffered a fatal apoplexy, and soon after, his estates and other properties were confiscated for his part in the rebellion. Once again widowed and impoverished, Frances was forced to flee to the rest of James's court in exile at Saint-Germain, where, once again, she found solace in the generosity of Mary Beatrice. It seemed to me my sister's life had become no more than a sorry testament to the unfortunate choices she'd made; I'd no notion then that our fates would cross one last time.

But the tale was different for John, who found the glory he so desired. Against the advice of William's foreign generals, he boldly laid siege and captured the ports of Cork and Kinsale, cutting off supplies and reinforcements that came by sea from France. His losses were slight, his victories complete, and much was made of how he was the most accomplished and skillful of the British generals.

Even the queen praised his bravery, and I walked through Whitehall with my head high and proud. At court there was talk of how John was sure to be named Master-General of the Ordnance, a position both powerful and lucrative, or made a Knight of the Garter, or granted a dukedom, or even all three. My fears eased, both for his safety and his contentment. As ambitious as John was, surely now he'd have no cause for complaint.

But after the Treaty of Limerick was signed to mark an Irish peace, and both William and John returned to London, I saw at once that nothing had changed between them. Despite the glorious victories that John had garnered for the crown, William still treated him like some low stableboy, unworthy of notice. There was no dukedom granted, no Garter, and the Master-General's post went to an inexperienced young colonel, the son of one of William's few friends. The king's distrust of John was obvious to all, his dislike equally apparent, and rumors skittered through London that the Earl of Marlborough was most grievously unhappy, and spreading his unhappiness among his soldiers. When, in passing, Shrewsbury mentioned that John was pressing his friends in Parliament to outlaw foreign officers over English soldiers, I knew my fears were grounded in truth.

John volunteered nothing to me and left my worried questions unanswered. Whether we were with the prince and princess in the Cockpit or our own home in Jermyn Street, among our closest friends or alone together in our bed, he breathed not a word more of discontent or misery with his lot to me.

I knew him far better than to accept such an unnatural silence. There must be more behind it, far more, and with each day without a voiced complaint, my dread grew.

By late January, I'd learned it all, and oh, dear God, how I wished I hadn't.

I came to the princess's bedchamber as soon as she summoned me, hurrying after the maidservant with my petticoats flying around my ankles.

Anne was sitting in her favorite armchair before the fire, her head lolling back against the cushions and her eyes closed. Her pale face was sheened with sweat, and with one hand she clutched the arm of the chair, the other pressed over the swell of her pregnant belly. I was certain she was gripped with the first pains of another miscarriage, and quickly I came to kneel beside her chair.

"Your Highness, I'm here." I took her hand, her palm clammy and damp. "Are you unwell? Shall I send for the physicians?"

"Lady Marlborough." Her eyes flew open, her head jerking upright. "Oh, you've come."

"Of course I've come, Your Highness," I said, my voice low and coaxing to calm her. "I always come when you send for me. Shall I send for Dr.—"

"No, no." Awkwardly she pushed herself straighter in the chair, seizing my hand in both of hers. "I'm well enough, at least of what any doctor can cure. What ails me is my sister."

Swiftly I glanced at the other women in the room, three maidservants and Lady Fitzharding. "Leave us."

The three lesser women retreated at once, but Lady Fitzharding remained, her pert nose in the air. "If you please, Lady Marlborough, I must remain to serve Her Highness as—"

"It's my wish, too, Lady Fitzharding," the princess said. "Leave me with Lady Marlborough."

Lady Fitzharding gave her skirts an irritated twitch as she curtseyed, but she had no choice but to leave us alone.

"You must be careful around that one, my dear," I said softly as the door closed after her. When Mary had gone to Holland as William's bride years before, she'd taken Lady Fitzharding's sister Betty as one of her ladies, and William in turn had taken Betty as his mistress. She held that position still, though the cold-blooded William prized Betty for her wit and cunning rather than any amatory talents. "She's a Villiers to the heart, and everything she hears goes to her sister's ear, too."

"And thus to Caliban's." Anne's eyes glinted with challenge. "Ask her back, so that he may learn all that his wife said to me today."

"I'll wager it's nothing he doesn't know already," I said. "Come now, it's not good for you or your babe to be so distraught."

"But you haven't heard what Mary said. She told me you and Mr. Freeman had too much control over me, that you'd inclined me to hate her and the king. Then she ordered me to dismiss you from my household, just like that." Anne paused for effect. "Not *asked* me as she has before, mind you, but *ordered* me!"

"Oh, Mrs. Morley." I'd suspected this would come, but that still didn't lessen the shock of hearing it. "She should never have done that to you."

"She *did,* as if she were queen of all creation, and I were no more than the meanest gnat."

"She'd no right to treat you that way." I sat back on my heels, knowing what must surely come next. "You're her only sister, and her heir. She should regard you with more respect and affection."

"*She* would tell you she's queen above all else, and must be obeyed in all things."

"Then she's left us no choice," I said, my heart quickening. Though long rehearsed, my answer would be a gamble, staking the princess's devotion to me against her sister's power over her. I'd make my little offer, and then she'd be horrified, and refuse it. "For your sake, I must resign my position at once, and spare you the ignominy of having to obey such an order."

"It's too late for that, my dearest." Anne raised her jaw defiantly, the soft flesh beneath it trembling. "I have already refused."

"You didn't." My empty offer to resign forgotten, I gasped with shock. Who would have dreamed the princess would suddenly become so decisive? "You didn't dare."

"I did," she said eagerly. "You would have been so proud."

"Would that I'd been there as witness." What had made her act so forcefully today? I'd felt sure that she and the queen would have continued to muddle along about me, hissing and spitting at one another like cats, with nothing ventured but nothing lost, either.

"I wish you had been, Mrs. Freeman, to see how outrageously she behaved." Her words were tumbling out now in a breathless rush. "She ordered me to obey her, and I refused, and refused *again,* until at last she bade me leave her rooms, she was so angry!"

"Oh, Mrs. Morley, that you would do this for me." No wonder she'd been so pale and quaking when I'd first come to her. For her to counter the queen like this must have taken more courage than I'd known her meek self possessed, but now I—I would be the one left with the consequences. "To refuse the queen's order as if you were refusing sugar with tea!"

"I did, didn't I?" Her smile was unsteady, as if she'd finally begun to realize the enormity of what she'd done. "Like sugar with tea—thank you, no!"

"You did indeed, dear, dear Morley." As much to hide my own discomfiture as to steady hers, I hurried to the sideboard and returned with a glass of the brandy she favored. "You were brave and strong for my sake, and I can never thank you enough for it."

"For you." She swallowed deep of the brandy, then with a sigh let her head fall back again. "I only pray I'll be as strong when she orders me again."

"She most likely will," I agreed, reaching out to stroke my fingers across her knotted forehead. "Her Majesty doesn't care for being denied."

"Especially not by me, with you as the reason." She sighed again and returned the empty goblet to me. "But I'll hold firm, Mrs. Freeman. You shall see. You're my dearest, dearest friend and love, and I will never be made to send you from me. Not even my sister can make me do that."

I looked down into the goblet, at the little swirl of murky dregs she'd left untasted in the curving bottom. To Anne, this was only one more quarrel with her sister in a shared life marked with many such skirmishes, but for me and for John and our children, too, it meant infinitely more: our future, our security, even, perhaps, our lives could be at risk.

How long would the princess be able to stand strong against her sister before she broke? And when the queen finally won—which, sorrowfully, I feared she must—then what punishment would Her Majesty extract from me for my constant loyalty to the princess instead of her?

The next morning, I walked with the princess and her ladies from morning prayer in the palace chapel. The sky was leaden and grey, with the sun reduced to a pale, watery glow behind the clouds and the promise of snow sharp in the air. We kept our gloved hands in our muffs and our heads bowed inside our fur-lined hoods to hold the cold at bay, and our shoes crunched over the frozen path as we passed through the arch of the palace gate with the old tilting yard on our left.

"Sarah! Sarah, here!"

I stopped and turned, my ears so muffled inside the hood of my cape that I wasn't even certain I'd heard my name called.

"What is it, Lady Marlborough?" Anne asked, perplexed that I'd stopped. "Come, it's far too cold for us to linger."

"It's Lord Churchill, Your Highness." John was walking towards me from the palace, his steps deliberate and his face so grim and set that I broke away from the princess's side without permission and hurried towards him. He stopped, waiting for me to come to him, and with each step that I drew closer his face seemed to grow more and more bleak. His scarlet coat seemed too bright on this grey day, too brilliant by half for whatever unhappy news he was carrying.

"John, my love," I said breathlessly. "What has happened? What's wrong? Dear God, is it one of the children? Has—"

"The children are well, to the best of my knowledge." He glanced past me to see if we were beyond others' hearing, and as alone as could be in the yard. "Sarah, I have been relieved of all my offices."

"Oh, John, no," I whispered with horror. I'd never guessed the queen would move so fast as this. "When did they do this to you? How?"

"Not a half hour past," he said, his voice hollow. "As always, I waited on His Majesty while he dressed. Once I'd gone back to my rooms, Nottingham came to me, acting as secretary of state, and delivered orders signed by the queen. I am dismissed from the court and relieved of all my offices, both military and civil. It's done, Sarah. I have nothing left to me."

"It's not done, not at all!" I slipped my hand into his, holding it fast, as much to reassure myself as him. "Oh, John, I won't let them do this to you!"

"What can you do to stop them?" he asked, the bitterness welling over his words. Everything he'd worked towards since he'd been a boy was gone with this single letter: not only his position as the highest ranking English officer in the army, but also his places as His Majesty's Gentleman of the Bedchamber and on Her Majesty's governing council, and the salaries and commissions of close to twelve thousand pounds annually that came with them.

"I must tell the princess at once, John," I said, looking back over my shoulder for her. "She won't allow this."

"This is not her affair, Sarah," he said bluntly. "She'll have no say in any of it. None. I served the king, not the princess, and it's the queen, acting for William, who has dismissed me."

"But Her Majesty has done this to you to force the princess's hand!" I cried, my frustration growing. "Can't you see? She's dismissed you because the princess would not part with me!"

"I don't see that it matters now." He took my arm, guiding me as he began to walk. "We must leave this place as soon as possible. At least we can be home at Holywell tonight."

"No." I pulled free. "You go, but I must stay with Anne."

"How long do you think you'll be welcome there, now that the queen's ordered her to dismiss you, too?"

"Anne's refused to obey the queen once, and I'm certain she'll do it again," I said. "Having you banished will only sharpen her resolve to keep me with her."

He glared at me, then took my arm again. "You are my wife, Sarah, not Anne's. You'll come with me to Holywell."

"And I believe I can do more good for us here at court than tucked away in St. Albans," I reasoned. "If it's my fault that you've been banished from court, why, then it shall be my penance to see that you're restored."

His eyes were as hard and flinty as stone. "Damnation, Sarah, do you really believe that this is entirely due to you? Will you claim credit for my disgrace as you would everything else?"

"I will, when I'm to blame," I said, reminding myself that he'd every reason to be distraught, that it had nothing to do with his love for me. "We've always relied upon one another, John, through the good and the bad, and I've no intention of shirking my share now. Did Her Majesty's letter give you any other reason?"

"There was no need. Her Majesty knows why, as do I."

"Then pray be so kind, John," I said, my voice brittle, "as to share the reasons with me."

"Very well, Sarah," he said, purposefully distant in a way that stung me to the quick. "You might as well hear it, since the rest of the court will likely know by nightfall. His Majesty believes I have undermined the army's faith in his foreign officers. That is true, and I've no regrets for serving England's interests over a foreign-born king."

"That's scarce reason for dismissal," I said, already planning ahead. "Once our friends in Parliament hear of this, why, then you'll—"

"Sarah, there's more," he said. "His Majesty believes I have sought to poison the princess against him and Her Majesty through the undue influence that you have with Her Highness."

I gasped, vindicated. "Didn't I tell you it was so? Now I will go to the princess, and you'll see what we can do to—"

"Hear me first, Sarah," he interrupted. "Most grievous to His Majesty, he likewise believes that I have been in close contact with the former King James in his exile at Saint-Germain. He has learned that I have requested full pardons for myself and for you, in the event that James or his son are returned to the English throne."

"Oh, what a slanderous lie!" I exclaimed, shocked. "How can William ever—"

"It's true, Sarah," John said, and at last his gaze met mine. "It's true."

"*True?*" I shook my head, not wanting to believe such a thing of him. "After everything we've gone through, you would do this? You hold the highest rank of any English general, and yet you would sell yourself to the *Jacobites?*"

"It's not like that, Sarah," he said sharply. "If I'd believed that William's reign had an honest chance of succeeding, then I wouldn't have gone to James."

"But you did go to him?"

He didn't hesitate now. "I did."

I turned away from him, overwhelmed. What he'd done was treason. There was no prettier word for it. I knew, for he and I had already been accused of betraying one king.

"Sarah, look at me," he said. "*Look at me.*"

Slowly I turned back and shuddered, my hand pressed to my mouth. Why hadn't I noticed that where he stood, his head was framed by the Banqueting House's crowned windows, the same windows that King Charles I had stepped through to his execution, beheaded for treason to his people fifty years before?

"Listen to me, Sarah," John said, taking me by the shoulders to keep me from turning away again. "William's popularity is failing throughout the country, and there are plenty who regret what was done. James has Louis's support, and if the French army comes to put James or his son back on the English throne, then William will be done."

I still couldn't understand. "But then it should be your duty to stop the French! What of your honor, John, your loyalty to your own country?"

He paused, each second he hesitated an anguished one for me.

"I chose my loyalty to you," he said hoarsely. "If I were killed, I wanted to die knowing that you and the children would not suffer for my sake, regardless of which side claimed victory. I did it for you, love. I did it for you."

I looked down at my muff and the fur ruffling in the breeze, and fought the tears I'd no wish for John to see. As much as I didn't want to think of his death, it grieved me more that he'd made such a serious decision without speaking of it first to me. "Why didn't you tell me you'd decided this?"

"I didn't want you to know," he said in that same gruff voice, so full of despair that it tore at my heart. "If they ever tried to force you to confess, you'd deny them in perfect honesty."

Such reasoning I could understand, and besides, it was easier to swallow than the rest. William's spies were everywhere, nor would he hesitate to condone torture for the sake of gathering information. I ordered myself to think, to plan, for nothing would be solved by foundering in misery.

"Then tell me this, John," I said. "Have they any real proof? Are there any letters that could be produced in a case against you?"

"Nothing," he declared with such certainty that I realized how foolish—and frightened—I'd been even to ask. "Everything was done through agents, with nothing left to chance. I've danced this jig long enough to know the steps by now, sweet."

"I know." That was some small relief. Without any hard evidence, at least John couldn't be charged with treason. "Then this is the worst they can do to you."

"For now, it is."

"We must do what we can to keep it that way," I said. "Does the princess know any of this?"

"Not from me," he said. "Doubtless the queen will give her some version of her own."

"Anne will believe us over the queen or king," I said. "For now it will be best for her to believe that you were dismissed without cause or reason."

At last I looked up at him. The face that had been so stern and unyielding now seemed filled with uncertainty, and I drew my hand from its glove to rest my palm gently upon his cheek.

He took my hand and turned it so he could brush his lips across my palm. My hand was warm from my glove and muff and his mouth was cold, yet still I felt the familiar heat course between us, the same bond that had been there from the first. Nothing that William, or James, or Mary, or even my own dear Anne did could ever change that.

"We'll set this to rights, John," I promised. "They haven't broken us yet."

That finally made him smile—not much, but enough to prove he'd not given up all hope. "Do you truly believe the princess will continue to stand against Her Majesty in favor of you?"

I nodded, my thoughts racing ahead. "Anne is determined, yes. And the longer she can hold fast, then the more foolish both the king and queen will appear. That's in our favor. If people begin to question why they're ordering Anne about, then they'll also question why a gentleman of your rank and achievements has been so rudely dismissed."

"That's a dangerous game, Sarah," he warned. "You can pull the tail of the lion—or the lioness—just so long before he lashes back at you."

"Not if I'm standing safely behind the lioness's sister," I said. "She'll catch the claws, not me."

"You would do that to the princess?" He studied me warily. "The queen's a ruthless woman, Sarah, and a stubborn one. Sisters or not, she'll gladly put Her Highness through hell."

I thought of Anne's limitless devotion, of how her hands would tremble and her eyes grow bright with longing when she kissed me. She'd sworn to do anything to keep me, her dearest friend and love. But my dearest friend and love was John: would I in turn be willing to do whatever was necessary for his sake?

I swallowed. Betrayal came far more easily than I'd guessed.

"Yes," I said softly. "For you, I will."

"What a perfect wife you are to me, love." He dipped inside my cloak and drew me close, his hand sliding possessively along my body. "Come with me now to Jermyn Street. We won't have long before I must go."

I knew he meant to make love to me, just as I knew I wanted him to. Intrigue was as exciting an aphrodisiac for us as ground Spanish beetles were for a jaded rake. Besides, John and I could be parted now for weeks, or months, or even forever, God help us, if things went ill.

Anne and her other ladies had long since gone on without me. Now I walked quickly across the park with my arm linked in John's, our disgraced heads high as we ignored the curious stares and pointing fingers of those who'd already heard. We weren't surprised. Nothing was secret for long at court.

And the first lazy flakes of snow began to drift to the ground.

Chapter Twenty-seven

KENSINGTON PALACE
FEBRUARY, 1692

"You are certain you wish to do this, Morley?" I whispered, my head close to the princess's as she leaned on my arm. She was seven months gone with her ninth child, and she wheezed and clung to me and to the prince, who held her other arm as we inched our way up the long flow of white marble steps. "It's not too late to turn back."

"No," she said, gasping for breath, her face near purple with exertion. "I've come this—this far, and I'll not—not give my sister any satisfaction by—by withdrawing now."

I nodded, sparing her the trial of a reply until we'd reached the withdrawing room, and she'd time to sit and compose herself before we went farther. Tonight the queen was holding one of her monthly drawing rooms, a formal gathering where courtiers, foreign visitors, and suppliants for favors would be introduced to Her Majesty and meet others of the court as well. Drawing rooms were too filled with ritual to be amusing, a tedious exercise in duty and obeisance. Anne's attendance tonight was neither required nor expected.

With a dish of hot tea brought to restore the princess—the cold, short drive from her lodgings to this palace, now the primary home of the king and queen, had been difficult, with the coach's wheels twice lodging in icy ruts in the road—she watched the maidservants unfasten my cloak and make final adjustments to my dress.

"Are you brave enough for this, Lady Marlborough?" Anne asked. "Do you have the proper zeal for what's before us?"

"Yes, Your Highness, I do." I smiled my confidence, and in fact I was ready for whatever battle might lie before us. Two weeks had passed since John had been banished from court. As I'd predicted, the princess had shared my outrage, while the queen had been outraged herself that I'd not decently removed myself to the country with my husband. Since then, Anne had refused to see Mary, pleading her health. But that would soon change, and so publicly that the scandal would explode like the most brilliant of Chinese fireworks over the city.

"I'm glad Lord Churchill's given you a measure of his courage, for you'll well need it to venture into Caliban's lair." She opened her fan, squinting at me. "What is that you're wearing?"

I stepped towards her chair. If every eye was going to be upon me tonight, then I'd decided to make myself easy to find: my gown was the finest thrown silk in brilliant yellow, with a crimson velvet sash tied around my waist, and I'd dressed my hair high, into loose curls twined with lace after the French fashion. My only ornament was pinned on the front of my bodice, where it would not be missed: a miniature portrait of John, as big as my palm and framed in gold and pearls. I tipped the miniature towards the candle so the princess could see it, and her eyes widened.

"Oh, that's as good as having Mr. Freeman here with us in the flesh!"

"Nearly so, Your Highness," I said, smoothing the fabric around the miniature. "I want everyone to remember how unjustly he was treated."

"No one will be permitted to forget our dear Mr. Freeman," she said, exactly as I'd hoped. "I remind my sister of how unjust her treatment was of him each time she deigns to speak or write to me."

She chuckled with relish as she pushed herself up from her chair. "That portrait will drive my sister to the most righteous fury imaginable."

I gave her my hand. "I should think we were bound to do that merely with our presence, Your Highness."

"We shall," she said, her eyes bright with scheming. "Oh, yes, we *shall.*"

All conversation stopped as soon as the princess appeared in the open door. She was announced, and in near unison the crowd bowed and curt-seyed, and remained that way as the princess made her interminable progress towards the dais where Mary and William sat, side by side, like new-baked pies set on the kitchen sill to cool. I measured my steps to follow hers, walking behind with her other ladies. I composed my face into becoming serenity, but inside I wished I could rejoice, for John's sake as well as my own.

I'd never seen the queen so furious, not since we'd all been young girls together. Her face was flushed the color of burgundy wine, and so tight that it was a wonder she could make her mouth form words. Not that she spared any words for me, nor did she chastise the princess before so many eager ears. Instead she waited until later, at her desk in her chamber, and let her anger flow through the nib of her pen.

And in a great many words, with a great many angry blots of ink—which I saw for myself, Anne having shown me the letter as we lay on her bed the next morning—she railed at her sister for daring to bring me with her to the drawing room, and ordered her to dismiss me at once from her service, and from court.

Of course the princess refused, in an equally vituperative letter the next day.

The queen's reply came not in a letter, but as an order delivered by the Lord Chamberlain: John and I were to vacate our rooms in the Cockpit at once. Doubling the insult was knowing that the queen was outside her rights to make this order. While the Cockpit lay within the boundaries of Whitehall Palace, the house had been given outright to the princess as a wedding present by Charles.

But the princess had already planned her next step. If I were no longer permitted to live in her own house, then she wouldn't live there, either. She asked one of her supporters, the Duke of Somerset, if she might make use of Syon House, his residence west of London. He instantly and graciously agreed, despite pressure from the queen to do otherwise, and at once we prepared to shift the princess's household.

But before we left, the princess had one final interview at the palace with the queen to plead for me and for John. It came as little surprise to me that the queen refused to be swayed, and remained as unfeeling as a statue. Thus we removed to Syon House, as fine a residence upon the Thames as any Englishman possessed, and a far happier place for us than the palace could be.

All of this I wrote to John, in our private code and cant in case of interception. I wrote that our case was progressing better than we'd dared to hope, that the princess was intent on proving her loyalty to me instead of to the queen. I wrote how our situation was often discussed at court, to the detriment of His and Her Majesties, yet with such great sympathy for us that I was certain we'd be soon vindicated and restored to our places.

I wrote that the princess continued to love me so much we couldn't be parted, and how she vowed she'd perish without me.

And I wrote that I missed him and the children and Holywell, and that I loved him more each day we were apart.

In late February, the queen removed the royal guards from the princess at Syon House, claiming Anne had lost the right to them by leaving the palace grounds. The princess said she did not care.

Next the queen sent numerous powerful lords to implore the princess to see reason and dismiss me. Anne listened politely, then told them no, and sent them back to the queen. The Archbishop of Canterbury and Bishop Compton also came as emissaries, and the answer they were given was no different.

From the princess's bedchamber, I watched the boat with the two white-haired bishops catch the river's current for the journey back to London. I was sorry to see them leave us. They were wise and venerable gentlemen, concerned with the good of both the princess and the country. I remembered how gallantly Bishop Compton had served us when Anne and I had fled James, risking his life in defense of both the princess and his country's faith. Could I truly now say the same? For the first time my purpose faltered and swayed with doubt, and I wondered if I'd pushed the princess too far.

Whenever the princess napped, I walked the barren winter grounds and gardens, striving to weary my legs enough to find contentment. I missed the bustle of London and the palace, and I missed being able to work towards the reinstatement of John's offices and ranks. I'd never been one to enjoy idleness; rather, I liked to be occupied in useful ways. Most of all, it rankled me to play the passive role of a pawn in the battle between the two sisters.

By the end of March, the queen was threatening to have Parliament revoke the princess's annual living grant. The princess declared that my dear presence was worth more than any sum to her, and that she'd rather live in the meanest of cottages with me than as an empress alone—the perfect vow, I thought, for a princess who'd never lived in a cottage with a smoking hearth or pails to catch the drips from a leaking thatch.

John's next letter to me was brief, only long enough to warn me against taunting or riling the lioness any further for fear of my own safety.

I went to the princess the next morning, while she still lay abed. Beneath her ruffled nightcap, her pale face was still puffy with sleep as she took her breakfast, the coverlet mounded over her pregnant belly. She'd had the curtains both to her bed and to the windows drawn so she could stare out at the river while she ate. She'd become so corpulent that this was her favorite pastime now, and one that bored me to distraction.

"You've risen early, Mrs. Freeman," she said, holding her hand out to me. "Come, greet me with a kiss."

I kissed her as she'd asked, her mouth stale from the night. "I've come to resign my post."

She gasped, her eyes round with horror as she scattered toast crumbs across the bed. "You can't leave me! I won't allow it. Oh, Mrs. Freeman, don't you realize how impossibly cruel such a notion is to me?"

"I don't intend to be cruel, sweet," I said, trying to remember the well-reasoned arguments I'd rehearsed in my rooms. "And I appreciate how much you have done for me, more than I can ever repay."

"But less than I can ever offer, less than you are worth to me." She caught at my hand, pulling me down to sit on the edge of the bed. "I know it's not enough, my love, but I—"

"It's more than enough, Morley," I said gently. "For my sake, you've made an enemy of your sister and her husband—"

"She made *herself* my enemy!" Anne wailed. "She expects me to embrace that hideous little Dutchman, yet in turn I'm to send away my dearest friend in all the world!"

"Oh, please, please, it's not like that," I tried to explain. "I mean it for the best, for you and your sister and England, too! Please, Morley, please don't distress yourself."

She gave a great heaving sob, shaking her hands in the air on either side of her face. "I—I know you love your—your husband more than you'll ever—ever love me, but I'd hoped to claim some—some small part of your heart!"

"Oh, sweet, you have. You *have*." I clambered onto the bed, gathering up my skirts as I crouched beside her and took her face in my hands. I felt the veins in her throat, and how her blood throbbed with distress beneath my fingertips. "Now you must listen to me, my own dearest princess, and you must believe what I tell you, because it is *true*. You are in my heart, and I do love you as no other friend, and not even this—this *raving* by you will ever change that."

She sobbed again, her face shuddering against my hands. "Then why—why do you ask to leave?"

"Because you have given too much for me," I said. "It's not that I'll vanish to India or Virginia. I'll still and always be your Mrs. Freeman. The only difference will be that I'm no longer part of your household."

"But I want you with me always," she whispered miserably. "My life is so dull and hateful without you in it. You—you bring me joy."

"You'll never have the chance to find joy in other places so long as the queen is punishing you on account of me." I leaned forward and kissed her again. "Let me go, Mrs. Morley. Let me go, so you can end the acrimony between you and your sister. Let me resign, and find peace."

I saw my reflection in the luminous tears that swelled her eyes. I didn't see the determination until it was too late.

"What of the day when I claim the throne as my own?" she asked, her voice low and urgent. "Will you wish you'd stayed with me then?"

"That could be years and years away!"

"Or it could be tomorrow," she said with a strange fierceness. "Their coach could overturn, and their skulls be dashed open. Their barge could sink, and they'd drown in the river. They could be assassinated by Jacobite agents, shot dead in an instant. And then I'd be queen."

She reached up now and took my face in her hands as I had hers. "Be patient, Mrs. Freeman, and wait with me for that day. You and Mr. Freeman told me it would come, and it shall. When *they* are dead, and I am queen, and can rule as I please."

I felt trapped by her hands, trapped by her love. Though the flames of our first passion had long since burned out, the heat had forged her devotion into a force that seemed impossible to escape. "Don't tempt fate like that, I beg you!"

"That sunshine day will come, my dearest," she said, "a day when all England will flourish and rejoice once again. And you and Mr. Freeman, too. You know you won't without me, any more than I will without you."

Oh, yes, I *knew*. My deepest ties at court had always been with Anne, and hers with me. From the first, when we'd both been girls, our fates had purposefully twined around one another. But like the vine that grows around and around the tree, who could say which of us now supported the other?

"You won't let me go," I whispered, a statement now instead of a question. What had become of her tears? I wondered. Where had they gone? "You won't let me resign."

Her fingers tightened around my jaw, the outsized ruby in her ring pressing into my skin. "Unless you wish to break my heart, my dearest, you must never, ever speak of it again."

There were voices in the hall outside, and she looked from me towards the door with eager anticipation, letting me go. "That will be my boy, come to see his mama."

I scrambled from the bed and shook out my skirts just before the door opened, and the nursemaid and three of the Duke of Gloucester's attendants entered with the young prince. He was three now, a seemingly happy child, but it was obvious to all that the seizures he'd suffered as an infant had left their mark upon him. He still could not walk or even crawl, relying on the nurses to carry him about, nor was his speech more defined than a chirpy babble. He'd inherited his mother's splendid dark eyes, but the effect was marred by a persistent swelling about his skull that distorted his face.

"Here's my boy!" cooed the princess, making a nest of the pillows in the bed beside her. With great care the nursemaid settled the little boy against them, but still he flopped to one side, startled and unable to right himself, and began to whimper piteously. Tenderly the princess swept him into her arms, holding him close and shushing him quiet as if he were a newborn.

It was hard for me not to think of how at this same age, my boy Jack had not only walked, but run, and how John had already placed him astride his first pony. Even my yellow-haired Charles, not even two, would tease and laugh and scurry to hide behind chairs. Yet this sad, wobbly little duke was heir to one of the greatest thrones in the world, the only one to survive of his six other siblings. Such was the hope to which I'd tied my future, and that of my family. No, more than that: such was the hope for all of Protestant England, and a precarious hope it was.

"Give a kiss to mama's friend," the princess coaxed gaily, turning the boy towards me. "Come, Lady Marlborough, grant my little gallant a favor!"

"Of course I shall," I said, bending down to press my lips to the round swell of his forehead. "Who am I to refuse a kiss to my handsome lord?"

Behind him his mother smiled her satisfaction. No matter what I might wish, it did not matter, nor ever would. For who was I to refuse her, either?

After a difficult night of hard labor in early April, Anne gave birth to another son, weak and pitiful, who died within an hour of being baptized. That same day, the queen came to the princess as she lay shivering in her bed, weak and feverish and full of grief. But instead of sharing her sorrow, the way a proper sister would, Mary told Anne that she had made the first move by coming to Syon House, and now she expected Anne to take the next move and obey her orders, and dismiss me. Somehow Anne found the strength to refuse Mary again, and sent her away. It fell to me to hold Anne as she wept, until finally sleep came and relieved her from exhaustion and the bitterest grief.

Sitting by her bed in the dark, I prayed for the princess and the innocent soul of her latest lost babe, his swaddling band now his winding cloth. And though none would know, I prayed for my own forgiveness, too.

Furious at being again disobeyed, the queen's next orders came at once. Now anyone who visited us at Syon would share my husband's fate and be banished from court. No one dared come to the princess now, and word was quick to reach us that there were plenty in the queen's camp who rejoiced at our humiliation. This seemed no real punishment to the princess, who was so morose and slow to recover her health after her last birth that she'd no wish for company. For me the days stretched long, and as the spring rushes began to green along the river, we were a lonely house indeed.

Yet our little drama paled before the larger one looming over the Continent. By the beginning of May, all reliable sources proclaimed that the French were planning an invasion of England. James was said to be poised at the French coast, ready to reclaim his throne, and word came to the princess through the old king's supporters that a force of five thousand men would be ready to return her to her father's side if she wished it. I was not surprised that she refused, for she'd held herself apart so long that I'd scarce expect her to go back now—though I'd thought the same of my own husband, too, much to my chagrin.

But the rumors of an invasion turned London upside down. The roads from the city were thick with those fleeing by carriage, by wagon, and on foot, desperate to escape from the ravaging French invaders. Those left behind were seized with a kind of madness, spotting phantom Jacobites in every street and rum shop. There was even a wicked tale running wild that I'd learned William's military secrets from John, and written them to my exiled sister Frances, who in turn had shared them with James and the others at Saint-Germain.

It was a foolish lie, of course, and easily tossed aside. But the next lie— ah, that one had roots that twisted too deep and ugly for me to destroy alone.

Soon after dawn on a bright May morning, two officers came to the door of our home in Jermyn Street and asked for John. The footman hesitated, for the hour was early, and Lord Marlborough had left no word about expected visitors. But the officers weren't friends or fellows, nor had they come to call on pleasant business.

On orders from Her Majesty, they had come to arrest my husband on charges of high treason.

Chapter Twenty-eight

The warder used both hands to turn the heavy key, and swung the thick oak door open for me. For a moment I hung back, not sure what I'd find on the other side. Then I saw John, standing with his hands spread before his tiny, cheerless grate. I dropped the hamper I'd brought and rushed to his arms.

"Oh, my love, how can they keep you here?" I cried against his chest. It had taken me five days to gain permission to visit him, and in that time he already smelled different, felt different, to me. With tears in my eyes, I searched his face for reassurance that inside, he hadn't changed.

"Ah, Sarah, I can't tell you how much good it does me to see you here," he said, his voice the low rumble I loved so dearly. "You know not a minute has passed when I've not thought of you."

"Nor I of you." I blotted my eyes with my handkerchief, determined that his new memories of me be of a happy face, not tears. He needed me to be strong and useful, not full of idle woe. "I've brought you your favorite things to eat."

I motioned towards the wicker hamper that the warder had just brought inside. At least as an earl, John had been granted a chamber that was more like regular lodgings than a prison cell, with a curtained bed, a table and chairs, an earthenware chamber pot instead of a bucket or straw, even several ill-drawn prints framed upon the wall. Yet it was still the Tower, with narrow barred windows and a box lock on the door, and the knowledge that most prisoners accused of treason went from these rooms to the scaffold was an inescapable nightmare.

"You must tell me if there's anything you need or want," I said, "and I shall do my best."

The warder was waiting expectantly by the door, rocking from foot to foot until John pressed a coin into his hand. At last the man swung the door shut and left us alone.

"I can have whatever I wish here," he said wryly, "so long as I'm willing to pay for the privilege. The staff's as obliging as at any inn, complete with a barber, a laundress, even, they say, a French cook."

"I won't let you want." I pulled the purse, fat with coins, from my skirts. It hadn't been easy to collect. John's income had ceased when he'd been dismissed, and though we'd always lived frugally for our rank, it was a challenge keeping our two establishments and six children on my moneys alone. "I had to bribe Nottingham's clerks to be allowed here now."

"Was there ever such a wife?" He tucked the purse away inside his waistcoat and kissed me again, turning me away from the door, and the warder likely listening on the other side. "Now give me what I need most, Sarah. Tell me whatever you know."

"It's such nonsense, I scarce know where to begin." I sighed, my hands moving restlessly across his chest. We'd been apart far more often than most married folk, but no other separation had been as painful as this one. "You're part of a 'villainous conspiracy,' brought before the queen's council. You and several other gentlemen—Salisbury, Cornbury—are accused of plotting to kill the king and queen at the bidding of the French."

He shook his head with frustration. "They told me that much when they brought me here. But what proof do they have, Sarah? What evidence against me?"

"Only the word of some lying parson named Robert Young, who claims that there's a signed bond of association to be found hidden in the bishop's house, tucked inside some wretched flowerpot," I said, unable to keep back my bitterness. "Only Devonshire, Montagu, and Bradford on the council claimed there was too little evidence."

"Wise, honest gentlemen," John said. "And the most honorable of friends."

"But though the bond's not been found, it's still not enough to keep the queen from signing the warrant to put you here."

"Of course the bond won't be found," John said, his expression grim, "because it doesn't exist. But if Her Majesty believes that trumped-up lies like this will be enough to distract the country from the French, then she deserves whatever comes her way."

"The princess fears that she'll be charged next. She says she expects the queen to place her and the prince under house arrest at Syon."

"The princess will be safe enough, and you may tell her I said so," he said. "Her uncle Rochester will see to that."

"Rochester," I said bitterly. "I'm sure he has his dirty Tory hands in this."

"Hush, love, hush," John said, sliding his fingers deep into my hair. "The one I worry for is you. Watch yourself, Sarah. Don't give them any reason to come for you, too."

"I'll petition William before they can." I understood his urgency. "They've no right to hold you without proof."

The door swung open, far too soon to please me. "Lady Marlborough, my lord." The warder cleared his throat for emphasis. "Her Ladyship must leave."

John nodded curtly, though his gaze never left my face. "Go first to the three who refused the warrant, and see what can be arranged to discredit the parson. Then write to Shrewsbury and to Halifax. If there's a way from this tangle, they'll tell you where to find it, and if—"

"If you please, my lord," the warder interrupted. "It's time, my lord."

"In a moment," I said, acutely aware of the fierce devotion I saw in John's eyes, of the four stone walls around us that could be the last he saw in this life, of how swiftly these final seconds together were flying past us. "I won't fail you, John. I swear to you by all we share, and all the love I have for you. I'll see you free, John, or perish myself in the trying."

Yet two days later, when I tried to arrange to visit him again, the first clerk I'd bribed so handsomely had been removed from the office of the secretary of state. His replacement sneered and told me that no ill-gotten garnish would make him cross his queen's order that the traitor Marlborough have no visitors.

My visit to the palace was equally fruitless, and even more insulting. William ignored my request for a private interview, and through his secretary made it known that my appeal would be treated as any other. Instead I was made to stand hour after hour in the long hall outside His Majesty's chambers, packed in among scores of other supplicants seeking a pension for a crippled grandfather, or a grant reinstated for a colonist, or a church living for a deserving seminarian, or a thousand other petty requests. I was the only woman petitioning for my husband in the Tower for treason, yet often the last supplicant called to present my case to the king—and always, without explanation, denied any satisfaction.

The fact that the infamous, incriminating bond was finally discovered in the Bishop of Rochester's flowerpot only blackened John's case more. When the bishop, a scattered, scholarly man with no inclination to intrigue, told the council that though he'd no memory of signing such a document, the signatures certainly appeared genuine, I felt weak with despair and fear for my husband. I couldn't help but recall how once before he'd conversed with the Jacobites and kept his secret to protect me. What if in his bitterness over being banished, he had in fact signed this dreadful pact? What if my constant, frustrating efforts were to save not only my dearest love and husband, but also a true would-be regicide?

Each day I ran between London and John, and the princess at Syon, pulled taut with worry on both sides. I was tortured with guilt over what I did know, and sick with fear over what I didn't, and dreaded to learn. I couldn't sleep or eat, and I lost flesh, my stays overlapping their lacings around my waist. Whether I went by carriage or boat, I was often stopped and my belongings inspected because of who I was, mixed with the constant terror of invading French and Jacobite armies.

Yet when John had been in the Tower a fortnight, news came to Syon that Admiral Lord Edward Russell had destroyed the entire French invasion fleet at La Hogue, and with it the threat to England. Our little household rejoiced, and watched as the footmen fired guns and set off firecrackers on the lawn to celebrate.

"You'll see," the princess promised, her arm linked fondly through mine. "This victory changes everything. Not even my sister's wicked Dutch logic can find a reason to keep Mr. Freeman in the Tower now. I'll wager he'll be free within the week."

I heard the same from John's friends who were working for his release.

But by the end of that week and the next, too, John remained in prison. The parson Young, an arrogant, lying rascal, had so boldly sworn against John and the others that the scaffold seemed an even greater threat. Still banned from visiting him, I figured which tower held him, and placed myself outside the walls. My face turned upwards beneath my sunshade, I prayed John would see me and be comforted by my loyalty, and never know how much my courage faltered.

At dusk I wearily stopped at Jermyn Street before returning to Syon, and there the messenger from Holywell found me. I thought I'd known dread, and I thought I'd known fear, but in that moment I realized I'd been ignorant of both.

My younger son Charles had been suffering from a putrid throat and a fever. He'd gone into convulsions and delirium. The physicians were called, and applied leeches and other certain cures to no avail. The nurse-maid and the housekeeper despaired, and sent word to me that my poor babe was in grievous danger.

By the time I reached St. Albans—ah, the longest journey any mother could make!—my curly-haired, teasing baby was dead and cold.

I waited alone in the carriage, with neither desire nor heart to see others. Rain pattered on the roof, and the famous ravens of the Tower cawed and complained of the weather as they wheeled in the brooding clouds overhead. I'd not share their displeasure: the grey June day suited my humor and sorrows too closely for that.

In this time of disgrace I had been saddened, if not surprised, by the number of people, once regarded as fond acquaintance, who had kept away through cowardly fear that our ill fortune could somehow shift to them by association. This was, of course, only another part of the grand, sordid game that was the court, but by that summer, I'd no longer the stomach for it.

As the princess and others had predicted, the plot against John had disintegrated for lack of real evidence. Parson Young was discovered to be not only a disciple of that old scoundrel Titus Oates, but also a bigamist, a scoundrel, and a consummate forger, finally admitting that the damning bond was his own creation. Even so, because of the queen's determination to discredit us, John was obliged to bring his case before the court of the King's Bench on a writ of habeas corpus, and required to ask his old and true friends the Marquess of Halifax and the Duke of Shrewsbury to act as surety for him.

I peeked through the curtains of the coach to see John come through the Tower's gates, his manservant and another following with his few belongings. He chose not to hurry through the rain or even to acknowledge it, walking purposefully with his head high, as if it were instead the sunniest of days. He was again a free man, and today not even the weather would make him go against his will.

Yet when he climbed into the coach, I could see how these last long weeks had marked him, his face drawn and carved with lines of worry, his coat looser than it had been. He sighed wearily as he sat beside me, and at once embraced me, holding me tight. My face pressed against his roughened cheek, into the stiff curls of his wig. Tonight I meant to love him until he lost that Tower scent of hopelessness, of despair. I'd strip away his clothes and take him to our bed, and love him and love him until he smelled like *us*.

Neither of us spoke; there was no need. We'd both suffered hard from Charles's death. Not only did we sorely feel the loss of our merry small son, but the guilt of our absences lay heavily upon us both as well. The physician had kindly told me that nothing could have saved Charles, that God had claimed him as his own. Yet still I couldn't help but believe that if one of us had been at St. Albans with Charles, instead of forcibly in London on account of the queen's hateful vengeance, then God might have been inclined to spare our son to us in this life a little longer.

As the trunks were lashed to the back of the coach, the footman latched our door shut.

"Forgive me, my lady, my lord," he asked softly at the window, loath to intrude upon us. "But what place, my lord?"

"Home," John said, and I knew he meant Holywell. "Home."

Chapter Twenty-nine

"You see the gentleness of the motion, Your Highness." The toymaker placed his hand lightly on the hide-covered rump of the rocking horse to set it into motion. The horse was a magnificent beast, a dappled grey with streaming black mane and tail, a saddle studded with polished brasses, and red-lacquered rockers set especially far apart to accommodate his new young master's difficulties with balance. "His Grace will be in perfect safety, yet experience the exhilaration of riding his steed."

Lying like the Queen of Sheba on her daybed—she was pregnant again, and as usual unwell—Anne clapped her hands with excitement. We had moved yet again, this time with Anne arranging with Lord Berkeley for the use of his house in Piccadilly. The Christmas holidays had just begun, and Berkeley House was rife with secrets regarding Twelfth Night gifts for the five-year-old Duke of Gloucester.

"Oh, yes, yes, he will adore it!" she cried. "My boy is as beguiled by ponies as any other English boy, Mr. Cartwright, and I'm certain your horse will be his favorite gift."

The toymaker beamed and bowed, knowing that as soon as he let it be known that he'd crafted the Christmas gift for the royal prince, his custom would soar among the peerage and the gentry. Providing toys to the young heir was a lucrative employment. While the feud continued between the queen and the princess, they'd arranged a truce where Gloucester was concerned. His mother and father might still be banned from the court, but several times a year he was invited to come visit his aunt the

queen at the palace, where he was severely spoiled even by princely standards. To me such visits were made with a cynical eye, a chance not only
for the queen to judge the boy's fragile health, but for her to have her generosity made public, with a list of the rattles and other playthings she'd
given him printed in the *Gazette*.

"Don't you agree, Lady Marlborough?" the princess asked, as always
craving my approval. "Won't my boy adore this horse?"

"I can think of nothing he'd like more, Your Highness," I said softly.
My Jack was seven, only a bit older than Gloucester, yet he'd long ago
traded his rocking horse for a live pony. I'd kept it, of course, intending
it for Charles, and even though it was two years since I'd lost him, I kept
the rocking horse still.

My melancholy should have been laid away, I know, but death had
seemed to haunt John and me since I'd buried our younger son alone.
We'd retreated to Holywell as soon as John had been cleared and freed,
and stayed there well into the fall. The princess had understood, having
lost a great many children herself, though still she pleaded her loneliness
and urged me to return as often as I could.

Yet it wasn't only grief that kept me from London. I felt that Charles's
death was a warning to me to cherish my remaining children, and not
leave their upbringing entirely to nursemaids and governesses. To my
constant sorrow, I'd conceived no more children after Charles, and I
feared that nature had deemed my breeding complete, though I was but
thirty-four. I read much, striving to improve my intellect, the better to
oversee my children's education, and to overcome the effects of so much
languish and torpitude spent in the princess's company.

I also believed it best to give more time to John. I could scarce fault
him for the bitterness he felt after his imprisonment, nor his ever-
growing frustration as news of William's disastrous foreign wars came
to us.

Under the inept leadership of William and Count Solms, the arrogant
and cowardly Dutch officer who had replaced John to oversee the army,
the British troops fighting at Luxembourg faced both defeat and stagger-
ing losses. The forces that John had personally chosen and molded into
the best of the English army were nearly destroyed, the majority of their

men killed along with the best of their generals. In Solms's stead, would he have won the day for the Grand Alliance? Would he have been able to stop the butchery of so many good men?

In impotent misery, John could only read the grim reports that came to him, mourning the losses of so many friends and fellow officers, and cursing the stubbornness of William to continue on so futile and costly a path of warfare. John offered his services and his loyalty to William on behalf of the country, and was curtly refused, to the outcry of many in Parliament. Other battles, with more casualties, followed—over twenty thousand were killed at Landen in 1693—yet still William left his best general to languish in St. Albans.

I'd one last private trial for myself at this time. Despite my mother's treatment of me as a child, I'd supported her since the time I'd first come to court, sending her a generous allowance against her every need. In the spring of 1693, her age and health finally gave way, and I had her brought to Holywell to spend her last days with her family. Illness subdued her temper and most importantly dulled her tongue, so that when she did at last find her peace in late July, I was at her bedside as a Christian daughter should be, with forgiveness and sorrow in my heart. Although she left me everything in her will, the sum of that legacy continued the Jennings' family tradition and consisted entirely of debts, which I dutifully settled.

And yet my first role in the great world remained unchanged: as the first Lady of the Bedchamber to Princess Anne of Denmark, the closest friend to Mrs. Morley, and the centerpiece of the rancorous, lasting quarrel between the two royal sisters. But during the Christmas festivities of 1694, one of those obligations was to vanish as surely as if it had never existed.

The toymaker had left us with the rocking horse and the princess had called for a fresh pot of tea when the messenger came from Kensington Palace. Written by the Countess of Derby, the Queen's Groom of the Stole, the note was brief for the shocking news it contained.

"Her Majesty has the smallpox." Anne's face was surprised, but without any other emotion, the way it so often seemed to be with her and momentous news of her family. "I suppose it would be to everyone's favor if I went to her."

"It may be your last chance, Your Highness, at least in this life." Small-pox was sadly almost always fatal, though the disease's slow progress would allow for the sisters to settle their differences. I'd learned from my mother's death not to take a grudge beyond the grave, and with so much more at stake between Mary and Anne, I prayed they would reconcile now, before it was beyond their power to do so. "Shall I write your reply?"

I copied the message just as Anne spoke it, with more cordiality and concern for her sister's condition than either had shown the other in years. Because Anne had long ago survived smallpox herself and therefore was immune, she even offered to come to the queen, if Her Majesty would only allow her that happiness.

Her Majesty would not.

The letter that Mary wrote in return was scarcely civil, accusing Anne of base flattery and false concern. She claimed she was too ill to receive visitors, and ordered her sister to keep away.

Disgusted, Anne tossed the letter on the table between us. "Well, that is *that*. Even in death, she will always be the queen before she is my sister."

I glanced at this latest page. Death had been too close a companion to me these last two years for me to be quite as callous, yet I shared Anne's disgust that Mary could remain so prideful even on her deathbed.

"Perhaps she believes she'll recover, Your Highness, as you did," I suggested. "In the event that she survives, then she doesn't wish the trouble of reneging on a reconciliation."

The princess sniffed with wounded disdain and sipped her tea. "I'll write to her each day she is ill to inquire after her. I know my duty, even if she refuses hers. But I must say that the only agreeable portion of that letter are the last lines added by Lady Derby, paying her respects to me."

I'd noted those lines, too, as well as their obsequious manner. Lady Derby was no fool. For her to add to the queen's letter like that made me conclude, more than if the entire college of physicians had told it to me, that the queen's disease was mortal.

And as the old year slipped away, so did the queen, dying on the twenty-cighth of December with her weeping husband on a cot at her side. Outwardly William had always treated his wife with distant regard, a necessary obligation to be tolerated, yet now that she lay dying, he was suddenly overwhelmed with remorse and grief. Her bedchamber was kept as warm as possible with roaring fires, and the room was close and crowded with scores of courtiers, dignitaries, bishops, physicians, nurses and necessary women. The only one absent was her sister.

Though the queen died in peace, she did not die without controversy. Many faulted the Archbishop of Canterbury for failing to coax a statement of repentance from her in regards to her part in the rebellion that had deposed James. The conclusion of these most pious folk was that the queen's early death—she'd been only thirty-two—was a meet punishment for her breaking the fifth commandment, and failing to honor her father. In the press and from pulpits, Anne was urged to heed this grim warning and beg her father's forgiveness before she, too, perished before her time.

If the princess learned of these warnings and considered them enough to look into her soul, I do not know. But she was acutely aware that now only William and his weak lungs stood between her and the throne, and she spoke of it often. Even in those bleak, grey, short hours of December mourning, Anne's famous sunshine day did not seem so very far away after all.

In our new mourning at Kensington Palace, we were as somber and cheerless as the ravens at the Tower, this small group of us who'd remained constant to the princess throughout her banishment. John, the Bishop of Canterbury, and I had gathered to comfort and advise Anne as best we could.

"It is true, Your Highness," the bishop began. "His Majesty is so overwhelmed by the loss of your sister that he will see no one."

"That seems a peculiar excess," the princess said, her hands and wrists uncharacteristically bare of jewels for mourning as she smoothed the black damask of her gown over her belly, "considering how he ignored her so thoroughly while she lived."

"But it's true, Your Highness," insisted the bishop. "At her death, His Majesty wept so that he could neither speak nor stand."

John sighed softly and shook his head. It was odd for me to see him dressed so somberly in black wool and white linen, without so much as a glint of a polished waistcoat button that could draw the queen's departed soul back to earth.

"Forgive me for speaking so plainly, Your Highness," he began. "But perhaps it might not be untoward for you to write to His Majesty in condolence."

I gasped with indignant surprise that he'd suggest such a thing. "Her Majesty refused to see Her Highness even as she lay dying. Why should Her Highness humble herself again?"

"Because it would be the proper thing to do, my dear," he said with that familiar, long-suffering patience of his that, in times like this, I found most irritating. "His Majesty and Her Highness share a loss in ways that we cannot."

"That is true, Lord Marlborough, very true," the princess said, nodding thoughtfully. "For all that he's a perfect Dutch Caliban, he was still my sister's husband, and my boy's uncle."

John smiled, not at me, but at the princess, and she in turn was gazing only at him. "Exactly so, Your Highness. It would be far better to reconcile over what you share in common than to continue to embrace your differences."

"Forgiveness is a most wonderful grace, Your Highness," the bishop ventured, not helping in the least. "I dare to believe such a sentiment lay in your sister's heart."

John nodded. "A brief letter, Your Highness, that is all."

"His Majesty won't accept it," I said tartly, unable to forget how that last ill-humored letter from the queen had pained the princess. "He will ignore it."

"I think not, Sarah," John said, and again smiled at the princess. "If you would wish advice in composing such a difficult message, Your Highness, then your minister Lord Sunderland and I are at your complete disposal."

She smiled back at him with such agreeable triumph that it nearly sickened me. "Then I believe I shall, Lord Marlborough. For the sake of England, I shall do it."

She wrote it herself instead of dictating to me as was her usual habit, leaving me to watch in idle silence while the gentlemen offered their counsel.

But I spoke soon enough when at last I was alone with John in the hall. "What mischief is this, having her write to William? You know he won't accept it, and then I'll be left to comfort her."

"Not this time, Sarah," he said. "The queen's death gives them both a chance for a resolution to this foolish warring between them."

I shook my head vehemently. "Must I remind you, John, that I was the cause of that warring? The queen would refuse the princess the solace of our friendship, simply because she was so jealous and proud."

"Sarah, Sarah," he said gently, taking my hand. "I should not have to remind you that sometimes it's best for us to put aside our own concerns, and consider instead the greater good of England."

"But the princess—"

"The princess, Sarah," he said so firmly I knew I could say no more, "must decide this for herself."

I still believed the princess did not so much decide as was led, with my husband holding the bridle. Now I did resent this; for years and years she'd turned to me for counsel, and for her to turn with trust to my husband and other diplomatic gentlemen instead was most difficult to bear.

Even more difficult was seeing that John had been right, and I wrong. The king's advisors had likewise suggested that he make peace with the princess, and in early January, she called upon him at Kensington Palace. Because of her pregnancy and raging gout, she was carried up the stairs in a chair to his presence chamber, and then, after greeting, they retreated to his closet for a more private interview.

The results of this conversation came quickly enough. The princess's guards were returned to her at Berkeley House. The king offered her the full use of St. James's Palace, where she could keep her court as if she were a crowned head. Word of this spread quickly, and at the princess's first drawing room at Berkeley House, the crowds were so thick there was scarce a breath to draw, with all those who'd kept away when we'd been in disgrace now as eager as honeybees for a fresh blossom.

Other wonders were to come. From being damned as the source of constant discord, John and I were now credited with restoring the harmony. Our favor with Anne was stronger than it ever had been. While William had yet to return John's military posts to him, he did restore John to the council, and as for the rest, we were resolved to be patient. Our doors in Jermyn Street were flooded by those wishing us well, especially those who had quite forgotten even our names when John had been imprisoned, and suddenly recalled them. We were granted new rooms in the southwestern corner of St. James's Palace, beside the prince and princess.

Some things, of course, remained exactly the same. Despite a public show of magnanimity, the princess continued to despise William, while William was as contemptuous of the Denmarks as he'd ever been, and as loath to grant them any genuine power. But to the rest of the world— most specifically to Louis in France—they'd reached a perfect, unifying understanding to support the Protestant succession from William to Anne, and then to her son Gloucester.

"I feel quite like a pagan Cleopatra, returning in triumph," the princess said, almost giggling with joy as we were driven from Berkeley House through the park to our new quarters—finally refurbished and ready—at St. James's. It was late in 1695, nearly a year to the day since the queen had died. With the guards riding beside us and the royal crest painted on the coach, we did make for a notable procession, and ragged cheers rose from the people we passed.

"You *are* triumphant, Mrs. Morley," I said, squeezing her hand. "And you didn't have to be bitten by some wretched snake, either."

She gazed through one window, and I through the other, and so she didn't see what I did. Chalked raggedly above St. James's Gate was a new inscription, put there by some wag or other: HERE REIGNS QUEEN SARAH AND KING JOHN.

I smiled. Anne's sunshine day might not yet have come, but John and I would be the first to welcome that dawn when it did.

Chapter Thirty

The princess sat beneath the small awning over her chair that had been rigged to keep her from the sun. The day held the fragile warmth of spring, and at my urging, we'd come outside to this palace garden to enjoy the heady fragrance of the first lilacs of the year. I'd hoped the air would do her good and help ease the sad malaise that plagued her almost constantly now. Who could fault her for it? Last month she'd miscarried another son, a six-month babe, and her thirteenth pregnancy.

She lay back in her oversized chair with her eyes closed and her lips parted, resting her head against a small cushion. She could be so still and her breath so shallow that anyone unfamiliar with her habits would surely believe her dead, though I recognized these little naps for what they were, a chance to escape the lethargy and pain of her ravaged body. Although only thirty-two, constant breeding with melancholy results had combined with gout, rheumatism, and lameness to make her a bent and bloated invalid, reliant on four chairmen to carry her everywhere.

I leaned forward to fan away an early fly from the princess's face. Her eyes fluttered open from the breeze, and she smiled. "Ah, Mrs. Freeman! You were telling me of this Mrs. Abigail Hill."

"The young woman wishing a position as a bedchamber-woman," I prompted. "A distant cousin of mine, driven into service by the misfortune of an impecunious father."

"Ahh," the princess said, nodding. "It's good to be able to assist those in need. You are familiar with her?"

"I took her into Holywell when she had no other home. She is calm and quiet and in perfect health, and of such a simple country demeanor that she'll cause no trouble among the male staff." To be truthful, Abigail was as plain as mud, with a large red nose and a pockmarked face, but she'd do well with the princess. Bedchamber-women were raised only slightly more than common servants, and though they had full access to the princess, they performed all the lower duties beneath a Lady of the Bedchamber. "No one will truly replace Mrs. Bust, I know, but Mrs. Hill will be honest and serviceable."

"Poor Mrs. Bust." Anne sighed mournfully for the memory of the late Mrs. Bust, her attendant for thirty years, whose recent death had created this convenient opening for my cousin. "If you believe this Mrs. Hill will suit me, then offer her the place. You always look after me better than anyone else, Mrs. Freeman."

"Thank you, dear Morley." I smiled fondly, relieved to have acquired both employment for my cousin and also a new bedchamber-woman for the princess. The demands of her sorry health made her care difficult and unpleasant, and she required a large staff to see to her needs.

But then the princess trusted me to look after her household, and I did it well. Little escaped me. I found out the servants who tried to cheat her, and the merchants who doubled their bills for royal accounts. I even discovered that her longtime comptroller—and a gentleman she'd thought a friend—had been making up the princess's accounts according to the figures before recoinage, and thereby costing her a third of her income. I also learned that this same rascal had been selling offices in her household, shamefully extorting sums from individuals who could ill afford it, such as the new undercook and the yeoman of the wine cellar.

I loathed such dishonesty, and I wasn't afraid to correct it, no matter how highly placed the villain might be, and because of this, the princess's trust and devotion grew even more. She might turn to John or Lord Sunderland and Godolphin for political advice, but in these years my rule of the princess's household was unquestioned, and unquestionable.

"Do I hear the boys?" she asked, twisting about in her chair. "I'm sure I hear their voices."

"I'll go look," I said, resting a hand on her arm to stop her. "It could be any children from the park."

"I'm sure it's my boy," she said, her face glowing at the thought of her son. "I'd know his voice anywhere."

I hurried across the lawn to peer over the wall, and in fact Gloucester was there, in the lower garden. With him were my husband and my own Jack. To please the princess, William had appointed John as Gloucester's governor in charge of the boy's household and his education, a position of considerable responsibility and honor. By now he'd also been reinstated to the Privy Council.

"Your ears are far better than mine," I said as I returned to the princess. "Mr. Freeman is there with both your boy and ours."

"I must see." She struggled to rise, using twin walking sticks to support herself. Leaning heavily on my arm, we made our way as fast as two snails to the wall. By then the two boys were sitting cross-legged on a long bench beneath a new-leafed tree. Arranged in formation between them were scores of miniature soldiers, which John was using to explain some complicated maneuver. The boys listened intently; whatever John was saying seemed to interest them so much that I smiled.

"What's he teaching them?" the princess whispered beside me. "Mark the fascination on my boy's face!"

"No doubt he's explaining the sort of military nicety that fascinates all males." After his slow beginnings, the eight-year-old young prince had grown into a grave but intelligent boy, more adept in the company of adults than the boisterous games of his peers. He was fragile, almost elfin, his uncertain balance occasionally making him stumble or walk with a drunkard's lurch, yet his narrow shoulders bore the weight of an entire country's expectations.

I couldn't help but look at my handsome, charming Jack by way of comparison. By fortunate chance, the young prince was devoted to Jack in much the same way as his mother was devoted to me, and they were often together. At ten, Jack was tall and sturdy from riding and climbing the willows at Holywell, so full of daring and high spirits that he dazzled Gloucester. I couldn't blame him. I doted on Jack as only a mother could, but also because he would be the next in line for the earldom, and the focus of all that John and I strived to achieve.

"My boy loves to play soldiers," the princess said. "Reviewing the troops with his uncle is his favorite part of staying in Whitehall."

She watched the boys with a hungry desperation. She'd hated having to give her son up for a proper education, seeing him leave her quarters for the palace, where he lived among men instead of women, and had his own household beside William's.

"John says His Grace is very quick to understand strategy," I said. "Perhaps one day he'll plot great battles."

The princess gasped with alarm. "I pray only from a distance!"

"Kings have that choice." She always needed to be soothed like this, whether there was any logic in it or not. "And His Grace is a good son. He'll never do anything to worry you."

"He's the best son imaginable," she said fervently, and I nodded. "The very best."

Sons, good and otherwise, were much on our mind at that time. Not only was Anne's ten-year-old half brother James Francis living in exile with his parents in St-Germain, constantly held up as the Jacobite hope and the true Prince of Wales, but there'd always been speculation that William might try to adopt James's son and convert him so as to make him a palatable heir. Such talk worried Anne no end, and she guarded the rights of her boy with a lioness's fierceness.

Another one of James's sons, the twenty-seven-year-old Duke of Berwick, raised far more mischief, much as Monmouth had done in his time. Raised as a Catholic in France, Berwick was one of Arabella Churchill's bastards and John's nephew, a connection made more difficult by Berwick's constant Jacobite machinations to restore his father to the English throne. Soon after the queen's death, he'd come in disguise to England to help plan the assassination of the king. John was named in a long, false list of noble conspirators, causing the king to doubt his loyalty yet again and continue to withhold his military offices.

One last son was often in John's conversation, too: the heir to the French throne. Mad old King Carlos of Spain was said to be dying, finally done in by his wickedness and venereal excesses. Childless, he'd leave no heir to his throne—a throne that King Louis thought would be quite excellent for his own son, the French dauphin. If Louis decided to seize

Spain after Carlos's death for his son, unifying the two great Catholic powers on the Continent, then England would be forced to interfere to protect the Protestant interests, and be at war once again.

And another war against France was exactly what John wanted. What better way to push William to reinstate him as a general, and give him real men to lead instead of these two boys and their toy soldiers, here among the lilacs?

"He's the very best son I could ever want," the princess said again, as if repeating the words like the chanted beads on a papist rosary would somehow make Gloucester taller, stronger, wiser. "The very best son in all this world."

"Then may His Grace be the king that England deserves as well," I said softly. "The very best in all this world."

Though those outside of court would scarce believe it, the next three years passed for John and me much as they would for common folk. Our children grew with the speed that surprises all parents, and when our friend Sidney Godolphin's son Francis asked for the hand of our Henrietta, now a fair young lady of seventeen, I could scarce believe that time had passed so swiftly. It saddened me to think of how little I'd seen of my children's youth. Because of my position at court and the demands of attending to Anne, I'd been away from Holywell far more than I'd been at home. Our children had been raised by nursemaids, governesses, and tutors instead of by their parents; in this they were hardly unique, for that was the way of nobly born families, but it still made me regret how much of their lives I'd missed. At thirteen, Jack was already badgering John and me with ceaseless determination to be permitted to leave school and join his father in the army, and just as ceaselessly, I was adamant in my refusal. Jack was heir to a peerage, and I intended for him to have a peer's education.

Anne had made an peaceable enough truce with William. They could both be pleasant for state occasions, and then avoid one another for the rest of their days: the same practical solution employed by most families, high and low, with testy relations.

The only subject on which they were in absolute agreement was the

Duke of Gloucester, Anne's only surviving child and William's heir. They both adored the boy, and lavished so much upon him that any ordinary child would have been spoiled beyond bearing. But Gloucester was serious and solemn, grave beyond his years in the way of a fragile child who'd spent most of his life in stuffy palaces among adults instead of running about with other children. William so doted on the boy that, on Gloucester's seventh birthday, he'd had him installed as Knight of the Garter at Windsor Castle, with far more pomp and ceremony than was usual for grown men.

In June of 1700, I celebrated my fortieth birthday, and considered myself well pleased at how I'd done with my life thus far. I'd a husband and children who loved me beyond measure, position and rank at court, and a dear and powerful friend who would be queen. England seemed as much at peace as it ever was in my lifetime, and for a soldier's wife, that was good indeed.

But within the month, that careful balance was rocked askew, and once again I was to bring out our mourning clothes, and wonder at the unfairness of life, and of death.

"I'll grant you're a woman of many talents, my love," John said as we walked together beneath the arching hedges, our arms looped familiarly around one another's waists. Excused briefly from our duties at court while Anne and her family had retreated from London to Windsor to avoid the summer heat, we'd come down to Althorp as the guests of our friends the Sunderlands. "But I'd never have guessed you'd show such a gift for matchmaking."

"They do seem happy, don't they?" Our second daughter Anne and her husband Lord Charles Spencer were walking before us, just far enough that we couldn't overhear their conversation. Yet without words, I could still tell from their postures—she leaning her head upon his shoulder, their hands clasped fondly and their feet in step together as neatly as if in a dance—that they were mightily pleased with one another, and their marriage.

"Not so happy as you," John teased, trying to kiss the side of my neck.

Laughing, I swatted him aside. "Why shouldn't I be happy? Because of me, the princess gave our Anne five thousand pounds more for her dowry, the same as she did for Henrietta when she wed last year. Besides, Charles is heir to a fine fortune and a finer title. What better ambition could I have for our daughter? He's an excellent husband to her; you can see yourself how even six months of marriage hasn't cooled his ardor for Anne."

"Six entire months, Sarah!" John exclaimed with mock horror. "I've been wed to you for nearly a quarter century, and my ardor hasn't cooled a single degree!"

I smiled wisely, and when he tried to kiss me again, I relented and let him. We seldom had the time or freedom for this kind of merriment between us anymore, and I'd missed it.

He pulled me closer, his hand making lazy, suggestive circles over my bottom. "Come off the path with me, sweetheart, beneath these trees, and I'll show you exactly how hot you still fire my blood."

I laughed again, softly, and glanced back up the path. Anne and Charles had passed from sight, or perhaps they'd slipped into the bushes as well. No one would know if the Earl and Countess of Marlborough decided to take their pleasure like common folk, nor would it be the first time, either.

"Come with me, Sarah." John's whisper was low and seductive. "Come lie with me, and—"

"My lord!" The footman came racing towards us, his breath short and the back of his jacket soaked with sweat from running hard. "Forgive me, my lady, my lord, but Lord Sunderland begs that you return to the house directly!"

"What has happened?" I demanded. Tidings brought by running footmen were seldom joyful. "Is there word from London?"

"No, my lady, from Windsor," the footman said. "The Duke of Gloucester has been taken grievous ill, and Her Highness begs that you come to her at once."

We raced to join Anne at Windsor Castle as fast as the coach could carry us. The news that greeted us was not good.

Of all the fears that Anne had had for her boy, she'd never dreamed he'd finally perish because of his birthday. An opulent banquet in honor of his eleven years and the excitement of fireworks viewed from the castle ramparts had led to a sore throat and chills and a delirious fever, then bleeding and blistering and cupping by physicians who had neither answers nor cures. Only a fortnight, and the poor little duke was dead.

I sat beside the princess in the black-draped room, the only one allowed to remain with her and her child's corpse in this last hour before the physicians would come again, this time to open the body to determine the cause of death.

There were countless rituals for royal death, rituals that must always be followed. His Grace's heart and entrails would be removed and placed in a separate urn packed with sweet-smelling spices. What remained would be rubbed with Indian balsam and spirits of wine as preservatives, its cavities filled with more spices, and embalmed and wrapped in perfumed cloths for the coffin. The candlelit procession to London would be led by John, as His Grace's last governor. The body would lie in state at Old Palace Yard before finally being laid to rest in the vault of Westminster Abbey, His Grace forever united with his sixteen other unfortunate siblings.

That was all to come. For now, it was only two women, old friends, silently grieving the loss of the small, dear boy who lay sad and shrunken and all too still in his last bed.

Chapter Thirty-one

I never understood why it was that deaths came clustered together, like poisonous berries clinging to a single stalk. But even before we'd put aside the heavy mourning for the Duke of Gloucester, news came of another death of grave importance to our world, and two more after that.

In November, King Carlos of Spain finally died, and as soon as he did Louis made his claim to the throne for his grandson. French troops invaded the Spanish Netherlands, and with the terms of the last treaties so blithely ignored, William and the rest of Protestant Europe feared what would come next. Yet William's health had become nearly as precarious as the princess's, his body so wasted by asthma and other ailments that he seldom could speak above a whisper, and certainly no match for the rigors of another French war.

"He's done it," John said, seizing my hands as soon as we were alone in our quarters. "At last, Sarah, at last!"

"Who has done what?" I asked. For a man usually so reserved in public, he'd a glow to his face that must have betrayed his news to everyone he'd met coming here to me. I grinned, sharing his joy without yet knowing its cause. "Tell me quick, John, for I must return to the princess. What has this fellow at last done to please you so?"

He grinned, too. "I'd make you guess, sweetheart, but I doubt I'd keep the secret long enough to myself. William needs me. He cannot deny it any longer."

"That's scarce a secret at all," I scoffed. "Everyone knows that—"

"But everyone doesn't know that he's appointed me commander in chief again."

I gasped, shocked. "He *has*?"

"He has, this very day." He grabbed my face in both his hands and kissed me hard and fast. "Commander in chief, Sarah, as we've prayed and hoped!"

I flung my arms around his neck, holding him tight. Nearly ten years had passed since his offices had been so unjustly taken away, and to learn that finally William had admitted he'd been led by his pride, not his wisdom, was almost beyond bearing. "Oh, John, I cannot begin to tell you how happy I am! To see you in your scarlet coat once again, with the power you were meant to have."

"We've waited long for this," he said. "Both of us."

I pushed back from his chest. "Does the princess know yet? May I tell her?"

"Why not, when all the court will know soon enough?" He laughed again. "But you must be certain to tell her that I'm also being sent as England's plenipotentiary, to negotiate a new Grand Alliance against the French before war is declared."

I pressed my hand over my mouth with shock at the haste of it all. Of course John would be the natural choice for such a position, given his experience in both diplomatic and military affairs and the respect he'd earned from the other countries involved, but it was still an honor to be William's choice—an enormous honor, considering how long John had been hovering in grey disgrace.

"There now, I've surprised you into silence," he said, so happy that he was almost giddy with it—a strange state for a general. "Surely I'm the only man in this land who can make a claim like that!"

Overwhelmed, I shook my head, now patting my hand over my mouth as I fought my foolish tears. Where were my thoughts to begin? To have John restored like this was the final vindication for us, returning us to all the power we'd previously had, and more. For William to name John the plenipotentiary was as good as admitting that he'd be the first statesman in the government when Anne became queen. We'd won by persevering. I was proud of John, and proud of us. No one would dare scorn the Marlboroughs now.

There was, however, another small and niggling part of me that longed to be like any other wife. I couldn't deny that I'd enjoyed having my husband safe near me, or if not by my side in London, at least safe at Holywell. For these last few peaceful years, I'd been spared the fear that followed all soldiers' wives, the sick dread of not knowing and the constant prayers. He could be gone with William to The Hague and away from me and England for months, even years, if the next French war began as soon as was expected.

But I would be strong; I wouldn't complain, or put my sentimental concerns first. John had been called to greatness and glory, and what kind of wife would I be to say I'd rather have him nodding in the chimney corner instead?

"Tears?" he asked, turning my face up so I couldn't hide. "Not from my brave Sarah."

"Tears of joy," I lied, linking my hand into his. "Come with me, and we'll tell the princess together. Though when she hears that the king has changed his mind and called you back to grace, she's sure to believe he's dying. You'll see. She'll vow that only death could thump such good sense into Caliban's head."

As if he himself had never called William a disrespectful name, John's face grew solemn, already practicing his diplomat's craft. "Then let the poor lady crow that His Majesty is dying, if it gives her some vengeful comfort. All one must do to know for certain is to look at the man, or hear that rattling, grave-bound cough of his. It will be a true miracle if he lives through another winter."

"The king is dead," I whispered. "Long live the queen."

He smiled and kissed my hand, his eyes full of the promise for more. "It's almost our time, sweetheart. Almost ours."

While John had rightly predicted the English king would die soon, it was James, not William, who next slipped from this life and into his Romish heaven in September 1701. He was stricken while kneeling at Mass, a most appropriate place, and died soon after with Mary Beatrice and James Francis at his side, and likely more priests than anyone could count.

When the first word reached us at the palace, the princess seemed un-
moved, as if the death of a father were of no consequence to her. Though
others at the court were shocked by her composure, I was not. She'd not
seen James for nearly twenty years, and before that matters had become
so cross-tempered between them that she'd refused to use his name in
conversation. I'd seen the last letter she'd had from him, too, the morning of Mary's coronation, when he'd damned her as an ungrateful and
disobedient daughter.

But the next day came a letter written by Mary Beatrice, and for some
unfathomable reason, this was enough to make Anne weep copiously.

"Poor, brave lady, to suffer such a loss in her exile!" she said, blotting her eyes. "She was always so gracious, and lah, how she did love my
father."

Since we were alone in her bedchamber, I couldn't keep from speaking plain as I handed her a dry handkerchief. "Your sympathy surprises
me, Mrs. Morley. You never did care for Mary Beatrice, not from the time
your father wed her."

"Don't be cruel, Mrs. Freeman," she pleaded, handing me the letter.
"How could I begrudge her my sorrow now?"

The letter was brief but beautifully written, as was always so with
Mary Beatrice. Yet I was disturbed by the way she alluded to Anne as her
half brother's supporter, and wondered that Anne hadn't noted that
herself.

"I suppose it's because she's grieving that she believes you'll preserve
James Francis's claim to the throne," I said. "I cannot fathom how else
she'd come by such a ridiculous notion."

But Anne looked away from me, uneasily fussing with the crook of the
walking stick beside her chair.

"You didn't promise you would, did you?" I asked, incredulous. "You
never even believed the boy was your father's son, and yet you said you'd
do that for him?"

"It was soon after Gloucester's death, when Mary Beatrice had kindly
written me upon my loss," she said with another sniff. "She asked if I'd
look after her boy, and your poor unfortunate Mrs. Morley saw no real
harm in agreeing."

"I pray she's not kept your letter!" Anne always betrayed her guilt to me like this, speaking of poor unfortunate Mrs. Morley as if she were another person wickedly given to dissembling and half-truths. "Have you forgotten that Louis has already chosen to acknowledge James Francis as the lawful King of England on your father's death?"

"That means nothing," she said, still avoiding my gaze. "Louis agreed years ago in the Peace of Ryswick that William was king."

"And what's a treaty to Louis?" I demanded, appalled. "Whatever has he done for England to earn such faith? You know how much he admires Mary Beatrice, and she him. Oh, Mrs. Morley! If he should ever have a letter written in your hand that says James Francis is your heir, why—"

"The succession is already settled by Parliament," she said, as defensive as a naughty child. "Louis knows I can't change that. It's William, then me, then my children, then Sophy of Brunswick."

Her children: a prospect so futile to contemplate that I marveled she'd dare speak it now. Since Gloucester's death, she'd not conceived another child, her poor womb finally exhausted. "But if Louis had possession of such a letter, written in your hand—"

"Oh, Mrs. Freeman, don't be so cruel to your poor Mrs. Morley, I beg you!" she cried forlornly. "I'm ordering the palace into deep mourning at once for my father, and you won't persuade me otherwise."

I caught my breath, for I was sure that Anne, with her great respect for ritual and rank, understood exactly the significance of such an order. "Deep mourning for your father? John wrote to me that William himself is only wearing violet, as if for the family, and no more."

"He was my father, and once England's king," she said, her voice trembling with emotion. "I will honor him in my home as I see fit."

"But there's already outcry against how Louis has recognized James's son," I protested, "not only here at court, but in Parliament, in the streets."

Desperate to keep her from such dangerous folly, I swept my arm through the air, reminding her of the rest of the city outside the palace windows. Although Anne had always been popular with the people, the people would see this not as filial respect but as sympathy with France, and an extension of Louis's imperious declaration.

"You must heed me, Mrs. Morley," I urged her. "I've heard that the few

Jacobites who dare drink a health to the new King James III have been covered with filth and rotten eggs, and tossed headfirst into the street."

"That was for James Francis," she insisted, "not my father."

"They wouldn't have treated James Francis so, if not for your father James II." She'd never seen the straw effigies tossed into bonfires; I'd never forgotten them. "Consider how others will see it if you grant the highest degree of mourning to the king you helped depose."

Her chin rose, quivering with stubbornness. "I *will* order high mourning."

"But you can't, Mrs. Morley, not when it's so patently unwise," I insisted. "When William hears of this—"

"Caliban will never tell me what to do concerning my father," she said, finally pushing herself up to stand on her unsteady legs. I stepped forward to help her as I always did, but she shook me aside, preferring to struggle clumsily with her sticks and prove her independence.

"In this and in all things, Mrs. Freeman"—her pale face flushed with frustration—"I am my own mistress, and will remain so."

"I never claimed you weren't, Mrs. Morley." I grasped her upper arm to steady her, whether she wished it or not. I'd put up with her moods for so many years that I'd hardly abandon her now, not with the greatest prize so near. "But better you save such declarations for the king than for me, who will always support you in every possible way."

"Yes," she said, breathing hard from exertion as well as anger. "I will tell him so as soon as he dares show his ugly face to me. He will not have his way, Mrs. Freeman, not now, nor ever."

From the safety of The Hague, William did in fact get his way, pleading to the princess through Lord Godolphin in London. Godolphin's gentler persuasion, combined with my own, finally made Anne draw back her orders about the mourning. Instead she added it to her personal reckoning of indignities suffered at William's hand, resolving to settle them with him as soon as he returned to England.

But William had more pressing thoughts on his mind. A new Grand Alliance was in place between Austria, England, and Holland with John in command, and war was imminent. William's health had deteriorated further, and John told me the king himself had said that the war would likely begin without him. In February, he suffered a broken collarbone after being thrown by his horse in the park. A more vigorous man would have healed from such a break, but William's fragile constitution could not bear the strain, and so came the last death in the cluster of my mythical vine.

The news was brought to Anne at St. James's in the last hour before dawn on the eighth of March, a Sabbath morn. At once she returned to full mourning, telling all it was for her father, with only the violet trimming in honor of William. Even that, she decreed, would last only until her coronation on April twenty-third, St. George's Day, and the same date as her father had been crowned seventeen years before. No one could cross her now. She'd outlived them all, and the throne was hers. Anne's sunshine day had come at last.

And so, I foolishly dared to believe, had mine.

Chapter Thirty-two

With her eyes closed to concentrate, Anne began to recite the well-practiced words one more time.

"My lords, I have come—I have come—oh, Freeman, I shall make a perfect fool of myself," she cried, squinting down at the speech in her hand again. "All those fine gentlemen want nothing more than to see me as an empty-headed, biddable woman, and that's exactly what they will see."

"No, Your Majesty, they won't, not at all." I came to stand beside her chair, my hands on her shoulders in the reflection of the tall looking glass, here in the antechamber. "They are already impressed that you have come here to address them."

I lowered my voice to a whisper, so no others would overhear. "Look at you, my dear Morley. *Look* at you. How can they think of you as anything other than England's queen and savior?"

She did look, as if seeing herself for the first time, and slowly smiled. The speech she was shortly to deliver would be the first and one of the most important of her reign, and between us we'd considered carefully how she'd dress. It had been Anne's own notion to liken herself to Queen Elizabeth, and the robes Anne had chosen for this day had been inspired by a portrait of that last great English queen. Her robes were red velvet, lined with ermine and edged with gold galloon, and in addition to her crown, she wore the heavy gold chains and St. George's medallion, and around her left arm was the ribbon of the Garter.

"I *am* the queen," she said, her eyes shining with unshed tears. "I may have lost my own children, Freeman, but I can still see England flourish, and be the mother to all my subjects."

"You must remind them of your English birth, Your Majesty." Her uncle, Lord Rochester, a blustering, crude man for whom I'd little regard or use, came to stand on her other side. "That should be the one idea that your listeners take away: that both your parents were born in this land, and that you're as English as any of them."

She turned towards her uncle, and let my hands slip from her shoulders. " 'As I know my own heart to be entirely English,' " she recited without so much as a glance at her paper, " 'I can very sincerely assure you there is not anything you can expect or desire from me which I shall not be ready to do for the happiness and prosperity of England.' There, my lords!"

The four gentlemen—Rochester, Godolphin, her prince and my John—applauded together, and she beamed and preened beneath their attentions.

" 'Entirely English,' " repeated Rochester, clasping and unclasping his hands. "As it must be. As *you* must be."

"Unlike Mary Beatrice," Anne said, running her fingers lightly over the gold chain, "or her son who pretends to be my brother."

Rochester laughed. All I could think of was how, not so long ago, Anne had pitied Mary Beatrice as another mother with a tragic son. Now with the crown on Anne's head and her wicked old uncle cackling beside her, her eyes were dry, and her pity was gone.

"You've always had a beautiful voice, Your Majesty," John said, standing beside Rochester. "Such a gift will bathe your words in glory."

The queen was grossly corpulent and too lame and twisted to walk, yet John had noted the one quality of beauty that still lingered in her. How like my husband that was, and how much the queen did enjoy it, blushing like the greenest of girls!

"Your own words are bathed with something less than glory, Lord Marlborough," she scoffed, but there was no doubting her pleasure in his compliment. "Surely it must be time for me to make my address. Where are the bearers to carry my chair?"

The chairmen hurried to slip the rods into their brackets, while the queen pressed her hand to her chest, steadying herself.

"Have courage, dear Morley," I said, but she'd turned again towards the men and away from me. All that was left for me to do was to join my husband as together we followed her chair into the main chamber where the lords were waiting.

Truly, what greater show of favor could there be for John and me, to stand there on either side of the new queen as she gave her first address? We were the only two thus honored, another among the many honors Anne had lavished upon us since she'd come to power. John had been made a Knight of the Garter and captain general of the army. I now held the top posts in the queen's household: I was Groom of the Stole, Mistress of the Robes, and Keeper of the Privy Purse, and my personal income was now over fifty-six hundred pounds per annum. I'd been given the Lodge near Windsor Castle, a handsome country house with a row of fine windows for the view, and I had ten rooms for my lodgings at Kensington Palace. I oversaw a staff of nearly sixty who served the queen, and I'd also been able to find posts for my daughters Henrietta, Anne, and Mary as Ladies of the Bedchamber.

Perhaps best of all, as Keeper of the Privy Purse, I had been given the Gold Key to wear from my pocket. This key opened most every room in the palace, both public and private, as well as the garden gates. Everyone who saw it sparkling at my waist recognized the confidence and trust placed in me by the queen, and each morning when I dressed I thought with pride of how far I'd come, and the power that at last was mine.

But as well as I'd done for myself and my family, I'd still hoped for more. I was not so foolish as to believe that a woman would ever sit in Parliament, but I still had thought I might have a voice in appointments, not for the promotion of friends, but to champion the Whigs and their causes. Anne had always found politics tedious and unpleasant, and suspected the two parties of bringing only strife to England. Worse still, she'd been fed the Tory diet of rich lies by her sister Mary and her uncle Rochester, that the Tories were the only friends of princes, while the Whigs craved their downfall.

Little wonder, then, that like a turtle tucking its head away, Anne had preferred in the past to avoid any questions of Whig ideals or Tory self-ishness. She hated conflict; it was not in her nature to do otherwise. Once she was queen, I'd believed she'd be as easily persuaded in such matters as she'd been in choosing the color satin for a new gown, or what courses should be served at a banquet.

But instead Anne seemed bound to decide her appointments with a sense of fairness that struck me as childishly simple. In place of merit or loyalty, she granted the places in her Cabinet evenly between Tories and Whigs as if portioning a savory venison pie among too many guests. There was no reason to it, and much that was troubling.

Now as I stood beside the queen in the House of Lords, doubts worried and nipped at my confidence like the shrillest of harpies. With an entire country of supplicants eager to bow and scrape before the queen, how much interest would be left for her Mrs. Freeman? Would her ears be so filled with the sweet flattery of rascals like Rochester that there'd be no passage left for my honest whispers?

Morley had sworn always to love her Freeman, and I'd never doubted she would. But would Her Majesty in her ermine and garter be so willing to pledge the same?

I sat before the looking glass at my dressing table in our house in Jermyn Street, rubbing my cheeks with a square of Spanish paper to redden them. For daytime I seldom had need of such tricks, my complexion always having been fair. But when I sat at table for dinner by candlelight, I could look as pale as a specter, not pleasing for any company beyond my own. Tonight was the first of a number of small dinners that John and I were giving to help solidify his command, and our new position at court, and I needed to look my best.

I smiled at my now-rosy reflection, tipping my head to make the large teardrop pearls in my ears swing back and forth to practice the effect for later. The new fashions flattered me. The gown I'd chosen for tonight had a deep, square neckline, edged with lace, displayed the whiteness of my skin, while the artful drapery of the heavy brocade skirts over the hips made my waist, sadly thickened a bit by age, appear smaller. The elaborate headdress of pleated Venetian lace that I'd pin on after my hair was dressed would give me height and presence, both of which I always needed to stand out in crowded drawing rooms.

I smoothed my fingers along the salmon-colored silk of my stays, easing the neckline a fraction lower over my breasts. Soon John must sail back to The Hague, and I wanted him to carry a pleasing memory of me when he left.

I unpinned and brushed out my hair myself before my maid came to dress it. At least that needed no assistance: though I would be forty-two next month, my hair remained my glory, without so much as a trace of white.

The door opened behind me, and I turned, expecting my maid.

"John, love." That sweet joy I felt whenever I saw my husband had not faded over time, either. He'd already dressed for dinner, the candlelight glinting off the brass buttons and bullion on his red coat and the silver-gilt hilt of his sword. "How is it that you're dressed so much sooner than I?"

"An officer has no choices to make." He swept aside my hair to kiss the nape of my neck. "Besides, I'll be so thoroughly overshadowed by your beauty and brilliance, no one will notice me anyway."

"My brilliance, ha," I scoffed, teasing, as I turned to push him playfully away, the full sleeves of my emerald silk dressing gown fluttering about my wrists. "They all come to court you, not me."

"They come to drink our wines, sweetheart, and court us both. As I would do with you." He slipped his hand inside my sleeve, gliding his fingers the length of my bare arm until he found my stays and smock, and grimaced. "Though I see I'm too late for true mischief."

"What, you'd have our guests find us dallying?"

He laughed. "Some would relish it. A reminder of old King Charles's days." He paused to kiss the inside of my wrist, as if I needed a reminder myself. "I sent word to the kitchen that we'll have another with us tonight. At Her Majesty's request, I've invited Rochester to join us."

"*Rochester!*" I cried, instantly furious. How dare John do this without asking me? "You know my feelings for that vile man. However can you invite him here after what he did to you?"

"What you thought he did, sweet," he said lightly. "The only proof you had was that he was a Tory."

"And that was not enough?"

"Not now, Sarah," John said. "Rochester's in the queen's Cabinet, and I'll need his support for the war. He's a useful man to us all, Tory or Whig or Hottentot."

I could not sit still another moment, nigh jumping to my feet before him, my hands clenched into fists at my side. "Do you truly believe that wooing and kissing will make me willing enough to welcome that man to our house?"

His expression was surprised yet irritated, as if clearly he *had* believed his idle nonsense would prove sufficient.

"What I believe, my dear wife, is that you will oblige both me and Her Majesty by making yourself civil to the guest I have invited to our house," he said, and though he smiled, his voice was more clipped than ever I deserved from him. "Please me further, and wear the cream lutestring gown instead, and the pearls I gave you last birthday in your hair."

He shut the door before I could answer, and I hurled my hairbrush after him. So he would like me to *oblige* him and the queen, and bend to his will for empty compliments, and wear his pearls in my hair as I smiled and scraped low enough to show my breasts in the cream-colored gown before that villain Rochester? Was that all the power I was ever to have, as Lord Marlborough's golden-haired wife?

Please *him*, for all the love we'd shared!

I jerked open the drawers on my dressing table, tossing out the contents until I found a pair of shears. With shaking hands, I grabbed the length of my hair, pulled it taut, and with the shears, chopped it from my head. Clenched in my fist, the hair drooped like the pelt of some lifeless creature. My head felt bare and light, the ends of butchered hair bristling against my jaw.

Still ruled by my fury, I threw open the chamber door, and flung the length of hair onto the table in the hall, where John would be sure to see it. Let *that* please him!

"Oh, my lady!" cried my maid at the top of the stairs, horrified. "Your poor hair, my lady!"

"If you'd come when you should have, Mowdie, this wouldn't have happened." Since I was a girl, I'd never before cut my hair, and now it lay in a fraying coil on the table, separate forever from me and my life. Breathing hard with my fading anger, I turned away, unable to bear the sight any longer. "Now you must make what is left as agreeable as possible so I do not shame Lord Marlborough before our guests."

The woman tried her best to cover what I'd done with the headdress, but all the lace in Venice could not disguise my butchery. Yet I would not weep; I'd done this to myself, and only I was to blame.

When I left my chamber to go below, the coil of my hair had vanished. I never asked the servants where it had gone, nor did they volunteer, and I suspected one of them had squirreled it away to sell to a wigmaker: fit and humbling punishment for my vanity, indeed.

I greeted our first guest with my head high and proud, as if to dare them to notice. None did so to my face, though I caught several of them stealing horrified glances at my shorn hair when they thought I wasn't watching.

And John—John was master enough of himself that all through the evening he kept his expression pleasantly benign. But at last we were alone together in bed, and what I'd done could not be ignored.

He leaned over me, a hand on either side of my shoulders. "For whatever I did, Sarah," he said, "I am endlessly sorry."

My anger was long spent, and tears of shame and remorse now stung my eyes. "Oh, my own love," I whispered, reaching up to pull him closer. "I'm sorry, too."

At last John was set to sail in May, and I rode down to Margate with him to wave him off. I know there are many who regard the sea and its shores as vastly romantic, the waves and violent sky combined to represent desirous passions. But for me the sea was only a perilous barrier that my husband must cross to reach some uneasy foreign place with a war where he would risk his life. Not even the bright blue sky full of wheeling white gulls could change my mind this morning, nor did the cheery sun sparkling on the waves.

Last week in London a solemn procession of heralds and guards, led by the King-at-Arms, had wended from St. James's through Charing Cross and the Strand to the City, to proclaim with trumpets and fanfare that war had been declared upon France. Now, on this day, my love must sail from me to fight that war, and nothing in all creation could stop my misery.

"Write to me often," John was saying, his arm tight around my waist as we stood beside the coach. "I would know everything of your life, however small."

"I always do." I tried to smile, my nose and eyes already red and swollen from weeping. So many times had we parted like this, and it only became more difficult. Neither of us was good at farewells, which was why we'd agreed to part here instead of on the quay, with all the world to witness the tears in the lord general's eyes.

"Write to me of Her Majesty, too," he said softly, slipping his fingers into my shorn locks. He'd never asked what had happened to my hair, and I'd never confessed it to him, yet still he'd understood. "That sad lady needs you, Sarah, more than ever. Be her friend, and keep me in her thoughts so she doesn't forget me, or my men."

"Oh, John, take care!" I cried miserably. "I must give you over to God's keeping, I know, but I won't rest for a moment until you're back with me."

"I love you, Sarah." He bent to kiss me, drawing me close. "You, and the children."

"I love you, too, more than I can ever speak!" I held him tight, unashamed to weep my sorrow. "Swear to me you'll come back soon as you can, John, with love for me and glory for England!"

"I swear it," he whispered, his crooked smile enough to break my heart. "I'll come back to you, love, with glory enough for you as well."

Chapter Thirty-three

KENSINGTON PALACE, LONDON
OCTOBER, 1702

"You would not refuse such an honor, Mrs. Freeman, would you?" Though it was still early in autumn, the queen always felt chilled, and sat at her desk close to the fire, with her skirts wrapped in furs. She looked at me anxiously, her pen clutched tight in her swollen, inky fingers. "I only wished to please you and Mr. Freeman as you deserved."

"As you always do, dear Morley." I glanced down at her last letter to me. With so many crowding and begging for her time as queen, we were seldom alone like this any longer, and I meant to make the most of it. "But this offer is too generous, even from you."

"How can that be," she said, incredulous, "after all your dear husband has done for England?"

"Because it *is* too generous," I said, echoing what John himself had told me, "even for my dear husband. *You* are too generous, Morley."

I came and sat beside her, drawing my chair as close to hers as I could. I slipped my hand inside her furs until I found her knee, and rested my fingers there in the old, fond way.

"My own dear Freeman," she said, her gaze so melting soft as she looked at me that I thought she might weep. "Where do my days go? What is so important that I must cut short my time with you?"

"I'm here now," I said. "And so are you."

"But for how long?" She fumbled through the furs until she found my hand, turning it so my slender fingers linked into hers, so puffed that her hand felt more like an animal's fleshy paw. "Oh, my dear, who would have dreamed a queen must toil so much that it keeps her from her friends?"

"I dreamed it, dear Morley, because I dreamed of you," I whispered, drawing her head onto my shoulder. I couldn't remember how long it had been since I'd been called to share her bed. Her illnesses and her heaviness had dulled her passions and made her self-conscious, too. But I knew the old loneliness still remained within her, perhaps more now than when she'd been a forgotten child, and that I could always answer.

"You would never settle for being half a queen," I whispered. "That is the kind of noble woman you are, and why I have always loved you so. You would insist on being the leader that England deserves, and you are."

She turned her head against my shoulder, and I felt her shuddering sigh as much as I heard it. "Oh, Freeman, you *do* understand."

"Of course I do," I said, my arms around her. "Of course I do."

How long we sat there together I cannot say. The shadows of the short October afternoon stretched across the floor, and the sun turned everything in the room to rich gold, yet still I held her, my lonely queen. Finally, beyond the closed door, the case clock in the hall chimed five times, and like a drowsy sleeper, Anne slowly raised her face from my shoulder.

"Oh, Freeman," she said, her voice thick as she rubbed her eyes. My sleeve had pressed a creased imprint into her cheek. "Where were we here? My letters, my letters."

"As you wish, dear." I drew back my hand from her knee and slid my chair apart from hers, letting her turn back to her desk. Long ago I'd learned that this was how it was with her: as much as she craved the intimacy of friendship, she could not let herself trust it, breaking away suddenly as if the kiss or caress had never happened. "I've no wish to take you from your affairs."

She stared down at the paper before her as if seeing it for the first time, and smiled slowly. "But this is no work, Freeman. This is pure joy. This is how I mean to reward Mr. Freeman for bringing us more victories this summer than in the whole of William's reign!"

I smiled at such a change of humor. How quickly she'd shifted back to the war!

And yet in a way she was right. The glories John had promised had in fact come swiftly, to the confusion of the French: Kaiserwerth, Stevenswaert, Venloo, Ruremonde, and Liege all had fallen to him, securing the Spanish Netherlands for the Alliance.

"I believe John would tell you his work has only begun against the French," I said, "and that such an honor as you propose comes too soon."

"And I believe that is you speaking, my modest Freeman, and not Lord Marlborough at all," she said—quite wrongly, in truth. "When he returns, I mean to offer him a dukedom, and you won't dissuade me otherwise."

I sighed, taking care with my next words, remembering what John had told me. "But so great a rank comes with more than honor, Morley. You know that as well as I. An English duke is expected to maintain a certain level of display and assurance that is beyond our circumstances at present. Our future is hardly secured. What of his income if John were killed in battle?"

"Oh, the heavens forbid it!" cried the queen, her gout-swollen fingers pressed over her heart. "We could not bear such a loss!"

"Nor I," I said. "But consider the burden that would place upon poor Jack, inheriting such a title without the means to support it."

"That is easily solved, too." The queen smiled with triumph. "I'll settle a pension on the title. What would be appropriate?"

I spread my hands as if I'd no notion, though this, too, was what John had predicted. There was little doubt that he'd earned this honor, risking his life again and again for his queen and country. But hadn't I done my share of earning, too, by keeping so much company with the queen? Hadn't I earned this title and living for Jack, too, by keeping silent when I wished to speak, and speaking when I'd rather have been silent, and following whatever path the queen had chosen for our long friendship? Though others would question why John and I deserved such an honor, my conscience would be clear. We'd *earned* it—John and me, and Freeman, too.

"You *are* too modest by half, Freeman." The queen smiled, as if reading my thoughts, and tapped her finger on the papers stacked before her. "I shall make it five thousand a year. I wouldn't wish Jack to go wanting. I suppose I must fashion him a marquess, too, if he's to be heir to a dukedom."

"And you are too, too kind," I said. I would have considered us fortunate for half the sum she offered, let alone the title for Jack. "Dear Mrs. Morley! I can never thank you enough."

"That's what I must say to you." Her smile was marked with the old familiar sadness that came when she thought of her lost son. "How is your Jack faring with Godolphin? What a bachelor house that must be!"

Now my own smile waned. While my daughters' rebellious ways had faded as they'd grown and married, Jack's had increased. Done with Eton and reading with a tutor at Cambridge, fifteen yet appearing older, Jack considered himself quite the blade, handsome and charming and lean as a whippet. All deemed him most promising, and congratulated John and me on having such an excellent son and heir. But once John had sailed, I'd been left to cope with all of Jack's energies myself. His heart's desire was still to leave school and join his father in the field, and his oft-untrammeled behavior seemed calculated to wear away my objections until I relented. Finally Godolphin had come to my rescue the way old friends do, and taken Jack to stay with him at his house in Newmarket.

"Lord Godolphin tells me his behavior is much improved," I said. "It's often so with boys, who will rankle beneath a woman's care."

"High spirits, that is all." The queen's melancholy was unmistakable. "How my boy did love to play with Jack! He claimed no other child could make any game as exciting as Jack."

"I fear Jack still has that power," I said wistfully, recalling, too, how much easier life had been when our two sons had been playmates.

"It will be his strength as a grown gentleman, and as a duke after his father," she said, then with a sigh turned back to the stack of letters before her. "Now come, Freeman, if you please, I need your advice on these petitions."

Although the queen maintained she could never repay John and me for our loyalty and service, the members of Parliament were of a different mind. With opposition led by Lord Rochester, the proposal for the hereditary pension to accompany the new dukedom of Marlborough was soundly defeated, though as a compromise, the five thousand pounds were settled on John for his life. The queen was mortified and furious at her uncle's presumption. She offered me an additional two thousand pounds from her own Privy Purse instead, which, of course, I refused, not wishing to seem greedy. Her open displeasure with Rochester was worth more than two thousand pounds to me. For now the dukedom itself would be enough, a splendid legacy for Jack and our family, and I'll not deny that it was fine indeed to be greeted as the Duchess of Marlborough.

But envy is a powerful emotion. For all of those who would cheer my carriage on account of John's victories, there were many others in Parliament and beyond who believed the war against France was a futile, empty pursuit, a waste of lives and moneys. Still more resented my friendship with the queen and claimed I'd undue influence over her. There were even cruel little ballads sung in the street about my low birth raised high, and how I led the queen about as if she were blind.

But the truth is this, as sure as any mortal might tell it: I worked day and night in my positions in the queen's household, harder than most folk would believe of a duchess. I did all that was asked of me, and whatever I realized that the queen had neither time nor inclination to do. I answered countless letters and petitions for her, from poor folk in need of charity to fine ladies seeking places at court, and for every one I pleased by granting them their favor, I must have made a dozen enemies for each I refused, no matter how just my reason. Not once did I sell a place or accept a gratuity in exchange for influence, and in all decisions on the queen's behalf I tried to be temperate and fair.

I read the queen my letters from John at the front, as well as the ones he wrote directly to her, and others between her and Lord Godolphin as Lord Treasurer. Because of this, I was as intimately informed of affairs of state as the gentlemen in her Cabinet, and though as a woman I was forbidden a seat in that group, I was still able to offer my own opinions to the queen.

She heeded them, too. Though Rochester's presumptions finally went too far, I knew I could claim some credit for informing the queen as to her uncle's true perfidy. In February, she ordered him as Lord Lieutenant of Ireland to reside in Dublin. In complete character, Rochester petulantly refused to leave London, and the queen dismissed him from both his position and her Cabinet—as neat a bit of business as ever I'd hoped to achieve, and one that heartened me, too.

But there was still more to my loyal attendance on the queen. I stood at her side at drawing rooms and other functions, offering my own quick wit to ease the demands placed on her. Her health was ever worsening, her shyness still that of a young girl, and she thanked me often and fervently for lightening her burden as only the truest and oldest of friends could. If all these services were perceived as influencing her overmuch, then so be it. *I* knew my worth, and so did Mrs. Morley.

But early in February the following year came news that turned all my work and care to the bitterest ashes in my heart. Every honor and reward that John and I had achieved ceased to have value. Nothing in the mortal world would have meaning now, nor ever would again.

Our darling son Jack had smallpox.

Chapter Thirty-four

With my body curled half on the bed beside my son, my cheek lay upon his silent chest, his stiffening fingers clutched tight in mine. My eyes were squeezed shut, yet still the tears flowed, more tears than I'd thought possible, yet never enough to mourn my dear, dearest Jack.

"Sarah, love, we must leave him." John's voice broke, as tormented by grief as I. He rested his hand on my shoulder. "They'll care for him now, and prepare him to be moved. He can't be left here any longer."

I pushed myself up, so weak that I'd doubted I could. I looked back at my son, and sobbed again. This was not how I wished to remember Jack: his handsome face distorted by the swelling pustules, his lips pale and cracked, his dark hair pressed flat with sweat from the fever, a body that was always in motion now horribly still. The room was small and bare and cold, a place where the school kept sick boys away from the healthy ones, the dead from the living.

The heir to the dukedom and the estates with it, the first Marquess of Blandford, a charming, dashing boy who was his father's hope and his mother's delight: how could such a gem be stolen from us like this?

"If only I'd come sooner, John," I whispered raggedly, smoothing the collar of Jack's nightshirt around his throat, the front over his chest. He'd lost weight in this last week, my boy, for I could feel his ribs beneath my fingers. "If they'd sent word to us earlier, then I—I could have saved him, I know it!"

"He had the best care imaginable, Sarah," John said. "The queen herself sent her own physicians as soon as she heard he'd been stricken."

"Oh, yes, those fine physicians of hers," I said bitterly. "They couldn't save her babies, and now they've failed with mine, too."

"Come, Sarah, we must go." John's arm was as strong as ever, lifting me to my feet and away from my son. "He's with God now. We must be brave, love."

"With *God*." My knees buckled beneath me, and I sagged in his arms. The keening wail was torn from me, forcing its way from my deepest grief. I would not be stoic in the face of such a loss, the way that Anne had always been. Bravery would not bring my son back to me. I would let the world know my pain, and care not who heard, even so far as London.

What happened next I could not exactly say. I was so hollow and empty that though I rose in the morning and went through my day, I'd no memory of what I'd done or seen, drunk or eaten, or how I'd come back to lie awake again in the dark. John was forced to return to the war within a week of Jack's death, and I retreated to Holywell, hugging my sorrow to myself.

The queen had been the first to write to me, but I hadn't the strength to reply. She offered to come to St. Albans to console me, promising that she could empathize with me for the loss of a child as no other. I wrote back that I saw no use in the unfortunate comforting the unfortunate, and told her to keep away. My daughters were likewise unwelcome to me, as were other friends. I did not dress, nor tend my hair, nor blot my tears, and as I walked through the empty fields surrounding Holywell I kept grief as my only company.

Most of all, I wanted nothing to do with the court or its petty concerns. I left my Gold Key in my traveling chest with my silk gowns, and I'd no interest in the duties I'd abandoned. How could petitions and politics matter to me now? What reason did I have to intrigue for power or riches when I'd no son to inherit my gains?

I returned to Jack's old school, unable to keep away. Shrouded in my mourning, I walked the cloisters he'd walked, watched the sun rise over the same slates and chimney pots that he'd seen from his cot. I stood apart and watched the other boys, laughing and shoving and jostling one another as they made their way to their meals or tutors, and wept the bitterest of tears at the unfairness of it, until at last I was gently, firmly, asked to leave.

Why did these boys live, while my Jack was dead? Why had I lost my son, while other mothers still basked in their good fortune? When so much of what I'd done was to secure Jack's future, what was I to do next when he was gone?

I could tell from John's letters to me that others had written to him of my behavior. Clearly they said I'd become addled and lost my wits, that I behaved like a madwoman. He told me to be strong for the sake of his love, and pleaded with me to take care of my health, to go with the queen on her annual journey to Bath and take the waters myself.

Instead I stayed at Holywell, and cared not what was said of my health or my sanity. I would heal myself my own way, or not at all.

Yet over that long summer, the hard shell of my grief began to soften. I walked often across our fields, dressed in homely linen with my face shielded by the same broad-brimmed straw hats the farmers' wives wore. I concentrated not on my loss or my sorrow, but on each step that I took through the tall grasses, on the warmth of the sun upon my back or the dew that flecked my skirts.

Godolphin came to see me, the only friend I'd tolerate, and he surprised me by bringing with him our shared granddaughter, the child of my Henrietta and his Francis. Little Harriot was only three, as innocent as could be of earthly grief. As I bent to take her chubby hand and show her the ducks on the fishpond, her happy chatter soothed me in ways that no well-composed condolence ever could. We laughed together as the ducks flipped topsy-turvy in the water, their tails turned to the sky. Slowly, slowly, Jack began to ease his grip upon me and slip into his rightful place in my memory. I began to think not only of gleeful little Harriot at my side, but of my daughters, my living children.

Most of all, I thought of John. Men were made to grieve in different ways from women, to bury their pain away. But hadn't he lost the same son as I? Hadn't he suffered, too, and yet found the courage to go ahead, one step at a time through the tall grass as I was doing? Our love had always been our shared strength. Why couldn't I draw upon it now, the way he'd begged me to?

I wrote to him with feverish impatience, eager to make him understand my new discoveries. He wrote back at once, and I could sense his relief and his devotion behind every word. I was cherished. I was loved, and I must never forget that. I knew I was changed from the woman I'd been before I'd lost my son, but I still had a place and a purpose in this life, too.

By summer's end, I began to write to the queen as well. I thanked her for her concern. I asked after her husband the prince, and if the weather was seasonable at Windsor Castle. I offered her my opinions of decisions before Parliament and new appointments that were pending. The days grew shorter, the long grasses in the fields dry and brittle beneath my shoes. I still mourned for Jack and always would, but my grief had dulled to an ache I could bear.

I tied the Gold Key back around my waist, and returned to court, and to politics.

I joined Anne at Windsor Castle in October. She received me with tears in her eyes, ready to share my sorrow, but I was determined to look forward, not behind, and eager to occupy myself again in a useful way. At once I plunged into the task of sorting through the piles of letters and reports that had accumulated in my absence. I'd been told a secretary had taken my place, but the more I read, the more I marveled at how little the man had done.

Each afternoon I joined Anne in her parlor, prepared with a fresh parcel of business for her attention while she took her tea. When the letters were finished, we'd often speak of politics.

Or more precisely, I would speak, and she would demur, and offer no opinion at all.

"You know my beliefs, Freeman," she said, rubbing one gouty, bandaged hand across the other. "I cannot accept that all Tories are bad, any more than I will swear that all goodness springs from the Whigs."

I shook my head at her willful blindness. "I agree, it's not so simple as that. But when one considers how the Tory leaders insist upon encouraging policies that harm the country—"

"You mean Mr. Harley." She sighed piteously. "It's always Mr. Harley with you."

"Of course I mean Mr. Harley." With Rochester gone, I'd turned my energies towards the Speaker of the Commons, a small, dry, lazy Tory whose special delight seemed to lie in attacking the army—which, for John's sake, I could not abide. "If you had but read my letters, then you would understand what a dangerous rascal he is."

"You know I read your letters," she said, wounded. She reached for the teapot beside her, her swaddled fingers fumbling with the handle. "More than it would often seem that Freeman reads the letters of her poor unfortunate faithful Morley."

I took the teapot from her clumsy hands and refilled her dish, adding the double splash of brandy that she always expected now, to ease her many pains. "How, pray, could I answer your letters if I'd never read them?"

She looked down at the tea to avoid answering me. She had changed much while I'd been away from court, and her most recent visit to the waters at Bath had achieved little. Her gout and rheumatism had worsened, moving into her hands as well as her legs and combining with her ever-increasing corpulence to make her most unpleasant to behold. As her limbs had grown more ponderous, so had her intellect, combining with her habitual stubbornness to make any sort of conversation more and more difficult.

And if she had changed, then I suppose so had I. Since I'd returned, I found I'd less patience with the queen than before, and with the workings of the court in general. If I'd learned any lesson from Jack's death, it was to value what little time we had in this life, and I'd no wish to squander so much of my span in listening to the queen's misguided logic.

"Mr. Harley is cautious over the funds spent upon the war, that is all," the queen finally said. "That does not make him the Jacobite you try to paint him to be."

"Jacobites burrow into power in many ways," I said, knowing full well how she still feared her exiled half brother James Francis. "They'll do anything to weaken England for a French invasion. Harley's so-called economy will cut our army off at the knees."

"I do not believe that's his intention."

"It's not so much what he and the Tories *intend* as what they have already *done*." While there had been some small victories this summer—

John had captured Bonn, Huy, Limburg, and Guelders, and freed the Spanish Guelderland and the bishopric of Liege from the French—the overcautious Dutch leaders had denied him a decisive battle with Louis's Army of Flanders. If only they had let him, John declared with considerable frustration, then he could have ended the war then and there. Worse for him still was the lack of support for his efforts in Parliament, where there were fools aplenty led by Harley and Nottingham who wished to cut funds for the army, and believed the war could be won with more economy by the navy.

"The war is most costly," the queen ventured hesitantly. "I know you don't wish your husband's troops to suffer, but I cannot ruin the country for their sake."

"Oh, bah, Morley, don't be so timid," I said with disgust. "It's a different tale when the messengers bring word of another victory. Then you order the church bells rung and the guns fired from the Tower to celebrate the new glory that's come to your reign. You can't have that without paying the piper."

She sighed again. "I've never said the victories have not been appreciated. It's only that Mr. Harley and the others believe there might be ways to accomplish the same good without spending so very much."

"Oh, I see!" I snapped my fingers together. "We'll pay for gunpowder with fairy dust, and sell pippins for cannon. Is there any wonder that Lord Marlborough writes to me constantly of quitting the army altogether and retiring to St. Albans?"

"I won't allow it," the queen said, aghast. "I've told him so before, that he and Lord Godolphin and you and I must remain together for England's sake."

"John would indeed quit the army, and resign his commissions," I said, my voice rising with emotion, "and so would I retire, and join him in the country. After all the service we have given, there's only so much we can bear."

The queen's face crumpled. "Oh, Mrs. Freeman, don't speak so, I beg of you! You know you are still my dearest friend! Why must you insist that I agree with you in all matters? Why can't I be permitted to hold my own counsel, and you yours, the way we once did?"

I rose from my chair, unable to listen to any more. "I'll be the same Mrs. Freeman when you can manage to be the same Mrs. Morley."

I did not wait for her reply, but swept from the chamber, the Gold Key swinging against my hip. To my surprise, I found Abigail Hill in the hall outside, so close to the door that I nearly knocked her over as I passed. Though she carried a wide basin of some vile-smelling brew in her hands, she still curtseyed to me, as was my due.

"Forgive me for being in your path, Your Grace," she murmured, eyes downcast as a good bedchamber-woman must. She'd not improved with age, her nose seemingly now of the shape and size of a turnip. But what damned her far more in my eyes was learning that as well as being related to me, she was likewise distantly connected to Robert Harley.

"What business do you have here?" I demanded. "Are you listening at keyholes?"

"Oh, no, Your Grace!" she said, playing the bewildered innocent a shade too well. "I was waiting until you were done with Her Majesty so I might change the poultice on the sores on her legs."

She raised the basin slightly towards me as evidence, and I recoiled with revulsion. I'd never performed such sordid attentions for the queen, and as a peeress, I wanted no part of them now.

"Very well, then, go in to Her Majesty," I said, twitching my skirts from her path. "But mind you, if I learn you're bearing tales to Mr. Harley, I'll see that you lose your position just as I saw that it was given you."

"Yes, Your Grace," she said. "That is, no tales, Your Grace, I swear to it."

But I didn't trust her then, and still less as time passed—with good reason, too. The kindness I'd once shown Mrs. Hill was repaid in the foulest coin imaginable, so traitorous to me that I came to wish I'd never brought that turnip-nosed serpent into my palace-nest.

Chapter Thirty-five

The morning of John's departure was fair and mild, and at his request the leather curtains of our carriage were rolled high so that we showed ourselves to the crowds gathering for the sailing in the streets and around the quays. For a captain general and a duke, he liked to be thought not so far removed from his men, an unusual philosophy that had earned him great favor among his troops. He was recognized at once. Excited cheers accompanied us, our progress slowed as some even pressed close to our carriage to wish him well. I smiled and waved cheerily, as the wife of so grand a man must, but there was no cheer in my heart on this morning, nor, I'd warrant, in John's, either.

His leave home had been brief, and though I'd welcomed him gladly, we'd begun quarreling almost at once. We fought over Nottingham's resignation from the queen's Cabinet, which pleased me, and on Harley's appointment as secretary of state, which pleased John. We fought over the queen's health and Godolphin's worries, our daughters' marriages and our son's headstone, even which apples in our orchard at St. Albans were sweeter for eating. We'd argued before and often in our marriage, but this marked the first time that we never made love—or peace—afterwards. Three nights into his leave, we were sleeping apart, and even last night, he'd not come to me.

And pride, I'd discovered, is precious little comfort alone in an empty bed.

"This makes for a warm farewell, doesn't it?" John said as he smiled not at me, but at those outside.

"How fortunate for you that they're here," I said, my own smile beaming and brittle. "But then, the passing warmth of strangers has far more to recommend it than the devotion of a loving wife."

"I've had no grounds for comparison," he said, "not in this fortnight."

"Perhaps if you'd deigned speak to me, then it wouldn't have been so."

He glanced at me, bemused. "What, speak, and risk having my head bitten off at the neck?"

"I'm not Jack Ketch, John," I said, trying hard to keep my temper. "But all this time, I've felt that you've stayed apart from me, that you wouldn't confide in me."

He shrugged, the gold lace on his shoulders swaying. "You've fancied that, Sarah."

The carriage stopped, and he climbed out quickly, as if to avoid any more questions from me. I followed more slowly, letting him hand me down to another smattering of cheers around us.

He could say what he would, but I'd fancied nothing. There'd been too many signs, too many rumors at court for me to ignore. I smiled again, but thought of the letter in my pocket, a letter I'd wet with my tears as I'd written it last night. Would I be so brave, so foolish, as to give it to him before he sailed?

I took his offered arm, and together we walked the length of the quay to the waiting longboat. There'd be no private farewell for us this day, as there'd been when he'd sailed from Margate two years before. This one would be as public as if we'd stood on the stage at Covent Garden.

At the top of the ladder he stopped and turned. The boatmen were waiting in the water below, the coxswain in the prow poised for a sign from John.

"Here we are, Sarah," he said. "Again."

My throat was tight, fair strangling me. "There's something I must say to you, John, something I—"

"No more, Sarah," he said. "No more. I've enough war waiting for me."

I blinked hard so I wouldn't cry, not before so many witnesses, and pressed the letter into his hand. "For later," I whispered. "Read it, then burn it."

He nodded, his face bright with anticipation, and then before I realized it, he was kissing me good-bye.

"I love you," he said. "Never doubt that. My love to you, and the children."

"I love you, too," I said, my whisper a hoarse croak of regret and remorse. "Oh, John, I love you!"

He settled himself on the bench in the bow as the oarsmen shoved off, and though the lieutenant beside him seemed eager to talk, he never once took his gaze from me. I dashed my tears away with the heel of my glove, not wanting to look away even to find my handkerchief. I stayed until the ship set sail, and found the wind, and finally disappeared over the crest of the horizon.

How long before he read my letter? I wondered. How long before he knew what I'd concluded must be the truth: that his distance from me in these last weeks could only mean what the gossips whispered, that the Duke of Marlborough had turned from his wife and taken a mistress. He would always be welcome to visit me in my own houses, but I would no longer live with him as his wife.

I went from Margate to Windsor Lodge, my house outside the castle. I'd not the strength to face the wags and wasps at court, nor the stomach for the tedium of the queen's company. I stayed there alone, but John's letters found me.

My accusation was false, confusing, causing him enormous pain and suffering. How could I ever believe such a lie of him? He loved me as no other, always had, and always would.

John's second letter came with the same messenger. I could believe what I pleased, but there'd been a reason he'd been distant, a reason he could not yet reveal to me.

Letter by letter, he was able to release the truth to me. In the greatest secrecy, the army was marching towards the Danube, and perhaps the largest battle of the entire war. If he found the victory he hoped, then his name would be glorious forever. If he was killed, his only regret would be that he'd not loved me as I'd deserved our last weeks together.

I remembered the devotion in his eyes when he'd looked at me on the quay, and felt my heart close to breaking at how cruel I'd been to him during his last leave.

I wrote at once and forgave him, and apologized for my doubts. The prospect of a great battle terrified me more than a score of mistresses. What if I never saw him alive again? What if he were killed, the way he seemed so gloomily convinced? What if my mistrust was repaid by his death? My thoughts were with him constantly now, this coming battle a secret almost too much to bear.

In early August I was back at our Jermyn Street house in London, amusing myself with my pet nightingales. I'd just set their Chinese cage beside the open window so they'd have a bit of sun and air when I heard the rider galloping towards our door. Curious, I leaned from the open window, and recognized Colonel Parke, John's aide-de-camp. Dreading the worst, I ran down the stairs to meet him in the front hall as he swept his dust-covered hat from his head.

"Tell me he's alive," I begged with desperate urgency. "Tell me he's not been harmed!"

"His Grace the captain general was as well as could be when I left him, Your Grace." Parke's grin broke through his sweat-streaked face. "I bring news of a victory, Your Grace."

He handed me a tattered, greasy tavern bill, and as soon as I saw John's unmistakable hand on the back, I felt relief wash over me. Even before the fighting was done he'd written, wanting to share his glorious news with me before anyone else. He entrusted me to make a copy of his note, and to see that Parke be rewarded as the joyful bearer of his news—such news!—to the queen.

Near a small Bavarian village called Blenheim, the English forces had joined with those of the Austrian Prince Eugene of Savoy, and under John's command, the combined army had crushed the French forces. It was the worst defeat suffered by France in two generations, and with this single masterful battle, John had changed the course of the entire Spanish war.

And yes: his name would be glorious forever.

All of England seemed delirious with celebration, mad with joy of so great a victory. For weeks there was talk of nothing else. Yet after the thanksgiving service at St. Paul's and the victory parades, the pealing church bells and fireworks were all done, the queen decided that John should receive a more lasting monument to what he'd achieved at Blenheim. She finally settled on the gift of a great house, to be built at the country's expense on the old royal manor of Woodstock, fifteen thousand acres of forests and wilderness that we could fashion however we pleased. The house would be called Blenheim Castle, and it would serve not only as a splendid home fit for England's greatest hero, but also as a tribute to the battle itself.

On a warm June evening with the stars just beginning to twinkle in the dusk, John and I gathered with the local people from Woodstock for the ceremony that would set the cornerstone in place. To represent the queen, whose infirmities kept her away from so wild a place, our daughter Anne, the queen's goddaughter, pressed the stone into place as two masons held it steady for her. While a crowd of local well-wishers applauded, Anne smiled sweetly for posterity, her pearly silk gown luminous in the twilight. There would be buckets of wine, punch, and ale, with cakes beneath the trees for all our guests, and we'd have music, and dancing, too, as part of the celebration.

"There now, it's fairly launched, or whatever is said of a house," John said beside me, his glass filled and primed for another round of toasts and his face flushed and happy. He had a small nosegay of white flowers tucked into his top buttonhole, the final gallant touch for a hero. "How long do you think we must wait before we can sleep beneath that roof?"

"Years," I said with my customary frankness. "We'll be fortunate indeed if it's done before we're in our dotage, and too daft to enjoy it."

He laughed, his arm settling comfortably around my waist. "So long as we're doting together, dear soul, I'll be content, here or anywhere else."

I smiled and rested my head back against his shoulder. I felt as close to content myself as I'd been since Jack's death. My husband had his glory, and I had his love, and now we would have this house— Blenheim Castle—that would be more a palace than many the queen herself possessed.

"This should keep you happily occupied for years, ordering Mr.

Vanbrugh and his builders about," John continued, half jesting, half seri-ous. "A more useful project for you than politics."

I twisted around to face him. "Are you still splenetic because my can-didates won, and yours did not?"

He snorted, his way of admitting that I'd guessed exactly right. The elections for Anne's second Parliament had been held in the spring, and I'd done my share of lobbying for my favorite Whigs with consid-erable success, both in the counties as well as at court and with the queen herself.

"You're jealous, that is all." I lifted his hand with the glass to my lips, tipping it so I could drink. "You wish you'd my skill at politics."

"What I wish, Sarah, is that you'd draw back from it, especially with the queen."

I frowned, surprised by his sudden shift in manner. "You know I'd be the greatest hero of Parliament House, John, if only I'd been born a man."

"How grateful I am that you weren't." He brushed his lips across my forehead, to mollify me, I know. "I'm serious, love. Godolphin tells me you've taken the habit of lecturing the queen, striving to make her hop to your bidding. That's not wise, Sarah."

"She seeks my opinions, and I give them," I said. "That's how it's al-ways been between us, John. The queen prizes me all the more for not being her sycophant."

"What I hear is that the queen would prefer more kindness from you, and fewer Jacobite bugbears."

I bristled at the part about the Jacobites, considering how much he'd dipped his toe in that particular pond himself. "You've never told me what I can and cannot do like this before."

"Because I've known you wouldn't listen," he said. "I've no guarantee that you will now, but I can pray you will."

"I cannot help myself, John," I said defensively. "You don't know what I must endure. The queen's wit has become every bit as slow and pon-derous and tedious as the rest of her."

He pulled me closer, as if that could change matters. "Once I believed you and the queen quite loved one another."

"You're the one I've always loved better than anyone else," I declared fervently. "I was her dearest friend, and she mine, which is not the same at all."

"No," he agreed, thoughtful, though I knew my answer pleased him. "But why no longer dear friends, Sarah?"

I scowled darkly. "No one could be her friend as she is now. All she wishes to discuss is the weather, or which gentleman dared wear the wrong manner of tie-wig to her drawing room. I want more than that, John. You can go conquer Vienna and change the world, but this—this is the one way I have to leave my mark."

"By worrying the queen about Tories?"

"By having a say in how this country is ordered." How I wished I could better explain my restlessness! "Since Jack died, and the girls are settled, and you are so often away, this is what I have left."

"Ah, Sarah, Sarah." That was no real answer, and we both knew it, with our lost son floating there between us. "But I believe this trial of yours began earlier than that, when the princess became the queen."

"What, when I took on so many more tasks in her household?"

"When she stopped listening to you alone for counsel," he said firmly. "When you were her world, your opinion was her law. But once she became queen, and turned to others with more—"

"She turned to men," I said bitterly. "Like you."

"She turned to those with more experience for the sake of the country," he said, his patient understanding maddening. "For better or worse, that means gentlemen."

I pushed myself free of his arm. "You can't forbid me to speak to the queen, John. I merely offer the Whigs' case to her as a reasonable balance, and hope I can overcome her stubbornness long enough for her to listen."

"You're stubborn, too, love," he said gently. "The queen has been most generous to us, but if you displease her, she could just as readily withdraw her favor."

"She won't." I smiled, confident. "I've been with her too long for that. Wasn't I with her when she fled her father? Wasn't I the first she called when Gloucester took ill? Why, she told me only last week that she couldn't bear to part with me."

But John was not convinced. "She told Godolphin that she feared you two would never again be friends as you once were."

That stopped me, for Anne had never before said or written anything so final to me.

Not my poor unfortunate faithful Morley . . .

"The poor queen is sick and worn and lonely, Sarah," he said. "While I am away on the Continent, I ask you to be kind, that is all. Recall that before you treat her roughly, or babble of your politics. And recall, too, that as much as she needs you, we need her more."

Though I was loath to admit it at the time, I later realized that John's advice was indeed wise, and for the remainder of that year and into the next, I did my best to follow it. I occupied myself much with the work on Blenheim Castle at Woodstock, taking lodgings nearby so I could consult with Mr. Vanbrugh, the architect, and oversee the progress. This proved no small task, as the building of so large a residence had become a murky tangle of carpenters and masons and plasterers and undertakers, sending costs far beyond original estimates and making the promised date for completion no more than a far-distant dream. Vanbrugh seemed so lost that I am certain he came to regard me and my plain speaking with as little fondness as I did his incompetence. But if my husband's noble tribute-house needed an advocate, then who better than I?

While I labored at creating this temple to John's victories, he was doing much the same on the Continent. In the fall of 1705, he was invested with the principality of Mindelheim by way of gratitude from the Hapsburg emperor. By this, John and I were now styled the Prince and Princess of Mindelheim, which amused us both vastly, and when we were alone we'd jest with each other about how high Prince Johnny and his Princess Sary had risen.

And through even greater effort, I managed to contain my enthusiasms for politics while about the queen. To be sure, I also stayed away from court as much as I decently could, removing myself from temptation, as it were. The queen continued to write to me whenever we were parted, but it did seem to me that Morley's protestations of affection for Freeman were but a pallid echo of what they'd once been. More often she accused me pitifully of neglecting her, or even of disdain, which I was quick, of course, to deny.

Yet I could accept that as well, or at least at that time I believed I could. Even the fondest of friendships did shift and change, and if the old passion and confidence between Anne and me was gone, then perhaps, I told myself, a different manner of regard would spring up into place.

But then, in the spring of 1706, my daughter Anne's husband, now the Duke of Sunderland, asked for my assistance as he sought to become the Secretary of the South, and all my best intentions scattered like the driest dust before a summer wind.

Chapter Thirty-six

"Oh, give the puppy another biscuit," the queen said, puckering her lips at the long-haired spaniel wriggling and whining at her feet. "Oh, yes, yes, the darling wants another, doesn't he? Give him the biscuit, Mrs. Hill, before he expires from longing!"

Dutifully Abigail Hill took another biscuit from the porcelain dish and dropped it into the dog's waiting mouth while the queen continued her babbling nursery talk.

I stood by the window and struggled to keep from bursting with impatience. I was a captive in the queen's favorite chamber at Windsor, a many-sided room with windows in one of the turrets. It should have been a pleasant enough retreat, if every window weren't sealed shut from the queen's fear of chills, and if the half-dozen ill-trained dogs didn't give it the stench of a kennel, and if Hill weren't obeying the queen's misguided request that she play, thumping away at the harpsichord in the corner. But then, Hill was always underfoot now, ready to bow and scrape shamelessly at every twitch the queen made, and I'd come to loathe her blank, ruddy face.

"What would you say, Lady Churchill?" the queen asked, still fussing with her dogs. "Don't you think that Blackie is the natural leader among the pups, and that Buttercup, though much the larger, is content to follow?"

"Perhaps we should have put Blackie up for a seat in the House," I said. "God knows there's a sore lack of leaders there."

The queen looked up at me warily over the edge of her tea. "I should not think you'd favor Blackie, for not being Whig enough to suit."

"Oh, why not?" I flung my arms out from my sides. "Blackie's no party man, which is far more important to you than experience or cleverness. Surely you must believe he'd make a better secretary of state for the South than Lord Sunderland. Surely you wish to do what is best for the country."

The queen looked down and patted her knee so that Blackie would jump into her lap. "I'd prefer not to discuss Lord Sunderland any further," she said, hugging the dog close. "I know your opinions regarding him as well as you know mine."

I sighed, folding my arms over my chest. "You shall have to make up your mind soon enough about him. You've put off your decision for months and months, and there's none better qualified. He is one of the first lords in the land, he has traveled much in the world and has engaged in extensive diplomacy on your behalf, he—"

"He is your son-in-law."

With my brows raised in scornful surprise, I stared at her for a long moment. "Is that such a grievous thing, for Lord Sunderland to have wed the daughter of your great captain general?"

Her mouth trembled. "It is not his connection to the captain general that concerns me."

"You would deny granting the place to the best man because of *me*?" I asked, incredulous. "Of *me*, Your Majesty?"

"I have heard he is of much the same—the same temperament," she said unhappily. "He is said to be radical in his beliefs. Mrs. Hill, I am cold. A shawl for my shoulders."

"That is preposterous," I said. "How can he have inherited any of my qualities when he is not of my blood?"

"I've heard it's so," she repeated. Hill wrapped a deep red shawl about the queen's shoulders, and Anne gave her such a look of fond gratitude that it nearly turned my stomach. As a bedchamber-lady, Hill was entitled to touch the queen's person, but the way she tucked the shawl around the royal arms and shoulders, her hands lingering, was more a caress than a service, and was beyond propriety. When they were alone, how much of

Harley's blather was Hill whispering into the queen's ear? How much Tory poison did she accept with that furtive touch?

"You might as well appoint Blackie, Your Majesty," I said with disgust. "At least you can be sure he's not one of my litter."

"That is *true*." She clutched the dog so tightly it squealed. "I won't be hectored, Lady Churchill, not by you or anyone else. I will *not*!"

"Very well, Your Highness," I said, sweeping her a cursory curtsey. "You will not."

I left then, not only the chamber, but Windsor as well. At least at St. Albans I would not be likened to a bitch, even if by the queen herself. It seemed safer to offer my opinions by letter, anyway, though even then the queen resisted logic. When Lord Godolphin pressed her to make her decision—and he the gentlest man imaginable—she burst into tears, which he confessed to me had discomfited him no end. I warned him not to be taken in by a woman's tears, not even from me: a notion which made him laugh heartily, as I'd intended.

The last thing that John and I desired was for the queen to drive our old friend so hard that he'd resign. Without Godolphin in office as a sympathetic treasurer, John was sure the war would be starved for lack of funds, and that the Dutch would sue for a separate peace with France. From the Continent, John wrote me letters full of worry and caution, and though I tried to heed his warnings as best I could, I likewise could not give up supporting my daughter's husband.

But at last the queen saw reason, and in late autumn, she appointed Sunderland as secretary of state. Godolphin was relieved, and content to remain as treasurer. John remained unhappy and unconvinced, and certain I'd overstepped. Later still, a plot by Harley to discredit John and Godolphin was discovered, and in disgust both of them swore to resign rather than share a ministry with so villainous a man. The queen was forced to dismiss Harley from his post to keep them, though he would remain in the House. Although I tried my best to be gracious in this double victory, there was a hollow taint about it that no measure of grace could wash clean.

But having taken nearly half a year of bitterness to settle her mind, the queen had showed the world her resistance to me, and to my husband. I was perceived as losing favor, and though I held my head as high as ever, I noticed how some at court began to treat me with less deference than before. As a famous lady at court, wed to the country's most honored hero, I had been daubed by the ink of Grub Street more often than any other woman save the queen. But now the pamphlets and penny-press sheets had a new bite to their mockery, their attacks and caricatures less subtle.

Yet further humiliation was to come. The following summer, Abigail Hill wed one of the prince's servants, a Colonel Samuel Masham, in a secret ceremony. Considering how I had raised her from nothing and brought her to court, I was stunned to learn of this marriage months after it had occurred. More shocking was discovering, too, that the queen had not only been in attendance, but had arranged it, and had given the couple two thousand pounds as a gift, taken from her Privy Purse without my knowledge. Soon after this, Colonel Masham was appointed to a post in Ireland, and the new Mrs. Masham was known to spend more and more time alone with the queen, even coming to her bedchamber late at night.

By the end of 1707, I could feel the sands beginning to shift beneath my feet, and for the first time in my life, I couldn't guess how to stop it. I struggled for my footing throughout the new year and into the summer, striving to find my place in a court that seemed increasingly turned against me. Yet worse was still to come, and in a manner impossible for even a saint to ignore.

In early July of 1708, word reached London of John's great victory at Oudenard, a battle that had brilliantly destroyed the remnants of the French army in the southern Netherlands and made Lille, the second-largest city in France, vulnerable to the allied armies.

As always after such a victory, a service of thanksgiving was to be said at St. Paul's Cathedral, finally rebuilt after its destruction in the Great Fire of 1666. No matter how weak her health, the queen made certain to attend these services just as old Queen Elizabeth had in her day. Anne desired to show her pleasure and acknowledge God's blessings on England, but also to claim her share of her captain general's reflected glory for herself. As the queen's highest lady as well as John's wife, I would ride in the open carriage with the queen to smile and wave at her side. The day was bright and warm, and though support for the war was lagging after so long, the crowds along the streets and hanging from the windows were sure to be large for the spectacle alone.

In my role as Groom of the Stole, I had laid out the queen's clothes and her jewels, making choices to her taste, and then gone to dress myself before meeting her in the carriage. I waited, my thoughts on John's safe delivery through yet another battle, and at last the queen was brought down and lifted into the carriage beside me. She nodded, all the greeting I merited from her these days, and I gasped.

She wore the gown and robes I had chosen, but not a single jewel. Her hair, arms, hands, and breast were as bare of jewels as a miller's wife, instead of arrayed as was fitting for a queen.

"Where are your jewels, Your Majesty?" I asked as soon as the carriage began to move and our conversation would not be as readily overheard. "I'd laid out the pieces we'd agreed upon beside your robes."

"I did not care to wear them," she said, no explanation at all as she stared straight ahead. "It did not please me."

"But to attend the thanksgiving service with none!" I said, scandalized. "Every ambassador in London will be in St. Paul's today, and every one of them will write home to his court tonight that Her Majesty wore no jewels."

"Let them," she said. "Their letters mean nothing to me."

This had never before been the case, for the queen had always cared for protocol and what others thought of her. "You know as well as I what they'll write. They'll tell their masters that you care so little for Lord Marlborough's latest victory that you didn't bother to wear your state jewels in his honor."

"I told you," she said again. "I cannot control what they write, and so their letters mean nothing."

"They mean *everything*," I said fiercely. "Do you care so little for what Lord Churchill has done for you? Are the lives of all the English soldiers who have died under your flag of so scant worth to you that you could not bother yourself to have a necklace clasped around your throat?"

She pressed her lips tightly together before she answered. She had spent most of the summer at Windsor with the prince. Although the prince was but fifty-five, over the last year his corpulence and chronic asthma had worsened so that few expected him to live much longer. The queen knew it, too, and her face had already taken on that settled cast she used to confront a coming death.

"The war has gone on too long," she said, her hand raised to wave as we passed into the street. "The people are weary of it, and so am I."

"The people would be a good deal more weary of speaking French," I said, "which is what they'd be doing now if not for the army."

Yet I smiled, and waved, and laughed as I caught a bouquet of white flowers tossed into the carriage. Could the queen truly be so willing to forget the war that had achieved so much? Did all that John had fought for and done mean so little to her now?

"Did you leave off the jewels because I chose them, instead of Mrs. Masham?" I whispered fiercely as we reached St. Paul's. Harley might be gone from the Cabinet, but he still had Masham's ear, with every other Tory striving to curry her favor, too. "Was that the reason? Did your Mrs. Masham tell you not to follow my wishes, and go without?"

She flinched. "This was not Mrs. Masham's decision to make."

"Oh, no, it was not, but that's not to say she didn't." We were being helped from the carriage, and the queen borne up the steps in a chair as I walked alongside, our smiles pasted bright on our unwilling faces. "If she told you, you would listen."

"That's not true," she insisted. "I obey no one but myself."

"None excepting the one we both know," I whispered as soon as she was helped from the chair. All around us the congregation murmured with anticipation, our conversation only one of many. "But then having no inclination for any but one's own sex can lead to all manner of wrongful decisions."

She jerked upright, her expression as outraged as if I'd struck her. "How dare you, of all women, make such an unfair accusation to me, when—"

"Be quiet!" I said sharply, not wanting this to be overheard. But to my endless misfortune, at the exact moment I spoke, a lull had fallen in the congregation's chatter, and all around us heard me as clear as if I'd stood in the pulpit. Too mortified to dare speak further, I took my seat, and the queen hers, and I'm certain neither of us heard a word of the paeans that followed.

Much later I tried to apologize in private and by letter, explaining that I'd only wished to protect her from others overhearing the unwise words of her answer. But her letter in reply was terse, with no forgiving, and no endearments. It didn't matter what I had believed, she wrote, for I need never be troubled with any answers from her again.

The letter was signed not by my poor faithful unfortunate Morley, but Anna Regina. Once again I left the court and retreated to the country, determined to continue my politicking from a distance through my letters. Both John and Godolphin urged me to remain and continue serving the queen, if for no other reason than to preserve myself from the enemies who would accuse me of negligence. But still I went to St. Albans.

There, at least, I knew my place was safe.

Chapter Thirty-seven

"How does he fare?" I whispered softly, the only voice appropriate to so dire a sickroom.

The queen turned from her dying husband, her face doleful. "Look at my poor prince, and tell me you cannot see for yourself."

I could see, and doubted not that I'd been right to come. The prince's asthma, always a trial to him, had kept him from the heart of London for years, but over the last weeks it had worsened and combined with a dropsical humor. Now his face was slicked with sweat and his hollowed eyes were squeezed shut, and his breathing so labored that the queen herself supported the pillow behind his head, coaxing every racking breath from his shrunken body.

To see this sad scene between them, and to recall them when they were young and vital and merry, dancing at Whitehall to celebrate their wedding, touched me deeply. Though the queen herself had not summoned me, Godolphin had written that the prince was close to death, and I had traveled all night from Windsor to join the queen in this sorry hour. Surely her grudges would be forgotten in such a time; surely as her oldest friend, I belonged here.

"I am sorry," I whispered, but the queen was too occupied with her dying husband to hear me. She was weeping now, cradling his face in her hands as she moaned his name and kissed him again and again. So frantic was her farewell that none of us in the room could say the moment when at last the prince slipped away, nor, I doubt, could the queen herself. But at last she realized he was gone, and with a quavering wail, she dropped her face beside his.

As the senior lady in the room, I motioned for the physicians, bishops, and numerous attendants and servants to leave and give the queen the privacy she needed. I knelt beside her, saying all that I could imagine to console her, both as a faithful servant and as a friend, but she seemed not to hear me. Instead she cried out and flung her hands and made other marks of woeful passion, her tears more free than ever I'd seen. At last she seemed spent, half conscious herself as she pressed against her husband's body.

"Come with me, Morley," I said, taking her by the shoulders. "We must leave him now."

Slowly she raised her head, her tear-swollen eyes dazed. "Where is Abigail? Send for Mrs. Masham, Freeman. That is who I want."

Her words struck me to the quick; why should she call for that vile, low creature at such a time as this? "Masham cannot come now. But you and I must go to St. James's, as is proper."

"But I do not wish to leave the prince!" she cried mournfully.

"I know, but we must." Not only did protocol demand that the queen return to St. James's Palace, but I'd no wish to leave her here alone at Kensington with Abigail. My own lodgings were still at St. James's, and there I could look after her needs. I took her by the elbow, helping her to her feet. "Come, my dear Morley. It is time."

She leaned heavily upon me, as she'd done in the old days between us, and I led her slowly, painfully from the prince's chamber. In the gallery, all her attendants and other staff stood in a line to pay their respects to the queen. I judged her too spent with grief to notice them, until we were halfway down the gallery. There in the line stood Masham, ostentatiously blotting a handkerchief to her turnip-nose. Then, though the queen leaned upon me for support, I found she had the strength to bend down towards Masham like a sail full of wind, and in passing by, went more steps than was necessary to be nearer to her.

And without a word, I knew that the queen was lost to me.

Chapter Thirty-eight

"So you have brought your latest treasure for me to review, Mr. Mayn-waring?" I smiled at the elegant gentleman sitting across from me, pleased that he'd come down from London so promptly when I'd bidden him. A fixture of Whig society, Arthur Maynwaring was a poet, a critic, a satirist, a journalist, and, as I'd quickly learned, a man most eager to employ his gifts for the cause. "I'm already certain it will be a true mark of genius."

"Genius of a special sort, Your Grace." With a flourish, he handed me the sheet he'd brought. "A new tune, to be published this very week, entitled 'The Ballad on Mrs. Abigail.'"

> *When as Queen Anne of great Renown*
> *Great Britain's Scepter sway'd,*
> *Besides the Church, she dearly lov'd*
> *A Dirty Chamber Maid.*

I chuckled with delight, forgetting the desperation that had led me to this action. "The entire city will be singing this."

"Read to the last, Your Grace," he said, waving a languid finger. "That's the best part."

> *Her Secretary she was not*
> *Because she could not write*

But had the Conduct and the Care
Of some dark Deeds at Night.

"The best, indeed." I tipped the sheet up like a fan in my hand, waving it back and forth. Perhaps I'd even bring it myself to court, and play the outraged friend when I showed it to the queen. She'd resisted every other argument to cast off Masham, but surely not even she could overlook this. "Having myself been on the receiving end of this kind of barb, I must say it's far more pleasant to be the one aiming the bow."

Maynwaring bowed. "Especially, Your Grace, when the target is such a broad one."

I laughed and pushed the small pouch full of coins across the table towards him. John would be horrified by this, but then, John need never know of it, any more than the queen would ever learn that I'd been behind it. "That should cover your publication expenses, as we agreed, with a bit left to feed the muse."

"A Whig muse, Your Grace." He tucked the pouch inside his coat and bowed. "And always, always your most obedient servant."

I knew that those little pouches given to Maynwaring were money well spent. Once his work was published and greedily devoured by eager readers, its effect was immediate, and efficient. A clever slander like Maynwaring's had the added benefit of being remembered for its cleverness and repeated beyond the usual life of a penny-sheet. Over and over I secretly funded his tuneful little attacks, enjoying for the first time being able to throw such darts instead of being only a hapless target. But the best part of employing Maynwaring in this way was how in perfect—well, perfectly feigned—innocence I could sit comfortably away at Holywell, and cluck my tongue with others over the wickedness of the press, my hands clean of the dirty work.

And successful dirty work it was, too. By summer I'd wager there were precious few people left in London who'd no notion of Abigail Masham, or her unhealthy influence upon the queen.

Maynwaring's accomplishments gave me more time to devote to the progress of Blenheim Castle. I was there often in August, to oversee the workers and the expenses with them.

Now, by 1709, the façade was finally done and presented a most brave appearance from this road, golden stone turrets and towers against a blue sky. I tipped back my head to study the latest tower to be built on our castle, keeping one hand on the crown of my wide-brimmed straw hat. Warm as it was, I was glad I'd made the walk for this vista. I had passed my fiftieth birthday—*fifty!*—earlier in the summer, and as I'd grown older, I'd learned to find pleasure in smaller joys as well as grand ones.

"Your Grace!" I looked towards the call and spotted one of the architect's boys running across the field towards me, a square of white in his hand. "Fresh news from his grace the captain general!"

I seized the letter from the boy and quickly retreated to a small shady coppice to read alone. My gaze raced over the words with the same haste that John had doubtless written them.

Another decisive victory, at a place called Malplaquet. But the losses had been very steep and bloody, bad indeed if John declared it so. Far worse for me was John's passing confession that he'd suffered a slight apoplexy from the stress of the battle. He'd had an extraordinarily lucky career for a soldier, and I realized the horrible irony that it had taken this, not a musket or sword, to send him to his cot. Surely this must be a sign for him to retire from the battlefield and return to England for good. Surely, for both of us, the end of this kind of folly must be near.

I pulled off my straw hat and read the letter again, more slowly. Its contents did not improve. There was much here that John had left unsaid, but that I understood with the heaviest of hearts. Though I shared John's conviction that only a complete victory would stop France, an honorable peace seemed no closer nor more tangible than a watery mirage on a summer's day. The carnage of this battle would serve the growing numbers of those against the war. It wasn't only in Parliament, either. The war was blamed for the rising prices in the markets, for too many foreign refugees taking too much work from Englishmen, for claiming too many men and casting too many widows and orphans onto the lists of parish poor.

But cruelest of all was how John and Godolphin were being blamed, even accused of prolonging the war for their own profit. I myself had fought to bring the Whigs to more complete power, but now they, too, were withdrawing their support. There were calls to stop the building on our great golden castle here at Woodstock. Even the queen, who had wanted the war as much as anyone, now countered all praise for John's courage with the snippy statement that he'd risked no more than any other common soldier would—a phrase that, I am sure, came directly from Masham's deceitful lips. I doubted now that the queen would call the bells to be rung for this victory, or a thanksgiving service said, she'd become that callous and ungrateful. Every question about the war in the House came down to money, and the Marlboroughs, and it both saddened and angered me no end that our loyalty would be so little regarded.

Yet just as John would never throw down his sword in battle, I would not give up this fight, either. I still would write daily to the queen, volumes, in the hope that I could undeceive her. At Maynwaring's suggestion, I had begun to write a frank and complete narrative of my life, with no details omitted. Through him, I'd let the world know of my intent to publish the work when it was done—a book that, I was sure, would make many quake with dread, even to the queen herself.

I pressed my lips to John's letter, as I always did, tucked it into my bodice, and headed back to sharpen my pen for another skirmish.

By the following spring, the attacks on John and me had grown too pointed to ignore, or to counter obliquely through Maynwaring or others like him. Not only was the queen being fed lies through Masham, but now also through the Duke of Somerset, who had showed his true knavery by putting his wife in the queen's household with the express purpose of becoming the new favorite. The queen had always been susceptible to flattery such as this, and with Masham away from court to drop another of the colonel's brats, it had been easy enough for the Somersets to insinuate themselves and begin spreading their own brand of poison. Once they had been so generous as to give the queen and me sanctuary in Syon House; now I would not trust so much as a crust of bread from them, for fear it would be dipped in ratsbane.

With the queen now trapped so tight between these two would-be favorites that she could scarce put her hand in her pocket, I realized I could wait no longer. I needed to speak to her alone, and defend John and myself from their odious charges. I wrote to her, begging a private hour to speak with her, and going so far as to tell her I couldn't with good conscience receive the sacrament on Sunday without saying what I must. Because it was Easter week, I suppose this last was what made her relent and agree to see me alone.

Yet as I walked down the long gallery to the queen's closet in Kensington Palace, my Gold Key still swinging gently against my skirts, I couldn't help but consider how I'd been forced to beg for this interview, for an hour of the privacy that had once been so free between us. Nor could I ignore that this meeting would take place on Good Friday, a solemn day marked by betrayal and redemption.

She kept me waiting, standing idle long after the page announced me. If she hoped to intimidate me or make me change my mind and retreat, she was mistaken, for the delay only steeled my resolve.

At last the door opened. The queen was sitting in her favorite chair, gripping the arms as if she feared for her life. The sun from the window was harsh upon her face, and I noted how her white powder and red cerise had settled like colored snow into the deep, grim lines on either side of her mouth.

She did not ask me to sit, nor was a chair provided, and so I stood before her, my hands lightly clasped with a lace-bordered handkerchief tucked inside.

"Your Majesty," I began softly, "I've come to defend my good name and loyalty, and that of my husband."

Her expression did not change. "Whatever you have to say, Lady Churchill, you may write it to me."

I smiled, hoping to coax the same from her for the sake of the past. "Indeed, I can't tell how to put such things into writing."

"You have never felt so constrained before this," she said, her words as cold and cheerless as January frost. "You may put your complaints into writing."

"Please, Your Majesty." I held my hand out in appeal, the handkerchief drifting from it. "I believe you never did so hard a thing to anyone as to refuse to hear them speak. Even the meanest person was granted that favor from you."

"I grant you the favor of writing your complaints," she said, "so that I may read them at another time."

Why did she insist on repeating this same odious line, like a schooled parrot that knows the words, but not the meaning? Why wouldn't she *listen* to me, the way she once did?

"There is too much to write, Your Majesty," I said, fighting to keep the panic from my voice. "There are a thousand lies made of me, which are so ridiculous that I should never have thought it necessary to clear my name. Especially not with you, Your Majesty, especially not with the long and devoted history that we share. Surely you must know that I am no more capable of what these lies accuse me of than I am of killing my own children!"

Still her expression remained hard and unyielding. "There are without doubt many lies told, Lady Churchill."

With considerable effort, she pushed herself up from the chair to leave, and I rushed forward to block her path.

"Your Majesty, please!" I cried, tears now spilling down my cheeks. "You know what has passed between us. You know I have never neglected my duties nor my loyalty to you."

But the queen only stared at me, her eyes full of chilly scorn. "Once you told me to be quiet, that you desired no answer from me, and I shall give you none now."

"Is it the Somersets who have turned you against me?" I begged, stopping short of clutching at her skirts. "Is it that—that other woman?"

The queen looked away, concentrating her energy pressing towards the door. "You may write to me your complaints."

"Is it that you have heard of the narrative of my life?" I cried, though I knew she would protect her gossips, and be silent. "Is that what has made you so distant from me? I have served you nearly thirty years, Your Majesty. *Thirty years!* Is that long loyalty and faithfulness of so little significance?"

Yet still she ignored me, considering the interview done. With only a scrap of my pride left for consolation, I drew back with my tears falling on my hem, and curtseyed as she lumbered past me. "Surely Your Majesty will suffer in this world and the next for such inhumanity towards one who loved you so well."

She gave me one final, unkind look over her shoulder as she passed from the room. "If I am guilty of inhumanity, Lady Churchill, then it is to myself, for having suffered you so long."

For a long time, I stood alone, letting my tears flow from my heart. I had lost my role as her friend and favorite, but more than that, I had lost her love.

I never saw her alone again.

Chapter Thirty-nine

Like a current that rushes forward when one vital stick of the dam is broken, after my last meeting with the queen, the entire careful construction of my world began to crumble and crash apart.

Of course I wrote to John at once, giving him my side of what had happened, and he wrote back within a fortnight. Though he often regarded my complaints about court or the queen with a large grain of salt, soothing me as best he could from afar, this time he must have understood the bitter truth of what I'd written. He was shocked by what had happened, and appalled that the queen would treat me so. His advice was to leave court immediately and spare myself further insult by going to St. Albans where I'd be less of a target. We both realized it was only a matter of time now before the queen would begin to take away our posts, and for the sake of the latest campaign, the siege of Douai, John hoped that we could continue at least until the end of the year.

But in June, our son-in-law Sunderland was dismissed. The queen had always resented him, and now emboldened by the support of both Tories and more moderate Whigs, she cast him out. Harley, Masham, and the Somersets all claimed to have the power of leading the queen now, and I've no doubt they celebrated together, too.

In August came the next blow. In a letter delivered by a groom from the royal stables, Godolphin was most shamefully dismissed from his post as treasurer. He had protected the queen for more than twenty years with all the selfless care and tenderness that her own father had never showed her, yet she in turn showed not a breath of remorse or gratitude.

I scrambled as best I could to reassure the ambassadors in London that John was still in command of the allied forces. The Dutch in particular were skittish, ably reading the signs of a shifting government.

In September, several of the highest ranking lords resigned their posts in protest of Godolphin's dismissal.

A week after that, the queen dissolved Parliament without consulting her council. I could see the high-handed imperiousness of her father in this, and could only pray that the same tumult that had followed James would not come again. The general election in October was a great victory for the Tories, as any suckling child could foresee. Yet while fools like Harley could gloat and smirk at their triumph, the news made the peace talks disintegrate on the Continent, undermining John's position further.

I watched, and listened, and shook my head from the safety of St. Albans, for though I was still in charge of the queen's private household, it had been made abundantly clear to me that I was unwelcome at court. When murmurings reached me that I might be investigated for thieving from the queen's Privy Purse, I let my outrage simmer for John's sake, and more seriously considered publishing my narrative in my own defense. This was not the blackmail that many called it, but simply my desire to bring the truth to the world, and the world back to my side.

Yet even I knew it was already too late for that. By the time John came home from the war in December, the crowds who loved him still cheered him in the streets, but there was little rejoicing to be found with us.

Soon after Christmas, the queen made it clear that I must give up my posts. I wished to resign, not be dismissed, and save what slight face remained to me. With John fair guiding my pen, I'd written one final letter to the queen, asking that I serve another few months, only long enough so that John could resign with me. It seemed, I thought, a humble enough request.

Now I stood by the front window of Marlborough House, watching the snow fall in St. James's Park as I waited for John to return from the palace. At last his carriage appeared, the wheels cutting dark stripes across the new snow. I rushed down the stairs to greet him, and led him to the fire in the drawing room.

"I did what I could, Sarah." He shook the snow from his hat, scattering flakes that melted at once from the fire, and with a grunt dropped into the chair. "I tried for all you asked, and more."

"What did she say?" I knelt on the floor before him to pull off his damp boots, heedless of the wet on my skirts. "Tell me. What did she say?"

"I asked for nine more months." He sighed wearily, supporting his head on his hand. "She said she could not bear to keep you so long, nor part with me so soon."

"No." I sat back on my heels, stunned. "She didn't."

"She did," he said. "I asked for an honorable retreat, saying that for her to deny us that would slander her reputation as a kind friend and a merciful ruler."

"And still she would not agree?"

"She would not even meet my eye," he said sadly. "She is at heart a Stuart, without a drop of gratitude."

I rose, turning away from him to stare into the fire. "Did she give no reason for why I must go?"

"I pressed her, yes, though got precious little in return. She said it was for her honor to remove you, but what exactly she meant by that, I couldn't tell."

"Her *honor*," I said, practically spitting the false word. "There is no honor with royalty."

"No, love, there isn't." I heard him come to stand beside me. "I'm sorry."

"There's no need for you to apologize, John," I said bitterly. "And the queen never will."

"That is true." He sighed again. "She's given you a fortnight to resign."

I looked down at the Gold Key at my waist, the symbol both of so much I'd had, and so much I'd lost. Everything I'd done had been first for the good of England, a claim the queen could never herself make. Without squandering another second of my life, I reached down and tore the key from my waist.

"Why should I waste fourteen more days in her service?" I threw the key skittering across the floor. "She can have it tonight, and all the ill will I can muster with it."

My key was accepted at once from John, but it took the queen another four months to make the last break. At last she wrote to ask me in May to vacate my lodgings at St. James's Palace and remove all my belongings. Since I'd already relinquished my posts, this seemed a reasonable enough request, nor did I have any earthly desire to spend another night beneath her roof.

I marched through the rest of my palace lodgings for what was sure to be the final time, my indignation still bubbling and my footsteps echoing through the empty rooms. All my effects had been taken away; I was nearly ready to leave.

Kneeling on the floor beside the door, the carpenter I'd hired looked up at me, his tools beside him. "The hinges, too, Your Grace?"

"The hinges, the locks, and every other scrap of brass you can find," I said firmly. The queen's last letter to me sat folded in my pocket as ready ammunition in the event someone questioned my actions. "I paid for this hardware to be put in here, and I've no intention of leaving it behind for another's free use."

Because certain improvements I was having made to Marlborough House had yet to be finished, I had asked if I might store my furnishings at the palace for another month or two until the house was ready. The queen had curtly refused, telling me to take a place for storage at ten shillings a week.

With a thump, two of the men lifted a door from its hinges and set it against the wall. I smiled, satisfied. I'd already taken away the looking glasses and the chimney stones, and the carpenters would be done with the hardware this afternoon. Though vengeful, this was perfectly in my rights, as I'd already asked the palace housekeeper to attest. No one ever left such costly improvements behind for those who'd come after, especially not if, as I suspected, my rooms had been promised to Masham and her ilk.

They'd certainly claimed the spoils of my appointments soon enough. The Duchess of Somerset was now Groom of the Stole, and Masham had been made Keeper of the Privy Purse. The rest of my appointments had been divided between them, with even Masham's two-year-old daughter being appointed the Ranger of St. James's Park.

Yet this was only a portion of my thoroughly public humiliation. Not only was Harley rewarded for his old villainy through Masham by being made Earl of Oxford, but he was also given the post as Lord Treasurer. Not content with this, he renewed his attacks upon John and me in the Commons and in the press, hiring the despicable Jonathan Swift to slander me in the *Examiner* and Daniel Defoe in the *Review*.

I was mocked as another Fulvia, that classical epitome of an evil, manipulative wife, and given as companions Envy, complete with snakes and whips, and Wrath in a robe stained with blood. Blenheim Castle was derided as a "House of Pride," built upon the "Tears and Groans of a People harassed with a lingering War." Another took its inspiration from the *Aeneid*, claiming I "frequented Public Assemblies, where [I] sat in the shape of an obscene, ominous Bird, ready to prompt [my] Friends as they spoke." In yet another I was shown to rival Medusa herself, "with a nose turning up, eyes glaring like lightning, blasted all she had power over with strange diseases."

At my own scribe Maynwaring's advice, I had resolved not to answer their lies, but to take Job as my model, and hold my head high. But the calumnies against me were so gross and yet so greedily devoured by the credulity of party rage that I found the road I'd chosen a hard and lonely one indeed.

My only consolation was that John was spared hearing or reading the worst of the attacks upon us. In February, he had returned to The Hague to begin plans for the coming season's campaigns. Although he now must fight with only the weakest of support from both a hostile ministry and queen, John was too honorable a man to refuse his duty, and too loyal to the soldiers who still called him "Corporal Johnny" with great fondness and regard. All he wished for now was the peace he'd fought so long to achieve, and, he believed, was soon to come.

"We're done, Your Grace." The carpenter tugged on his forelock. "There be nothing left, as you said."

"Very good. You may go." I waited until they were gone, then took the last key from my pocket. The lock to the outer door I'd scrupulously left in place, for I'd not replaced it while I'd lived there. I turned the key for the final time, trying not to think of how, after having lived in St. James's since I'd been a child, I was now leaving it for good.

The letter I sent that evening to the queen was as short as hers had been to me. I had left the lodgings as she'd requested. If they wished the key, they might have it, for the sum of ten shillings.

Though in my wrath I'd thought this clever, the queen, in a fury of her own, did not. She retaliated by ordering the construction of Blenheim halted, vowing that she'd not build the duke a house while the duchess was busy pulling hers down.

She'd left me with no rejoinder, of course, infuriating me further. Yet this action of hers was petty compared to what followed.

I'd believed that I had seen the very worst of the queen when she'd summarily dismissed Sidney Godolphin from the Treasury with the coldest of notes. I'd thought that her manner in requesting my resignation through John to be a low and dirty trick, calculated to shame me beyond all measure. But what she next condoned, with Oxford as her prime henchman, was truly beyond conscience, and bearing.

While John was still in the thick of the campaign, having brilliantly crossed the *"ne plus ultra"* lines that the French had believed to be impenetrable and laid siege to Bouchain, the queen had already begun the most traitorous act of her career. With great secrecy, she had authorized unilateral peace negotiations in Paris. When at last three preliminary articles of peace were signed and announced, they broke the earlier treaties that the Whig ministries had made with their allies. Instead these new articles broke the contract between England and the Austrians, Dutch, and Germans, for the sake of commercial concessions and trade advantages with the French. It was clear enough that this new ministry had deemed a peace so necessary to the preservation of their power that they had agreed it must be had at any rate.

It was also painfully, obnoxiously clear to me that, with this so-called peace in place, there would no longer be need for John as captain general. Why would they wish to keep a man whose very brilliance and honor would only remind them of their own knavery?

When I wrote all of this to John, he thanked me, but also asked that I refrain from any further mention of the government, or this peace. Try though he might to concentrate on the end of his final campaign, I knew he was disgusted and disheartened, and now when he wrote to me of a retirement in the country, I believed him. When he returned home in November, I had never seen him look so weary, nor so old.

But one last battle remained before him, and it would be the ugliest of his entire career.

"You are ready?" I asked John softly on the chilly December morning when he'd been called to speak before Parliament. The carriage was waiting for us outside the door to Marlborough House, but still I tarried, wanting these last moments alone with him before we must go to the House, where everything we did or said would become common to all the world. "You have your speech?"

He smiled, grimly determined, and tapped his forehead. "It's in here, Sarah. I don't need a written scroll to speak my own defense."

"You shouldn't need to defend yourself or the war at all."

"I shouldn't, but I will," he said. "And I also mean to call upon the queen to admit that the charges are slander."

"Yes," I said fiercely. "Do that."

"I will, only if you promise to behave yourself and not leap from the gallery spitting fire in Her Majesty's face."

"I'm serious, John," I said. "She should be accountable for what she has done."

"She is but one," he said lightly, but I understood. Oxford's greatest achievement had been to fund a scurrilous booklet by Jonathan Swift called *The Conduct of the Allies*. Presenting itself as honest fact when in truth it was far from it, Swift's booklet had openly accused John of peculation and endless greed, of thriving on the "harvest of war," even of single-handedly having begun the War of Spanish Succession for his own personal gain. Over eleven thousand copies had been sold in two months.

Oxford understood how much the book's message would appeal to minor country gentry and other such Tories, the ones who most protested the cost of the war, and at his own expense, he'd made certain that copies were sent to landowners in the most remote counties throughout the country. Now these same men would be sitting in Parliament, as hostile and ill informed a group as I could imagine. I knew all too well the power that such press could carry, and though John was confident he could defend himself with success, I was full of worry: not because I doubted John's goodness, but because I feared the strength of his adversaries' evil.

I ran my hand lightly over the front of his uniform coat, over the medals and ribbons that reflected a lifetime of victories. "I hope every one of those cowardly members sees these," I said fervently. "I hope each one feels shame for how disgracefully you've been treated."

"Oh, yes, and the Thames will run with Rhenish wine instead of water." He took me gently by the shoulders and kissed me with great tenderness. "You'll see. We're not done yet, my dear soul."

Though the gallery was crowded for the opening of the session, I sat apart, by choice and by circumstance. No one wished to share my taint of disgrace, though I could tell by the endless whispered conversations behind hands and fans that I remained a source of fascination. I didn't care. I was there for John, and no one else.

He spoke brilliantly, as I'd known he would. He spoke for every soldier who had done no more than follow his orders to the best of his abilities. He said that while he had always wanted peace, for England to settle for a separate treaty with France would put the safety and liberties of the rest of Europe into jeopardy. As he'd promised, he did call the queen to admit to the slanders against him, raising a murmur of amazement from the audience. Of course the queen herself did not so much as blink, her face as impassive and lifeless as a holiday pudding. Yet to my surprise, it was our old Tory adversary Nottingham who called for the fighting to continue, predicting that those who settled for this dishonorable peace would face impeachment when George of Hanover, the German prince who had been chosen to become the Protestant king after Anne's death, finally came to claim his throne.

The vote was close. The peace proposals were defeated, sixty-two votes to fifty-four. When John and I drove home, our carriage was cheered in the streets, while Oxford's was pelted with snowballs.

But it would take far more than snowballs to stop Oxford. With both his brother and his brother-in-law holding key posts in the government auditors' office, Oxford ordered a full inquiry into John's accounts. Impeachment proceedings were believed to be imminent. The rest of Europe—even France—was appalled that England would dare treat the greatest hero and leader of his generation with such shameful disrespect, but though in public the queen said she was shocked and saddened by the investigation, I'd heard from most reliable sources that in private she gleefully urged Oxford onward with his conniving wickedness.

Without John's knowledge, I waged a defense on his behalf, writing tirelessly for support to every friend and acquaintance we'd ever had at court, in Parliament, or in the army and navy. Disgraced as I was, there were still those who cocked an ear for me, and I did my best.

But on a dim night in January, as we sat before our fire, the footman brought John a letter from the queen.

"What is it?" I asked, though I could guess too well. "What has she written you?"

He turned the sheet over, as if to see if it contained more than was written on one side, then crumpled it and hurled it into the fire.

"I am dismissed from all my posts," he said, and for the first time in our life together, I heard his voice break. "As easy as that. I am no longer captain general."

The charges that Oxford and his cronies had contrived to bring before the House were as preposterous as they were false: that John had taken bribes from army bread contractors, and that he'd skimmed a percentage of salaries paid to foreign troops in his command. Worse still were implications that John had also diverted money from the army's surgeons, and abandoned countless wounded Englishmen to suffer and die. For John, who had always put the welfare of his soldiers first, this was the cruelest and most ill-founded charge of all.

As much as Oxford wished it, the House of Commons could not commit a peer to prison. While the government could conduct a trial of impeachment, the chances for a guilty verdict were considered too unpredictable to risk. Besides, beyond Oxford, the ministry was turning skittish, realizing too late the magnitude of what they'd begun against England's favorite hero, and thus decided merely to censure him instead.

I attended every long day of the debate in the House, never knowing what new calumnies would be sworn against my poor husband. Yet for every fresh lie hurled at him, another old friend or colleague spoke up in his defense, gladdening me near to tears. I dared to hope that the truth would win and John's honor be vindicated. How else could such a monstrous scandal be resolved? I had never been so proud of my husband, nor so loathful of his enemies.

Yet when the final vote was taken, Oxford was the one who smirked with victory. He had called in every favor and seen to it that the Tory majority had voted by party, not by reason or intelligence. Dr. Swift's hateful pamphlet had done its work. The final count among the members for censure was 270 to 165.

Afterwards John spoke not a word to his disappointed and angry supporters, nor did he acknowledge the cheers of the belligerent crowds gathered outside the House. I walked proudly on his arm, and he with me, our heads high with the knowledge that, unlike the queen and her Tory toadies, we'd done no wrong.

Yet once we were alone in the carriage, John finally let his pain and anger show, his face flushed and his eyes fair glowing with it. "I am done with them all, Sarah. *Done.*"

"Then it is just as well you still have me," I said wearily, curling against him. "This way you know you've at least one person in this country who loves you as you are, with all her heart."

"Grace to God for that." He pulled me into his arms, holding me so close that I could hear the furious beating of his heart. "I'm done with England, too, love. There's no place left here for me."

"Nor me," I said softly, with more sadness than anger. "Nor me."

It was decided then between us, in that carriage. Our pride might have remained unbent, but our bodies and souls were exhausted and worn. Soon after we sailed for the Continent.

And never did an exile feel so like the sweetest sanctuary.

Epilogue

DOVER, KENT
AUGUST, 1714

"I told you they'd remember you, John," I said. As our little sloop drew closer to shore, we could see the crowds gathered on the quay, waving flags and cheering.

"They remember *us,* sweet." John kept his arm around my waist, heedless of what the young sailors might think of us fond old folk. "What a grand homecoming for this sorry pair of wanderers, eh?"

I was smiling so hard my mouth hurt, and my eyes stung with tears of happiness at this first glimpse of England. For two long years, we *had* been wanderers, living in exile in Antwerp, Aachen, Frankfurt, in unclean, inconvenient houses that were not our own. Though John and I had been treated with the same high honor and regard as if he were still captain general, I'd been desperately homesick. I missed our daughters and our grandchildren, our own beds and gardens and orchards, even the very English air that was so different from the Dutch, and when the letter had come to John calling him back, I'd danced such a jig of joy that I'd quite terrified our chaplain.

And why shouldn't I? Prince George of Hanover, who would become King George I of England at the queen's death, had respected and favored John since the Battle of Blenheim. As soon as word had spread that the queen was most grievous ill, the prince had invited John to return to London, promising that he'd be restored to all his former ranks and positions. Already we'd heard that our old enemies—Oxford, Bolingbroke, even Masham—were said to be in abject fear for their futures, and rightly so, for all they'd done to us. There were rumors, too, that the queen in her final delirium had called for Mr. and Mrs. Freeman, but that I could not bring myself to believe.

Though I was as pleased as John to be returning now, I could not give myself over to delight just yet. To me, the queen had been "grievous ill" for at least the last twenty years, and despite what all these clever great lords might believe, I knew she could just as soon live another twenty after this. I believed in coaxing fate rather than daring it, and thus this day I wore a miniature of the queen pinned to my bodice, a little memento set with diamonds that she'd given me long, long ago. I touched the stones now, trying to remember exactly when. Had it been at Windsor, or Tunbridge, or maybe Syon?

At last the sloop bumped alongside the quay, and the gangplank lowered. John and I collected ourselves at leisure, not wanting to appear overeager, and we'd only just made our way to the waiting carriage when a small, black-clad man came pushing his way through the others. He thrust past the footman, bowing deeply with his hat in his hand as he introduced himself as the mayor of Dover.

"Your Graces, I have the most terrible news," he intoned over the cheering crowd surging around the carriage. "Her Majesty the queen is dead."

I gasped, not from grief or shock, but sheer surprise that Anne had finally lost the will to keep death at bay.

At once John rested his hand over mine to comfort me, or, because he knew me better than anyone, to silence me. "When?"

"Yesterday, Your Grace." The mayor nodded solemnly. "They said she went with peace, Your Grace."

With *peace*? I bit back my laughter. What peace could Anne have found on her deathbed? She had stolen her father's throne from him, and earned his damnation as an ungrateful, deceitful daughter. She'd lied to him and to her stepmother about preserving her brother's claim to follow her to the English throne, the same brother she'd never admitted was her blood. She'd let the bitterest of feuds and ambitions destroy her only sister's love. She'd ordered the jackals in her government to drive John from office and from England, and turned her back on the general who'd brought more glory to her reign than she ever deserved. Worst of all, she'd broken every promise she'd ever made to me, the one person in her life she'd sworn she loved.

"I thank you for telling us," John said gravely, and with a reluctant nod, the mayor retreated. The footman latched the carriage's door shut, and slowly the driver began to guide the horses through the crowded street.

While John waved at the window, I unpinned the miniature from my breast to study the tiny painted face. Like everyone else, the artist had flattered her, and I wouldn't have recognized her save for the yellow gown trimmed with ermine that she'd always favored. Yet I had known her when she'd been no more than an unpleasant child whom no one noticed, a royal princess who had needed a friend. I had obliged, and in the end, my loyalty had been cast off like a worn stocking, full of holes.

I looked down at the ring of diamonds, twinkling in the sunlight: rose cut, and of good quality, too. Only four thin prongs held the silver setting in place over the painted ivory oval. By wedging the weakest prong under the latch of the door, I was easily able to pry it back and slip the oval free. Never one for careless waste, I tucked the diamond setting into my pocket for another use.

"Mark that, Sarah," John said, pointing from the window. "They've hung garlands of flowers for us, but not a single scrap of mourning for Her Majesty. Poor lady! The queen is dead. Long live the king."

I looked one last time at the little portrait in my palm: a queen I'd never see again in this life, a friend I'd already long ago banished from my heart. I joined John at the carriage window, and without another thought, I tossed the miniature into the churning crowd of faces before us.

"The queen *is* dead," I said softly. "Long live the king, John, and long live us!"

Afterword

Few common-born men or women in English history have made so much of life's opportunities as Sarah and John Churchill. Their return home in 1714 after their self-imposed exile was no exception. On the road to London, they were met by jubilant crowds and showered with flowers, their homecoming completely overshadowing Queen Anne's death.

After a stroke had left Anne bedridden earlier in July, she had agreed to appoint Lord Shrewsbury to replace Oxford, her final act as queen. Knowing death was near, she had also haltingly asked for Mr. and Mrs. Freeman before a second stroke left her unable to speak. The Churchills' arrival was three days too late. Anne died on the morning of August 1, 1714, having made no last confession and leaving her will unsigned. Only her favorite Anglican clergy were at her side; she had neither family nor friends left to comfort her.

Even Abigail Masham deserted the queen on her deathbed, and reportedly spent the last hours before Anne died looting the royal quarters for whatever she could carry away (though it would seem entirely in keeping with Sarah's character if those last "reports" about her rival had somehow originated from Sarah's own pen). Abigail then disappeared from the palace, and from history.

The supporters of Anne's half brother, James Francis Edward Stuart, never abandoned the empty hope that Anne had somehow made a final acknowledgement of him as her successor. A weak, pathetic figure, the Old Pretender was the constant center of futile Jacobite plots to regain the English throne. He died in 1766, in the same exile in which he'd lived his long and wasted life.

James Francis Edward's single significant achievement was to marry a Polish princess named Maria Clementina Sobieski, who in turn gave birth to his only son Charles Edward Stuart in 1720. (Soon after, Princess Clementina abandoned James Francis, and retreated to a nunnery for the rest of her life—much as James Francis's mother Mary Beatrice had once longed to do.) More commonly known as Bonnie Prince Charlie, or the Young Pretender, Charles Edward was blessed with all the charisma that his father had lacked, and he soon became the rallying leader of the remaining Jacobites. But though he gallantly led his supporters in the Scottish rising of 1745, his hopes for the English throne as well as the Jacobite cause were forever destroyed in the disastrous battle of Culloden Moor. He died in exile in Rome in 1788, a tragic figure immortalized in romantic fiction and poetry.

While John Churchill may have been disgraced by the English Parliament, Europeans still revered him as the most brilliant general and diplomat of their time. Prince George of Hanover, soon crowned King George I of England, immediately reinstated John as captain general. All of John's honors and privileges were returned to him, and construction on Blenheim Palace was ordered resumed. Sarah grandly—and somewhat gleefully—resumed her place at the top of Whig society, and Marlborough House in St. James's Park was crowded day and night with well-wishers and those seeking favor with the new regime.

John had little time left to enjoy his restored glory. Sixty-four when he and Sarah returned to England, his health rapidly deteriorated, and two strokes in 1716 left him partially paralyzed and deprived of speech. Sarah nursed him faithfully, their love for one another still famously strong, until he died in 1722, aged seventy-two. He was buried in Westminster Abbey with full military honors.

When Sarah sorted through John's most private belongings after his death, she found the long switch of her hair that she'd so furiously cut off to spite him long before. All she'd known was that the hair had disappeared after she'd thrown it away. Now she discovered he'd kept the hair for over twenty years, coiled and tied together with her love letters in a silk ribbon.

Was it any wonder that she never remarried?

Though John's death left an enormous vacuum in Sarah's life, she was not prepared retire as a grieving widow in the country. At sixty-four, she was still remarkable for her beauty and her lively mind—and her infamous gift for quarrels. Summoning the most powerful gentlemen of the day to her at Marlborough House and at Holywell, she continued to be active behind the scenes of Parliamentary politics, and her widespread network included Henry Walpole and William Pitt, and even Voltaire.

She persevered tirelessly to see that Blenheim Palace was at last completed in 1727—the permanent tribute to John he'd wanted—and exhausted (and outlasted) two architects and countless workmen in the process.

Always the one who'd handled the family accounts, Sarah developed a shrewd eye for investing her already large fortune, and was one of the few who made enormous profits (rumored to be as much as one hundred thousand pounds) from the infamous South Sea stocks in 1720, predicting the exact moment to withdraw her funds before the bubble collapsed. In time she became the wealthiest woman in Britain, and one of the wealthiest in all Europe, including royalty.

Sarah's relationships with her daughters, sons-in-law, and grandchildren were always turbulent. None ever seemed to live up to her standards, or act as she wished, and her family quarrels were filled with endless manipulation, long-lasting grudges, name-calling, and periods of furious silence. She outlived all but one of her children, her youngest daughter Mary.

Perhaps Sarah's single greatest disappointment was that neither of her sons had survived to inherit the title and fortune that she had labored so hard to achieve. But even that was settled with typical Sarah determination: she lobbied Parliament hard to permit the dukedom of Marlborough to descend through the female line, and upon John's death, their oldest daughter, Henrietta, became the second Duchess of Marlborough.

But what makes Sarah still so vivid today was her very modern concern for how she would appear both to her contemporaries and to future generations. In a time when ladies were expected to stand silently in their husbands' shadows, she boldly presented herself as an equal at the sides of both John and Queen Anne, and seized her own share of fame.

She was one of the first to understand the power of the press in creating a public personality. To this end, she alternately courted and vilified some of the greatest writers of her time, and there is no other lady who can claim to have been lambasted by Daniel Defoe, Jonathan Swift, *and* Samuel Johnson. She kept all letters written to her, and copies of all she in turn wrote, saving everything with an eye to presenting herself to posterity in the best possible light—or, if necessary, in a court of law.

Finally, in 1742, the eighty-two-year-old dowager duchess published her ghostwritten, tell-all autobiography. With the unwieldy title of *An Account of the Conduct of the Dowager Duchess of Marlborough, from her First Coming to Court, to the year 1710,* the book named royal names and supplied juicy details, even if not always entirely true. To Sarah's immense satisfaction, her *Account* became an instant bestseller, and for the last two years before her death in 1744, she was once again bright in the public eye.

And while Sarah might have been disappointed in her own children, surely certain of her qualities passed through her descendants. Born in 1874, her great-great-great-great-great-great-grandson began his career as a soldier with a good measure of John's courage, and finished it with such legendary statesmanship that even Sarah would have been proud: Sir Winston Churchill.

More recently, a shy, golden-haired girl descended from Sarah through her daughter Anne's marriage into the Spencer family rose to prominence. This lady combined Sarah's bright beauty and boundless charm with a celebrity that made her the center of attention wherever she went. Crowds cheered and tossed flowers to her, too, just as they once had to Sarah: Diana, Princess of Wales.

A NOVEL OF

SARAH CHURCHILL

SUSAN HOLLOWAY SCOTT

QUESTIONS
FOR DISCUSSION

1. *Duchess* is told exclusively from Sarah Churchill's point of view, and both events and other characters are colored by her strong opinions of them. How would this story differ if it were told by Queen Anne instead?

2. Although Sarah was regarded as a beautiful and much-desired woman at court, she often lamented that she hadn't been born a man. What do you think she meant by this? What would she have achieved as a man that she couldn't as a woman?

3. From their penniless roots, John and Sarah managed to amass an enormous family fortune. They were undeniably lucky, and gifted in court politics. Do you believe they were avaricious, as many of their peers accused them of being, or simply ambitious?

4. Many readers will be familiar with how Henry VIII's difficulties siring a legitimate male heir to his throne changed English history. His daughter Elizabeth I chose not to marry at all. Charles II, William and Mary, and Anne were likewise "cursed" by having no surviving sons. How differently did the Stuart and Tudor monarchs deal with their childlessness? How did each choose to secure their successors?

5. As an impoverished but beautiful maid of honor, Sarah was unusual for not marrying a rich, titled gentleman, or becoming such a

man's mistress, but instead wedding John Churchill for love. Even after his death, she refused all suitors, saying that no other man "could ever come close to John Churchill." Considering how calculating her personality is, does marrying for love seem in character, or out of it? Why do you think she chose John?

6. Sarah's relationship with Anne and her role as the royal "favorite" was openly acknowledged at court. How would Sarah's position have varied from that of a king's mistress? Would she have had more or less power with a man than she did with Anne?

7. Many of the Churchills' more cynical contemporaries believed that the secret of their long and famously happy marriage was easy to identify: because of their separate careers, John and Sarah were often apart for months at a time. Do you agree or disagree?

8. While both Anne and Sarah loved their children, they were also traditional upper-class mothers of their time who gave their children to nursemaids, governesses, and tutors to raise. They regarded these children not only as cherished sons and daughters, but valuable possessions and symbols of power and prestige, and pawns to be used to cement important relationships with other noble families. How do their attitudes towards children and child rearing differ from those of modern mothers? In what ways are they the same?

9. While the Great Plague of 1666 is the most famous seventeenth-century epidemic, smallpox claimed far more victims, cutting across all classes and ages. How did smallpox affect the characters in this book? How are their views of death and disease different from our own?

10. Sarah's generation was the first to understand and use the press to manipulate public opinion. Both she and her enemies hired journal-

ists and other writers to attack one another, often with blatant disregard for the truth. Compare Sarah's methods with how modern politicians use contemporary media.

11. Seventeenth-century childbirth was perilous to both mother and child, with nearly a third of all babies failing to survive their first month. Anne suffered through nearly twenty pregnancies in her lifetime, with no children living to adulthood.

The rate for mothers was not much better. Both Sarah and Anne routinely updated their wills during the last stages of pregnancy, and John often said he feared more for Sarah's life in childbirth then his own in battle. How would such a high mortality rate affect views of motherhood? How would families cope with the constant threat of losing new babies and their mothers? In a time when birth control was largely unknown and unpredictable, do you think the high risks that came with pregnancy would have served as a deterrent to sexual activity?

12. When at last Blenheim Palace was completed, the chapel included an elaborate family tomb that, at Sarah's request, featured statues of John, Sarah, and their two sons. Their daughters are pointedly not included, continuing a pattern of disregard that had begun at their births. By Sarah's death, only one of her daughters was still speaking to her. Why would she have so blatantly favored her sons? Why do you think she held her daughters in such low opinion?

Susan Holloway Scott is the author of more than thirty historical novels. A graduate of Brown University, she lives with her family in Pennsylvania. Visit her Web site at www.susanhollowayscott.com.